THE BLACK MASK LIBRARY

THE EARLY YEARS (1920–26)

The Man in the Shadows: The Complete Black Mask
Cases of Terry Mack *by Carroll John Daly*

THE SHAW YEARS (1926–36)

Blood on the Curb *by Joseph T. Shaw*

Black Harvest: The Complete Black Mask
Cases of Jules Tremaine *by Norvell W. Page*

Boomerang Dice: The Complete Black Mask Cases of
Johnny Hi Gear *by Stewart Sterling*

Dead Evidence: The Complete Black Mask Cases of
Harrigan *by Ed Lybeck*

Laughing Death *by Raoul Whitfield*

Luck: The Complete Black Mask Cases of
Oscar Sail *by Lester Dent*

The Price of a Dime: The Complete Black Mask Cases of
Ben Shaley *by Norbert Davis*

South Wind: The Complete Black Mask Cases of
Jerry Tracy *by Theodore Tinsley*

THE LATER YEARS (1936–51)

Dead and Done For: The Complete Black Mask Cases of
Cellini Smith *by Robert Reeves*

Let the Dead Alone: The Complete Black Mask Cases of
Luther McGavock *by Merle Constiner*

Murder Costs Money: The Complete Black Mask Cases
of Rex Sackler *by D.L. Champion*

SOUTH WIND

The Complete

BLACK MASK

Cases of Jerry Tracy

1932–35

THEODORE A. TINSLEY

introduction by Boris Dralyuk

illustrations by Arthur Rodman Bowker

cover by Fred Craft

BLACK MASK
2021

Table of Contents

Introduction

TED TINSLEY WAS a superman of the pulps who never shed his Clark Kent–like attire. He was the most ordinary looking of fellows and he neither cared nor did anything about it. In fact, he seems to have taken a certain pride in putting the lie to the romantic image of "Author" writ large. He knew that image well, as he demonstrates in a hilarious piece for the May 1934 issue of *Writer's Digest* titled "But Mister… You Don't Look Like an Author." When he prods a "dazzlingly beautiful girl, a graduate of Bryn Mawr—oh, all right!—she's a suetty blonde, quite bosomy in black satin and she really works in Gimbel's basement," about an author's proper mien, the lady responds:

> I—I dunno… I always kinda thought… Well, somehow, kinda flashy and handsome in a dissolute way. Gray at the temples, sorta. Puffy eyes, kinda deep an' full of—uh—glamour. The kinda eyes that makes a goil feel like a frightened little boid watchin' a soipent… A tweed suit all rumpled an' baggy and—uh—interestin'. And—oh yeah—smoking a pipe… Kinda fatherly an' awful sympathetic; but bold eyes like I said—make a goil breathe deep an' feel that she might hafta—

Needless to say, by this point Tinsley's lost her. Our man, as the editor's note to the article tells us, "looks like an investment banker. Put him behind J.P. Morgan's desk, and all the moneyed widows and orphans in the country would just naturally flock to him." No one would suspect a J.P. Morgan banker of writing riproaring yarns for *Black Mask Magazine* and countless other pulps; Tinsley, a veteran of the Great War, liked to defy expectations and to fly under the radar.

In fact, the prim-and-proper banker look—the cleanly parted hair, the neat moustache—was a kind of front. Some of Tinsley's most memorable series characters also defy expectations, and employ similar fronts. As he wrote in a letter to Will Murray in the late 1970s, his characters "were what Ezra Pound called 'Personae,' actually Masks." For starters, there was that obvious master of disguise, the Shadow; Tinsley wrote twenty-seven Shadow tales, beginning with 1936's "Partners of Peril," the first one not penned by series creator Walter B. Gibson.

But Tinsley's own characters don subtler camouflage. The war-hardened gangbuster Major John Tattersall Lacy, who took on Manhattan's wiliest racketeers in various pulps from 1932 to 1939, "was clean-shaven except for a trim, sandy mustache that imperfectly concealed a scar that curved like a small white crescent from his upper lip past his nostril."

His pioneering female hardboiled detective, Carrie Cashin, who debuted in the November 1937 issue of *Crime Busters*, uses another kind of front: She knows full well that her clients aren't likely to trust a "frail" with rough cases, so she partners up with a big lug named Aleck Burton and forms the Cash and Carry Detective Agency. She puts Aleck in the front office and has him play boss, for appearance's sake.

And then there's Jerry Tracy, who is as unlikely a crime solver as a J.P. Morgan banker is an author. Tracy is a gossip columnist (read Walter Winchell) on the staff of the New York *Daily*

Planet (read *Daily Mirror*), who has a heart that's unusually marshmallowy for his profession. Outwardly cynical, he's a man of ideals. Physically unimposing, he packs a mean punch and can handle a Remington pistol as skillfully as he can a Remington typewriter. Like Clark Kent, a later employee of the *Daily Planet,* and like Tinsley himself, Tracy is a man hiding in plain sight.

TED TINSLEY AND Jerry Tracy entered the *Black Mask* stable in October 1932 with a story titled "Party from Detroit." Although he was a born New Yorker, Tinsley's dour and somewhat milksoppy appearance had fooled a few colleagues into thinking that the fellow knew nothing of the Big Apple's nightlife—or of its underbelly. In his rather fanciful memoir, *The Pulp Jungle* (1967), Frank Gruber wrote, "I don't believe Ted Tinsley was ever inside a nightclub himself. He was an extremely conservative man, a plodding hard-working writer, not given to frivolous things." The trouble was that, as Tinsley asserted in a letter to Murray, "I had small association with [Gruber], knew little of his professional or social life—and vice-versa—his knowledge of me amounted to considerably less than zero." Gruber had simply fallen for the disguise.

Even a brief dip into the Tracy stories demonstrates that— even if Tinsley wasn't a nightly visitor to the 21 Club—he sure knew the scene. No one but Damon Runyon himself had trapped the lightning of Broadway's glitter and grit in the bottle of finely honed, punchy prose as well as Tinsley in the Tracy tales:

" 'Lo, Bum!"

The flippant greeting was Jerry's cynical trade-mark along every roaring alley that radiated from the Main Stem. Jerry was the Main Stem. Once a day he dished up his hot column of copyrighted chat for the Planet, consisting of leers, winks, a sprinkle of dirt, a bit of phoney mystery stuff such as: "What prominent chip-shot will be found in a vacant lot next Thursday, according to torpedo wireless? Somebody Stole My Gal is a swell tune—on the radio...."

"'Lo, Bum!" indeed. But Jerry's no bum, and nowhere near as low as the man who inspired his character—Walter Winchell. Unlike Winchell, Tracy is a "queer mixture of public executioner and good-time Charley [who] withheld a dozen dirty items for every one he printed." The real Winchell was a lot closer to the slyly nefarious J.J. Hunsecker of *Sweet Smell of Success* (1957), penned by Clifford Odets and brought to reptilian life by Burt Lancaster.

No, as much as he'd like to claim otherwise, Jerry has a heart of gold. He and his trusty palooka, Butch, would go to the ends of the earth—OK, as far as Penn Station—to help a dame or a kid out of a jam, or to spare an old Southern coot's feelings, as he does in Tinsley's second *Black Mask* offering, "South Wind" (November 1932). When Major Geo'ge Fenn—a down-at-the-heels patriarch from Thunder Run, No'th Ca'lina—calls on Jerry to find his long-lost granddaughter, Alice Anne Fenn, the columnist quickly recognizes the innocent girl in the high school graduation picture as "Lola Carfax," a nasty little actress on the make. With the help of Butch and Veronica Mulligan—a jaded but supremely ethical Vassar grad on the *Planet's* staff—Jerry teaches "Lola" a lesson and makes a hero out of Alice Fenn in order to let the Major down gently. He sends him packing for Thunder Run with a tidy sum from the Alice Fenn "estate." When Veronica confronts Jerry about shelling out his own money for the Major, our man replies in his typical half-sweet, half-cynical, and exuberantly colorful manner:

> "I went to the proper window for it. Carfax. I pumped her for every nickel she had."
>
> "Are you lying, you ——?"
>
> "Stop snuffling and show sense. Do I dig for ten grand of hard-earned Tracy jack because some old bozo comes drifting in to put the bee on me? Grow up, baby; you're living in a big town."

Jerry toes the line between hard and soft with perfect balance, while Veronica takes the plunge to the downy side. It turns out she's had enough of the "big town" and is headed down south with the major:

> "Jerry... Hey, hardboiled..." Her eyes were soft. "Any time you get sick of this crooked game, come on down to Thunder Run. I'd be awful glad to see you... Anytime...."

But Jerry has work to do—twenty-three more stories' worth, to be exact. It's no wonder that these snappy, goodhearted tales appealed to Joseph T. "Cap" Shaw, the great *Black Mask* editor who brought Tinsley aboard and included "South Wind" in his *Hard-Boiled Omnibus* (1946).

It's also no wonder that Jerry Tracy attracted Hollywood's attention. Three of these highly cinematic *Black Mask* stories served as bases for successful B pictures: "Five Spot" (November 1935) was filmed as *Panic on the Air* (1936); "Body Snatcher"

(February 1936) was adapted as *Alibi for Murder* (1936); and "Manhattan Whirligig" (April 1937) became *Manhattan Shakedown* (1937). A fourth film, Murder Is News (1937), was apparently based on a Tracy story written directly for the screen.

What sets the Tracy tales apart from most other *Black Mask* series is Tinsley's brilliantly evocative depiction of the "Main Stem" and the sprawling metropolis around it, and the color and liveliness of his prose. The stories are rich with excitement, local color, and the author's wit, by turns sharp and gentle. Jerry Tracy has stood the test of time, and is a refreshing hero for our era, which is beset with its own unscrupulous Winchells and conniving celebrity fakes.

THEODORE ADRIAN TINSLEY was born on October 27, 1894, in Manhattan, to Francis B. Tinsley, a coal yard owner who had emigrated from England, and his wife, Gertrude. The family was a large one, with Ted being the first of six children. The Tinsleys made their home in a spacious private brownstone at 159 East 116th Street, which belonged to Gertrude's parents, Theodore A. and Alice M. Theban. Both Theodore and Alice Theban were native New Yorkers born in 1839, he to a French mother and German father, and she to an English father and Irish mother.

This well-heeled family made a double contribution to the pulps. Ted's younger brother, Francis Xavier Theban Tinsley (1899–1965)—known as Frank—would become an important illustrator and cover artist. The brothers had something else in common: They both served their country in the final year of the Great War. Ted Tinsley registered for the draft on

June 5, 1917, at the age of twenty-two, and is described in the report as a tall young man of medium build with black hair and brown eyes. He joined the Second Anti-aircraft Machine Gun Battery in Meuse-Argonne, France.

Back in the States, Ted tried to put his excellent education to good use. In 1916, shortly before he was drafted, he had graduated with an AB in English from the City College of New York. He worked for a while as a teacher and (you guessed it) insurance salesman, while his brother, Frank, who'd served as a draftsman in the War Department's design section, struck out as a freelance artist, eventually finding more-or-less-steady employ as an illustrator for Fiction House's Action Stories. As Will Murray reports in his introduction to *The Crimes of The Scarlet Ace: The Complete Stories of Major Lacy & Amusement, Inc.* (Altus Press, 2012), this is how Ted got his own start in the trade, selling his first story "Cross Words at the Circle K," "a Western inspired by the crossword craze then sweeping the nation," to the fledgling pulp in 1925. Writing late in life in a letter to Murray, Tinsley peered into his "cloudy 1940 crystal ball" and described his career choice as follows: "I was a Liberal Arts graduate of CCNY, with a background of Latin, Greek and English literature… I found writing fiction to be easy and profitable for me."

In the 1930s, Tinsley married an Alabaman named Mary Ethel White, who was then an editor of *Breezy Stories*. Mary Tinsley became her husband's constant companion and supporter.

Tinsley's career in the pulps spanned just under two decades, ending in the lean years of WWII, when paper could no longer be spared for the likes of John Lacy and Jerry Tracy. In 1945,

Tinsley headed to Washington, DC, following in the footsteps of his eccentric friend, the pulpster Norvell Page. He first took a post in the writers' division of the Office of War Information. As he wrote to Murray, Page and he knocked out "government public relations stuff (tactfully called 'Information' by the bureaucrats)." The war soon ended, and so did his stint writing "Information"—or, as Tinsley put it, "then came the Bomb and bang! went the OWI." He stayed in DC and took a post at the Veterans Administration, where he wrote speeches for Gen. Omar N. Bradley; radio material for U.S.O. regulars Bob Hope and Bing Crosby; and "a million or so 'routine' messages of condolence, praise, congratulations, special events and the like for the White House (in connection with the VA) from FDR down, to A.D. 1960." That was the year he retired. In his introduction to *The Crimes of The Scarlet Ace*, Murray quotes the VA's citation commemorating Tinsley's departure:

For his writing genius, for his good nature, for his sound judgment, for his constant willingness, for his refreshing wit, for his dependability, for his other attributes that have endeared him to us over the past 15 years. There is only one Theodore Adrian Tinsley and we shall miss him.

Mary Ethel was a native of Auburn, Alabama, and after Tinsley's retirement, the couple moved to her hometown. It wasn't New York, and not quite Thunder Run, No'th Ca'lina, but it suited the couple just fine. Ted Tinsley died of lung cancer on March 3, 1979, at the age of eighty-four. Writing to Murray in 1979, Mary Tinsley left a powerful and moving portrait of her husband in his final agonizing year, when cobalt treatments had left him weak and helpless: "How he has remained so cheerful and considerate is almost hard to understand except that he is a man of great faith, is widely, widely read and has a truly philosophical mind."

Ted Tinsley's daughter, Dr. Adrian Tinsley, had by that time built a career that surely made her father proud. In 1969, she filed a dissertation on the plays of Eugene O'Neill at Cornell University, taught and served as an administrator at a number of institutions and, in 1989, was named the first woman president of Bridgewater State College in Massachusetts. Times had changed and, unlike Carrie Cashin, she needed no Aleck Burton for a front.

Further Reading:

Goulart, Ron. *The Dime Detectives.* New York, NY: Mysterious Press, 1988.

Gruber, Frank. The *Pulp Jungle.* Los Angeles, CA: Sherbourne Press, 1967.

Murray, Will. "Introduction." In *The Crimes of The Scarlet Ace: The Complete Stories of Major Lacy & Amusement, Inc.,* by Theodore A. Tinsley. Boston, MA: Altus Press, 2012.

Murray, Will. "Theodore Tinsley—Maxwell Grant's Shadow." In *The Duende History of The Shadow Magazine,* edited by Will Murray, et al. Greenwood, MA: Odyssey Publications, Inc., 1980.

Tinsley, Theodore A. "But Mister… You Don't Look Like an Author." *Writer's Digest* (May 1934).

Party From Detroit

Introducing Jerry Tracy, the newest member of Black Mask's *remarkable band of characters—a group that cannot be matched in any other magazine in the world. You'll welcome Tracy and enjoy being with him on his various adventures as keenly as you do any of the others. And you won't find his like elsewhere—anywhere.*

JERRY TRACY OPENED A groundglass door and stepped into the dingy little Broadway office maintained for him by the *Planet*, New York's goofiest Tab. A hard-faced man in a derby hat sat tilted back in a swivel-chair, his big feet crossed comfortably on a battered roll-top desk. The soles of his shoes looked like twin billboards. He had the massive head and muscle-bound shoulders of a palooka heavyweight. At sight of Jerry he grinned like a St. Bernard dog and lowered his feet to the floor.

"Hawzit, Mr. Tracy?"

" 'Lo, Bum!"

The flippant greeting was Jerry's cynical trade-mark along every roaring alley that radiated from the Main Stem. Jerry *was* the Main Stem. Once a day he dished up his hot column of copyrighted chat for the *Planet*, consisting of leers, winks, a sprinkle of dirt, a bit of phoney mystery stuff such as: "What prominent chip-shot will be found in a vacant lot next Thursday, according to torpedo wireless? Somebody Stole My Gal is a swell tune—on the radio...."

In the course of his night and day rambles Jerry Tracy met everyone in New York sooner or later, from the Mayor to the scrub-ladies at the Palace; and his invariable gay salute to rich and poor, male and female, publicity-seeking crooks and publicity-seeking churchmen, was always the same. Hello, Bum! A queer mixture of public executioner and good time Charlie, Tracy usually withheld a dozen dirty items for every one he printed. A sucker at heart, he told himself ruefully. Brokendown actors wore his suits and overcoats. Occasionally he larded his column with a phoney scandal paragraph about some poor, tired kid in a honkytonk for no other reason except that her thin whine for the favor excited his compassion, and the dirt-clipping might help her to a better job.

Jerry removed his gray snap-brim and slipped out of the trick overcoat.

"Any fire-bells?" he asked carelessly.

"Nope."

"Okey, Butch. Gimme a light."

He lit the fag, blew a gray funnel of smoke and went into his private hide away. A bare, messy little place. Desk, two wooden chairs and a dusty couch. A "World Almanac" and a phone directory. In a corner, a dictating machine set on a contraption like a tea-wagon, with rubber wheels and a lower shelf piled with cylindrical records. The columnist pulled a notebook out of his pocket and flipped the pages rapidly. His patent leather toe jerked the machine closer to his desk. There was a partly used record in place; and he snapped the playback switch and listened to his own nasal voice retailing bits for the next Monday column:

"Hello, Bums… Leap year makes the calendar long, but the depresh keeps everything else short… One of Jack Curley's wrestlers has a headache and, boys and girls, that's news… The medicine at the *Silk Sandal* is as smooth as a Scotch panhandler on Park Avenue…."

He grinned. He owned a piece of the *Silk Sandal* and all Broadway knew it, but the puff would pull 'em in hopefully just the same. The thundering herd! Better call up Marty and tell

him to cut down on dance space. He ran through the familiar gossip and dictated a fresh item:

"Peggy Maloney—the Broadway Nightingale to you—is choo-chooing West to renovate… The new papa will be a prominent architect… An architect ought to appreciate Peggy…."

He thought, cynically: "She handed me that last gag herself, the cheap little tramp!"

The phone rang and he reached negligently for the receiver.

" 'Lo? Oh, hello, Pat… How's the Commish? Yeah, in and out—mostly out. Believe it or not, I'm busy. How's tricks?" He grinned. "I told your noble predecessor he was crazy when he threw out the spittoons from headquarters. You can't turn a cop-house into a furniture department without turning dicks into ducks—if you get what I mean… What's new?"

His face assumed a deadpan expression as he listened to the Commissioner's low metallic voice. He said, once: "Don't be silly." And again: "You're not kidding me, are you, Pat? Sure thing. I'll hop over to Zogbaum's office. I breeze in there a dozen times a day—which is more than I can say for the little gray home in Centre Street. Right!"

He shrugged into the trick overcoat, grabbed his hat and stepped into the outer office.

"Going for a walk, Butch. Stick around."

"Okey, Mr. Tracy. Any message?"

"Sure. Keep away from single women with husbands."

He went downstairs and took a cab a few blocks south and east to a shabby building on a side street just off Sixth Avenue. Most of the floor space was occupied by *Footlight Topics,* the greatest amusement publication in the world. *Footlight Topics* was bible and prayer-book to a host of professional readers, from star prima donnas and millionaire comedians right down the line to five-a-day acrobats and roller-skate acts. Morrie Zogbaum was the founder and editor. His office was on the fifth floor. The tabloid columnist barged in without knocking.

Jerry noted with a grin that there were three hot numbers—a brunette and two blondes—waiting on Zoggie's hard bench for a chance to get the great man's nod. The bench was always warm. Zoggie's nod carried weight with producers; he had no use for salami and he never recommended a snide performer.

The dapper little hook-nosed man who guarded Zoggie's inner portal smiled fulsomely. "Hawzit, Mr. Tracy?"

" 'Lo, Bum. Zoggie in?"

The brunette on the bench said hopefully in a fluted, baby voice: "Oh, hello, Mr. Tracy!"

" 'Lo, kids." He glanced at them. That olive-tinted brunette—had he seen her before somewhere? Maybe. Couldn't place her. Broadway was full of little twists on the make who had once said hello to Jerry Tracy.

He stepped into the inner office. The spindly little publisher glanced up, jerked his thumb backward over his shoulder and said dryly: "Inside. Don't try to kid her. She's on the level."

THE LITTLE INNER room was Zogbaum's out whenever he chose to scram discreetly. It opened on a rear corridor that ran in L-fashion to a back stairway. As Tracy shut the door he thought cheerfully: "Two-line gag for the column. What good's a front without an exit? The bigger the front, the slicker the exit!"

A massive bespectacled man sat silent and alone on an overstuffed chair, staring intently at the pattern of the rug.

"Hello, Pat," said the columnist. "Take off the cheaters. You wouldn't fool me, would you?"

Pat Donovan was a big man with iron-gray hair and shoulders like a bull. He removed the dark glasses without a smile. His habitually deep voice was low and metallic Jerry liked this tall Mick who had risen from pavement pounding to the main desk in Centre Street without any crooked cadging or political tap-dancing.

"I'm worried," Donovan growled morosely.

"Good sign. The last guy never worried."

The tall man shrugged. He was not in a jovial mood.

"You know every grifter along the axle, Jerry. Who's the biggest chiseler of them all?"

"Which mosquito sucks the most blood? That's easy. Solly Weinzer."

"Listen! Did Weinzer ever use a short length of pipe? Did he ever stick a gat in anyone's vest?" Donovan growled.

The columnist's eyes narrowed. "Don't be sil. Weinzer's a business man. Show him a rod and he'd turn as blue as a mandril... Worried about this new guy?"

"What new guy?" the big man barked.

"Oh, I hear things. From Chi, they tell me."

"From Detroit," Donovan corrected. "That's all I know. Just rumors. The telegraph's a joke. The stools don't click. We can always put the finger on Weinzer if we need him—but this fella! He's the party, I'm dead certain, that plucked the vaudeville crowd opposite the Fillmore Hotel last week and shot Izzy Turkel through the neck with a soft-nose. My Broadway Squad is going to miss Izzy. He was a damned valuable little Hebe... That's not for the column, Jerry."

"So what?" Tracy smiled vacantly. "You asking me to stool, Mister?"

"Stop clowning. What do you know about Detroit?"

"Detroit?" He chuckled. "Not a thing. I'm just a Broadway heel. My beat's between Third and Eighth. When I go as far north as Harlem I wear snowshoes and carry blubber. Detroit's just a place where Ford works. Never heard of it... And I don't stool, even for you, oldtimer."

"Nobody asked you to stool. Just the usual, Jerry. Pass the word along to your army of stooges and get 'em to lay an ear to the ground. All I want's a lead."

"I seem to see headlines," Tracy murmured. " 'Detroit Killer Slain by Rival Gang. Body Found in Bronx Vacant Lot.' "

Donovan shrugged. "You're old enough to vote. What else can we do?"

"I'm not arguing," Jerry stated calmly. "I'll see what I can do. You're a good Irishman and a square cop, Pat… I tell Hizzoner that once a week regular, just to watch him squirm."

The big man got to his feet, unlocked the rear door and stuck his head out. Immediately he drew it in again, closing the door softly.

"I knew I was tailed here," he snapped. "There's a dame down the corridor. What the hell's that mean?"

The *Planet* man jumped to the knob and looked out. The rear corridor was empty. He walked down the hall to the tarn to make sure.

"I saw her," the Commissioner insisted.

"Doll, eh? What'd she look like?"

"Black hair. One of them funny tight hats. Hat was gray. Gray coat, cheap yeller fur—looked like imitation fox."

"X-Ray speaking," said Jerry lightly.

His mind jerked to the gray-clad brunette doll he had seen in Zozbaum's front office. Again she tickled his memory. Somebody had pointed her out casually to him a couple of weeks before—was it in Harlem? He couldn't be sure… Pinky Schwartz's thick murmur flowed suddenly in his mind: 'Lamp that dame in the corner, Jerry. She usta play around wit' a high-yaller band-leader; now she's gunnin' for somebuddy else. The boy friend musta saved all his heat for the trombone…' Hold on, though! That wasn't Harlem; wasn't that the broad down in East 53rd, with the absinthe and the orchid bouquet?" The fogged picture refused to focus.

He said: "Scram, Pat. She mooched, whoever she was."

"Help me on that Detroit angle and I won't forget it, son," said Donovan slowly.

"Uh-huh." His hand closed briefly on the other man's shoulder with a faint pressure. "Ankle along."

He turned the key in the door. "A grand old guy," he thought grimly. "One straight spine in Crookedtown! I'll lay a small bet the dark babe has pulled her freight from Zoggie's hard bench. One went away an' then there were two...."

He smiled as he entered the outer waiting-room.

"What happened to the girl-friend, kids?"

"Oh, *her?*" The blonde on the left sniffed with malice. "You mean that *Spanish* broad? Somebody went by the door jingling two quarters and a dime and she scrammed."

The blonde on the right smiled sweetly.

"Don't be a mug, Claire. We wouldn't kid you for the woild, Mr. Tracy. The girl-friend went into that booth over there, right after you come in. She made a quick call and lammed."

"Thanks. I'll be seein' you somewhere, kids."

The sugary one plucked at his departing sleeve. Her eyes looked suddenly haggard and hopeful. She fumbled for words; he knew what she wanted.

He said, with a humorous inflection that was tinged with something more than mock anger: "Big-hearted Jerry! Always a sucker. Tell you what I'll do, babes. You and Claire be in the *Silk Sandal* about 2:30 a.m. tomorrow. Put on a short sketch. Yank hair with the girl-friend and sing a few high notes. Write down your names and your last show on a hunk of paper and leave it at the door with Marty. I'll give you three lines in the column. Slip an original gag into the act and I'll make it a paragraph. S'long...."

He breezed out, leaving a soft twin cooing behind him like the tinkle of bells.

ON THE SIDEWALK he paused for a moment and glanced about. The afternoon was waning fast. There was no sign of the jane who had made the phone call and the quick sneak. Was there a tie-up between her and the party from Detroit? For all of his wisecracks to the Commissioner, Jerry's scouts hadn't tabbed a single reliable muscle item.

He decided to drift over to Barney's. Barney was his favorite speake. Everybody went there sooner or later; he'd pile in and say "hawzit" to the Dutchman.

Barney rubbed his pink pate and nodded glumly. He was in one of his pessimistic moods. He rang up "no sale" and mixed an old-fashioned. The *Planet* man sipped the drink with slow pleasure and listened to his own idle queries and Barney's morose grunts. He eyed the cash register and grinned faintly. "No sale" on Detroit either! He mooched out and stood staring idly into the dusk from the top step of the speakeasy stoop.

There was a Paragon taxi at the curb and a girl was emerging from it with taut, angry lips. She stood on the sidewalk and the hackman lounged sidewise to face her. He had alert eyes in a stolid, dirty face.

He said gruffly: "Argue wit' the meter, sister. I can't add."

Her face flushed. "I can add up five blocks—and it doesn't come to sixty cents, either!"

"Oh, no?"

He unlatched his door and stepped down. He gestured briefly with a cupped, dirty palm.

"Sez you. Come across, you cheap little floozie! I got no time to stand here arguin'."

Tracy watched without much interest. Squabbles over gyp

meters were a dime a dozen so far as he was concerned. He reached for a butt.

The cabby was crowding the girl against the side of the hack, his palm urgent.

She said shrilly: "I'm not gonna pay a cent more than—"

He grinned as he leaned closer. Deliberately he began cuffing her, shoving her coolly around.

Tracy, to his own blank amazement, found his patent-leather feet descending the speakeasy stoop, crossing the sidewalk. He thought, swiftly: "I'm nuts! What's wrong with me?" As his fist swung he threw the weight of his body behind it. His knuckles tingled. A couple of pedestrians stopped to watch. The taxi driver got to his feet slowly, rubbing his numb jaw.

"Just for that," panted the white knight of journalism, "you don't get a damn' cent!"

"Who says so?"

"I said so!" There was a pleasant glow in his right fist. "Beat it!"

A big man in vivid pink shirtsleeves came out of the Dutchman's and walked across to the curb.

"Whassamatter, Jerry? Gyp?"

"Yeah. One of these fast clock boys."

The taxi driver's eyes shifted from the pink sleeves to the lumpy face. He began to mumble as he backed towards the door of his cab. The lumpy jaw jerked coldly. "Amscray!"

With a muttered oath the hackman clicked up his pirate flag. The cab rolled.

"Thanks, Mike," said Tracy.

"Aw, hell!" Mike shrugged and gave the girl a lidded once-over.

"He hurt you, kid?" Jerry asked her. "Come on in and have a drink."

"I'd—I'd rather go home. Sorry I hadda bother you this way."

"Don't be silly. Where do you live? I'll grab a cab."

She murmured an address. The diplomatic Mike said dryly: "I'll be seein' yuh, Jerry," swung his big shoulder and went up the speake's stoop.

The girl's long cloth coat was wrinkled but not exactly shabby. She had the thin, flowerlike face and full-curved figure so often seen in casting offices. A red-head. Good make-up. Not too prosperous.

The columnist thumbed a 15 and 5, climbed in beside her and gave the wop the address.

"Show bizness?"

"Yeah."

"Whatcha name?"

"Alma—uh—Murphy."

The cab crawled through the West Fifties and pulled up in front of a cheap theatrical boarding-house. Tracy paid off the wop and went in with her. Up three flights. Turkey-red carpet with rubber treads. She unlocked a door and smiled hesitatingly.

"Come in for a minute? I can't give you a drink. It's all gone."

"Off the stuff, eh?"

"Not that. I'm busted; or I'd have paid that yegg and saved you a lotta trouble. I—I wanta thank you."

He walked in after her and shut the door. He was mildly curious.

She was, she told him, a hoofer—a good one, too. Jerry appraised her as she removed the wrinkled coat and tossed her hat on the dresser. Swell figure and a sweet mug, The poor little rat looked hungry. Maybe he could do something for her. His glance swept the room. Pretty bare. An empty bottle, beside a glass, on a small table, bore mute evidence to her statement on drinks.

"Where you from, Alma?"

"Detroit."

Tracy's heart jumped oddly. Detroit! His mind hopped to Zoggie's office and the big Mick Police Commissioner in the back room. The brunette in the corridor and the quick phone call—plenty of time to plant the cab and this little redney—a phoney!—the act was phoney!

He rose and reached for his hat.

"Wait a minute," the girl begged. "Don't go yet. You're Mr. Tracy, ain't you?"

"Right now I am. A minute ago I was John J. Dope, One side, baby."

She paced him to the door. There was panic in her voice: "Swell hoofer—honest to Gawd, Mister Tracy—don't know the ropes in this burg—need a job—gimme a break—I can dance...."

She kicked the thin grass-rug flying. With her eyes fastened desperately on his she went into a swift tap routine on the bare boards. Looka this—an' this! The silken legs flashed like pistons in the froth of her raised skirt. No music; she didn't need any. Those shabby strap-pumps of hers were drums and cymbals and hot, moaning brass. They slapped, whispered, raced, crawled. Into Jerry's mind popped a swift close-up of Sam Spellman. Sam could use a spot like this in the second act of the new show. Spot, hell! The kid was good—a four-alarm riot.

The connoisseur in him overshadowed his suspicious hunch.

He watched with approval as she worked up to the bang climax. A pause. Then four slow tops like the tired sneer of a sax—'At's all....

"Am I lousy?" she panted.

Her eyes hadn't moved from his. Her hands hung stiffly at her thighs, still twisted in the folds of her hoisted skirt.

ABOARD CREAKED FAINTLY in the hallway outside and Tracy glanced at the door. It opened; two men stood in the gap blocking his exit. The rear man closed the door and leaned against it. He had a silenced gat in his stubby hand. They both had 'em. The man in front said: "Okey, sister," and walking up to the girl, gave her a swift palm-shove into the corner.

The *Planet's* playboy stood stock-still.

He had never seen either of the pair before. Out-of-town gorillas. Couple of time-table heat-men. A big guy with flat ears and a snag tooth; a medium guy with a spongy nose and pale, whitish eyes.

He said grimly: "So what?"

The yegg with the white eyes laughed.

"Why, you lousy stool—you know damn' well what! The big-time gossip man—wise guy Jerry Tracy—rattin' for the cops!"

"You've been seeing movies, sonny. I'll have to cut down on your allowance."

They all laughed together.

"Hand it to him in the belly, Sid," said the man at the door.

"Wait a second!" Tracy protested. There were beads of sweat on his forehead. He caught a glimpse of the girl's white face in the corner. "This thing sounds screwy. You boys sure you're in the right church?"

"He's killin' me wit' those comic gags o' his," said the flat-eared man. "Let him have it, Sid, for —— sake."

The barrel of the gun lifted. The motion brought a sharp gasp from the girl.

"Gawd, you're gonna kill him—I wasn't told that—they said he was gonna get a good goin' over—just a beatin'...."

Tracy twisted his head. He said, thinly: "Thanks!"

She came forward a step at a time, her hands clenched.

"That dago lied to me—you're gonna kill him...."

"No foolin'? Git back, sister!"

He shoved out his left palm, but she dodged suddenly, sprang inside his arm, clawing fiercely. Her nails tore his face. She caught at the gun and bent it upward. Her face stared under an armpit at Tracy. She shrilled at him: "Scram!"

She was hanging on desperately; the panting thug shook her like a rat but he couldn't tear loose.

He snarled at his partner: "What the hell yuh laughin' at? Let her have it!"

His partner was grinning as he stepped closer. For the moment he seemed to have forgotten the crouched newspaperman.

Jerry's hand swept behind him, caught up the empty bottle. He jumped.

The gunman's hand swerved a fraction too late. Tracy caught him side-wise and off balance. The bottle landed with all of Jerry's strength at the back of the flat ear. He tripped over the fallen body, dropped the neck of the bottle and came to one knee with a clutched pistol in his shaking hand.

The man struggling with the girl gave a shrill yelp of dismay and tore himself free, hurling her backward so that she struck the wall with a thump. As he whirled, Tracy's finger fired the silenced gun blindly. Scarcely a sound. The thug's body shivered. He said, faintly: "Hey!" and went over backward on the edge of the mattress. It bounced him sidewise to the floor and he rolled on his face.

The knockout victim was trying dazedly to get up, one palm flat on the floor, the other groping weakly like a flopping fish. Tracy ran over and clubbed downward at the skull with the barrel till the threshing stopped.

He picked up the girl and set her in a chair. She was chalk-white, her clenched hand crammed into her open mouth.

"Don't squawk, kid!" Tracy begged. "We're sitting pretty."

He was shaking like a leaf himself. There was a faint smoke-haze in the room and a smell like smoldering rags. He took a handkerchief from his pocket and wiped off the gun he still held. He tossed it on the bed and tiptoeing over to the door, opened it a crack and wiped both knobs. Then he shut it softly and went back to the girl.

He slipped an arm around her, Stroked her red hair, patted the clenched hand. They rocked back and forth together like two scared kids. He drew the hand downward from her mouth.

"Looks like you're on my side, honey."

She buried her face in his coat and began to cry. He dabbed awkwardly at the wet eyes with his handkerchief.

"I swear to Gawd, Mr. Tracy—"

"I know. It's okey... Who hired the act?"

"A—big slick-haired greaseball. He said he—he come from Detroit and we got chummy, talkin' about places an' people

we knew out there. That cab was a plant. I got a phone call…
I was dead hungry—haven't had a square for a week—eatin'
fifteen cents a day in *Coffee Pots*—an' he promised faithful there
wouldn't be no—"

"Sure, sure… You don't know his name?"

"No."

"Remember him if you saw him, eh?"

"I—I think so."

Tracy glanced at the slumped figures on the floor. Assurance
flooded back into him like a warm wave.

"This ain't your room, is it?"

"No."

"I thought so. Let's breeze."

"I'm afraid."

"Bunk! Shove on a little make-up, sweet. You're all right."

SHE CLUNG TIGHTLY to his arm as they crept down
the dark, creaky stairs. A yellow light burned in the entry. He
grinned at her in the cracked mirror of the ancient hatrack
until her frozen reflection melted in a wispy smile. From the
basement stairs came a warm gush of fried onions and the
mellow tootling of a soprano sax running the scales. Jerry shut
the door softly behind them.

It was quite dark outside. His mind was racing at top speed.
This tough party from Detroit—this greaseball chiseler—if
he was like all the rest of the small-timers he'd be on the prod
tonight in some flashy ankle-joint, smirking like John Napoleon, looking the Big Town over. All these guys were alike—
hot trombones and giggle-water and a great big smile for the
ladies!

He glanced at the girl and said abruptly: "Listen—you're hungry, kid, and so am I. We'll put on the feed-bag in a nice quiet place off the stem. I know a dozen…" The voice hardened. "After that we'll go places. Whaddye say? Got an evening rag?"

She nodded tremulously.

"That's swell."

They walked west and he flagged a cab. The restaurant he picked was a dingy place under the clatter of the 9th Avenue L. No music, no celebs; a pot-bellied chef named Andre, who lived upstairs with a wife and nine kids, and whose meat sauces and gravies were almost unique on the island of Manhattan.

Tracy ordered for both of them, and excusing himself politely, went to a glassed phone booth in the rear where he could easily watch her. He called up his man Butch.

When he returned to the table the girl was eating ravenously. He grinned sympathetically and touched her arm. "Slow down, babe; we've got an evening ahead of us."

Butch arrived before they were finished. He brought a suitcase with him.

Jerry answered the girl's eyes. "My valet. Leave the bag here. That'll be all for tonight. Beat it!"

Butch blinked calmly, gave the columnist's guest a stolid once-over and walked out.

"Trip?" said the girl. She glanced at the bag and there was a shadow in her eyes.

"Work clothes." He paid the check. "Take another puff on that butt and we'll roll… You haven't told me where you live."

THE ROOM WAS a small one. A battered wardrobe trunk

stood in one corner; there was a shallow closet, two cane-seated chairs and a scarred oak dresser. Beyond the bed, a half-opened door showed a peep of dark, tiny bathroom.

Tracy put his suitcase on one of the chairs.

"Still scared?"

"Maybe."

"Maybe, hell. You're all tuned up like a fiddle. We've got lots of time, so for Pete's sake, be sensible." He glanced at the bathroom. "Turn on the tap in there. Toss in a big soap-cake. Make it hot and steamy. Close your eyes and soak."

She didn't say anything. He picked up a copy of *Variety* from the cluttered dresser, dragged a chair towards the light and began studiously to read. He heard her, after a while, moving about in the bathroom. The gurgling splatter of water sounded and the door closed. Jerry grinned as he heard the curt snick of the lock.

He scrutinized his face in the mirror, fingering his chin. Smooth enough! He pulled down the shade, heaved the suitcase to the bed and opened it. The efficient Butch had packed thoroughly. His employer stripped and changed. When he had finished, the gleam of his shirt front was irreproachable, his silk lapels faultless, the set of his bow tie smoothly trig. He was studying the principal exports of Yucatan in a torn almanac when the bathroom bolt clicked.

She held the robe folded about her. The shabbiness of the thing made a curiously effective sheath for the draped mold of her slim dancer's body. She flushed suddenly and he stopped staring.

"Climbed into my overalls while I was waiting. Feel better?"

"Lots."

She moved over to the open wardrobe trunk and hesitated. "What's the matter?"

"Oh, I don't know—I've only that one *damn'* rag...."

"Break it out. Let's have a look at it, girl-friend."

She held the thing against her body. Not so good, Jerry thought. Effective as hell, though. Like the dressing robe, its very dry-cleaned shabbiness was an effective contrast with her red hair and the cream of her throat.

"Swell," he announced. "Stop frowning and crawl into it."

The bathroom bolt didn't click this time. Tracy rummaged through his opened suitcase. He uncorked a bottle of rye, filled a silver flask and pouched it on his hip. When the girl finally reappeared she looked at him smilelessly, steadily.

"Shoot," he said.

"Just exactly what are we doing tonight?"

"I told you once, sweetheart. We're going to cover an assorted bunch of ankle joints from the Village to Harlem. We're looking for a certain party from Detroit. You're going to point him out for future reference—or are you?"

"And after that?"

"After that we'll shrug happily and let a big honest Mick with iron-gray hair and square-toed shoes take care of him."

"Then you're a police stool?"

"What of it?"

Her eyes fell before his. "I don't know," she admitted.

"You don't know," he repeated coolly. "I do. There's the difference. Listen. I'll probably shake hands and say hawzit! to about fifty assorted mugs tonight—some of 'em killers, all of 'em grifters and wrong guys. Not one of 'em belongs outside of a jail-house, but they're all pals of mine and the Commissioner—up to a certain point. They tell me things and I tell them things... Oh, hell, what's the use of talking—you point out the guy and leave the code of ethics to me... Here!"

He held out her fur-trimmed coat and she slipped her arms into the sleeves. He donned his own coat and reached for the snap-brim gray hat.

THEY STOOD BY the railing in the *Club Timbuctoo* in darkest Harlem and Tracy glanced moodily at his watch. Quarter past two. No dice—it had been that way all evening.

The girl's glance moved quickly over the crowded floor, among the tables, into every dim corner. It was hard to see dearly; the air was thick with cigarette smoke and heavy with the odor of perspiration and cheap gin. Drowsy couples moved like corpses in a slow, sticky rhythm. On a raised platform a semi-circle of sweating bandsmen rocked in unison, eyes closed, black skulls gleaming. The music was raw jungle.

Tracy looked at the girl. She shook her head slightly.

"I don't see him."

"Let's go."

They walked towards Lenox Avenue.

"Tired, kid?" he asked.

"A little."

"Me, too; my pups are numb. Tell you what we'll do. There's a couple of joints we really ought to cover before we quit. If we can't spot him then we'll call it a night." He grimaced.

He whistled a cab to the curb and helped her in. As they sped southward he slipped his arm about her and her head drooped drowsily. He glanced down at her. Poor kid! She must be nearly dead! He hadn't tabbed her wrong at all. He liked the way she kept her mouth shut and her eyes busy. And he wasn't forgetting those strap-pumps of hers, either! He'd get her a hot spot in that second act of Spellman's new revue—or tear off both of Sammy's ears!

He lit a cigarette.

"About this next dive," he said tonelessly. *"Club Humpty-Dumpty*—it's a tough puddle. Tip me the wink quick if he's there. If he isn't, we'll move right out"

Her head turned on his shoulder.

"He's a snake, Jerry," she warned. "Be careful."

He laughed. "What have we got cops for?"

"I wouldn't know," she said jestingly, but her eyes remained grave.

"Not many do," he told her. "Why do you s'pose there's a half dozen big shots in this town that nobody bothers? Graft? Don't be nuts. There isn't enough dough in Manhattan to square that fella in the Commissioner's office. The big shot operators are business men. When they bump a mug—and they've bumped plenty—the ordinary citizens of this burg are getting a break, sister. Sounds screwy, but it's true. Innocent bystanders don't get killed as often as you'd think. I'm not kidding…."

The *Club Humpty-Dumpty* was a weathered brick structure in the middle of a short block.

A slot opened in the heavy door and a shadowy face peered.

" 'Lo, Bum! Open up!" said the newspaperman.

The face split into a sour grin. " 'Lo, yourself."

They stepped into a dim hallway. From behind a long wooden partition wall came the steady bleat of tinny jazz.

"Anybody around?"

"Jist a few."

"Keep your wraps on," Jerry told the girl.

They walked down the passage towards an open doorway framed in draped black velvet, tied back in dusty folds. The girl's hand vised on Tracy's arm.

"The guy in the middle," she breathed into his inclined ear.

There were three of them at a table across the tiny dance-floor. The man in the middle sat directly facing the entry. A swift flicker crossed his face as he saw the girl and Tracy. The corner of his mouth jerked inaudibly to his nearest companion. His face was unfamiliar; he looked like a Spick—sleek and dark. Black hair, jet eyes, pale olive cheeks. There was a stiff poise to his head and neck, a lidless quality in his stare that made Jerry think of a snake regarding a robin.

The newspaperman was in a tough spot and he knew it. He didn't dare walk out, so he walked in. His feet felt like lead. He waved the waiter aside and stepped behind the girl, pushing her chair in as she sat down. As he bent over her he breathed: "Sit tight. If they go for me, scram!"

He needed a drink badly but he didn't dare to reach for his hip-flask. A thin, hatchet-faced woman at the next table peered owlishly at him; the man with her was moodily intent on a pair of sugar-cube dice that he kept rolling monotonously across the tablecloth with a neat flick of his hairy wrist. Jerry didn't know him; he couldn't see anyone that he knew. The dance-floor was empty but the music blared horribly without a pause. It hurt his head to listen but he prayed silently for it to go on and on. He had a queer certainty that the moment it stopped, the man with the jet eyes was going to rise and stroll across. He was settling his check now, carelessly peeling a bill from a thick roll that he hardly looked at.

His eyes suddenly lifted past Tracy towards the velvet-draped entry.

A hubbub was going on in the hallway. A noisy crowd came spilling in—a half dozen couples, girls and men—skylarking, playing drunk, bumping against tables and waiters with cold-sober hilarity. A girl squealed out shrilly: "I smell rye! Gimme, gimme, gimme!" and the waiter jerked his tray backward as one of his glasses crashed to the floor. He wriggled away with a feeble grin; no flying wedge appeared to rush these hard-faced jokesters to the sidewalk.

Tracy saw a red moon of a face in a kind of foggy blur. He could hardly breathe. He smiled wanly and waved a small, stiff salute.

"'Lo, Dan," he quavered.

The big fellow crowed with elephantine delight. "Look who's here! Hello, yuh little bum! I'll buy yuh a drink—whaddye think of that!"

"Just a second," Jerry whispered to the red-headed girl.

He squeezed her cold hand and got up and walked over. Danny Murtha's eyes narrowed soberly.

"Whassamatter, kid? You look sick."

The columnist's voice raced. "Listen, Dan. I'm on the spot. They got the finger on me. Those three guys—easy—don't look."

"No kiddin'?" Danny's whine was flat, barely audible. "Them guinzos, you mean?"

Tracy whispered urgently.

"Dee-troit?" said Danny. "I'll be darned! The t'ree little guinzos from Dee-troit... So *that's* them!" He shrugged and the smiling eyes blinked sleepily. "Okey, Jerry. Thanks for the tip... Gitcha doll and scram!"

The *Planet* man's back crawled as he laid a five-dollar bill on his table. He helped the white-faced girl twitch her arms into her coat sleeves. As they walked towards the draped exit the three Detroiters rose without haste. The black-haired chiseler crossed the dance-floor to head them off. He bumped into Danny Murtha. Danny's hand was in his pocket; he rocked on his toes and shoved slightly with his stomach.

"What's th' rush, monkey?"

The dark man backed up a step, his eyes cold with venom. His two companions moved quietly forward until they stood on either side of him. Other men came slouching in on either side of Danny. The trio saw that they were blocked off from the doorway by a small semi-circle of hard faces.

A voice called: "Hey! What's goin' on here?" and the jazz orchestra stopped suddenly.

Murtha glared sidewise at the frozen piano player.

"Well lousy, what'rye stoppin' for? Go ahead an' play!"

He crouched as he saw a sudden motion of the trio in front of him.

Tracy heard the roar of the shots as he shoved the girl helter-skelter to the sidewalk. Her feet dragged. She was like lead on his arm. She cried stridently: "Lemme go home! Lemme go home!" There was a night-hawk cab at the curb; they flung themselves into it and the chauffeur gagged a frightened oath and stepped on his starter. The cab rolled.

AS IT SPED east a moon-faced man came leisurely out of the *Humpty-Dumpty* and helped his girl-friend into an automobile across the street. The rest of his party scattered in twos and threes and walked west. No flurry at all....

"Lemme go home!" the girl in Tracy's cab kept moaning to herself.

He shook her grimly. He felt as funny as hell. He wanted to choke her and kiss her—beat her into pulp, bury his scared face in the red mop of her hair. Poor little dead-game kid, with paper-thin soles and a pair of million-dollar dancing dogs—Hal LeRoy in step-ins—a smash hit for Spellman's lousy second act!

"Listen, dope!" he said, with an odd snarl in his voice. "The war's over. Snap out of it or I'll whang you in the ear! I'll be around for you tomorrow, understand? And for —— sake, stop sniveling! Sing a prayer to those sweet pups of yours, baby; they're gonna tap you right out of the *Coffee Pot* circuit. If you've got a loose dime, bet on it."

He left her staring frozenly at him in the dingy hotel lobby and rolled away in the cab. He was dead tired and his brain felt as thin as a razor blade.

He stopped in front of a dark theatre building in the middle of a side street. There was an alley alongside of it and he walked through to a doorway and rang the bell—two longs, two shorts. He went aloft in a tiny self-service elevator.

There were three men upstairs playing cut-throat poker.

"Thought I'd catch you guys before you quit," he told the white-haired man with the large nose.

"You look lousy," Spellman grinned. "What's new?"

"Plenty! I've got a plug for that second-act hole you've been crying about. Laugh that off, Sammy."

Spellman laid down his cards with a throaty grunt.

"Oh, yeah? He better be good, sweetheart."

"Guess again. This he is a she."

"I'll do you a favor," the producer shrugged. "I'll look her over some time."

"Play cards!" somebody growled.

Spellman picked up his pasteboards with inattentive fingers.

"What's the kid's name?" he asked.

The *Planet's* playboy grinned foolishly. What in the hell *was* her name? He didn't know; he didn't care. A silly tune was jingling in his brain. "Redhead, red-head; gingerbread-head…."

"Big secret," he grinned. "I'll tell you in plenty of time for the billboards!"

South Wind

*Jerry Tracy, maker of wisecracks, cuts
in on a bit of Southern tragedy*

BUTCH'S BIG FEET always shuffled when he was worried or puzzled. As he led the old man into the private Broadway cubby of the *Planet's* famous columnist, he squirmed his huge shoulders sidewise and his soles dragged like twin ashcans.

He shot a brief glance at Jerry Tracy and resumed his fore and aft scrutiny of the visitor.

In the canny experience of Butch old guys like this worked the novelty grift between Longacre Square and the lobby of the Republic Theatre. They were hired by the Minsky Brothers or maybe Luckyfield cigarettes. Every few yards on their strolling they pressed a button and an electric sign lit up on their shirt-front, or maybe on the seat of their pants. They all wore crummy Prince Alberts like this in the daytime and changed to dress suits with shiny shirt-fronts after dark; and they all sported that white, goatlike whisker under the lower lip. Must be a rule of the union, Butch figured.

Butch waited stolidly to get the office from Jerry—either a discreet scram for himself or a swift bum's rush for the old bird.

"Mistuh Je'y Tracy?"

A soft, blurry voice. Southern. The columnist looked at the straight back, the mild eyes. Sixty, he guessed. His gaze dropped to the veined back of the hand resting on the knobbed cane. It was puckered and fragile looking, spotted on the skin with faint brown marks like overgrown freckles. Jerry changed his guess. Seventy, at least.

He answered the formal query with a brisk: "Check. What's the complaint?"

The old man sat down.

"Why, no complaint, I reckon. It's merely that I've been info'med, suh, that you're in a position by virtue of yo' knowledge of theatrical matters and Bro'dway, to render me a kindly service—"

Uh, uh! Here comes the bee, Jerry thought He could almost hear it buzz. In a moment it would alight painlessly on his wallet and fly away with a buck. Well, maybe two, damn it! The old fella looked pretty tired; the hand that mopped his face was trembly....

"I've come to see you about my granddaughter, Mist' Tracy. I tho't—I've been reliably info'med—that you could probably help me find her."

Tracy's eyes narrowed. Might be the McCoy; might be a

build-up. Too hot to speculate. The dead pan of his bodyguard wasn't much help.

"Outside, Butch," he suggested curtly.

The old man was fingering the edge of an inner pocket. "I've got a photograph—"

"Just a minute, Colonel."

"Major, suh," he corrected courteously. "Major Geo'ge Fenn."

"Okey by me... What makes you think I find women? Somebody tell you I was a private op? And who gave you the address? Been over to the *Planet* office?"

"Yes, suh. I forgot—I saw a gentleman named Hennessey, I believe, and he gave me this yere note."

"Let's have a look, Maje," said the columnist grimly. Dave Hennessey was getting to be pretty much of a lousy nuisance lately! Him and his nose for news! Jerry would put a cover on his can the next time he saw him!

He ripped open the envelope and read the thing with a scowl.

The attached prise package has been getting under our feet and walking around presses looking for you. He refuses to spill the plot except to Mistuh Tracy, suh. Maybe there's a gag in the guy. If there isn't, toss him to Butch.   D.H.

Jerry crumpled the message disgustedly and flipped it into the waste-basket.

"That makes everything as clear as the depression," he grinned. "Who sent you over to the *Planet* in the first place?"

"The clerk at the hotel. Mr. Collins. A ve'y nice man. Most helpful an' courteous. When I explained to him that Alice Anne was in the theatrical profession he said that—"

"I know. He said Jerry Tracy, just like that. He's not Snitch Collins, by any chance, of the dear old San Pueblo?"

"That's right. That's where I'm stoppin'. I like it first-rate, suh. Ve'y quiet. No noise. The cab driver recommended it."

His wrinkled eyes smiled.

"New Yo'k is a real homey town. As nice an' friendly folk as you'd find in the hull of No'th Ca'lina."

Tracy nodded absently. Friendly, all right… The friendly hackman, cruising around Penn Station in a gyp-wagon, hauling fresh meat to the San Pueblo, pulling down his commission. The friendly Snitch Collins, steering the old guy to the *Planet* on the off chance that his joint might horn in on some publicity for a change. The friendly Hennessey, his Irish nose alert for a cheap hot-weather gag for his lip-reading customers… Just a great big friendly town!

And quiet! You couldn't find a quieter spot than the San Pueblo Hotel if you started at the Aquarium and walked all the way to Gun Hill Road. The San Pueblo specialized in dense silence. The hard-pan dicks who dropped in for an occasional chat with the guests and the management, did all the loud talking. A month back they had carried out a small blonde exhibit from a room on the fifth floor. The Tabs made an awful noise. *"Dance Hostess Slain by Fiend!"* But the San Pueblo merely said: "Tsk, tsk!" got a pencil and a *Racing Form* and stretched out in its underwear to study the Pimlico results with the shades discreetly pulled.

Tracy said, in a flat murmur: "Yeah, it's pretty quiet… The granddaughter's in show bizness, you say—her name's Alice Anne Fenn and you say she's been up here—"

"Fo' years, suh. But I haven't had any letters since—"

"Let's see the photograph."

He studied it with a scowl. The picture was about as helpful as ear-muffs in August. A faded three-quarter pose of a girl about sixteen in a fluffy white dress, with a white ribbon, on her hair and a rolled diploma in her left hand.

"Her graduation picture," said the old man proudly. "First in her class. Smart as a buggy whip."

"What's her stage name? Never told you, eh?"

"No, suh. I always wrote to Alice Anne at general delivery. She wasn't much hand at answerin' letters and for the last two years—"

"I know."

Damn' right, he knew! An actress, eh? That meant she might be anything. A waitress in Quids, a salesgirl in Gimbel's basement. Or she might be demonstrating corn-razors or opening day-beds in a store window. Pounding the sidewalks of Sixth Avenue or doing a strip act in a cheap burlesque show. Hell— for all he knew she might have a coupla kids and be living in the Bronx, married to a shoe-clerk. Try to find a stage-struck kid from the South in this burg! New York was lousy with Southern gentlewomen trying to get their monickers up in the lights.

HE PICKED UP a sheet of paper, folded it, tore a semi-circle out of the crease. He opened the paper and laid it flat on the photograph with the girl's face in the hole.

He studied it, looked away with eyes closed, studied it again. There was something vaguely familiar about that isolated head in the center of the white sheet. Add a few years, subtract the schoolgirl simper… Hmm… Lower-lip pout, round face and movie chin; moonlight and honey-suckle in the slow drawl of that famous second act exit....

Behind his own closed eyelids jigsaw letters joined hands and formed a name. Lola Carfax, by ——! Lola....

When he opened his eyes his face was wooden.

"Can't place her at all, Major," he said. "Some more dirt, please."

"Suh?" The old man looked puzzled.

"Details. Dope. Information."

Major George Fenn wiped his moist face and began tremulously to recollect. Jerry sucked a pencil end and listened.

Alice Anne was the only kin—his only granddaughter—all he had left—he was gettin' old, powerful lonesome. Smart little tyke; she used to play with his watch-chain an' call him Marse Geo'ge. The Fenns came from Thunder Run, in No'th Ca'lina. Not much of a place, but pretty, suh... Saggin' fences an' houn' dawgs blinkin' lazy, with their paws couched in the red dust o' the road. Thunder Run warn't much of a crick but it certainly did thunder, by Judas Priest! when the stars made everythin' else quiet an' the spray kep' brashin' an' gurgling in the dark over them flat stones. An' the hills—blue, suh!—with hawks driftin' like dots an' fat white clouds that never moved....

"So Alice Anne packed up and left," Tracy reminded him.

That was correct. She went No'th. Grandpap couldn't hold her, not after she married that damn' Jeff Tayloe. Only seventeen, she was. Headstrong as a colt.

Jerry stopped sucking the pencil abruptly. So La Carfax was married! Well, well—and also, hum, hum!

Jeff Tayloe was a scamp, it seemed. A damn' cawn-pone hillbilly with white teeth an' a big laughin' voice—an' she ma'ied him. Three months later Jeff was in jail and Alice Anne smiled calculatin' an' far-away, packed up and went North. Plenty o' spunk. She wrote letters for a while, then they stopped coming. Never told him her new name—he always wrote to Alice Anne Fenn at general delivery, and after a while his letters came back with big carmine rubber-stamp marks all over them.

"How long since she left, did you say?" Tracy murmured.

"Four years this Fall."

Humm… Lola Carfax—seventeen and four—check! Three years since Hymie Feldman picked her out of thin air and gave her the juicy lead in "Southern Charm." A natural! Couldn't act worth a plugged dime, but her drawl—oh, man! And her luscious innocence in the second act—oh, ma-a-a-an! And her wise, case-hardened persistence in the part after the smash-hit closed. Little Lola knew instinctively what the vise critics didn't—that Southern Charm was a golden racket in a big evil-minded burg, if you played the role on Park Avenue and met the right people and your voice was as soft and velvety as pollen on a bee's thigh… A luscious peach from the Southland with a small, rotten pit tucked snugly away in the fruit. Jerry knew the outlines; Patsy would know a hell of a lot more!

He said, absently, "Beg pardon?"

"—my declinin' years," the old man was saying in a slow, stately murmur. "The last prop of my house. If you could only find her—"

"I thought you said she had a brother," Tracy lied in an odd voice.

The old man hadn't said anything of the kind, yet he nodded.

"Did I mention him? Her brother, Henry Fenn, made the supreme sacrifice in France, suh. She's all I have left."

"Check," said an odd, gasping voice in Jerry's brain. "No brother to guide her. Then who whelped Buell Carfax? And—holy sweet hominy!—can it be that young Massa Buell has white teeth and a big, laughing voice? Also, how tight are Southern jails, I wonder?"

He was burning with a desire to get to Patsy and soak up her slants on the subject. Patsy could spear a fish like Lola Carfax with a dozen well-chosen words.

He got to his feet, smiled, held out his hand.

"Tell you what, Major. You've got me interested. I don't recognize the photograph but I'll keep it, if you don't mind. You wait for developments at the San Pueblo—I'll have Butch ride you over in a cab. It may take a little time to trace Alice Anne—"

"I was hopin' you might find her for me in the next fo'ty-eight hours," Major Fenn said faintly. "Circumstances at Thunder Run make it impe'ative, I'm afraid—"

Busted. The old fella had his fare probably and a small, carefully counted roll....

"We'll do the best we can, Maje," said Tracy cheerfully.

He stepped into the outer office and leaned over Butch's cauliflower ear.

"Take this guy over to the San Pueblo. After you've parked him, go up to Snitch Collins at the desk and tell him I said to keep his hooks off the major. Tell him if he doesn't I'll send someone over there that'll take him by the ears and smash every—chair in the lobby with his heels! Tell him that from me."

Butch made a slow spittle-noise with his lips. He pulled his unfailing joke, a high-pitched falsetto: "Is that a promise?"

He went out with the major and Tracy walked to the window and stared across at the dirty façade of the Times Building.

He put on his hat after a while and went out.

TYPEWRITERS WERE CLICKING busily in the *Planet's* big news room. Hennessey looked up from the city desk as Tracy breezed by.

"Hi, Jerry! Get any belly laffs outa the old gempmum?"

"Shut up, you ape, or I'll raise a high hat on your skull!" Tracy grinned. "Patsy around?"

"Where d'yuh get that Patsy stuff? Lay off! I happen to know she don't like it."

"Brrr! You happen to know? You wouldn't know if your collar was unbuttoned, Dave. See you later when you got money."

He turned a corner, went down a corridor and stepped into the third cubby on the left.

"Hawzit, Patsy?"

"H'lo, Bum." She sat back. "Lousier an' lousier. This place makes me sick. I could be fired right now for what I think I've been toying with the quaint notion of expunging myself from the payroll."

"So what? And if same occurs?"

"I could try newspaper work for a change."

"Ouch! That hurt!" He looked at her with alert eyes.

"No kiddin', Jerry," she said gravely.

She was tall and slim, almost loose-jointed. Nice face, dark hair and eyes, small mouth. She dished up society news and could write with a cruel, jewel-like hardness when the need arose. It seldom did. Her customers rode in the Bronx Express and liked prose poems about Piping Rock. She could turn that stuff out in her sleep. She and Jerry were the twin stars that made the circulation manager of the *Planet* sing in his bathtub. Doris Waverly's Chat, syndicated....

She bad been born in a beery flat on Tenth Avenue. Kicked loose, saved up, pulled a grim A.B. out of Vassar—talked nice to strangers and tough to friends. Her real name was Veronica Mulligan. Tracy called her Patsy and she liked it. Hennessey, the city editor, tried it once and she curled him like Cellophane with a brief, pungent description of his type, straight out of the Elizabethan drama.

"Ever hear of Lola Carfax, of the ole Southern Carfaxes?" Tracy asked her.

"Ah reckon Mistuh Beauregard... Why ask me? You've got the rat assignment, Jerry."

"Come, come, child! Poppa wants the dirt."

"Want it brief?"

"Uh, uh."

"I'll say it slowly. She's a wise, crooked, honey-drawlin', little—"

"I getcha. B as in bird-dog."

"And not the Poppa, either..." She grinned. "Why the sudden interest?"

"Her grand-pappy's in town. The real name, if you'd like to know, is Alice Anne Fenn. Take a long look and say yes or no."

She studied the photograph.

"It's Lola, all right. That's one dame that can make the hackles rise on me. She and her pretty brother!"

"What's he like, this brother? Wait—don't talk! Has he got nice strong, white teeth and a big laughing voice?"

"That's Buell. Add the professional drawl and the phoney courtly manner and he's yours."

The columnist's smile cut a little crease in his face.

"What makes you think I want him? Listen, Patsy! She married him when he was Jeff Tayloe, when she was shy and seventeen, in the dear old deep Southland."

"Tell me some more," Patsy said slowly. Her dark eyes were like agate.

He told her a lot. When he had finished she nodded.

"I've often wondered about Buell Carfax," she admitted. "He's only been on the scene for a year or so. Her graft is no mystery but I never could figure brother Buell. They're smooth workers. Right now I'd say they're both definitely in the inner sanctum. I've only heard one 'no' since Lola gave Park Avenue the office. It came from old Miss Lizzie Marvin of Sutton Place. Somebody said: 'Dear little Lola! Such a sweet child!' And the ancient virgin from Sutton Place smiled her wise old smile. 'The little girl in white? Ah, yes… She fairly stink-ks of Southern charm!' I had all I could do to keep from hugging the old warhorse!"

Jerry lit a cigarette, leaned over the desk and blew smoke against his trick Panama.

"Scene changes. What about this Doctor Altman? Profile, please."

Her lips curled.

"There's a suspicious nose in the profile, but the good doctor is Church of England. Edgar Louis Altman. He gets around. Surgeon, polo, squash—maybe Lola Carfax."

"Why maybe?"

"There's always a big maybe about matrimony—did I tell you the girl was smart? She's been in the money for months, but like old Robert E. Lee, she wont surrender without a ceremony.

If I were you I'd bet on matrimony. Altman has sunk enough dough already to make a wedding look like good economy. He's chasing her hard, Jerry."

"I'll make a note of that," he grinned. "The little girl is chased!"

She said irritably: "Stay sober. How about Buell Carfax? The big brother with the nice teeth."

"You asking me, Patsy? A nice boy like Jeff Tayloe gets out of a North Carolina jail, sees something in a rotogravure, reads something else in the social chatter, picks a few pockets and comes North. What a lovely reunion *that* must have been! I'd say the split was 50-50, but we know Lola is smart so maybe he's only cutting a straight 10 per cent. Even at that, he could play ball—it's a life job, Patsy, and a handsome brother with a smooth line is worth 10 per cent of anyone's dough."

Her face clouded. "And the old grand-pappy's in town? He sounds nice. It's nice to find someone that's McCoy once in a while… Where's he parked?"

Jerry chuckled. "You'd never guess. San Pueblo. Nice and quiet, he says."

"Holy cats! Well—what are you going to do?"

"None of your damn' business."

"I'd like to talk to the old fella."

"You'd *better* like it," he said. "You've been talking to too many phonies lately. It spoils your temper. Go on over and pump him. It's a tonic. Tell him I've got a lead. If you have time you might drop in on the Carfax suite and smell the air… What would you like to do tonight?"

"You wouldn't understand, you heel."

"The hell I wouldn't! I'll shoot an arrow, just to show you.

Let's go yokel for the evening."

"Are you kidding?"

He pulled on his Panama, snapped the trick brim, waited.

"A corned-beef dinner," said Doris Waverly, Inc. "With cabbage, or you can go to hell! A ride on the Staten Island Ferry. We'll sit on the top and you'll keep your mouth shut and hold my hand. Did anyone ever tell you you talk too much?"

He leaned over and kissed her on the tip of her sharp nose.

"You simple-minded ape," he said, and went out the door, grinning.

She's got the summertime heebies, he decided mentally. The poor kid looked seedy, tired. He'd siphon a coupla drinks into her tonight and try to wisecrack her out of the gloom.

BUT PATSY WASN'T to be blarneyed. She was glum over the corned-beef, sour on the boat ride. She borrowed his butts and stared morosely at the lights of St. George. The boat thudded monotonously; the vibration added their feet.

"How'd you enjoy Lola and the boy friend?" he inquired.

"Dead fish," she snapped. "Must be a few more in the Harbor tonight. Get dat sweet whiff! Do you s'pose it's true that Indians used to paddle around this lousy burg in clean water before the smell era?"

"Don't go Noble Redman," he grinned. "Friend of mine went to Taos once. According to him, the Injun kids learn to smell long before they learn to eat."

"I wouldn't be surprised... I saw a clean show today, Jerry."

"You're telling me! How'd you like the old fella?"

He watched the slow smile come and go.

"Ni-i-ce. An old-fashioned road show crammed full of

hoke… I don't think it was good for me. Made me think of Dennis Aloysius."

"Do I know Dennis?"

"Why should you?" she said, sweetly. "He was the respected sire. The ancestor. Tenth Avenue. Waterfront whiskey. Beer by the scuttle for a chaser."

Her cigarette end glowed jaggedly, once, twice, and then went over the rail in a long arc.

"You're swell company," said the columnist feebly.

They stood outside the gaunt cavern of the South Ferry Terminus and a hackman threw open his door invitingly.

Tracy said: "You need a coupla highballs, cheerful!"

"No." She hesitated. "But if you knew where we could get a tall glass of good old-fashioned beer—"

Tracy grinned. "With pretzels."

"And some Roquefort and crackers—and a slice of Bermuda onion."

Jerry turned to the chauffeur.

"Okey, Rocco. Click us uptown till you hit Third Avenue. I'll tell you where to stop."

They downed a couple of tall ones, found out they were hungry, and fixed that too. They walked over to Fifth.

On the downtown bus the girl said, suddenly: "What are you going to do about Anne and the last of the Fenns?"

"Have I got to tell you that again? None of your damn business."

"You always were a consistent rat!" she said with cold rage.

Tracy chuckled without rancor.

"Here's the schedule. Go over to see Massa Geo'ge Fenn tomorrow morning. Tell him that Old Sleuth Tracy knows all and that the search has been successful. Take him over to the Consolidated Ticket Offices and if they roll Pullmans as far as Thunder Run, say Pullman as though you meant it."

"Any other little jobs?"

"Sure. Check him out of the San Pueblo. See that Snitch Collins behaves himself on room extras. Then I'll let you bring the major over to me. I'll be in the Times Square hideout. Any questions? Dismissed!"

He pressed the stop buzzer.

She wrenched around to look at him. Her voice was a whisper, a mere thread.

"You lousy heel, if you do anything or say anything to hurt that old man, I swear to I'll—"

"My corner. I get off here," said the columnist.

He tipped his hat, swayed down to the rear of the bus and swung off. He called up from the sidewalk: "So long, Babe."

She leaned over the rail and gave him a furious farewell—a loud and rather fruity bird.

"Ding, ding," went the bell. The grinning conductor leaned way out to stare. He hung like a swaying chimpanzee for the next five blocks.

MR. BEULL CARFAX was tall, handsome, with cold eyes and a small ashblond mustache. He bowed briefly to Tracy and shot a quick flicker at the stolid Butch. Tracy had forgotten to mention Butch over the wire.

"I hardly think, Mister Tracy," said the courtly brother of Lola, "that Mis' Carfax would care to be interviewed. Any news of plans, social engagements and so fo'th is, of co'se, sent to yo' readers regularly by Mis' Carfax's secretary."

Tracy said: "This is different."

"If there is anything that I personally might—"

Tracy said, again: "This is different."

The cold eyes focused on him. After a moment they blinked.

"Very well. This way, please."

Nobody said anything to Butch. He trailed after Tracy. Lola Carfax was standing on the far side of the room, examining a small hunting print on the wall. She didn't turn around.

Buell said, in his stately drawl: "Lola, honey, here's that newspaperman."

She paid no attention. Tracy walked swiftly across. His smile was as thin as a hacksaw blade. He stood and looked at her back for a moment. He caught her eye reflected in the glass of the picture frame.

He said, deliberately: "Turn around, you cheap little grifter!"

She whirled. Her beauty was like the flash of a blinding ray. Tense, wordless, carved in ice. Her red lips were parted slightly, she seemed scarcely to breathe. Her eyes had the cold, hard glaze of a cat's.

Across the room, Buell Carfax gave a thick bellow of rage.

"Why, dam' yo' filthy Yankee—"

As he sprang forward his hand came away from his vest pocket. The light glinted on the muzzle of a tiny derringer. Butch's hand thrust out with the speed of a striking snake. His hairy fingers closed around the slender wrist and bent arm and weapon upward.

There was a muffled report; a short, straining tussle; Carfax squealed shrilly as his pinioned arm snapped.

Butch's left hand caught the slumping man by the throat and pinned him upright against the wall. He held him there almost casually. His attention was on the little derringer in his own right palm. Butch had never seen a toy like that before. He stared at it with the absorbed curiosity of a monkey.

Tracy smiled into the lovely eyes of Lola. She was lifeless, stiff, except for the candle-flame in her eyes. There was something eerie and horrible in the intensity of her fright. Her voice was barely audible.

"Is this a hold-up?"

"You're damn' right"

"What are you after?"

"Everything you got."

They were like conspirators whispering together in a dark cave.

"You can't get away with this. You must be insane. You're a madman."

He said to her: "No, I'm not—Mrs. Jeff Tayloe."

The flame he was watching was quenched for an instant and then blazed up brighter than before.

"I don't know what you're talking about."

"Oh yes you do, baby."

There was no humanity in Tracy, either. Two lumps of ice whispering together.

He paused a moment.

"Thunder Run," he said. "It's in North Carolina. No comment?"

She watched him with that horrible immobility.

"Just an old-fashioned story about an old-fashioned gal. Once upon a time there was a gal. Pretty name. Alice Anne Fenn. Lots of brains but no judgment. She was always a sucker for white teeth and a big bass voice. So she married a lousy hill-billy home from the wars, name of Jeff Tayloe—and Jeff carved a yaller gal in a particularly nasty way and went to jail—and little Alice Anne saw the Big Town beckoning, packed her cotton underwear and scrammed North."

Tracy grinned like a wolf. Butch had pocketed the derringer. His left hand still pinned the boy friend against the wall. He was listening to the bedtime story with a puzzled interest.

"Only trouble was Jeff Tayloe was smart, too," the columnist resumed. "He wangled a pardon after a while and saw a photo and read the papers. He had pretty sharp eyes. It all worked out swell after the first dirty argument. Then they got down to business. Jeff got a break; Alice Anne got a well-built husband that she had kinda missed; Lola Carfax got a brother and a protector. Background means a lot on Park Avenue. Brother Buell was well worth the percentage he held out for."

His voice sounded friendly, quite cheerful.

"A swell arrangement for all hands except the fish. But the fish has dough, so who cares? This fish even thinks about marrying, believe it or not. Good old Doctor Edgar Looie Altman. Let's see; he lives at the *Mayflower*, doesn't he?"

The movie chin trembled. The little-girl eyes were grown up now and haggard. A bead of sweat gathered in the hollow under the red pout of her lower lip.

"Blackmail," she whispered stonily.

"You tellin' me?"

"You can't prove it. He'll throw you out on your face."

Tracy said, mildly: "I forgot to tell you. Grandpa's in town. Major Geo'ge Fenn. As innocent as a child—proud of his race and his lineage—as simple and honest as they come. I thought I'd take him over to see the Doctor."

Her throat made an ugly rattling sound.

"Damn your soul, if I had a knife I'd rip your belly—"

Slow tears welled from her eyes. He waited.

"How much?" she said, finally.

"I told you once. Everything you got.

"Five thousand, cash."

Tracy laughed at her.

"Put on your hat, lousy. Go get your bankbook. We're gonna take a walk and close an account."

"It's all I've got in the world. You'll strip me."

"That's a good start. You'll get along… Keep an eye on the boy friend, Butch. We'll be back. Look this joint over."

Butch nodded and his big forehead creased with a self-conscious and intelligent frown. "Sure, sure." Buell Carfax's face was a dull purple. He was out on his feet. His broken arm hung limply.

She looked at him with a cold loathing as she went out. Tracy held open the door ceremoniously. He had a brief case with him. He had brought it along because he preferred cash.

When they returned Butch was sitting alone in an armchair, smoking a cigar. The top of his breast pocket looked like a pipe organ of Havana Specials. He nodded towards an inner room.

"On the bed in there, Mr. Tracy. I hadda slough him. How'd yuh make out?"

"Fair. Did you go over the joint?"

"Yop. Small change… Got a baby roll outa his hip pocket Coupla saw bucks in the bureau, wrapped up in a silk pantie."

He grinned, got up and took the heavy brief-case.

Lola Carfax watched them go. A faint moaning reached her ears from the inner room. She stood rigid, listening to the monotonous sound for a long time. A haggard face swam back at her from the small antique mirror on the wall.

She screeched at it suddenly. Sprang at the mirror and wrenched it down. Whirled, flung it viciously with both hands. Then she stood there shaking, looking dully at the jagged fragments.

PATSY BROUGHT MAJOR Fenn into Tracy's little Times Square office with a slow, solicitous smile for the old man and a quick, stabbing scowl at the bland columnist. There was not much of Doris Waverly about her—and a whole lot of Veronica Mulligan. She looked worried, vaguely suspicious.

Tracy sprang up and gave the old man his chair. He hooked another one closer with his toe and Patsy snapped shortly: "Thanks," and sat down.

Tracy fiddled with a pencil and laid it down again.

"I, er… I promised Id try to find your granddaughter, Major. It's been quite a search. I, er… I've been successful."

"You've found Alice Anne?"

"I've found out about her," Tracy said evenly.

"Where is she? Have you her address?"

The *Planet's* playboy hesitated.

"Do you want the truth? You'd like to know the truth, even if it—hurt?"

The shaggy eyebrows twitched. The pink face went gradually gray.

"I reckon the plain truth will suit me, suh."

The girl at his side made a sudden hopeless gesture.

"Listen, Jerry! You didn't find her. You're lying. You made a mistake."

"Shut up!"

His shaking voice became even again.

"I found her under her stage name. The identification is proved. The photograph of Alice Anne and the facts you gave me were conclusive evidence... Did you ever hear of the Arcadia Theatre?"

No. George Fenn hadn't heard. Neither had Veronica Mulligan, from the look on her face.

Jerry told them about it. It stood on Fifth Avenue and 59th Street, opposite the Park. The pride of New York—the old Arcadia Theatre. It housed nothing but the best, the finest, the cream. Alice Anne was its greatest star—its last glorious star.

The girl was staring at Tracy with amazement.

"A little over a year ago," Jerry said, "Alice Anne played her greatest role. In the middle of the second act there was a blinding flash backstage, a sheet of flame shot out from the proscenium... There's a new hotel where the grand old playhouse stood. The theatre was totally destroyed."

The columnist's forehead was glistening with sweat.

"Alice Anne Fenn was standing in the wings in costume, waiting for her cue, when the flames came. She refused to leave the theatre; shook off the hands of rescuers. She knew there were two chorus girls, hemmed in by flame in a blind corridor on the dressing-room level. Alice Anne gave up her life in a vain effort to save those two girls."

He added, tonelessly: "When the ruins were searched she was not—found."

Patsy's palm rested suddenly on the back of the major's veined hand. Her eyes were hard and bright, enigmatic.

"Thank you, suh," George Fenn managed to articulate. He

drew in a deep breath. "I certainly want to—to thank you for your—efforts—"

"Why, that's all right… There—there were a few legal matters connected with your granddaughter's estate. I took the liberty of acting as your agent, signing for you. The trust officials were quite sympathetic, friendly."

He touched the fat brief-case awkwardly.

"The estate, of course, goes to you. I thought you'd like it in cash. It's here—a little over ten thousand dollars."

The columnist shifted slightly in his chair to avoid the angry challenge in Patsy's eyes. The old man wasn't listening at all; the talk of money was a meaningless buzzing on his ear-drums.

He said, gently: "She could do no other, being Fenn. She was suckled on gallantry, suh… She used to twist my watch chain with her little fat fingers, call me Massa Geo'ge… My dead son's child…."

"You've got his ticket bought?" Tracy whispered to Patsy. "Yes."

He pressed a buzzer with a fierce, fumbling jab.

"All right, Butch. Take care of the brief-case. Go over to Penn Station with him. See him aboard."

The major got slowly to his feet. He turned at the door and Patsy turned with him. Her arm braced his.

"I want to thank you," said the major, "for yo' kindly help. New York's been mighty fine to me. Nothin' but friendliness in the two days I've been here. I'd feel it remiss not to thank you, not to let you know my deep gratitude." He patted the hand his arm. "You too, Mis' Waverly."

They passed outside and the columnist heard Patsy's strained voice. "Wait a minute, Butch. Just a second."

She came back and closed the door.

"Listen, Rockefeller! I'm in on this. Your damn' dough's no better than mine! I've got a half interest in the racket or I'll swing on your lip right now!"

He grinned at her in startled wonder.

"——! you're as pretty as a picture, Kid… Don't be silly. It's not my dough."

"Whose?"

"I went to the proper window for it. Carfax. I pumped her for every nickel she had."

"Are you lying, you ——?"

"Stop snuffling and show sense. Do I dig for ten grand of hard-earned Tracy jack because some old bozo comes drifting in to put the bee on me? Grow up, baby; you're living in a big town."

"It stinks," she shrilled suddenly.

"Who said it didn't? So does Thunder Run. So does every other damn' burg. You're still soft, baby; get back in the water and boil some more."

She stared at him with brimming eyes that jeered at him.

"Tell your friend Hennessey to run a *want-ad* in the *Planet*."

"What do you mean?"

"I'm through with this lousy town. I'm going where I can breathe clean air."

She fumbled in her handbag, threw an envelope on the desk in front of him. Jerry could see Pullman tickets—two seats—to Thunder Run.

She looked at him defiantly. "What the hell do you think of that!"

She swept the tickets into her purse and the door slammed.

A moment later it opened slowly.

"Jerry... Hey, hardboiled..." Her eyes were soft. "Any time you get sick of this crooked game, come on down to Thunder Run. I'd be awful glad to see you... Anytime...."

The door swung with a small click.

Tracy leaned back in his chair, cupped the back of his skull with his clasped hands. After a while he grimaced wanly.

"I'm not so tough," he thought. "I gotta be careful or they'll have me pitchin' hay in Wichita—or wherever the hell you pitch hay!"

He dragged a notebook out of his pocket and flipped open the pages to a recent entry. He got up and went over to the dictaphone.

He shrugged and spoke nasally into the flexible tube of the instrument:

"Harvey Smith, feed and grain impresario, and his wife, the former Claire La Tour, are ffft-ffft... Mrs. Smith has left for Reno to establish legal residence... It's a girl...."

Park Avenue Item

*Jerry Tracy, wisecracking columnist,
knows tragedy when be finds it*

THERE WERE TWO or three angles to that phone call from McNulty that made Jerry Tracy decide to roll up Park Avenue and have a look at the place. Jerry had a high regard for the old man's judgment; and the flat, singsong voice on the wire sounded quite positive: "Me think velly much on level okey. Boss. Where hell you stay all night?"

McNulty was Tracy's butler, major-domo, conscience and guide. An enormously fat and unsmiling Cantonese Chinaman, he ran the domestic affairs of Libel's End—which was Tracy's penthouse—with a wise and stolid tyranny. His ancestral name was Mei-Now-Lee, or something of the sort—so Jerry called him McNulty and so did everybody else. He had, it seemed, been trying to locate Tracy since two o'clock that morning.

"Make tlenty calls," he complained. "Hab bleakfast. Make tlenty-four. Where hell you go? You dlunk?"

Jerry grinned. He was, he told the Chinaman, stone sober. He had been out to an impromptu brawl with Hart Schaffher and the Four Marx Brothers. Just dropped into Frank's place for a tonic... His smile hardened.

"Did Johnny Vega make the call himself?" he asked. "Or did some friend of his pass the tip along?"

"Me think Johnny Vega. Not sure, Boss. Sound quick, sound velly unhappy."

"Okey, McNulty," the *Planet's* columnist grunted. "I don't have to tell you to keep your mouth shut."

He stepped out of the speake's soundproof booth, nodded to the tall man polishing glassware and started for the door.

"Gotta go home and prove I'm sober," he chuckled.

"That Chink's a darb," said the tall man morosely. "S'long."

On the way uptown in the cab Jerry glanced again at the address and apartment number he had scribbled in his notebook.

There were two or three angles… In the first place, Jerry had never wholly subscribed to the town's theory that Johnny Vega was the guy that had slipped the heat to Kane. It was a mug's trick any way you looked at it—a hop-head stunt to drill a first grade Dee like Marty Kane who, everybody knew, was a sob'd, plainclothes veteran with six kids and a million friends. Yet the circumstantial evidence and the whispers all pointed to Vega, and then Johnny had taken that quick, panicky dive out of sight.

The Department gave Kane an inspector's funeral and for six weeks now there had been a steady editorial yelp from the anti-administration sheets to nail down the coattails of the vanished Johnny Vega. Up to now the harassed commissioner had been unable to oblige—and here was a phone call, apparently from Johnny himself, telling a Chinaman named McNulty in a scared voice that he hadn't killed Kane, that he had found out who had, and would Jerry Tracy for God's sake come around, grab the confidential info and slip it to the commish for a quick pinch?

Jerry frowned as his cab swung north on Park Avenue. The yarn clicked. Vega was a wrong guy, a grifter; but he wasn't a crazy hood, a cop killer. Not in Jerry's album anyway. The phone call proved that he still had his head on right, that he trusted

the columnist. And why in hell shouldn't he? They had always played ball together until the murder of Kane gummed the works. The withdrawal of tie dark-eyed little Vega from circulation irked the *Planet* man. It was no coincidence that for the past six weeks the column hadn't tabbed a single muscle item that was worth printing.

Jerry dropped the cab and walked up the east side of Park Avenue for two blocks with a grimly sour feeling that Detective Marty Kane hadn't helped anybody a nickel's worth by sticking his big, honest belly in line with a hot slug.

The apartment building was typical of the neighborhood—eighteen stories, square as a drygoods box, built to turn in a profit on every last foot of rentable space. With a shallow entry, a canopy and a lazy admiral. Only there wasn't any admiral.

No taxi-stand outside, either. Funny... The doors were shut tight—they were locked.

Tracy eyed the pushbell at the side of the door-frame. He had just made up his mind, for no reason at all, not to push it when a voice said mildly: "Lookin' for somebody?"

A big bluecoat was grinning at him from the sidewalk; a spruce, good-looking young cop. The smiling eyes glanced with approval at the columnist's tricky light overcoat and made a shrewd and wrong deduction.

"You won't find her here, Bud. She's pro'ly at the Canopus. Next corner, across on the other side. They moved all the tenants over to the Canopus Hotel two months ago. Didn't she tip you off? The place here is closed up tight. Nobody around but a caretaker."

Tracy blinked. He said, slowly: "What's the idea? Small-pox?"

"Depresh," said the patrolman, and amplified with a bored air.

"No new leases, d'ye see? Owners tryin' to keep up the old rent scale. Only a dozen lease-holders in the whole buildin'. So what does the wise big shot in the realty comp'ny do? Moves the tenants over to furnished suites in the Canopus Hotel— signs an agreement to pay all expenses—fires all help except the guy in the basement—locks up the whole place, so help me... It's cheaper, d'ye see, to carry the handful o' tenants in a hotel than it would be to keep the joint goin' with heat an' hot water an' elevators an' doormen an' all the rest of it. Both sides save money."

Two months ago, the cop said... The columnist's eyes gleamed at the thought. You could put six weeks into two months very nicely; and it was just about six weeks since they lowered big Marty Kane to rest in Calvary. A guy in the basement, according to the cop. And, if you believed in telephone messages, a guy maybe in apartment 12-B. Not a bad idea if you were under the hatches and your name was Johnny Vega.

Tracy didn't bother calling at the Hotel Canopus. Instead, he turned the corner and took a slow, leisurely stroll around the block. The cop was well up the Avenue now, his broad back a dwindling spot of blue. Jerry halted casually at the service entrance and tried the grilled gate. It wasn't locked. He closed it behind him, went down a long sloping ramp through a whitewashed tunnel, descended steps to a sheer-walled courtyard, walked into the basement.

A DIM, QUIET labyrinth. A few yellow bulbs burning. Through an open door he could see the tubs and dryers of the laundry. His nose crinkled at the faint smell of heat—a funny smell. A turn round a corner showed him the service elevator with its door open and a light burning. He stared at it speculatively and lit a cigarette. As he exhaled expensive smoke he heard the scrape of hurrying feet and a voice growled: "What the hell d'yuh want?"

A little fellow. Looked like a Swede. Brown dungarees and a big wrench in his right hand. Johnny Vega's lookout, probably. Scared as hell, too! The wrench was trembling visibly in his fist.

The Swede took in Jerry's sartorial splendor with a quick gulp, and added placatingly out of the corner of his mouth: "Was yuh lookin' for somebody Mister?"

Tracy studied him silently. He knew this guy—he'd place him in a minute... His mind clicked suddenly. He didn't know him—it wasn't the face that was familiar, but the signs. The hunched shoulders, the cocked head, the pasty phiz, the words clipped out endwise. This mug was an ex-con; he'd been in stir somewhere. Under the stress of his queer panic he was broadcasting The Prisoner's Song like a brass band....

"I'm a friend of Johnny Vegans," Tracy said.

The little Swede gulped nervously. "Dunno who yuh mean, Mister. They ain't no one livin' in the house now. The whole place is closed up."

Tracy shook his head, smiled blandly.

"Booshwah... I said I'm a friend of Johnny Vega's. That means I'm not a dick, a nose, a stool or a screw. Just a friend— get me?—a pal."

"Never heard of him, Mister, an' that's Gawd's truth."

"That's funny. He called me up from this building last night and asked me to come over and see him. How do you figure that?"

The Swede's quick shrug was like a gooseflesh shudder.

"Okey. I gotta be careful, y'unnerstan'. The guy's on the lam and it you're a pal of his, you know why." He paused a moment and licked his lips. "Johnny ain't here. He breezed last night."

"Where'd he go?"

"Don't be silly, Mister. Would he tell me?"

"What time'd he pull out?"

" 'Bout midnight." The Swede studied the expressionless face of his visitor. "Maybe ha' past twelve. I didn't notice exactly."

Damn' right you didn't notice, was Tracy's thought According to McNulty, Vega's call came through a little after two a.m. The Swede was a punk liar and a lousy guesser.

Tracy said aloud: "Okey. Maybe he'll gimme a ring from his

new dive. If he's got sense, he will."

"Sure. He'll pro'ly do that. That's what he'll pro'ly do."

They both nodded sagely at this ideal solution and Jerry dropped his cigarette and crushed it under his sole. As he turned away his palm rested for an instant on the whitewashed firebrick wall beside him. The firebrick was quite warm—hot, in fact. The smell of heat was quite perceptible. He sniffed a couple of times.

"Pretty early for steam," Tracy said mildly.

"Yeah. Just a touch o' pressure to keep out chill an' damp. These big buildin's are like tombstones when they're empty. They git pretty chilly."

To prove it he wiped his moist forehead. Jerry said: "I wouldn't know about those things," grinned, waved a polite gesture and walked out through the basement.

The Swede stood watching him from the concrete arch outside the laundry door, with the Stillson hanging loosely a his thin, bony hand. Tracy turned out of sight into the long paved courtyard and went up the steps to the sidewalk ramp. There were eighteen steps. He climbed twelve of them and marked time for the remaining six. Then he turned around on his rubber heels and stood there, a thin grimace on his lips. He was going to have a look at apartment 12-B, no kiddin'. He was quite sure about that. If the Swede's head showed in the courtyard he'd walk down again and ask him something. Take a chance on the wobbly wrench. He wasn't a hell of a lot impressed with the caretaker's toughness.

The Swede didn't show. After a while Tracy descended gingerly, rubber-heeled it across the courtyard, removed his hat and took a cautious one-eyed peek. The nervous caretaker was gone. There was a faint clanging going on in the sub-cellar below. Jerry listened for a few seconds and grinned. Just a mug from Scandinavia! He slid into the open service elevator and closed the catch with a mild click.

He rode up to the twelfth floor. 12-B was at the end of the service hall, close to the big fire-door that led to the tenants' hall and the main elevator. The columnist opened the metal door, looked through and closed it again. The main elevator was probably locked and dark. Johnny Vega would be more apt to use the service shaft. He had become damned leery of Mr. Johnny Vega in the last ten minutes. What was it all about anyway? For no reason at all his belly was contracting nervously. He hated to press the buzzer on 12-B.

After a brief hesitation, instead he rapped boldly—three times. Nothing happened and he rapped again. After a while he heard the slap of approaching footsteps—sounded like bare feet.

A nasal voice, a woman's voice with a nervous saw-edge to it, cried petulantly: "That you, Nick?"

Tracy gargled unintelligibly.

"—— sake!" the voice shrilled fiercely. " 'S a wonder you wouldn't use your key, you dumb—"

The door opened partly and he saw the staring, bloodless face of a woman under a green rubber bathing-cap. Instantly he put his foot in the door.

Jerry knew his little piece by heart now. He watched her curiously as he recited it. "I'm a friend of Johnny Vega's."

Her pale face went paler and she stared at him. After a moment she smiled at him mechanically and allowed him to push the door a bit farther. "You had me scared, brother, jammin' in like that… I thought for a minute you was a flattie."

He laughed. "Since when do dicks wear coats like this? Believe it or not, it came from London—and I don't mean London, Ohio."

She laughed, too; not a good laugh. "You say you're a pal of Johnny's?"

Tracy nodded. "Johnny and me are just like that."

She said: "You're too late, brother. The kid ain't here. We was tipped that the place was gettin' hot and he breezed. How'd yuh know he was here?"

"He called up my dump three days ago. Needed half a grand. I was out of town and just got the message. He been gone long?"

"Coupla days. Musta raised the jack somewhere else. Thanks just the same. If you wanta slip me the dough—I'm his babe."

She was his babe—and he left two days ago—he must have come back and left all over again according to the Swede in the cellar. What the hell were they all lying about?

Tracy looked keenly at her eyes, the nervous hands, the pale lips with the sagging flesh-lines at their corners.

He said, coolly: "Nix. This is Johnny's dough. I'll hold it for him. I'm not staking his babe to a trip through Switzerland."

She grinned at that. Her right fingertips jerked suddenly to her left forearm with a slow rotary movement of which she was entirely unconscious.

She said, sneeringly: "You're a pretty wise jasper, at that. Only I don't sleigh-ride. Morph's my dish, dearie."

This whole thing was screwy, Jerry decided suddenly. Screwy as hell. The jane was alone and trying hard to bounce him away with a bluff. Well, he didn't bounce… He'd give this joint the once-over.

The girl backed away as he pushed through the door.

His narrowed eyes flicked from the woman to the room, back to the woman. Her face was like soft putty. She was quite obviously in a state of near nudity except for the silk negligée and the green rubber cap. She had no slippers on her bare feet. Every shade in the room was drawn. A kerosene lamp burned smokily on a side table. The whole place reeked with it.

"Didn't get you out of the bathtub, did I?" he said idly.

The glassy eyes focused sharply. She drew in an audible breath. The fear that had ebbed for a moment came spilling up through her eyeballs. Like a wave on the beach, Jerry thought.

She grimaced and took a step towards him.

"Be a nice boy. Scram, like a good fella."

He didn't move from her push. Just stood there. "Why?" he asked her.

"Because—well—I ain't exactly wearin' overcoat an' hip-boots—an' if Johnny came back for somethin' an' seen us together—he's a jealous bimbo—"

Tracy laughed, a chuckle of amusement.

"You wouldn't lie to me, would you?" he asked.

"What do you mean?"

"Who's Nick?"

"I don't getcha." He heard her teeth grind.

"Sure you do. You thought I was Nick. That's why you opened up."

"He's—he's the guy downstairs." Her voice blurred. "The Swede in the basement. He's coverin' us. I thought it was him with a letter from Johnny. Jeeze, you're suspicious, honey."

Nick—that Swede in the basement? Not on your tintype,

thought Jerry; but he only said: "Aw, no… Mind if I take a look around?"

He thought she was going to faint. He hoped she would. But she didn't.

He could barely hear the flat whisper: "I guess I can't stop you."

"You're damn' right you can't… What's that door? A closet? No, you show me…."

CLOSET, EMPTY. HE followed her. Passage way, pantry, kitchen. About face and back again; bathroom. Three bedrooms; more closets. As he followed the soft slap-slap of her feet on the floor he felt the skin prickling on the back of his neck. It was exactly like the childish game of "search.""You're warm; now you're getting cold; warm again; warmer…."

In that third bedroom he had strongly me feeling that the game was getting damn' hot. The top drawer of the dresser was half open. Slippers and a par of stockings on the floor and a dress, a girdle and a crumple of underthings in a heap on the chair next to the dresser. The woman in the negligée stood near the chair, staring at him with about as much animation as a drugged dummy. He crossed the room, opened a closet door, gave it a lightning scrutiny. A few dresses and hats; not many. Nothing else.

When he turned he was sure that the woman hadn't moved. Just a drugged dummy next to the chair with the soiled clothing. Yet he saw at once that her right hand was in the pocket of her robe; and the top drawer of the dresser that had been half open, had slid miraculously a third farther out.

Tracy didn't say anything, and after a moment she seemed

to come awake. He followed her out of the room with ice in his knee-caps and practically no belly at all. He kept pretty close behind her.

There was one more room at the end of the passage.

She muttered dully: "Maid's room. Don't wanta see that, do yuh?"

"Might as well."

The room was bare. No furniture at all—and still *another* door. With a ground-glass panel.

"Maids bathroom," said the thick, sleepy voice.

She padded submissively ahead of him, turned partly as though to beckon him. He saw her feet spread a little and brace themselves. He swung at her, and as the gun came out of her pocket his fist connected. It was like kicking a cat—no sound from her at all. Her paralyzed fingers scrabbled on the floor, trying vainly to raise the gun. He kicked the thing loose, scooped it up.

He sprang to the bathroom door and wrenched it open. His hand stayed on the knob. For a long eternity of seconds the watch on his wrist went *tick, tick, tick*.... Then he stepped back from the threshold and gently closed the door. The blood had drained from his face, leaving it a curious mottled white; his cheeks and jaws looked suddenly dirty and unshaven. He stared at the semi-conscious woman on the floor and muttered: "Nice girl... Just a nice girl...."

The private phone in the front room was dead, as he had feared. Probably a single trunkline open on the deserted switchboard in the main hall downstairs. He caught the girl under the armpits and walked her like a wobbly sack to the room where her clothes were, where she had palmed the gun.

He dumped her on the bed and tied her ankles and wrists with ripped lengths from the pillow-case, anchored her hands and feet to the bars.

She squirmed a little; her breath was like a drowsy gust of hate in his face.

He crammed a gag in her mouth and stood there thinking hard. There was that damned Swede in the cellar. Had he really foxed the mope? He'd have to get downstairs in a hurry and buzz Harry Wilkie—Marty Kane had been Harry's partner—Harry was the logical man to look in the bathroom and switch his red bloodhound beak from Johnny Vega to a guy named Nick. Meanwhile the Swede hadda stay dumb and this half-naked jane hadda stay put....

With a grin Jerry remembered the incinerator hopper in the service hall outside. He cleaned out her clothes closet, picked up the junk from the chair. It made a double armful.

The elevator outside was just where he had left it. The incinerator hopper was set in the wall on the right of the corridor. He flipped it open—and knew with a sick certainty what the Swede was up to. Tiny sparks danced, there was a hot, tinny smell. The Swede was in this thing up to his eyes! Johnny Vega obviously wasn't going to stay very long in the bathtub—and by the same token a guy named Nick certainly had unfinished business in apartment 12-B.

The *Planet's* columnist shoved the girl's clothes down the warm flue, left the door of the apartment wide open and went down in the elevator.

He got out on the street floor, tiptoed through to the public hall and sat down at the deserted switchboard. The place was like a silent tomb; a single light burned wanly and the only sound he could hear was the dim, bee-like humming of the motor traffic on the avenue outside.

He got headquarters, gave his name and asked for Wilkie, listened feverishly to a bit of kidding from his friend on the desk, was switched finally to the 98th precinct house. More kidding, and—

"That you, Jerry? Wilkie talkin'. 'Smatter, kid?"

"Listen! Write it down fast!" He gave the address. "Kane case. Keep your mouth shut. Hop over quick if you want the lad that cut down Marty Kane."

He heard a faint gasp. "You got Johnny Vega there? Is this a gag?"

Tracy swallowed fiercely. "Get over here, you louse. No squad car. Take a cab. I'll let you in the front door. How soon?"

"Fifteen minutes."

"Make it ten, Harry, for —— sake."

He was sweating as he sat back. His face was yellow under the light. He wiped off his forehead with a tremulous hand. Back in the dimness of the service hall a shadow retraced noiseless steps towards the elevator. The Swede's face was puckered in a frozen, nearsighted glare. Ten minutes—he had heard that! He hesitated at the elevator, changed his mind, sped up the boxed stairs without a sound....

THE STREET DOOR darkened with Wilkie's bulk and Jerry sprang up and let Kane's partner in. He was a big man with a pouty lip, a barrel chest and thin legs. He uncovered a dull-blue gat without haste.

He said, in a low voice: "What's the lay?"

Jerry nudged him round the corner to the elevator and they

rode up. The apartment door was still open. Wilkie looked puzzled at that. He went in first. There was no one on the bed. The knotted slips had been hurriedly slashed with a knife. The detective took one look and his bull voice roared:

"—— sake! Yuh let Vega scram?"

"No. He's here."

"Where 'bouts?"

"Maid's bathroom. Down the hall there."

"Bathroom? Say, what is this—a comic strip act?"

"Take a look, Harry," said the columnist in a weak voice.

Wilkie wrenched open the door, rocked slightly upward on his toes, said very briefly: "——!" He came back to Jerry, his pouty lips working with a snarled undertone.

"Who done it? Who was here? Gimme the dope."

Tracy talked fast. He gave him a swift outline. "She can't be far away. She's half naked! Just that robe of hers. Bare feet. I shoved her clothes down the incinerator."

Wilkie grinned nastily. "What of it? You'd git far away, wouldn't yuh, with a thing like that in the bathtub? Jeeze, wotta girl-friend! The Swede musta been wise—heard yuh come back maybe, or got a flash of you phonin'... If you think they're still in the buildin', you're nuts. Gimme a quick description of them two. I'm gonna hop down to the switchboard for a secon' and have a fast look in the basement, too. Stay here."

"Don't mention the bathtub or Nick," Tracy begged. "He's coming back—he's got to! He doesn't know the thing's busted. If he sees a flock of P.D. cars outside—"

"Don't worry any," said Marty Kane's partner grimly. "Jist a routine alarm for a wench and a Swede. The rest is my party. I'll take a chance on a police trial for withholdin' information."

He was gone in a flash. When he showed again he said harshly, "You say this guy Nick has a key to the joint?"

"Yeah. She bawled me out for not using it when I rapped."

"Okey." Wilkie shut the door and turned the lock knob. "We'll jist stick around." His chuckle held no mirth. "Entertainment committee."

"I can't figure her on the street in that outfit she's wearing," Tracy muttered.

"Can'tcha? What's the matter with the Swede flaggin' a cab from that dam' service alley, carryin' his sick sister out, takin' her to his wife's mother—or anybody else he can think of? He's had over ten minutes to stir his hump while you were sweatin' downstairs at the switchboard. You shoulda taken that wrench off him and nicked his skull in the first place… Huh! Let's glom this dive!"

They found a fresh ugly stain on one of the mattresses after they had ripped off the clean bed-clothes and turned the mattress over.

"Vega got his payoff right here," said Wilkie sourly. "He ain't improved any since he got it. I s'pose I oughta apologize to th' corpse if your slant is right."

His big body teetered about the room without sound on his thin legs like an overbalanced cat. There was nothing much to play with except the irregular brown stain on the mattress. Johnny Vega's clothes and the soiled sheets had probably gone down the incinerator. The two men flopped the mattress over and re-made the bed.

They tiptoed back to the maid's room and Wilkie fixed the door slightly ajar. The bathroom was still open and, with a faint grimace, Tracy went over and closed it without looking in.

Wilkie's low murmur hummed in his ear.

"A swell layout, hey? The girl and Nick and the janitor in cahoots. Vega's been the fall-guy from the start—right from the time poor Marty Kane got the heat. It's all a guess—the girl mighta had an apartment in this hive and tipped Nick the news when the tenants were moved over to the Canopus. Nick braced Vega an' it pro'ly sounded like heaven to a mug with a general police alarm on his tail. Wotta dump... Phones dead, shades drawn, oil lamps—an' the Swede for a lookout man. He's the guy that pro'ly spilled the beans. I noticed his phone's working; plugged in with the switchboard trunk-line. If Vega sneaked down at two a.m. this morning to make a call, an' the Swede listened in, it would be just too bad for Johnny, hey?"

"It's a fair guess, I s'pose."

"Sure it's a guess. It's all guess. The finger was out for Johnny and he was panicky as hell—he *should* be! I'd of plugged him on sight!—so Nick played the good, er, Samarian an' got him under the hatches, figgerin' that while the cops hunted Johnny they wouldn't be apt to hunt Nick. It'd work swell unless Vega happened to git wise to who bumped poor Marty Kane... Looks like he got wise some time yestiddy."

Wilkie's pouty lips closed. He stood tensely, quietly for a moment, listening, his eyes on the crack of the door. After a while he grinned and relaxed. His grin lingered at Tracy's whispered question.

"I'm still guessin'," he admitted. "But I gotta hunch I'm ringin' the cane. How could it happen? Well, they're both dopies, see?—Nick and his gal—an' six weeks is a long time. Yuh git careless. And don't forget yuh feel like a king in Babelong when yuh got a skinful o' high-power. Yuh might begin to drop woids—maybe boast what a hell of a clever fella you are. Yuh might—holy Jeeze!"

A flush mottled his heavy face. He took out his handkerchief and mopped it off.

"*That* might be it, for —— sake! If the murderin' louse had *that* in his pocket an' Vega got a flash of it—sure, he'd have it! Why didn't I think—only a dopie'd take it in the first place. He'd like to play with it an' laff long an' satisfied, an' think what a coupla cheap two-dollar punks Napoleon an' Caesar was... By ——!"

"What do you mean?" Tracy whispered uneasily.

"Never mind what," Harry Wilkie husked. "I'm prayin' the fella shows, that's all. I gotta notion I'm gonna roll him an' scrape out his pockets. I gotta notion—"

HIS HARD FINGERS bit suddenly into the columnist's forearm. The metallic sound was faint but unmistakable. A key was fiddling in the lock of the service door of the apartment.

It opened and shut again with a slam. Wilkie's gun looked big, even in his big hand. Both men held their breaths and watched through the crack. The murderer was tall, bony, built like a lath. He was grinning a mile a minute, talking to himself. His eyes glittered in the semi-darkness, a fixed glitter of satisfaction.

"Hey, Myrtle! Hey, Kid! Where are yuh, yuh li'l ——?"

He meandered around, always laughing softly.

"Where are yuh, Myrt? I gotta deck for you... Huh! Gone out for a hop sandwich—couldn't wait for Poppa's groceries. Awright, Baby—I'm happy. Hell with you...."

He came noisily down the darkened hall and Tracy's mouth

was wide open. Wilkie's fingers had uncurled from the columnist's forearm. It was just as though the big homicide dick wasn't there at all.

The visitor disappeared into one of the bedrooms and they heard a chair creak. In a minute a shoe thumped on the floor. The second one clattered. Jerry stood frozenly, wondering with a kind of insane calm, why dropped shoes usually roll topside on the sole nine times out of ten. Wilkie was still fast asleep with his eyes open.

The man came out of the bedroom presently—stark naked— and padded down the hall with a soft slip-slap. He went into the kitchen.

Wilkie's drowsy eyes gleamed. He couldn't resist a brief threadlike whisper: "Remember the roomin'-house case in Brooklyn? Same thing all over. No stained clothes."

Goose flesh crawled up Tracy's neck.

The man Nick came out of the kitchen. He had a big knife in his hand. He walked down the hall, swung open the door to the maid's room. It screened the two hunters in the corner. The murderer took four steps towards the bathroom and then Wilkie's arm slammed the door.

Nick whirled, screeched once, and lunged at them with a downward sweep of his knife.

Wilkie didn't say anything. He grouped four holes well above the navel. Then he opened the door, walked out and went into the bedroom.

He riffled through the pile of clothing with a face like stone. He held up his palm for Jerry to look. A flat shiny thing with a coat of arms on it and a number.

Wilkie swayed up on his big brogans. He was blinking

rapidly. He said, suddenly: "Kane was a good man—one square dick…."

He whirled with a strangled oath and went clamping into the maid's room where the body lay. When he came lack Jerry didn't make any comment.

"Let's get the hell downstairs," said Wilkie. "I gotta put in a call."

The deserted switchboard was buzzing monotonously as they got out of the elevator.

Wilkie grinned at that "I gave 'em the number just in case. Wonder if they've nabbed them two… Hello? Yeah; right here."

He talked a while and then listened.

"Right Sweat 'em some more and see if I care. Listen, Eddie—hold everything—I got Johnny Vega. Dead, yeah. An' a mug name o' Nick, ditto. Found Marty's shield on him… Okey; send over the works. You aught flash the bozo on this beat; there'll be a mob outside, pretty soon."

He hung up with a small, finicky gesture.

"They tripped Swedie an' the gal. Add one for the flatfoot boys. He seen she carryin' act goin' into a dump on East a Hunnerd an' Tenth right after he got the G.A…. Yuh look lousy, Jerry. You crazy to be in on this?"

"——! no!"

"Okey. You don't need to show. Take your runout while you got the chance. How do yuh feel?"

"Not so good."

Wilkie's laugh rumbled. "None of you newspaper guys can take it. You make me think of a joke I heard once—remember it? The one where the doctor says to the patient: 'Trouble with you is you got a weak stummick!' Scram Jerry; you're a good guy."

He unlocked the door and Jerry went out into the afternoon air. He thumbed a rolling cab and relaxed on the cushioned seat.

"Up Fifth," he told the hacker.

At Seventy-odd he got out and went into the Park. The little lake was alive with kids' boats.

He thought, "——! I never want to see a grifter or a cop again!"

A voice said: "Nice day, sor, ain't it?"

A paunchy old flatfoot was grinning at him, reaching down with a lazy grunt to untwine a kid in soiled shorts who was trying to climb his uniformed leg. A bloated old Mick cop with a cheerfully creased phiz, a comfortable belly, comfortably flat feet. He whacked the kid softly on the tail with his gloved palm.

"Git off wid ye, ye monkey!"

Tracy looked at him queerly. "What's a good way to lose a grouch, Officer?"

"Well, sor," he grinned amiably and considered, "I wouldn't call that a poser by anny means. I'd have a dhrink or two, maybe—shtep out wid the old woman, telephone aroun' teill I found a party goin' on wid a real good accordeon player—"

"Thanks. Have a cigar."

Tracy hurried out the Park entrance and hooked another cab with a brisk gesture. "Down to Fifty-ninth and then west."

He'd have a Chinaman named McNulty shake him up a couple of extra specials. He'd crawl into a stiff shirt and have dinner out. With whom? Somebody decent—somebody with a clean line of charter. A red-head... Stella—that crazy little bimbo with million-dollar dogs and a laugh like a tall drink with bubbles. One swell Broadway child and as straight as a string.

He watched the cars scud by, going north.

A nice dinner—pick up a gang somewhere—drag 'em over to the penthouse. Organize a kazoo orchestra and let Stella tap for 'em—oh, man! Get Abrams and Manny Field to put on the great Rival Stooge act. Hold on, for —— sake—Schnozzle himself was in town....

He leaned forward with a blurred smile and slid back the glass panel in the front.

"Step on it, mug!" he told the hacker. "Papa's on the prod!"

Beyond All Light

What the world doesn't see, it doesn't believe. A blind man judges without sight and believes he is always right.

A DRIPPING, SLATE-COLORED afternoon—brrrr! The slow squishy, filthy cold downpour was one of those icy, skin prickling drizzles, scarcely more than a smoky mist but it was falling steadily and freezing underfoot. The sidewalk as a paste of frosty slush.

The beggar at the curb said no word at all as Tracy went by. He stood patiently aloof, as quiet as a stone. Tracy was sloshing along in the very devil of a hurry, but he paused instinctively as he caught a sidelong glimpse if the man's extended cup and his wide, sightless eyes. There were two wet pennies in the cup and the fingers that held it were blue with cold. Jerry fumbled a moment, dropped in a quarter with a brisk *plink!* and walked on.

The beggar's left hand moved upward from his side with a lightning dart, probed deftly for the quarter, slipped it into his pocket. He said in a rasping singsong: "Thank you, sir!"

Tracy was already two or three paces away when he heard the growled acknowledgment of his gift. He stopped short, hesitated, turned, came slowly back again. His mouth was twitching faintly with the mirthless grin of Broadway—a trick done mostly with the lips and teeth, compounded equally of cold amusement and colder wisdom, with a grim dash of "sez you!"

He said to the man: "I like to know things. I'm funny that way. That was a pretty good quarter I slipped you… Just how really blind are yuh, Bud?"

"Blind?" said the beggar. "You're a wise guy with a quarter and you'd like to know how blind am I, Bud?" He laughed harshly for an instant. "Blind?" he said again. He seemed to derive a kind of tortured pleasure from the repetition. He played with the word, terrier-like. "As blind as a bright red fire-plug. As blind as the side of a whitewashed barn. A velvet mole with whiskers and a tin cup... Is that a quarter's worth, Mister?"

He stared at Tracy through the freezing mist and people went skittering past the two of them, heads down, elbows shoving; a swirl of damp ghosts in a slippery, endless maze. The beggar's wide-open eyes were milky and unwinking; they looked unpleasantly like chinaware. His short-clipped beard was a scraggly, fuzzy brown. Water trickled down his forehead from the sodden brim of him hat. The upturned collar of his cheap overcoat was beaded with twinkling drops.

He shivered suddenly and the two pennies in his cup clipped together in a faint scuffle.

"You said 'thank you, sir'," Tracy said. "I wondered how you knew it was a man and not a woman."

"Thought maybe I was peeking?"

"I just wondered," Tracy said nasally.

The man's jeering laugh was so low it was barely audible.

"Very simple, Watson. The night has a thousand eyes—surely you remember that. You walk like a man; longer steps, fainter clicks. You smell of tobacco and soup. You didn't open and close a handbag when you took out your quarter... And women always give pennies—never less than two or more than four— and that's all, Watson. Put your whistle away."

"I'll be damned!" said the newspaper columnist. "A nice, smooth lecture. Where did you go to school, Mac?" His eyes narrowed. "You smell 'em and you hear 'em. Is that it?"

"Mostly smell," said the harsh whisper. "Close your eyes some time and try it. You'll drop about half your friends. In the dark thieves stink and so do liars… Move on brother; you're discouraging charity."

"Okey, Central," Tracy said coolly. "Put me through for another call."

He fished leisurely in his pocket and dropped another coin in the cup. The beggar's finger swiftly filched it and stowed it away.

"How long have you been on this grift?" Tracy asked him.

"Not as long as you, brother. You're sitting pretty."

That made Tracy laugh. "How do you know?"

"For one thing, you're too free and easy with your quarters.

For another, you stink of highballs and silk underwear. You belong on this street; you've got the damned Broadway whine in your voice. Laugh now and tell me I'm guessing. You're one of the boys and you've got plenty of easy cash and you don't work very hard."

"Let's have some more professor," Jerry said. "Bring your lecture right up to date. What do I work at?"

The blind man shivered suddenly. "—— I'm cold!" His teeth chattered.

Jerry reached out and took hold of the wet sleeve. "Let's move over to a doorway. I'm still interested. A buck says you can't tell me what I work at."

"You're a persistent louse, aren't you?" the beggar sneered.

He allowed Tracy to guide him across the slushy sidewalk. He walked with short, shuffling steps, his crook-handled cane swinging loosely from the bend of his arm.

"You're offering me a buck if I call the turn on your racket?"

"That's right."

The man chuckled. "That eliminates one guess. You're not a card and dice man or you'd have made it a straight bet—made me risk a buck of my own."

He closed his dead eyes with a muttered oath.

"Let me concentrate… One of the boys. Broadway native. An actor, maybe… Or a newspaper man?"

"You're asking me?" Tracy clipped pertly. He was watching the man with narrowed, incredulous eyes.

"Shut up! I'm thinking. I think I'm going to say newspaper… You don't smell like an actor. You have the vaudeville whine all right, but you talk tight like a mouse-trap. And you're more interested in me than you. That doesn't sound like an actor…

You heard me say 'sir' and wondered at my choice of sex. An actor might wonder but he'd let it go at that. A newspaperman would stop and ask questions. They're curious lice... Well?"

His eyes opened wide again with their level, disconcerting stare.

"IS THAT THE final guess?" Tracy asked him.

"That's the final guess."

Tracy folded a dollar bill lengthwise and slipped it between the stiffly extended fingers.

"Satisfied?" said the harsh voice.

"Yeah."

"You're a liar," the blind man sneered. "You're still wondering about me and my smooth line. You've had your money's worth; now you'd like to stay a while and hear the customary story of how I first came to lose my virtue."

"How did you?"

"Not on Broadway."

"Where are you from?"

"Kentucky," He laughed with a horrible jocularity. "I was born in Mammoth Cave. Catch wise, Mister? Just an underground fish."

Tracy shuddered. "You're cold-blooded, all right."

"Just blind, Mister," the voice grated.

"What's your name?"

"None of your damn' business... Wait, I'll be fair; after all, you paid cash on the nail... You called me professor. All right, my name is Jefferson Brick. I used to be a professor of chemistry in a Protestant Episcopal university. I lost my eyesight in a laboratory explosion. I left home because I didn't care to be a burden on my beautiful young wife. Besides, I knew she was secretly in love with the professor of history, who was a man of independent wealth and very handsome in a sinister way. So I took a tin cup from the pantry and stole away in the night… Try that on your city editor. It's not true, of course. But it wouldn't be a bad bet for the movies."

His bearded lips twitched haggardly.

"And in number two yarn," Tracy suggested with a grin, "you're probably Sergeant Amos J. Sparrowcock in a shell-hole on the Ourq with bullets whining overhead—"

The columnist ducked his head back with a distant grunt. The blind man had lashed out wildly with a clenched fist that caught the newspaperman flush on the mouth. They scuffled clumsily together in the dark doorway and Tracy caught at the arms and held them tight.

He panted: "What's the idea of that, you mug?"

The man stopped struggling suddenly and Jerry let go of his arms.

"You son of a ——!" the beggar whispered softly. He bent down and felt with his hands for his fallen cane. Tracy let him alone. The beggar turned unerringly and took a swift tapping step towards the sidewalk where icy rain blew and pedestrians slopped through the gray slush.

Tracy blocked him off. "Listen a minute, will yuh?"

"Let me alone! Let me go or I'll smash you with the cane!"

"Oh, no, you won't. Who do you think you are—Gyp the Blood?"

His captive gave a short despairing cry. His blank eyes seemed to bulge from his head. The columnist's own eyes were gleaming. He could use this fella—this blind monkey with the

wise ears and the accurate nose. Jerry always played hunches—
and he had a hunch right in front of him cornered tight in a
wet doorway.

It'd be worth a little dough to get a hard-boiled nose-and-ear
verdict on Daisy. That babe had Tracy worried. He wasn't sure
about her. And he *had* to be sure! If she was on the level and
he broke her story in the column—good ——! what a story!
And verification all over every sheet in the town in three days.
——! he'd slay Manhattan with the hottest news prophecy
since Croker left for Ireland.

But if Daisy was a double-crossing little liar… The thought
made him sweat. If little Daisy happened to be a patient, dewy-
eyed Judas, working in cahoots with Tom Hoyt of the *Sphere*…
They'd laugh Tracy off the earth and the *Daily Planet* would be
caught belly deep in libel….

"Let me go!" the blind man snarled.

"Will you shut up a minute? Look… I'm making you a proposition."

"Lemme go!"

"All you have to do is listen to someone while she's talking—a
woman, see? In my office, not two blocks away. Twenty-five
bucks for you. In advance. Right now and in your mitt."

"Lemme go!"

"Jeeze, I'll smack you in a minute! Listen, all I want is a
verdict on this dame. Is she crooked or straight? Is she a louse
or the best friend I've got? She has something to peddle, with
no proof except her unsupported word. Twenty-five bucks—
two tens and a five—and all you do is listen and say yes or no
when she's done. She's as smart as hell, blind man!"

There was a pause.

"What's your own personal opinion?" said the other man sullenly.

"I don't know. I've been checking and re-checking and snooping—and I'm still absolutely—"

"Blind?" said the beggar in his razor-thin murmur.

The fellow's bitter self-torture made Jerry's fists clench with a helpless, impotent anger.

"—— you sure love to pick at the scab, don't you?"

"As long as I can bleed, I'll know I'm still alive. That's horrible, isn't it?… Now go ahead and tell me all about Helen Keller. Nice ladies with a candy peppermint smell press my hand on an average of twice a week and tell me all about her."

"And?"

"She was born blind, wasn't she?"

"What of it?"

"I wasn't," said the dusty murmur.

There was a silence. Tracy took a deep breath. "Will it make you feel any better if I bust out crying?" he said brutally. "Let's go back to business. I don't think you're a bum and I do think you got brain. Wanta sell out for twenty-five bucks?"

"Two tens and a five, you said."

"Yeah."

"You might slip me singles. I couldn't tell."

"That's your problem," Tracy said. "Sniff hard and tell me whether I'm an insect or an angel."

"You're a louse, all right… Which one is the five?"

Tracy laid the bill in his palm. He folded it and stowed it away. He put the two tens in another pocket.

His blank eyes rolled vacantly towards the newspaperman.

"Better tell me what it's all about, hadn't you?"

"Not in a wet doorway, sonny. Grab hold of my arm… And for —— sake, throw that tin cup down the sewer and I'll buy you a new one."

They stepped out from the doorway's shelter and plodded southward through the slippery slush. Of the two, the blind man had the surer footing.

BUTCH—THE FAITHFUL BUTCH of the cauliflower ears and the oversize feet—was lolling in the outer office of Tracy's Time Square hideout. He pinched out his butt and stretched massively, yawning like a hippo. He stared at Tracy's brown-bearded companion without much change in his leaden eyes.

"Any phone calls?" Tracy asked him.

"Nothin' fancy. Just chopped meat. There was a drunk in a speako that Hennessey thought maybe might—"

"Hell with him. I got a frill coming here pretty soon. You know her. She'll breeze right by you when she comes in. Let her breeze."

"Okey, Boss." He rolled his big head lazily toward the columnist's sodden companion.

"Who's the pencil merchant?"

Tracy ignored the query and grinned. "Let's have a quick tintype of Butch," he suggested.

The blind man's lip curled. "Quarts of blood," he said thickly. "Offal. A prehistoric brain."

"Oh, yeah?" Butch gagged helplessly for an oath and then gave up the struggle. "Is zat so?" He growled. "Yuh don't tell me!"

Tracy led the blind man into his private cubby and closed

the door. He took off his companion's hat and overcoat and hung them up on a hook in the corner. He swept a phone book to the floor and swept the empty chair close to his desk. He prodded the back of the man's knees with the chair edge and the blind man sat down.

The columnist felt suddenly diffident, uncomfortable.

"Have a cigarette? Or is that—er—"

"It is. Don't worry; I'm used to it. People don't smoke much in the dark. Inhaling helps, but not much… You don't believe me, do you?"

Tracy looked incredulous. "I don't get you on that. I've done it myself plenty."

"Try it without your optic nerve sometime, my friend. Or just close your eyes so you can't see the red glow when you draw. It's not quite—satisfactory." He said the word purringly. With a brief wrench of a smile. "I'd rather you didn't light up until the girl I'm going to listen to has gone. And please don't offer her a smoke. I'd like an unblurred impression. What's her name?"

"Daisy Crandall. I'll give you the scenario right now."

The *Planet's* columnist leaned forward.

"I've known her for six months. She works on another paper—the *Sphere*. Tom Hoyt's sheet. I wouldn't trust Tom for a drink of water. There's no query on *him*—he's the town's dirtiest so-and-so. We'll talk about Daisy who works on his paper. A sweet kid, or I'm cock-eyed. I like her plenty and she me. For six months she's been giving me news tips, good ones—selling out Tom Hoyt, if you like, but *giving*'em to me, not selling 'em. For six months, see? Not a kick-back or a libel suit, and I'm taking her word on every item she hands me."

The blind man's eyes were closed. He made no comment.

Tracy reached for his cigarettes, swore faintly, and shoved the case back in his pocket.

"She's dug me up a scandal tip. I've got it in the desk here right now. Smoking under hatches. Hot as hell. The story is due to break in three days—Daisy's unsupported word for that—and when it breaks old man MacMadden will be sorry he ever canned his *Gazette* of departed memory... You gotta get the picture clearly—I'm talking about a ripe news prediction—my column breaks the tape three days ahead of the gun, get me? Hell, I'll read you the working squib!"

He unlocked a drawer in his steel desk, took out a sheet of paper on which was typed a long single-spaced paragraph. He read the thing aloud:

> What lovely little dancer of Park Avenue, the Lido and the more expensive musical comedy stages is about to cross the Equator and go native, by request? What middle-aged husband is about to go into the public laundry business? Blame it all on the vogue for sun-tan, folks. But in this case they do say, so they do, that the sun-tan came straight from Harlem. The little lady's male parent turns out to be as chocolate as a Hershey bar. The husband's lawyers—and what lawyers!—have Uncle Tom dotted and signed and under key somewhere between here and Cincinnati. The dancer still thinks he's safely hidden in West 137th Street. The egg will be cracked in three days. Phooey! See you in the courtroom. Or do you go for our more colorful dirt?

He put the thing back in the drawer. "That's a rough outline of the tip. The question is—"

The blind man nodded and said slowly: "What a filthy dung-fly you are! What a slimy roach! And sweet little Daisy? Where does she fit in?"

Jerry smiled wanly.

"Why get nasty? She's newspaper. So am I. If you pinch either of us we'll turn black and blue. We're human sweetheart."

"True enough," the beggar said. "Add me too. We're all members of the—damned human race aren't we?"

He relaxed after a moment and the thin hand unclenched in his lap.

"Just what are you afraid of? Don't you trust the girl?"

"Listen," Tracy said nervously. "There's Tom Hoyt to consider; the owner of the *Sphere,* the guy she works for. He's as wise as a family of foxes, and if he got a chance he'd like to burn me and the *Planet* to death with matches—one at a time. Six months would be a half minute to that guy if he thought he could frame me. He knows I'm a sucker for women. It'd be a slow, careful build-up."

"Verify the tip yourself."

"What do you think I've been doing lately? Layin' dead drunk in a cellar somewhere? No sale on that angle. Or should I crash the dancer's penthouse with a big lead pencil, tip my hat, and ask her if she's a dinge?"

"What's your friend Daisy say?"

"She says it's absolutely the McCoy. She's seen the documents—won't tell me how or where. She says the divorce suit will be filed in three days."

"But you don't trust her."

Jerry snarled irritably. "Don't keep saying that! I do! Look—do you see what'll happen if I print the squib and there's no suit filed—just a plant? I'm no guinzo peanut vendor. I'm Jerry

Tracy. There's lots of people would commute in from China to see me fired out like a monkey and plastered for criminal libel. I can understand where this damned Gloria—never mind her name—but I can understand just how she'd help the plant along so she could go into a courtroom with a battery of lawyers headed by Moe Steeger, and bare her back and flanks and weep for the sound cameras. She'd love it—provided she's lily-white and Daisy's a liar."

"Why not wait three days and see?"

"Because I want to print that squib!" Tracy said fiercely. *"It's my business to predict the blow-off!"*

THE MAN WITH the maimed eyes laughed at him with a grim and quiet mockery.

"And you tell all this," he murmured, "to a blind bum with a tin cup. You don't trust Daisy and you want me to listen to her. I'm to make the great decision because I'm blind and can smell thieves and hear them lie… Well, I've smelt plenty. You'll get your money's worth; I have a wide gutter practice… I don't see yet why you've honored me with your confidence. I might double-cross you and tap-tap my way to your pal Tom Hoyt if I think the girl is telling the truth."

"Stop clowning or you'll have me in stitches." Tracy told him morosely. "No matter what happens you'll go with Butch to a nice quiet place and stay there three days at my expense. How's that, professor? Incidentally, you're not kidding me a nickel's worth. You usta be a professor, didn't you? I've got that yarn of yours tabbed. Too slick to be all fiction. Coupla fact nuggets in the story, hey? And I'm not forgetting you pasted me in the jaw when I mentioned bullets—or was it shrapnel?"

He watched the man's knuckles whiten as the thin hand closed into a fist. They were staring at each other when they heard Butch's ponderous feet scrape suddenly in the outer room. The unseen bodyguard's voice roared a playful announcement. "Hello, Babe! Lookin' for somebody?"

There was a pause. The blind man was still staring at Tracy. Then he said with grinding effort: "Why not ask the faithful Butch about—my personal—history? He might be psychic."

The door opened and a girl came in.

She said, smilingly: "Hello, Jerry m'lad."

"Hello, kid."

The blind man sat forward in his chair. He was bent over a little, with his eyes closed tightly. Daisy gave him a quick puzzled glanced. She looked interrogatively at Jerry.

She was small, birdlike, rather pretty. Gray eyes and a wide mouth. A pert hat at a frivolous angle. Her heavy coat was damp, her loose galoshes shiny with moisture.

"Got your call, m'lad," Daisy said. "Anything new?" She looked at the man in the chair while Jerry took her coat.

"He's a friend of mine," Tracy said. He grimaced slightly. "Mr. Peter Mole."

"Not a bedtime-story man! What is this, a gag rehearsal?"

She swished forward with a smile.

"Wake up, brother. I'm being introduced."

He opened his eyes and looked at her. She stopped dead, with a quick indrawn breath.

"Oh! I—I beg your pardon… I didn't—I'm sorry."

Tracy came forward with a dusty chair. "Sit down, kid."

She said to him jerkily, without anger: "That was a lousy piece of humor, Jerry."

Her voice was low and husky; a curious flat contralto as though she had a frog in her throat. It imparted a flavor of metallic cynicism to her speech. She spoke in jerky phrases like spurts from a faucet.

Tracy said to her: "I'm still worried about that dirt special, Babe. There's one or two angles about it—Listen!"

"What good's listening? You're at bat, boy friend. It's up to you to hit the ball or strike out."

"I know, but—"

"Don't print the item if you're worried."

"Oh, for —— sake!" he growled. "I know it's my play. I got my share of guts. But honey, when you hop flat-footed into print with octoroon news—"

She interrupted him instantly. Swung around and glared at him. Her jerky voice was hard with a suppressed fury.

"I see, sez the blind man. Meaning me. You've spilled him the outline, haven't you? That's why he's here. How lovely! Who is he?"

The man with the closed eyes sat impassively. Neither Daisy nor the columnist paid any more attention to him than if he were a suit of armor standing in a corner.

Tracy said: "He's a friend of mine."

"Thanks. I heard that before. I'm trying to see where he fits in and I can't. You've spilled the tip to him, that's all I know. Who is this bum? Oh, Jerry lad, are you going crazy in the head to spill out a confidential think like—"

"I'm not crazy," Jerry snapped. "He'll be under Butch's palm for the next three days. Forget it."

"Forget nothing," the girl cried in husky undertone. "Why is he here at all? There's something screwy about the whole thing. My ——! sweetheart, are you crossing me up?"

Tracy replied unevenly: "Don't be silly."

They were both silent. Daisy's eyes were bright scalpels, cutting, slashing through flesh and tissue to get at Tracy's remote mind.

After a while Daisy said: "Get my coat for me, please." She stood up. Her voice rasped viciously. "Will you—get—my—coat?"

Tracy got up, too. He looked at the brown-bearded sleeper. The columnist was trembling. "What do you say, mug? What's the answer? Come out of your trance!"

The eyelids lifted.

"You want a definite answer?"

"I want a yes or no. Shoot!"

"Give her her coat," the blind man sneered. "You're lucky to get rid of her. She's crooked. Crooked as hell."

Tracy was over him suddenly, whispering at him out of contorted lips.

"Are you sure? How do you know?"

"That's none of your damned affair. You wanted my verdict. You got it."

The girl was wrestling blindly with the sleeves of her coat. She shoved Jerry away and got it on by herself. There were tears of rage in her eyes but her voice remained steady.

"I gather that the prediction won't appear in your column, Jerry."

For answer he opened a drawer of his steel desk, took out a sheet of paper, scratched a matched and watched the flame transfer itself. He held the sheet till it burned thumb and finger; then he allowed the corner to drop writing into the metal waste-basket.

They looked at each other like ghosts.

The girl nodded dully. "Thanks for the buggy ride. It was nice to know you, Jerry. I wish you had decided yourself, though. I—I hate a yellow ba—"

Her hand was on the door-knob. She pulled herself together visibly and laughed a little. Tracy was staring woodenly out the window. Her voice went hard.

"Dumb Daisy, the girl that can take it. A sucker for a left hook. Punch drunk for six months and never knew it. Cherrio, m'lad!"

She went away fast.

Tracy turned around from the window. He said harshly: "Butch! Git in here!"

"Okey, Boss."

"Take this guy over to my place. Throw his clothes in the sink and see what you can find for him. You and he are mustard plasters for the next three days, see? Just like that!" He held up two parallel fingers jerkily. "I'll phone McNulty that you're coming."

He snow-shoed across the floor to his desk. Sat down heavily. Unhooked the receiver with a fumbling hand.

LATE IN THE afternoon on the third day of the blind man's captivity Jerry Tracy came home from the office in his usual fast cab, but the speed was all in the wheels of the machine. He wasn't in any hurry himself. He paid off the hackman with maddening deliberateness. He slouched into the building, said "Hawzit?" and rode a city block vertically.

He didn't bother ringing for the Chinaman. Instead he played aimlessly among his keys and unlocked the door himself. The

Chinaman heard his slow step in the foyer and met him with a glare of indignation for the obvious breach of the employer's code.

Tracy smiled wanly at the old fellow. "Okey, McNulty. Butch here?"

He walked down the hall. Butch came out of a doorway, said: "Hawzit, Boss?" and stepped out of the way.

The columnist paced slowly towards a leather chair in a corner of the room. His right hand closed up and lifted backward a little."

"I oughta smash that —— damned skull of yours," he said thickly. "D'yuh ever look at the papers?"

"You know how it is with me," the guest said acidly.

"Yeah… I know… Well, I'll read 'em for yuh!"

He wrenched a sticky tabloid out of his pocket. He read the first headline: *"Brands Society Dancer Negress!"* He read again: *"Husband Alleges Color Taint; Sues to Nullify Fraud Marriage!"* He read some more and then tossed the paper fluttering and sailing.

"Does that sound like a sure enough news item?" he snarled.

The man in the chair uttered a shrill, incredulous sound and started gropingly to rise. Tracy shoved him down again.

"How do you explain it, wise guy? Smell it and hear it. Chew it and feel it and taste it—it's still a news item! You can tell a horse's leg from a pig's whistle through a twelve-inch plank, can't you? That girl was straight—clean level straight… Damn you and your nose."

"Impossible," he whispered. "I couldn't be wrong."

"Oh, no? Well you were wrong plenty! And Daisy was right. The kid was honest. Square. She had the goods—and the proof

of it is splattered on the front page of every sheet in town...
And I was sucker enough to go for your mud-gutter mind-act."

"Impossible!" the man with the brown beard was mumbling.
"It couldn't be. I was too certain..." He groped out and rose
swaying to his feet. "Get her here! I must know. Call her up!
Drag her here! Tell her I've got to—"

"Fat chance."

"You've got to!" Don't you see what it means? I can't be
wrong—don't you see I can't be wrong? If I was wrong—God
help me if I was wrong—" He was babbling.

"I turned my back deliberately on home and friends. I though
that those who loved me were liars out of pity for me, Sorrow
for a useless hulk, pity for a helpless burden! I could hear lies in
their words of affection. So I fled deliberately to the gutter—and
I lived in the gutter for twelve years —— help me!—because no
man ever dies who jeers at every breath of air he draws.

His gaunt body quivered.

"And now you tell me that the girl, Daisy, is decent. How
can that be? If Daisy's decent, *then I'm crooked!* Have I always
been wrong—stewing in a make-believe hell for twelve long
years? Have I been imagining lies and filth where none existed?
Was I a self-deluded fool when I fled in black despair from
my own home?"

"You're rotten, all right," Tracy spat. "You've got crooked
ear-drums. Pretty damn' easy to smell filth when the stench is
in your own nostrils, brother!"

The blind man whimpered. Beat at Tracy with his two fists.

"Get her! Will you get her? If you don't, I'll smash out
through the window! I'll crawl on hands and knees till I find
her and get the truth. Can't you see what it means to me?"

"To hell with you. Who cares about you?"

The beggar tried to wrestle him aside. Jerry caught at him and hurled him back into the chair.

Tracy's face felt stiff. As though his lips were frozen. Hard to frame words. He stood there, breathing heavily, his fingers still clenched. He laughed suddenly.

"Okey," he said. "I'll call her up. I got it coming to me."

He turned on his heel and went out of the room.

When he came back he sat down heavily. He saw Butch peering with dumb bewilderment from a doorway and he hurled an ashtray at the lumpy face. Butch receded without a sound.

The clock went *tick, tick,* for a long time—like the steady tap of a pick on rock—and suddenly a bell was ringing faintly, the Chinaman McNulty said gravely: "Lady say hully up, go way, shut up!"—and Daisy was standing small and white-faced in the room's doorway.

She broke the silence with a flat, expressionless murmur. "Hello, Jerry, m'lad."

She came forward a step and the blind man rose. He stumbled mistakenly away from her, peering horribly, till she said: "Well?" and then he turned.

He said in a cringing whisper: "Will you answer me truly, as God is your judge?"

"What do you want?"

"Was—I wrong?"

She looked at his face.

"I'm sorry for you, my friend. You were wrong."

He swayed on his feet and his hands went out and she stood quite still. His thin questing fingers brushed her forehead, explored cheek and mouth, slid tremulously along the smooth line of her jaw. She allowed it, her eyes averted from his. She was like ice.

He said thickly: "Will you please—Tracy—leave me here—have a moment alone with—this girl?"

Tracy hesitated, went out. He bounded back when he heard Daisy's muffled scream. She looked daunted, weak; there were tears in her eyes.

She cried: "Jerry, please—Tell him it's all right. Talk to him, Jerry... This poor devil's in hell."

"Hell?" the blind man croaked. "Twelve years of it. And wrong—blind wrong. Doubly blind. In a hell of my own filthy making."

They heard him whimpering with terror like a frightened child.

"Lost... Blind... Beyond all light...."

The girl said to him, tremulously: "That's not true, is it, when you've come out, when you've come back?"

"Out?" he whispered bleakly. "Back?"

"You've been lost in the dark. You know it now. Could you know it if you were still lost?"

"Sit down," Jerry said to him. He touched him with a chair. The man obeyed like an automaton.

"You don't belong on Broadway with a tin cup. Where do you belong?"

No answer to that.

"Can't blame you for not trusting lice," Tracy said deliberately.

He jerked: "Don't—for —— sake!"

The girl's hand touched him. "There are two of us. You're only one. And we're trying to help."

"It wasn't shrapnel," Tracy said. "Was it?"

"No… Not shrapnel. Nor on the Ourq. I was gas… In a gulley. Beyond the dynamited bridge-head at Dun."

"And was there a Protestant Episcopal university, or was that—"

"That's true. I'm a poor hand at fiction, as you thought. Only there wasn't any professor; he was an instructor. And his branch wasn't chemistry; he taught a less exact—" He shuddered painfully. "They re-offered him his place—afterwards—but he didn't want their charity, pity…."

"Who said it was pity?" Tracy interrupted. "You came back with the same brain, didn't you? You have a voice. Were your eyes so necessary? What branch did you teach?"

"Literature." He began to laugh at the thought of literature. Gaspingly. "Lyric p-poetry! Shelley's Ode to a Skylark—after dark!" his laughter shook.

"Quit it, or I'll slap you in the jaw! Wife?"

"No. A mother and—and a sister—please! Let me alone, will you?"

"And you sneaked like a rat. Ran away."

"Do you think," he cried fiercely, "I'd lie on their doorstep? A bag of soiled laundry? A burden?"

The girl spoke suddenly. Her metallic voice was low, fiercer than his.

"What makes you think, damn' fool, that you'd be a burden to a sister who happened to love you?"

The blind man said brokenly: "Stop! Stop! I want to think. I want to sit quietly—you've torn me open, bleeding…."

"Easy, old man," the columnist murmured. He turned to the girl and jerked his head towards the doorway.

THE WONDERING BUTCH saw them cross the corridor

together and go into another room. Tracy walked to the sideboard and poured himself a drink. Daisy was dabbing at her eyes with a handkerchief. Tracy looked at her for a moment in the mirror.

He said to her, jerkily: "You came around when I asked you, kid—and that's the puzzle to me."

"Is it?"

"Maybe it isn't. I dunno. I feel dopey."

"I feel," Daisy said quaveringly, "as though I'd been blown through a vacuum cleaner," She tried to smile. "I guess, between us, we'd make a fair Boy Scout—good deed a day... How'd it ever start, Jerry?"

"I dunno." His smile matched hers. "Funny, isn't it? I'm supposed to be a newspapermen. But if some mug was to hand me a bass-drum, I could feel like the Salvation Army."

He leaned a little and slapped her lightly on both cheeks, shook her a bit by the shoulders and slapped her again. She seemed to now what he meant.

He stepped away from her, grinning stiffly at nothing.

"Butch!" he howled. "Butch! Git in here, mug!"

Butch said in a relieved voice: "Coming, Boss."

"Fold your arms," Jerry told him.

He did, and the columnist swung hard and cracked him in the jaw. Butch backed away with a pained yelp.

"Easy, Boss! What's de big idea? You nuts, or somethin'?"

"I gotta get hard in a hurry or I won't be worth a dime to anybody. Just getting tough, that's all. See what I mean?"

Butch rubbed his jaw slowly and digested the idea. His massive brow darkened. His mind groped visibly for a satisfactory oath. For twenty seconds he struggled for the *bon mot*.

"Is zat so?" he said at last. "Yuh don't tell me!"

Ball and Chain

A sharp story of Jerry Tracy, wisecracker

JERRY TRACY, WISECRACKING columnist for the daily *Planet*, crossed one knee over the other and made little swinging circles in the air with his patent-leather toe. He eyed his faithful bodyguard, Butch, with a kind of sour impatience.

"I'm beginning to think there's a depression," he grumbled.

Butch didn't say anything. His lumpy jaws continued their slow mastication of what had once been spearmint gum.

"People don't eat any more," Tracy growled. "And when they don't eat there's no garbage. And when there's no garbage—where do I come in? Stop that damned chewing, sweetheart; Papa's talking to you!"

Butch's gum made a sticky crackle. He said: "Huh?"

"What's a good way to pad an empty column?"

Butch's forehead wrinkled with concentration. He hiccoughed faintly.

"How's this, Boss? Them three little dots you always use—you know what I mean? How 'bout writing 'em?"

"Writing them?"

"Sure thing. Write 'em out. Dot, dot, dot! See what I mean, Boss? Think of all the space yuh'd—"

"Oh, my ——!" Tracy said wearily. "One lonesome squib left in the locker—and he tells me to use dot, dot, dot!"

He dragged out a notebook and flipped open the pages. "Listen to this one. Bum." He read the squib aloud: *Observed on Park Avenue: Charles Spencer, of the boot and shoe Spencers, dining at Pierre's with his ex-wife, Kitty... Tucked away at a small corner table and v-e-r-y feckshnate... The decree was made final last week... And that makes it FUN...."*

Tracy paused and looked expectant.

"Lousy," said Butch.

The big bodyguard was grinning. If he had said any other word Tracy would have crowned him. It was a little game they played together. Whenever the boss was in the dumps he always read a squib to Butch; Butch always said: "Lousy!" and Jerry came instantly out of his gloom with a grin a mile wide. No sense to it at all, Butch thought, but so long as the crack made the boss happy....

He lumbered outside to the outer office, closing the door softly behind him. Tracy chuckled, pulled open a drawer in his desk and started riffling through selected mail. It was a little after eleven o'clock in the morning—early for Jerry to be on the job.

The phone rang and he scooped it up.

" 'Lo? Oh—hello, Garbo!"

Garbo was the child on the switchboard in the *Planet* office. A carrot-haired baby with seven freckles and a temper like a keg of loose nails. She handled all calls through the *Planet* shop to Tracy's hideaway. An efficient little gamin. Nora something or other. The first time Tracy called her Garbo she got up and kicked him in the shins. Nowadays she contented herself with a grin that matched his and a soft: "Nerts to you, boy friend!" They got along swell.

Tracy said to her: "What's new?"

"Mysterious party with a dirt-nugget for the colyum."

"Male?"

"Fe."

"What's the dirt?"

"How the heck do I know? This is the third time the dame's called up. McCurdy said ask you. Wanta talk to her?"

"She on now?"

"Yeah."

"Okey. I'll take it."

"I didn't think you could," she chuckled. A buzz, a click, then: "Mr. Tracy, the columnist?"

"In the flesh, sweetheart. Eardrums and all."

"I have an item for you about a famous Broadway comedian."

"All right, Blondie. Let's have it."

"How do you know I'm a blonde?"

"Don't be silly. You said Broadway comedian, didn't you?"

"Oh!" She sounded puzzled. "I've got it all written out. I'll read it to you. Can you print it tomorrow?"

The columnist's eyes narrowed. "Let's hear the story."

She read off the statement in a stilted tone: "What well-known Broadway comedian is in a tough spot if he doesn't listen to reason? His first name is Harry but according to the wise gossip his last name is mud."

"Who's the victim?"

"Can't you guess?"

"Sure, I can guess—but I don't print guesses; I print facts, darling. What's the dirt on Harry? And what's his last name?"

"You're a wise guy," said the thin voice in the instrument. "Find out yourself. I'm handing you a hot tip. Does that make you mad?"

"It makes me curious. Just for the fun of it—where do you check in on this thing?"

"I don't," said the voice. "I check out."

The line clicked and Jerry swore softly. A frown gathered on his forehead. He kept the receiver against his ear. Garbo came back.

"All through, Jerry?"

"I am *not!* Listen, honeyball. I want that call traced. If there's any trouble getting the info, tell McCurdy to put it up to the main squeeze in the front office. I want a name and an address, get me? Buzz me when it's ready."

"I'll do that little thing. So long, Gable!"

He grinned at the unseen carrot-top. "Nerts to you, Garbo!" he said and cradled the receiver.

He got up, lit a butt and walked to the window. He stood there staring down at the helter-skelter of Times Square; at the hats and overcoats shoving north and south like twin currents, boiling into eddies at the crossing. A man with an unwieldy white parcel dodged a truck and dived for the sidewalk—like an ant dragging a captured bread-crumb. Ants. Tracy thought moodily. Out in swarms to beg a dime or chisel a dollar; out to sell a business or see a show or pick up a lady-ant.

The columnist wondered what new kind of jam Harry Wexler was in. The dame on the phone was right about one thing—Tracy didn't have to guess much about the victim's identity. Poor Harry Wexler was a soft mark for anything under twenty-two, with a blonde transformation and syrup eyes. Tracy liked Harry a hell of a lot. What a genius of a comic the guy was! A natural zany. And no baggy pants or funny hats—all in his eyes and the play of his expressive hands and that rolly-bolly voice of his.

Blackmail, was Tracy's guess. Someone had the hooks into Harry Wexler and was trying to use the *Planet's* gossip column to scare him.

After a while Garbo reported and Tracy made a notation on a scrap of paper. He sat staring at the scrawl: "Muriel Slade, 902 East 54th Street, 1208." The name didn't mean a thing to him. He didn't worry much about it. He'd attend to that part later.

He was thinking right now of the Ball and Chain. The Ball and Chain was out in Hollywood, on the Metwyn lot—thank God for that! One more mess like Harry's last escapade and two damned good troupers would be washed up for keeps. A rotten shame if it ever happened!

He shoved the scrap of paper into his pocket, put on his hat and the tan overcoat and went outside. Butch said: "Okey, Boss," in an eager voice and reached for his derby. He moved like a big dog being taken out of his kennel for a run among the cowslips.

Tracy shook his head. "Nix, Bum. Stick around. I won't need you."

"Okey, Boss." His eyes looked sorrowful, hurt.

"I'll be back later on. Are ya listenin'?"

"Sure."

"Look out for gas inspectors and exterminators with little leather satchels. They might be jewel thieves—see what I mean?"

"Okey, Boss. I'll make 'em show their badges."

"Attaboy, Butch!"

Tracy walked out as sober as a judge.

THE VERY ENGLISH man-servant with the graying mutton-chops, the correct waistcoat and the decorous and subdued little cough that he had developed in the service of the late Duke of Albermarle, opened the door.

"Good morning, Mr. Tracy. Is Mr. Wexler h'expecting you, sir?"

"Hello, Bum." He tossed the servitor his coat and hat. "Is the Marster in bed yet?"

"H'I—er—h'expect so, sir."

"So did I." He raised his voice in a stentorian yelp. "Hey, Harry! Crawl out, Bum, and take a bow!"

From the closed bedroom a muffled voice replied thickly: "Hi, Jerry! That you?"

Bare feet padded to the door and Harry Wexler's tousled head peered out. "What the hell's the idea? The house on fire?"

He looked like the comedy husband in a black-out sketch. His graying hair was a rumpled bird's-nest; the comic door-knob eyes were red-rimmed and sleepy. He wore Russian

Cossack pajamas with a black sash and an embroidered double-eagle on the pocket. He caught Jerry's amused grin and went instantly into an effortless pantomime, with the doorway framing him like a proscenium arch.

"Clowning," Tracy thought. "Harry would clown in his own casket, the little mug!"

Wexler cocked a bleared eye at the polite man-servant. He made gestures of dismissal.

"Okey, Cornwallis. Whaddye standin' there for? Mix us up a couple of factory whistles."

"That's out!" Tracy snapped. "Get him a glass of water and an aspirin."

The servant looked wooden and departed.

Wexler said: "Wait a second, Jerry," and reappeared in a moment with a futuristic bed-quilt draped about him. He padded into the living-room with the quilt trailing behind him like a bishop's train. He flopped into a wide chair, swathed himself like a mummy and lit a cigarette with a shaky hand.

He grumbled: "What's new, you hellion?"

"You took the words right out of my mouth," Tracy replied easily. "What's new, yourself?"

"Haven't got a thing for you, kid. We throw it down the incinerator as fast as it collects. If you hurry you might catch the wagon."

The butler came in with a glass of water and a folded dressing-gown. Wexler said, irritably: "Go 'way, Burgoyne, and surrender somewhere," but he took the two aspirins and washed them down with a grimace.

Tracy said: "Know any women, Harry?"

The quilt slid away from the comedian's shoulders and he

made no effort to pull it back. His mouth quivered at the corners.

"Cut out the kiddin', Jerry. I'm jumpy."

Looking keenly at him the newspaper man saw that worry and not booze had rimmed Harry's eyes with red. Worry was making the bare toes curl on the rug. Behind the expressive face of the comedian apprehension was running riot. It made him appear oddly juvenile, appealing. He looked like a small boy with painted wrinkles and a gray wig—a small boy on the way to the woodshed and scared stiff.

"Whaddye mean, women?" he blustered.

Tracy got up and walked over to his friend. He pressed the nose and chin together with his thumb and forefinger. Then he sat down again.

He said, with a faint smile: "I thought I'd drop in and cut your throat, Harry."

"Thanks, pal, thanks," Wexler grinned.

The tension went out of the comedian's eyes. It was as though, under the surface of their talk, they had just sworn fealty to each other. Or rather, renewed it—because on Broadway, when you talked about Jerry Tracy and Harry Wexler, you held up two parallel fingers and said: "Just like that!"

"Who's this Muriel Slade child?" Tracy asked him.

The round eyes bulged. "Oh. Lord!" he groaned. "Is it in print? Is it out on the street already?"

"East 54th Street. Apartment Twelve O Eight."

"Jerry, it's a frame! I can talk about it to you—we know each other. She wants ten grand. But I'm paying it—I promised her. I told the little rat I'd pay!"

"Yeah? Figure this, Harry—she called up the column this

morning. She thought I'd print a squib and scare the hell out of you so you'd hurry the check along. That's what brought me over. What's she like?"

Wexler grinned foolishly. "You know, I guess."

"Yeah, I know. Blonde, shy, nice eyes and an outcurve like Lefty Gomez throws. What happened?"

"Not a thing, Jerry. I've been on the absolute up-and-up ever since—"

He was silent and they both thought of the same thing: the Ball and Chain. The greatest old character actress in shoe leather. The amply built mother of the seven little Wexlers. Out on the Metwyn lot in Hollywood, making the callous electricians and prop men invent excuses to sneak around the set and watch her sure-fire art in "Gum Drop Sadie." A grand old trouper, the lighthouse in the gray-haired comic's existence. A year ago she had blown up plenty. Tracy was the only outsider present when they patched things up. He had seen the tears in both their eyes. Gray-haired and pathetic children, both of them. He had heard the ultimatum.

Tracy said tonelessly: "What's the plot? The blonde trying to queer you with the Ball and Chain? One of those pay or 'else' things?"

Wexler nodded miserably.

"Tell me about it."

"I dunno. Believe it or not—laugh if you want to, Jerry—you remember what I promised? Well, I kept my word and I'm still straight."

The comedian clenched his two fists and stood up in his rumpled Cossack suit. There was dignity and sincerity in his shaking voice.

"Before —— Jerry, it's a frame."

"All right, kid. That makes it more pleasant for me. How did the blonde twist work the scheme?"

"I met her in a speake. Somebody or other introduced her… ——! what a sap I've been! I don't mean no harm—I can't keep away from 'em. The Ball and Chain knows what I'm up against. I got used to it when I worked for poor Ziggy… I like to listen to the baby voices, watch their eyelashes, have 'em sway close and tell me what a grand comic I am. You get used to it, to their vampy ways and their perfume. It's like incense, Jerry. I—I can't explain, I guess."

"Go ahead. Stick to the plot."

"Well, we were kidding about that damned English butler of mine. I've been using him a lot for radio gags on my Cocoa Hour."

"Air-Tight Cocoa," Tracy said dryly. "Brought to you in sealed tins by fast airplane from the certified cocoa tree. Every tree dated or your money back… Talk blackmail; I haven't got all morning, Harry."

"So I took her home. We both wanted a decent drink."

"Whose home?"

"Here."

"You—dope!"

The comedian looked foolish. "Don't I know it! She ribbed me up that she wanted a drink of the McCoy mixed by a real English butler. And the next day she called up and said ten grand."

"Why did she say ten grand?"

"Because the slick little blonde —— went into the bedroom to primp up before she left, and she walked out with the Ball and Chain's diamond earrings. Took 'em out of the bureau. Proof she'd been nice to me, see? She's got 'em, all right I looked and they're gone." Jerry grinned sarcastically. "Doesn't that put little Muriel Slade in a tough spot? I mean you could send her to jail for theft."

The comedian swore in a high-pitched voice.

"Don't kid, Jerry! What the hell do I care about jail? She's got me, don't you see? The old lady wouldn't listen to me or you—she'd look at the earrings and she'd know where they came from and she'd—"

His head dropped into his hands.

"Jerry, if the old Ball and Chain gets hep and quits on me, I might just as well walk down the nearest sewer-hole and die. I'd be washed up—drowned."

"I know."

"No, you don't. You couldn't, Jerry. We grew up in the same tenement in Rivington Street. She married me when I didn't have a dime. We worked hard; batted all over the country in old-fashioned tank-town vaudeville. Got any idea what I'm talking about? You couldn't know—you weren't born.

"We usta lay in bed in some lousy hick hotel and talk quiet together in the dark about how we'd build up the act. You could hear the switch-engine snorting over by the freight depot. The wife always fell asleep first, and then I'd lean over and kiss her easy so's not to wake her, and I'd whisper in her ear: 'Sarah, old kid, you're the best —— —— little trouper in the world!' She gave me seven kids, Jerry... That's my Ball and Chain."

He made a harsh, jerky noise in his throat. Tracy looked away, fiddled with his cigarette case, lit a butt and laid the burned match carefully in a tray.

"I think I'll go over and say hello to Muriel," he said in a brief, manicured voice.

"I'll pay her the ten grand. Make her see that, Jerry! Tell her I won't make trouble—she'll get the dough. Only for ——'s sake, get those earrings!"

"I'll say hello to her, anyway," Tracy muttered.

He walked out to the foyer. Wexler followed him in his bare feet. Tracy took his hat and coat from the stolid butler.

Wexler's voice sounded fuzzy. "We don't have to talk, Jerry. This is friendship."

"We don't have to talk," Jerry agreed.

He leaned suddenly and slapped the comedian briskly with a flat smack of his palm.

"Go on back to bed, dope, before you catch cold!"

He said to the butler: "The king, God bless him!" replaced the derby he had lifted reverently from his head, and went out.

THE MAN BEHIND the desk said: "Who did you say sir?"

"The name is Wexler," Tracy smiled. "Tell her it's Mr. Wexler, on business."

"Thank you," he said with more interest.

He spoke into the phone, glanced side-wise for a dubious second, and said: "Just Mr. Wexler, ma'am. No; no one else… Very well."

He hung up with a brisk click. "Twelve O Eight."

"Thanks. I know." Tracy smiled dimly and slouched into the elevator. Wexler seemed to be welcome so long as he came alone. The little lady upstairs must be worried. A friend with Wexler might be a private cop, a cop with a warrant, a strong-arm thug—anything. Tracy's smile widened. Uncertainty upstairs didn't make him mad.

When the door of the suite opened he shoved hard and walked in.

She was a little taller than he had pictured—closer to show-girl than pony. An orchid child in a lovely negligée with wide sleeves and a loose sport-collar effect at the throat that hinted, rather than disclosed, the creamy cleft of her bosom. Her eyes were unblinking and steady but her hand flew tremulously to her mouth.

"All in the spirit of clean fun, sister," he said. "Just a prank. I wanted to see you. The name is Tracy."

He folded his coat on the back of a chair and crowned it with his hat.

She said, carefully: "Tracy? You don't mean Mr. Jerry Tracy by any chance?"

"None other, child. Just a good egg with a nose for news. Call me Jerry and I'll love it."

"Why did you lie your way in here, Mr. Tracy?" Very upstage. Very regal.

"Scandal items, beautiful. I print 'em before they happen. You've got something on Harry Wexler. You called me up—remember? I want to run that squib you telephoned in—but I can't print it unless I know *exactly why* Harry's got the arrow in his back."

"Aren't you a friend of his?"

He gave her the musical note. "I'm a friend of the circulation manager of the *Daily Planet*. Catch wise?" The mirth went out of his eyes. They were level, boring. "There's a brain behind that lovely pan of yours, or I'm all wrong. Listen—if you've got a juicy item for my column, Harry Wexler's out of luck. Or anybody else."

She digested that for a while. Her eyes stayed on his. "Will you run the item in tomorrow's paper—I mean if I explain to you about the arrow? It's in his back, all right." She laughed shortly. "Up to the feather!"

"Then the blue-print reads as follows—or am I wet? You get dough, lovely; the column gets the squib; the customers get a dirty laugh—and the roof falls in on Harry Wexler if he don't give. Am I right?"

"That's the scenario, boy friend. And if you have any idea of double-crossing us—"

"Us, sweetheart?"

"Me and Frankie Stork." She stared at him with hard eyes.

"Frankie Stork?" He whistled softly.

"Yeah. Frankie Stork. He's the partner—I thought you might like to know."

Tracy swallowed a moment. He said, faintly: "Now I'll tell one."

She groped down the front of her negligée, fished out a locket, snapped it open, held it below his eyes. He looked at the tiny photo. At the glossy hair, pinched nose; the sallow face with the skin taut over the cheekbones like the covering on a drum. Frankie Stork, all right! Even in this tiny replica of the gunman's face the eyes showed the flick of killer's insolence, the assassin's smile.

She snapped the locket shut and Tracy said: "Nice picture."

"Nice guy, too… All right, now, listen!"

About what he had figured, it turned out. The Ball and Chain was the threat to pry the dough out of Harry Wexler. Actually, it would never get that far—Harry would squeal at the thought and disgorge. The tip in the column was to show him that they meant business.

Tracy nodded to the girl with the creamy skin, the candid throat and the hard eyes.

"It sounds negotiable, Muriel."

"How about tomorrow morning for the squib?"

He looked innocent and thought fast. Today was Friday.

"Capital N——. Capital O. No."

"Why not?" Like a machine-gun.

"Libel laws, darling. Do you think the *Planet* prints everything I toss carelessly over my shoulder? Come, come. You know better than that. My columns get looked at by a brace of high-priced *Planet* lawyers before the customers stand in line with their two cents. It takes time, darling, and I write 'em ahead. Tomorrow's is locked, sealed and delivered. How about Monday?"

"No later."

"Then it's settled. Goody, goody. Shake?"

He grinned as he squeezed her hand The predatory glance he gave her was subtle with flattery. She smiled back and allowed him to retain the hand.

"Care for a drink?"

"No hurry, beautiful."

She murmured pensively: "So you're the great Mr. Tracy!"

"Am I a disappointment?"

"No-o-o-o. I wouldn't say that."

"What would you say?"

She laughed. "Okey, Uncle Sam!"

"Silly trade-mark, isn't it?"

"I think it's cute."

That made them both laugh. He cupped the silken clad shoulder with his left palm. She said to him in a baby voice:

"It must be something terrible to have the power you got, Mr. Tracy."

"Terrible?"

"Yeah. Havin' people's reputation right in the palm of your hand—and all that. You know what I mean, Mr. Tracy?"

"Terrible is no word for it—and the name is Jerry, sweetheart." The cupped hand slid down her arm.

When he left the apartment he was grinning like a monkey. He nodded genially to the man at the desk downstairs and went out.

It was getting much colder outside; a windless, biting chill. He rumpled his overcoat collar about his throat and shoved both hands deep into his pockets.

He was thinking hard. The time was a little after one o'clock. Eleven, twelve, one—three hours difference in time. Mmmm… What the hell was the name of that movie director? He couldn't remember. The Ball and Chain would know. Three hours… Plenty of time to grab a bite to eat and still catch her when she knocked off for lunch.

He grinned at the memory of lunch-time in Hollywood. He'd been out there once! He remembered the suggestion he had made to Old Papa Weintraub: Why not build a swell minaret, hire an extra with a white beard at ten bucks a day, dress him in robes and turban and have the guy blow the lunch call from a silver trumpet? *Ta—ta— Whah!* Papa Weintraub gurgled with delight at the idea and made a notation on his Nile-green memo pad… Cr-raazy people….

FOR SOME STRANGE reason Tracy was hungry. He went to a speako where they lost money on the food and made it on the drinks. He had an absinthe cocktail—millionaire's dream. Then he polished off with leisurely enjoyment: antipasto, minestrone, spaghetti, veal covered with tomato sauce and strips of cheese and the whole baked to a glorious brown. He washed the meal down with a tall bottle of white wine and finished with Gorgonzola and crackers. Okey, Emil! Emil brought him a brandy and soda on the house and he toyed with the drink and thought some more about the Ball and Chain.

She was the key to the whole thing. If she got wind of the conspiracy, the thing would flop like a house of cards. But Muriel and her gunman partner knew darn well that Harry Wexler would mortgage his house in Great Neck before he'd let them poison the mind of the skeptical old trouper out in Hollywood. But on the other hand, if Jerry got her ear—and got it first....

She was a good sport, the Ball and Chain. And the thought of a blonde wench rooking Harry of dough that ought to go to the seven little Wexlers would make the old girl snort like one of Jake Ruppert's horses and reach for a meat-axe.

Tracy sighed, patted his distended stomach and grabbed a cab back to Times Square.

He picked up the phone and called the genius of the singing wires over in the *Planet* office.

"Listen, Garbo! I want a long distance, person to person, Hollywood, Cal. Metwyn Studios. Sadie Hollister."

He heard her prompt laugh. "Well, well... The famous old Ball and Chain!"

"Sadie Hollister to you, maiden."

"Okey. Want me to drag her off the set?"

"Dope! Time it for the lunch hour. And get busy—or I'll get mad and agitate your permanent!"

He slammed down the instrument, lit a butt, closed his eyes dreamily and allowed digestion to proceed.

After a while the phone buzzed and Garbo's professional whine said: "All set, Mr. Tracy. Here's your potty."

He growled: "Hello? Sadie? Jerry Tracy."

A surprisingly distinct voice said: "Hello, you little rat! What's the matter?"

"Listen, Sadie! It's about Harry! And for —— sake, hold your temper till I get through."

"Harry?"

"He's in a jam. He's been put on the spot by a blonde."

The yelp she let out in Hollywood made him pull the receiver away from his ear.

"Take it easy, Mama! Lemme explain. It's a phoney—a plant—a job. Harry's scared stiff; he doesn't know I'm calling you. *Shut up a minute, damn you!*"

He shot her the yarn with staccato speed and newspaper clarity. He heard her puffing and snorting clear across the continent. He stared at the flat surface of his desk but all he could see was the Ball and Chain's fleshy, good-natured face—as clearly as though he were staring at an advance still from "Gum Drop Sadie."

"How much is the blonde —— into him for?" she barked.

"Ten grand—she hasn't got it yet, old girl."

"Ten grand! Oi, yoi! Ten grand! And me slavin' out here with a lousy script to make money for mein babies. And then that fool husband of mine—"

"Will you listen?"

"Ten grand! She should deprive little Maxey of his pony-cart, hah? She should make little Holman give up his English tooter from Oxford! She should maybe—Ten grand! I'll give the dirty yeller-haired —— skin treatment!"

"Fine!" he sweated. "We can fix it, Sadie. I got it all doped out. Who's that director with the speed job—you know—that low-wing thing? The fella that likes to take baby stars up and show 'em altitude?"

"Morrie von Haldemann."

"Right. Grab him and talk turkey. You can start this afternoon the minute they finish shooting."

"Oi, would I love to! I can't, Jerry. We're behind on production."

"Nerts. It's a racing ship, Mama old girl. You can be back on the set Monday… Poor old Harry's crazy with worry—it's a lousy shake-down. Come on; I'm betting on you."

A long pregnant silence. Then: "You're a good guy, Jerry. I'll fade your bet."

He wiggled with relief. "I'll meet you at Newark airport. Try and keep it under your hat. Gas up and scram the minute you can. You can wipe off the grease-paint going over the Rockies."

"You're a good skate, Jerry. If Harry had a coupla more friends like you—"

"Rats! Go on back to the sound stage and slay 'em for a couple of hours more. And—don't worry, Sadie. It's in the bag."

He hung up with a gentle, faraway precision. He said smilingly to the wall; "What a gal! When the old Ball and Chain quits Harry I'll be writing clean serials for the *Fireside Companion*."

THE WELL-GROOMED JUVENILE at the airport looked up inquiringly.

"Ship due pretty soon?" Tracy said.

The tailored shoulders shrugged prettily. "Sorry, sir. She's grounded at Cleveland. Low ceiling; poor visibility."

For a second Jerry looked crestfallen and worried: then his eyes lighted.

"What show are you talking about, sonny? You mean the regular passenger ferryboat?"

"The scheduled tri-motor. Yes, sir."

"Phooey! What about the special—the low wing?"

The man's face turned eight shades more obsequious. He became aware he was talking to a big shot.

"The private low-wing, sir? The job from the Coast? She's coming through, sir—how, God only knows! Everything east of Cleveland has been grounded. Amazing performance. We're all frightfully thrilled about it here. Do you realize that she'll come *damned*—" He whispered it. "—*damned* close to breaking Doolittle's record?"

Tracy wasn't interested.

"We've been ordered to clamp down on publicity. Must be someone from the Industry." He said the word reverently. "We're all curious to know who's aboard."

"Santa Claus," Tracy said "I'm a friend of the family—one of his brownies."

He walked around aimlessly and people peered out of doorways at him. He was on his third cigarette when a signal sounded somewhere on the field, and the clerk cried out: "That must be her, I think!"

He followed Tracy outside. Earth and sky were a gray, cheerless monotone. It was freezing cold. Airport employees stood around, stamping their feet and whacking their chests. The clerk at Tracy's elbow was bareheaded and his teeth kept clicking like dice. His finger pointed but Jerry could barely see the ship. A tiny speck in the leaden half-light.

It grew amazingly fast. He saw it whizz like a bullet till it was directly over his head. Life size. Roaring. A thing of streamlined beauty; a clean arrow from tip to tail. Silver wings with dappled red tips.

Dark blobs appeared suddenly under the ship's smooth belly and the man at Tracy's elbow yelled: "Retractable landing gear! What a job! What a *swwwweeeet* job!"

She circled the field twice and dipped. Touched the frozen earth and taxied into the apron. Her tail swung about and a hail of pebbles and sand stung Tracy's shins. The engine blipped, the propeller kicked over stiffly—once, twice—and stopped. In the gray haze the poised blade was like a silver lance pointing skyward.

The landing steps were trundled forward on a wheeled dolly. A man in uniform reached to open the door. He didn't quite get there in time. Someone inside the ship flung the door open.

The Ball and Chain stood in the gap, grinning. Her fat face was one vast smile. She stood there, arms akimbo, and her shrewd eyes lit on Tracy.

"Whoops! Hello, and how are yuh, you little punk?"

Her face jerked backward for a second, towards the unseen pilot.

"If I ever buy one of these things, you're elected, young fella! Thanks for the buggy ride. Whoops! *Am I dizzy!*"

People were buzzing around like flies. Sadie Hollister! In

the flesh—uh-huh—in from the West Coast on almost a record-breaking trip! A grimy grease-monkey ran alongside and howled, daringly: "Hello, Sadie!"

"Hello yourself, sonny boy!" She ate up that crowd stuff.

Laughter followed her like an eddy. Tracy hooked arms with her and got her away to the car. She was royalty—a rowdy queen kidding with her devoted subjects. Completely at ease and happy.

She waved her beefy hand to the crowd as Tracy's chauffeur meshed gears. "I'll see the pack of you in 'Gum Drop Sadie,' kids! Don't miss it if you have to go hungry!"

As the motor spurted she dropped the professional gayety like a cloak. She looked suddenly older, haggard.

"I'm a workin' woman, Jerry. I got no time for long vacations. Where's that blonde —— live?"

"Take it easy."

"She's got my diamond earrings, the dirty little trollop!"

"Okey. That's what we're going after. Lemme tell you about Harry."

The blazing eyes filmed and softened. She patted his hand.

"Harry's all right," she said. "I know what he's up against. I keep him scared for his own good—the softhearted slob! Don't you worry about us, Dirty Minded! You couldn't pull old-timers like us apart with a tractor, sonny boy."

Her laughter bubbled oddly. "Can you imagine a little wart like Harry giving me seven beautiful kids? Mama loves Papa—and don't you forget it!… Now shut up and let's go places. I'm tired…."

Neither of them said another word on the long drive to Muriel's apartment. They got out at last, walked rapidly across the freezing sidewalk and ducked into the lobby.

Tracy nodded, picked up the desk phone and told the clerk curtly: "Get Miss Slade's apartment. I'll talk to her myself."

He could barely hear the blonde when she came on the wire. She sounded muffled, like hot potatoes.

She said: "The *same* Mr. Wexler? The *nice* Mr. Wexler from the *Planet?*"

"In person, honey. Everything's lovely. I'm coming up."

The low voice became urgent.

"No, no... Don't—please don't, Jerry! Make it tomorrow like a good boy. Be nice to baby and make it tomorrow!"

"Fine. I'll be right up."

He nodded to the Ball and Chain and they got into the elevator. As it rose wheezingly he could hear the phone on the desk ringing furiously. He grinned. Muriel wasn't to stall Mrs. Tracy's little boy!

His grin solidified suddenly. She wasn't stalling—she was *scared.* Maybe... Good Lord, there *wasn't* any maybe! A sickening picture flicked inside his skull. Frankie Stork! The gunman with the parchment skin and the arrogant smile. Upstairs— and in the complete dark about a guy named Jerry. The blonde was scared. She had tried to whisper Jerry away. That was it!

The elevator continued to ascend wheezingly. Frankie and Jerry—it sounded like a song. The whining cable of the lift was pulling them together. No way out. Jerry couldn't *get* out of it. He glanced at the Ball and Chain's face. She'd crash forty Frankies to *get* her hands on the blonde. He hadda go through with it. Sweat gathered on his smiling face.

"Corridor down to the left," said the operator. He descended with a bored stare.

Jerry's rap on the apartment door was barely audible but the door opened instantly. A mere crack. Muriel's face peered. She looked ugly.

"Scram!" she whispered. "I tried to tip you. He's in the bathroom, shaving."

The Ball and Chain gave the door a titanic shove and sent it crashing open. She barged in with a roar of rage.

IT ALL HAPPENED together. The blonde screamed shrilly, took a smack on the jaw from Sadie and went over backwards like a hosiery ad. Frankie Stork came racing out of the bathroom in a dressing-gown, his face covered with soap lather. He was almost blind with the stuff. He couldn't see Jerry at all; the door screened the columnist.

The soaped gunman bent over his piled garments, fumbling fiercely. As the gun jerked into his hand Tracy sprang from concealment and drove his fist into the stooping face. He heard a dull *plop!* as the blow landed, and blobs of white lather flew.

Frankie Stork fell over the chair and dropped the gun. Jerry grabbed it, swung it upward like a flash and clubbed the gunman's skull—twice.

The startled Ball and Chain was standing like a mountain of frozen incredulity in the center of the room. The blonde had turned over and was on her hands and knees, glaring venomously at Jerry like a snake.

She squalled at him: "Wait'll Frankie comes to and sees who done it! Your life ain't worth a dime no more, dearie!"

Tracy shut the apartment door softly and locked it. He put the key into his pocket.

"That's right, beautiful. Frankie never did get to see me, did he? That's a break."

He walked coolly across to the bed, yanked off the coverings, tore a sheet hastily into strips. The blonde didn't hinder him. She was watching the Ball and Chain out of narrowed eyes. She got up and smoothed her hips. One look at the Ball and Chain's famous phiz had told the blonde that the blackmail scheme was fatally queered. It was her personal safety now that was worrying her. She stood very quietly, watching the older woman.

Jerry tied the gunman's hands and feet, slipped a gag over his jaw, bandaged the closed eyelids. He dragged Frankie Stork across the rug and flopped him on the bed.

He told the blonde: "If you've got any sense at all, lovely, you won't remember a thing. You were clouted on the head and passed out in a flurry of undies before Frankie got his. It's all a mystery to you, beautiful. Frankie Stork would be apt to misunderstand if he knew I was here."

She snarled: "Git outta here—the two o' yuh—before I screech for the cops!"

The Ball and Chain blinked and came suddenly out of her brown study.

"I want two diamond earrings out of you, tramp! Hand 'em over!"

"Haven't got 'em. I pawned 'em."

"Hand 'em over!"

Her hands sprang out and the blonde's head began to wobble drunkenly. There was a ripping sound and Jerry pulled the old character trouper away. He threw a blanket at the blonde.

"Is that nice, Mama? You're making me blush. Don't be like that. We'll find the earrings ourselves."

"Damn' tootin'," she growled.

She ranged around the room like a female rhinoceros, pawing furniture, pulling open bureau drawers, tossing stuff helter-skelter over her shoulder.

"Ten grand! The gall o' the skinny yeller carrot! Blush? She couldn't make a door-knob blush—the skinny little whelp! Takin' my diamond earrings! An' me with seven kids and a swimmin' pool not yet paid for! Ten grand! Looka this— got better underwear than I can afford! No wonder—stealin' people's diamond earrings!"

She snorted and threw the offending garment aside.

Tracy came in swiftly from the adjoining room. "This what you're after?"

She took the earrings from him with a grunt of satisfaction.

"I'll have to send 'em to the laundry for a scourin' after the hands they been through!"

Tracy piloted her to the door with difficulty. He unlocked it. The fettered gunman was still dead to the world on the bed. Tracy was shaking like a leaf with nervousness. He was trying to get Sadie away in a hurry and it wasn't easy.

The Ball and Chain turned for a parting shot. Her finger pointed disgustedly at the blanketed shoulders of the blonde.

"Look at her! How Harry ever said hello to her is a mystery to me. Beanpole! She could double for Slim Summerville in the nude and nobody'd know the difference!"

He said, soothingly: "Sure, sure."

They rode down in the elevator together and she giggled suddenly like a plough-horse. "Ain't I the excitable old idiot! Wait'll I tell Harry—he'll split a rib!"

Tracy didn't witness the complete reunion of Papa and

Mama. He saw only the overture. They stared at each other like two gray-haired kids.

"Papa, I'm ashamed of you. You oughta be wearing diapers!"

"Mama, you took the words right out of my mouth!"

They didn't miss Tracy for nearly twenty minutes. By that time he was back in his dingy Broadway office, pulling a sheet of paper from his typewriter.

He read the typewritten squib with a mild grin:

"What little blonde started to take a stroll up Easy Street and got all tangled in a Ball and Chain?"

Help Wanted

*Jerry Tracy, hardboiled wise-cracker,
pulls two grand out of the snow*

DESERTED SEVENTH AVENUE WAS a blurry wilderness of flying white. It was unexpectedly quiet and lovely. The snow was falling steadily, eddying downward in thick gusts. Jerry Tracy took a deep breath and the cold wind burned in his lungs like wine. It whipped away the memory of the late poker game and the stale dregs of cigarette smoke; made him tingle from head to foot.

A belated taxi went scudding past with a faint *slap, slap* of its skid chains. The drowsy hotel doorman fingered his whistle and glanced at the *Planet's* columnist. It was late—or perhaps early; about 3 a.m.

Tracy said: "The hell with a cab. I haven't seen snow like this since I first hit this lousy burg. I'll walk."

He turned up the velvet collar of his Chesterfield, tilted the expensive derby low on his forehead and shoved his gloved hands deep in his pockets.

He started southward along the deserted avenue. His patent-leather shoes kicked up the feathery snow in little puffs like frozen smoke.

He skidded around a windy corner and plodded east. He was halfway towards Sixth Avenue when he saw a figure ahead of him.

Unconsciously, he quickened his pace. A girl—no kiddin'. All alone in a blizzard at this grim hour of the morning! Having a hard job to navigate, judging from her bent back and her uneven trail in the snow. She was going in the same direc-

tion he was—head down to the sharp claw of the wind—and moving unsteadily. Looked like a liquor stagger. He grinned faintly and fished professionally for a flip headline: *Just a broad abroad. Not a bad pun; hey, Jerry? The hell you say; it's lousy!*

He had no trouble overtaking her. As he came abreast he gave her a quick once-over and the grin went out of his eyes. Again his brain buzzed. *No booze there, Jerry! Sez you. Sez me. All right—so what?*

He slowed down and kept in step with her.

"You look all in, baby. None of my damn' business, of course." He hesitated. "Got far to go?"

She made no sign whatever to indicate that she had heard him. Her head didn't turn; it continued to push obstinately against the wind as though dragging the rest of her numb body along like a trailer.

He eyed the pinched profile curiously. Her chin was jerking with the cold like a paralytic's; he couldn't tell whether she was a hot-house beauty or a hag. Plenty young, though—and plenty weak on her pins. She wasn't taking a short stroll, either. The front of her skimpy cloth coat was crusted white from collar to hem; her shoes were sodden.

He said: "Listen, kid!" and that didn't get him anything.

He stepped around in front of her and stood there. She ran right into him like an automaton. Her hands came up and clawed mechanically at his chest trying to push him away. He had to bend his head to catch the words.

"Not for—sale —— damn you!"

"Don't be that way. Listen, kid! You broke?"

She raised her head dumbly. The lips writhed away from her chattering teeth. She looked wolfish, wild.

"Not—for sale—Mister."

"Cripes sake!" he snarled. "Stop talking movie… You haven't got a thin dime—and you're not used to it. How about a beef stew with a flock of potatoes?"

Her hands made a weak clutch at his lapel and missed. She fell forward. Her weight threw him off balance and he went awkwardly to one knee in the snow with his arm about her. She hadn't fainted; she was conscious, with bleak, wide-open eyes.

He got her to her feet and held her braced close so that her head lolled on his shoulder. —— damn the snow! He winked his eyes and stared desperately up and down the deserted street. Try and find a cop!

His mind worked swiftly. A flock of unpleasant thoughts:

What a sucker I am to bother my head! Nerts; you wouldn't leave a dog out on a night like this. The poor little rat's all in! Damn right; she might croak on me right here—wouldn't that be swell! What the hell, Jerry; be decent; flag a cab. Try and find a hack in this lousy blizzard... Maybe I could walk her down to a drug-store. That's a laugh, too....

His eyes veered down the street with sudden hope. Head-lights were boring through the snow under the Elevated structure at Sixth Avenue. He saw the beams bounce up and down as the car crossed the tracks.

Tracy waved his free arm and yelped. "Taxi! Hey, Taxi!"

It pulled towards the side drifts. A yellow cab all splotched over with snow. A wop with a fat face and a sheepskin coat. Tight little eyes like hard black show-buttons.

"Pile out here, fella, and gimme a hand!"

The hackman didn't move. Just sat still and peered at the two of them.

"What's the matter with the dame, Mac?"

"She just keeled over in the snow. She's starved—half frozen. Some poor little two-bit dame on her uppers."

The hard eyes blinked and got smaller.

"Are yuh sure she ain't dead, Mac?"

He crawled out and looked at the girl closely. He shrugged. "Okey, Mac, so long as you come along wit' her. I ain't takin' no rap for nobody." He studied Jerry's face, his silk muffler, the wing collar, the black bat-wing tie. "An' it's gonna cost yuh a buck over the meter, Bigboy. Tonight's no night for hackin', what I mean—I'm on me way to the garage right now."

"Am I arguing?" Jerry grated. "Gimme a hand!"

Together they got her into the cab. Tracy dropped down

next to her and slammed the door shut. The shoe-button eyes looked back from the driver's seat.

"Where yuh wanna dump her? Polyclinic Hospital's the nearest."

There was a "Heated Cab" sticker on the door of the taxi but the cab's interior was as cold as Greenland. The newspaper columnist shivered as he peeled off his coat and tucked it around the girl.

"You're a swell advertiser," he growled. *"Heated cab, nerts!"*

"Where yuh wanna dump her?" repeated the sullen voice. "Polyclinic?"

"No; I don't!" He gave the wop the address of the towering hive on whose dizzy pinnacle rested "Libel's End," the Tracy penthouse.

THE CAB LURCHED ahead through the snow. Jerry braced the dazed girl with one arm, reached with the other for his silver flask, uncapped it, tilted it carefully to the girl's slack mouth. A lot of the liquor ran down her chin on to his prize English overcoat; but she swallowed some of it. He sat back, satisfied. *"Old Doc Tracy. No diploma but lots of brains!"* A moment later he swore softly as she quivered, gagged feebly and vomited the liquor.

Cripes, he thought, she's empty as a drum… Can't hold two swallows of smooth, honest to God rye on her stomach… Jeeze, she must be starved! He kept patting her shoulder with a kind of futile, monotonous gesture. He kept telling her: "Okey, kid. That don't mean a thing. We got 'em licked; hey, kid?"

The cab stopped presently. A uniformed doorman hurried down a shoveled path under a long sidewalk canopy. He carried an opened umbrella in his hand. He threw open the door and beamed at the columnist. "Good evening, Mr. Tracy. Be careful getting out, sir; it's slippery at the curb."

The cab's dome light glowed and he saw suddenly the extra huddled passenger. He stood there smiling woodenly, holding the umbrella over his head like a black toadstool.

"What the hell are you standing there for? Hotfoot it inside and put a call upstairs to McNulty. Tell him to start some hot coffee. Tell him I want it ready by the time I get up there. And send the elevator man out here to give me a hand."

"Yes, Mr. Tracy." He closed the umbrella with a snap and departed on a trot, his plum-colored coat-tails whipping in the wind.

Jerry leaned forward and peered at the dimly lit meter. He counted out the fare, added a dollar to it and thrust the money in the hackman's grimy paw.

The doorman and the elevator man loomed outside in the snowflakes. Together they lifted the dazed girl out of the cab, caught hold of her on either side and walked her into the warm lobby.

McNulty was waiting upstairs in the penthouse foyer, his yellow Oriental face wooden and impassive. He led the procession into the beamed living-room and Tracy smelled coffee and the acrid odor of wood-smoke. Crackling flames were licking at the fresh logs in the fireplace—good old Chink, McNulty!

The columnist became a swift demon of energy. He yanked a deep leather chair over to the fire, plopped down a footstool, slipped a bill to the waiting housemen and gave them the office to scram. Then he propped up the girl and pulled off her snow-covered coat.

"Okey, McNulty. Gimme the Java!"

The Chinaman shook his head without excitement.

"She plenty cold, eh, Boss? Velly much no eat. You go way. Me take care."

He fed her a teaspoonful of coffee, watched her narrowly, gave her a couple more. She kept the stuff down; and bit by bit he fed her the whole cup and filled another. Tracy yanked off her thin shoes, ungartered her stockings and peeled them off.

He began to chafe the bluish feet and ankles with brisk palms.

McNulty said calmly: "Be back bime-by. You wait see," and disappeared without haste.

What a guy, Tracy thought admiringly. That Chink would look just as wooden if I brought in a giraffe and asked him to cut its head off. He'd say, "Can do," and bring in a stepladder and a meat saw!

He kept rubbing the bare feet briskly, watching the girl's thin face. She looked ruddy in the firelight, less witchlike. Her chin had ceased its ugly quivering.

After a while McNulty was back with a steaming bowl containing a clear straw-colored soup. She smiled wanly and drank it down with eager little gulps. She started to rise.

"Sit still a minute," Tracy ordered. He raced into his bedroom and came back with a brown fuzzy bathrobe and a pair of slippers. "Get out, McNulty, and stay out!" He put the slippers on her bare feet. "Can you stand up all right, kid? That's swell! Now just hold those arms up for a second...."

He pulled the dark dress over her head and tossed it aside.

She stood there, swaying a little, looking at him with troubled eyes. He was holding the brown bathrobe wide to the fireplace, toasting it in the dancing heat. His head turned briefly.

"Not afraid, are you, kid?"

She shook her head weakly.

"You shouldn't be. Got to get to bed quick or you'll have a swell case of pneumonia… Almost ready with the robe! Just turn your back to me. Kick off the rest of those things."

He spoke casually. She hesitated. Then her back turned. There was a swift, candid glimpse of white skin; then he whipped the warm robe around her, picked her up bodily and carried her into the bedroom. He slipped her under the covers, bathrobe and all; piled more covers on top.

He stepped outside for a moment and reappeared with his flask. "Try and keep some of this down, baby; it'll start you sweating."

She smiled glassily at him. "You're a prince, Mister…."

"Shut up and go to sleep!"

Her eyelids looked heavy. They drooped. She began to breathe rhythmically. After a while he put both her arms under the covers, doused the light and tiptoed out. He found another quilt, slipped off his clothes and stretched out on the couch in the living-room.

He lay awake for a while watching the flickering shadows from the fireplace. The girl had called him a prince. A prince, eh? He might turn out to be a prince of saps… He hadn't the faintest idea what the kid was. She might run any one of a dozen games on him in the morning… Then he thought of her bare, bluish feet… Swirling snow… Nothing phoney about that! *You might be a sap, Jerry; but for once in your life you did the right thing!* The thought made him feel oddly light-hearted, happy. He grinned in the darkness, turned over and went to sleep.

IT WAS ALMOST noon when Tracy awoke. He took a stealthy peek in the bedroom. The girl was still dead to the world. She looked good for hours. "Let her sleep it out," he told McNulty. "If you wake her up, you're fired!"

He downed a quick feed, grabbed a cab for his Broadway office and spent a painful couple of hours banging out a long glittering column, full of wise winks, hot-cha and snappy gags. When he got back to the penthouse it was mid-afternoon.

The girl was awake at last, staring up at the ceiling with drowsy opened eyes. The sleep had done her good, he thought with approval. The wolfish pinch was gone from her face—an unexpectedly pretty kid. Younger than he had thought; twenty-two or so, probably. Brown eyes. The eyes were shy, youthfully grave. She lay quite still under the covers.

"Who are you, anyway?" she asked softly.

"Kris Kringle's favorite nephew. How do you feel?"

"Warm and sleepy—and kinda weak." Her eyelids blinked rapidly. "I—I dunno what's the matter with me. I'm—I'm gonna cry, I think."

"Hey, nix! Nix!" He made a gesture of comic concern. "Let's talk sense. Are you hungry?"

"I could eat," she said drowsily, "a cow, a bull and a roasted soldier...."

He chuckled at the old nursery rhyme. His fingers made a cheerful snapping sound.

"Okey. Can do. Now listen. There's some clothes over on the dresser. Dressing-gown and slippers on the chair. That door leads to a hell of a swell bathroom. I know because I paid for it. Are yuh listenin'?"

She nodded.

"Fine," he said. "Hop in the tub, fill the place full of steam. You'll find plenty of towels and four kinds of soap. No bath-salts; I'm not that kind of a guy... When you get finished, climb into these brand-new silkies and join me in the dining-car. Can do?" He grinned ruefully. "I'm beginning to talk like a damned Chink! That's the McNulty influence."

He backed out, his hand on the knob. "If you're afraid of burglars, sweetheart, there's a key in this door."

He buttonholed the passing Chinaman. "Tea for two, McNulty. The kid hasn't eaten lately, so use your own judgment."

McNulty smiled one of his rare grimaces. He patted the columnist on the arm approvingly, muttered something that sounded like "clazy sunny peach" and padded off to the kitchen.

The meal was ready long before the girl. She wore a flowered silk dressing-gown that covered the embarrassment of borrowed underthings. Pink satin mules on her feet. Level brown eyes, brown hair neatly brushed; slim little girl figure. Tracy gulped and revised his earlier judgment. Pretty—hell! She was beautiful—a soft-eyed little knockout.

She was speaking her piece again. "I—I don't know how to thank you or—or I suppose your wife—"

"Why bring that up?" he grinned. "Oh, I getcha! You mean the borrowed garments—you mean the silken thisa and thata... Wife, hell! I'm just a bold, bad man-about-town, equipped for all emergencies... Draw up to the groaning board; I'm kinda hungry myself."

There was plenty of thick soup and thick gravy, and mashed potatoes, with some kind of a savory Chinese mystery-meat that made the salivary juices gallop all over your tongue... She cleaned up with a relish, slowing down on the attack whenever she caught Tracy's worried glance.

The Chinaman watched her too. He clapped his hands presently, said "Feenish. No more. Get hell out," and Tracy chuckled and the girl went with him to the beamed room with the huge snapping fireplace.

They sat down together on a couch and watched the play of the orange and purplish flames. The *Planet's* scandalmonger lit a cigarette. After a few puffs he tossed it into the fire.

"I'm going to get nosey and inquisitive, if you don't mind."

"Mind? You've bought the right to ask—anything, I guess." Her mouth was tremulous but the brown eyes were clear and clean.

"I'm asking questions, kid, and nothing else," he said sharply. "Maybe I can help you. I don't want any lies or heroics. If I get too nosey, just tell me. That fair enough?"

"Go ahead."

"What's your name?"

"Lily Carson."

"Age?"

"Twenty-two."

"Where you from, Lily?"

"Pennsylvania."

"Parents? Relatives?"

"No."

"What do you mean? All dead?"

"I don't know," she said in a low tone. "I grew up in a big red-brick building with four hundred other kids. We wore pig-tails and gingham uniforms. Little Orphan Annie from Pennsylvania—that's me."

"Nix on the cynical stuff, sister! It's cheap and it gets you nowhere. Leave the hardboiled line to clever guys like me."

"Are you a crook?" she asked him suddenly.

His eyes narrowed instantly. "Why ask me that?"

"I met a crook once. He was always telling me how hard-boiled and clever he was."

"Did you play the game with him?" Tracy countered.

"No. I didn't have guts enough."

"You had guts enough to play straight. Isn't that what you mean?"

"I don't know. Maybe."

He shrugged irritably. "Listen, Lily. We're getting nowhere. Suppose you start with the old red-brick asylum and bring yourself up to date. And incidentally—I'm not a crook."

He sat back and closed his eyes. Listened to the low-pitched murmur at his side. Small-town stuff... The job here, the job there. Factory, bakery, drygoods. The Pitman stenography class at night. The fat real-estate man who wouldn't let her out of the inside office till she cut his bald head with a ruler. No job. The dough dwindling. Gulp, sniffle—chin up, finally—millions of steno jobs in the big town! Choo! Choo! and the West Shore Ferry....

Tracy opened his eyes and grunted morosely. "Go ahead, Lily."

Cheap hotel. Want ads. New job. Three bucks a week in the savings bank. Blooie—no job again... Furnished room. Coffee and beans twice a day. A thousand gals fighting for one job—and not fighting clean, either. After a while, no furnished room, no suitcase....

"And a blizzard for a fadeout," Tracy muttered. He looked

at her for a minute. "You left out the crook, Lily. I'm sorta interested in crooks. Where did he proposition you? In New York here?"

"Yes."

"How long ago?"

"Not so long."

"Who was he?"

"His name is Georgie Gray."

"The moniker doesn't mean a thing to me, sweetheart. What's he look like?"

"A little man. About my height but kinda solid and heavy in the shoulders. He has jet-black hair but his eyebrows are gray and kinda bushy."

"And a busted nose, maybe?" Jerry shot at her eagerly. "You know—bunchy looking? Smeared a little to one side?"

"Why, yes. That's right." She stared wonderingly. "Do you know him?"

"Uh-huh... Just distant friends—pretty damned distant."

He rubbed his own nose slowly. Georgie Gray, hell! Georgie Grecco sounded more natural. Georgie Gray to the kid here—George Grecco to the homicide squad. A finicky little Greek chiseler on the wrong side of fifty who liked to dye his hair black and carry a perfumed handkerchief. He never used a gun; he had long muscular fingers.

Jerry said huskily: "You were sure sensible, baby, to turn that mug down. He's *mean!*"

She nodded dully, without comprehension.

"He made me a proposition," she said. "Said he was taking a quick trip to Boston and he'd be back Wednesday. I told him I'd think it over. Thought maybe I could get another meal out of him before I turned him down. It was last night when I got to the end of things and—and lost the hallroom and the suitcase. I—I just kept walking around in the snow... Just yeller, I guess."

"Yeller, your aunt fiddle-de-dee! What was Grec—er—Gray's proposish?"

It sounded screwy the way she told it.

Gray met her in a cheap restaurant on Broadway, got friendly right off the bat, took her out a couple of times and then sprang his scheme. He had a swell idea to nick a wealthy playboy for plenty jack. He'd stake Lily to a swell evening rag, tow her to a speak where the wealthy sucker usually hung out. After a while Gray fades, Lily smiles and lets the prospect pick her up, lets him taxi her home—not his home. Lily feeds him a couple of drinks—and bingo!—in comes Gray from the next room. *"My wife, you hound!"* The playboy's legal Park Avenue wife is hot for a divorce excuse; he pays sweet to hush up the mess. And a grand in cash for Lily's cut... Sez Gray!

It sounded screwy as hell to a case-hardened Broadway snoop-and-peep artist like Tracy.

The old-fashioned badger game! Whiskers on it. A throwback to Little Egypt and strip dancers with petticoats. The gay Nineties... Georgie Grecco wasn't pulling any cheap jerk like that! What *was* his racket? Whatever it was, Lily wasn't hep. Grecco's proposish undoubtedly called for a pair of saps, including Lily....

"WHO WAS THE proposed sucker?" the columnist asked. "Did Gray say?"

"He gave me a photo from a newspaper. The name on the bottom was cut off. Just a clipping from a paper."

"Still got it?" Tracy snapped eagerly.

"Why, yes… I think I had it in my handbag."

He gave a shrill snort like a pony and jumped up. His eyes scanned the room. The cheap black handbag was on a side table. Tracy scooped it up and gave it to her.

"See if you still have the picture, honey!"

Wealthy playboy was right! It was Freddie Hullen. "Boots and Saddle" Hullen. Polo, horse-flesh, fox hunts, stable smell— and about ninety-two millions in his own right. A fish for liquor; a fool for women.

Tracy gave the impassive girl a curious look.

"You're a nice-looking number, Lily. And when I say nice I mean beautiful. But what makes you think this wealthy coot would be apt to pick up an unknown little gal on her uppers? How did your old pal, Georgie Gray, figure that slant, sweetheart?"

"He said that was the easiest part of the whole thing," Lily Carson said in a low, embarrassed voice. "He—he said I was a natural—made to order. He said that the playboy was the kind of bird that got friendly with nightclub flower-girls, girls with cigarette trays…" She flushed. "Young, he said, and—er—slim and…."

"I getcha. The boyish form divine—and no educated chatter to make his head ache."

Her flush deepened and so did Tracy's funny smile.

He watched her profile silently as she stared at the crackling logs in the fireplace. Why did Grecco *deliberately pick* poor little Lily Carson? There must be a reason for it—but what? There were plenty of slim dames for a bunco steer of that sort. Syrup-eyed wenches with straight little bodies and crooked little minds. Tracy could name a dozen offhand; Georgie Grecco probably knew fifty. Then why try to line up a decent little brat without dough, without friends, nameless....

His heart skipped a beat and he sat quite still.

He said, in a gentle, faraway voice: "I want to ask you something, Lily. Think hard."

She turned a little. Her eyes were round with wonder at his manner.

"Did you," Tracy purred, "tell this man Gray, at any time, what you told me a while ago? I mean about the redbrick asylum in Pennsylvania? About being alone in the world, without a friend or a relative?"

She nodded. "We got pretty chummy. I told him. Shouldn't I? It's nothing to be ashamed of."

"No. That's all right. It's okey, Lily."

Her throat was like a slim white column rising from the silken V of the negligée. Like her name it was—lily—slender, graceful. Tracy shuddered as he saw for a dreadfully clear second of fancy the white skin blotched with purplish marks; the edge of a man's shirt-cuff slowly withdrawing; sinewy fingers curling and relaxing....

"You look so funny at me," she cried out. "What's the matter?"

"Nothing, Lily. Nothing at all. Lemme think a minute."

The badger game—the silly yarn that Grecco had spun for Lily's benefit—began to blow away like a smoke screen. Underneath it, coming slowly into focus, was the real racket.

Tracy's case-hardened newspaper brain had no trouble fashioning the correct picture. Suppose... And suppose still further... She'd pick up the millionaire sucker, all right; that part was true. Her slim, virginal type was made to order for a wealthy decadent like "Boots and Saddle" Hullen. Okey, she leads the sap to the kill! Feeds him drinks. Fake husband in next room? Fake husband, nerts! All right, what then?

She feeds him drinks… Remember one thing, Jerry, oldtimer: Grecco's a sure-thing squeezer and he's after real dough. Lily's a corpse from the minute Grecco gave her the first once-over… So she feeds Hullen drinks. Drugged, of course. And then?

He shut his eyes to see the filthy thing the clearer.

Grecco comes in from the next room. All smiles, little pats for Lily's shoulder. *"Swell, honey; swell!"* Hullen out like a light. All set… And then—the red blaze of hell in Grecco's eyes, the hands shooting out to quench her scream of terror, the clamped fingers on her constricted throat. Soft hiss of Grecco's breathing. His fingers tightening….

Jerry shuddered. He was cold all over.

There's your answer, his mind shrilled triumphantly. No crude knockout drops for Hullen. A quick buzz. A little nap for him—the old *"One minute, please, while we change reels."* Hullen wakes up when Grecco comes in and shakes hell out of him. Grecco's no comedy husband; he's a city dick and there's a warm corpse on the floor, and Hullen is sick and scared and can't remember what happened. He holds his aching head and there's a warm corpse on the floor in an evening gown—purple marks on the still throat… *"God in Heaven, man! I tell you—I swear—"* Maybe it could be fixed for a prominent fella like "Boots and Saddle" Hullen. Does he pay? *Does he pay? With ninety-two million?*

Jerry Tracy walked across the soft rug and poured himself a stiff peg of rye. There'd be a crumpled Lily to get rid of some-how—a nameless brat in a torn evening gown… Maybe a plank across a narrow airshaft; a freight elevator, maybe… *Wake up, Jerry! You're going dime novel. The hell I am—and I'm nobody's innocent orphan, either!*

He went back to the lounge.

"Don't mind me, kid. Just woolgathering. The fire here always makes me dopey."

"That's all right," she said listlessly.

"Are you—" He sounded casual. "Are you planning on anything for—Wednesday?"

"Wednesday?" She had forgotten.

"I mean about Gray—the fella we were talking about a while ago. Remember? He was going to Boston, you said, and you were going to meet him when he gets back Wednesday and say yes or no to the proposish. You left him up in the air, figuring you might get him to buy you a few more meals. Remember?"

Her shoulders jerked as though he had struck her.

"That's finished! You—you did that much for me last night in the snow. I might have caved and gone to him—but not now. Not after—"

Her eyes filled with tears and Jerry said awkwardly: "Sure, sure. Forget it."

He tried again: "Suppose I ask you to meet this guy Gray and play ball? I mean, pick up the wealthy sucker and go through with the play. Would you do it if I told you it was on the level? I mean—"

He floundered.

"On the level?" she faltered. "How can that be?"

"I can't explain exactly. It's straight crooked, or crooked straight—or something… Listen, kid: I told you I wasn't a crook and I'm telling you again. Do you trust me, Lily?"

"Does that matter particularly?"

"It might matter a hell of a lot. Will you do as I ask?"

She saw his eyes watching her throat as though fascinated. She misinterpreted the look and her face flushed. A tide of crimson spread down her neck. "It's your right. You've fed me and sheltered me."

"Oh, yeah?" he snapped. "Put it that way and I ask nothing."

"What do you mean?"

"You're free in this thing, Lily. Get that in your dome! You either trust me or you don't."

She turned slowly so that she faced him directly. Gave him a long level look.

"I never met a man like you before."

He said: "I like your eyes, Lily; they're clean."

Neither of them was smiling. His gaze was as steady as hers. Steadier.

"So are yours," the girl said. "Clean eyes… I'll meet Gray on Wednesday night and tell him yes."

Tracy leaned suddenly and brushed her lips lightly with his own.

"You've just paid me one hell of a sweet little compliment, Lily," he growled huskily.

DETECTIVE HARRY WILKIE turned the knob of the hotel door softly, carefully, with an even pressure of his big red paw. He had waited patiently at Tracy's whispered request. He knew Jerry was holding back some of the story—always did, the little bum!—but the girl inside was a very special friend of Jerry's and the big City detective was deep in Jerry's debt for a flock of authentic police tips. Nice info that had pulled Harry Wilkie high in favor with the Gruff Guy in Centre Street.

So Wilkie waited. Then he heard a faint, funny noise and a thump and his big hand turned the knob.

Through the widening crack he could see part of a table. There was an overturned bottle on it and a man in evening clothes sat slumped forward with his head on his extended arms.

The detective couldn't see the girl. She was on the floor beyond his vision. Lily's eyes were wide open and protruding. A man was crouched above her on both knees, his fingers clamped on her throat. Georgie Grecco's face was a sweating mask of relief and satisfaction. He gloated to think how neatly he had timed his rush to quench that terrified scream of hers. His nostrils flared and he inhaled air with a soft, hissing sound.

Wilkie bounded in with a blue-steel .38 special in his paw. One hundred and ninety-two pounds of hard meat. He saw the killer squatted low like a hunched ape and dived at him. He struck at the bobbing black head with the barrel of his gun. It was an awkward blow but it tumbled the man five feet away.

Grecco squirmed, monkeylike, to his feet—and stopped. Stood there frozen and glaring with a trickle of blood on his cheek and his hands raised, palms outward.

Wilkie panted: "Stay that way! Are yuh here, Jerry?"

"Right behind you," Tracy murmured. He had closed the hall door as he came in. There was another door, wide open, leading to an adjoining room of the suite. He skipped hastily over and looked in. Empty.

The girl on the floor was getting to her knees, one hand fumbling at her throat. She was chalk white with terror. More scared than hurt, Jerry saw at once, to his immense relief. The Greek's fingers hadn't had time to do more than bruise the flesh.

"Take it easy," he begged.

The drunk in evening clothes was still slumped over the table, his face hidden between his extended arms. Tracy clutched him by the hair, peered at his face, dropped it with a bump. "Boots and Saddle" Hullen, all right! Tracy wrinkled his nose disgustedly. The guy smelled like a prohibition distillery.

"Who is he?" Wilkie growled. "Know him?"

"Nope. Drunk as a coot. Hell with him."

Wilkie was grinning balefully at the crook in front of his gun. "Little Georgie Grecco! Well, well, well… How d'yuh do an' please t' meetcha an' how are all the folks?"

"You got nothing on me, fella."

"No? I might think up a few. How 'bout unlawful entry?"

"She invited me in. Whaddya think of that!"

"Oh, yeah? You mean a conspiracy to commit a felony?"

Grecco shut up suddenly.

"How about the mugg in the soup and fish? Attempted robbery, maybe? Extortion? Blackmail? An' this pretty little dame in the evenin' gown—would yuh call that felonious assault, assault with intent to kill—Hell, I'm forgettin' the good old Sullivan Law."

He leaned forward and slapped Grecco's body expertly with his free hand. He frowned.

"Too bad. We got enough without that, anyway. Stick out your mitts, sonny boy, for a pair o' cuffs and a nice little ride in the wagon."

"Wait a minute," Tracy said. "The girl is a particular friend of mine, like I explained to you, Harry. She doesn't want to be mixed up in a whole lot of notoriety if she can help it. Lemme talk to her."

HE WENT OVER to her, bent close and whispered seriously: "Buzz, buzz and a couple of more buzzes. Stall a little bit, honey. Recite the alphabet to Papa. Argue a little bit, and take it easy."

He nodded and straightened up. "Just as I thought, Harry. She doesn't want her future ruined by a lot of tabloid publicity. She's got half a mind not to press the charge."

"Let her press and see what it gets her," Grecco sneered. "The whole thing's a frame."

The detective chuckled. "The State can use her testimony fine. Come to think of it, there's a law in this State concerning life sentences for habitual criminals. How many convictions have you got chalked up, Grecco?"

Sweat stood out on the Greek's forehead. He swung towards the expressionless face of the *Planet's* columnist.

"Maybe she wouldn't wanta make a charge, hah?" he muttered thickly. His bushy gray eyebrows crawled with anxiety.

Jerry looked at the big detective.

"Mind stepping outside the door a minute, Harry?" His hand dropped into his overcoat pocket. It came out clutching a squat automatic. "I can take care of this guy all right."

Wilkie scowled, stared at him; then he opened the door and stepped out.

Jerry's eyes never left the prisoner. "Proposition me," he said.

Grecco licked his lips nervously. "If the kid don't make a charge, there's no rap against me—that the idea?"

"That's the general idea. Talk arithmetic."

"Half a grand—cash."

"Fourth offense means life in this State," Tracy said.

Grecco swore. "I'll make it an even grand."

Tracy glanced over at Lily. She stared back at him dumbly.

"The kid says," he reported, "that she won't take a nickel less than two grand. She says she wants it now and it's up to you to figure how to get it here."

The Greek hesitated a moment. Then he nodded. He looked corpse-like. "You got me right. Lemme use the phone."

Tracy's gun gestured towards the desk in the corner. The crook drew a notebook from his pocket. He riffled the pages briefly and then picked up the instrument.

The girl, close beside Jerry, faltered in a low voice: "It's rotten money. I don't want it. I can't take it."

"Wrong," Jerry rejoined in the same low murmur. "It's plain ordinary money. Neither good nor rotten. In Grecco's palm I'll admit it's pretty damned dirty money. In yours it's whatever you choose to make of it... As we say in dear old Harvard, don't try to personify an inanimate object... Any comment?"

She was silent.

"Then shut up!" he grinned.

He heard the click as Grecco replaced the receiver.

"It's okey," the crook snarled. "Two grand on the table and it's the last —— —— cent I got."

"Fine. Details, sweetheart!"

"In about ten minutes. He'll come right up to the room."

Tracy lit a cigarette with his left hand and puffed a while. "Boots and Saddle" Hullen stirred briefly at the table and mumbled something faintly. Nobody paid any attention to him. After a while Jerry looked at his watch. The time was almost up.

Suddenly he heard the deep murmur of Wilkie's voice in the hall. The door swung open and Wilkie's head thrust into the room. "Guy out here with a package, Jerry. Know anything about it?"

"I'll take it, Harry," the columnist said. He walked over and held out his hand. He shut the door on the waiting dick and turned back into the room. He tossed the manila envelope on the table.

"Count it for me, Georgie."

Big bills, little bills; all kinds. It added up to two grand. Tracy slipped it in the inside pocket of his overcoat.

"Oke?" asked the crook sullenly.

"Oke."

Grecco reached for his hat and coat and started for the door. When he opened it Wilkie's huge bulk blocked the exit. The detective looked seriously at Jerry.

"Listen! I can't let him get away with this!"

"No? How are you going to hold him? The girl absolutely denies the assault. So does Grecco. So do I. The drunk saw nothing at all. You're up a tree, Harry."

He was grave, dead in earnest. Wilkie frowned and scratched his head.

"Tell you what, Harry," said the columnist smoothly. "Walk him over with you to the precinct house, like a good fella."

"Why, you dirty—" Grecco's face was livid with fear. "What is this—a cross?"

Jerry grinned amiably. "Nope. Go on, Harry; take him over to the station. You ran into him somewhere and picked him up for routine questioning, see? Maybe he's the guy that shot Lincoln. Hold him an hour or so and then kick him and turn him loose. I don't want Lily worried when we go out."

Detective Wilkie met the girl's troubled gaze. He said

grimly: "You ran into one hell of a good little guy, lady, when you bumped into Jerry Tracy!"

The columnist flushed. "Don't talk so much, Harry! Go on home with your prize package!"

When the door closed behind the pair of them, Tracy gathered up the girl's wraps hastily. He'd hurry her along before the reaction set in. She was getting shaky already.

She was pointing hysterically at the recumbent millionaire at the table. "Boots and Saddle" Hullen was swaying up on his elbows, mumbling foolishly. His eyes were glassy. His clumsy movement overturned the chair and he tripped and sat down on the floor heavily where he fumbled helplessly.

"Money in the wrong hands," Tracy muttered. "Remember my sermon, Lily? Look at him! Back in his sty! That's where his whole breed will be in one more generation. Back in its sty!"

He shrugged. "He'll be all right in another five minutes. Cut out the weeps, honey. Come on!"

Lily didn't let go till he got her in the cab. He stopped off at Stella Kahn's home in East Fifty-third, pushed the kid into Stella's capable arms. He stood around, scowling and worried, until Stella snapped: "You still here? Beat it, Jerry! Can't you let the kid cry in peace? Gwan, beat it!"

He had time to think a bit on the way to his penthouse. His thinking was characteristic of Jerry Tracy, the pride of the *Daily Planet.*

When he got upstairs he went into his soundproof den, snapped on a droplight and pulled the cover off a portable.

There was a fresh sheet of paper in the cylinder and his fingers began picking at the keys. He wrote:

According to the latest chatter in underworld circles, a celebrated perfumer with pre-hen-sile fingers dropped two grand at the races and was forced to bum his way outta town. Tsk, tsk! These gamblers....

What celebrated amateur jockey and first-nighter took a mixed drink last night and slept right through the best show he'll never see?...

Add prosperity signs: According to Department of Labor reports, the total number of stenographers from Pennsylvania with brown eyes, gainfully employed in industry, will be increased o-n-e in the current month. Or so I hear....

He yanked the sheet out of the machine and flipped it into a drawer. He cocked both feet around the typewriter, leaned back comfortably and raised his voice in a shrill, ear-splitting yelp.

"Hey, McNulty! What the hell have we got to eat in this —— —— dump? I'm hungry!"

He Asked for It

*Jerry Tracy goes to a lot of trouble
to find if he is really yellow*

JERRY TRACY, FAMOUS little wisecracker columnist on the *Daily Planet,* was in anything but a wisecracking humor as he emerged from the shabby entrance of the *Club Picador.* The flame of his pocket lighter jerked uncertainly as he held it against the end of his cigarette.

It wasn't fear—nobody that knew Jerry would ever accuse him of being yellow. It was something more vague than fear, and for that very reason twice as uncomfortable and unpleasant. A sense of dread. It had been growing stronger all evening. No reason to it that he could fathom. A whisper in his blood without words and without sense.

"You've got the horrors," he told himself jeeringly. "You're not used to inhaling the *Picador's* brand of paint."

But he couldn't kid himself. He hadn't downed enough booze to give a pup the jitters. This was something different, something....

Tim, the doorman, was out at the curb making shrill music with his whistle. The hour was late; no sign of a taxi anywhere. Tim shrugged and tried again.

"Stick around," said the warning voice in Tracy's skull. "You're in no hurry. Play safe. Wait for a cab."

He swore suddenly. Squared his shoulders. He said grimly to the doorman: "Nevermind. Don't bother. I'll pick up one on the avenue. 'Night, Tim."

"Good night, Mr. Tracy."

The columnist turned up his coat collar against the bite of the

night wind, balled both hands deep in his pockets and strode off. He walked down the dim length of the street with a brisk stride. And with every impact of his heels on the quiet sidewalk the warning whisper baited him with uneasiness.

To his annoyance his eyes kept veering sidewise as he walked. He was passing a huge automobile parking lot that ran clear through to the next block. Behind a low wire fence that paralleled the sidewalk were long rows of dark cars parked fender to fender. A yellow light burned dimly on a tall iron pole. The dark cars were like sleek headstones in a quiet graveyard.

Tracy found himself walking quietly, listening. And because he was listening he heard a faint sound that wasn't the wind. The brief scraping crunch of a shoe on gravel.

He stopped short instantly and his face screwed around over his shoulder. He saw a dim peering face—saw the stretched arm—and threw himself headlong.

As he fell forward flame spurted from the parking lot. His hat flicked from his head. Bullets fanned above his shoulder. He dropped in his tracks as though struck by lightning.

He didn't stir. His legs were stiffened awkwardly; one hand was still in his pocket. It hurt him to lie twisted on the pavement with his wrenched muscles held tense; but he didn't move. His hat with its torn brim lay a scant six inches from the stiffened fingers of his free hand. He was flat on his face, his lips a taut grimace against the icy sidewalk.

The fear that had enveloped him all evening whipped from his brain like smoke. His heart was thudding savagely. This was real! This was deadly!

He heard again the faint crunch of gravel—that would be the gun punk making his quick sneak. A distant yelp and the sound of running feet—that would be Tim, the doorman of the *Picador*. Heavier feet, slap, slap, slap—that would be the cop on the beat. Or would it?

It was. The bluecoat's gun was a dull glint in his big red fist. He was puffing as he bent over the prone columnist.

"Did they get yuh, buddy? Where'd they go—through the lot?"

Tracy sat up. Stared at the oldtimer with a slow smile. "Hello, Riordan."

"For —— sake! It's Mr. Tracy! Are yuh hurt, sor?"

The columnist got to his feet and dusted himself off. He picked up his hat and held it with his fingers over the torn spot on the brim. The cop wheeled and ran towards the low wire fence of the parking area.

Tracy snapped at him: "Wait a minute, Riordan!" He said to the *Picador's* doorman, who had reached him: "Hello, Tim. What's all the excitement?"

"Jeeze, Mr. Tracy, I heard the shootin' an'—"

"What shooting? Are you two guys *both* crazy?"

They stared at him queerly. Tim's eyes became instantly wise and alert; the patrolman, Riordan, looked puzzled.

Tracy chuckled mildly. "Don't be silly, boys. I'm sorry to disappoint you—but there wasn't any shooting. What you boys heard was that Buick pulling out of the other entrance to the lot. Backfire, sweethearts."

Tim didn't say anything. The cop grunted slightly. "If it wasn't shootin' what th' hell was yuh doin' on the sidewalk?"

"I'm funny that way," Tracy said. "I get dizzy spells. If you insist on it, I'll take a little walk with you over to the cop-house and you can spill any charge against me to Lieutenant Krantz. He's on the night desk, isn't he?"

"That's right, sor."

"By the way, Riordan, this is a pretty good beat you got along here. Pretty good precinct, too, I'll bet."

"It is that, sor." Riordan looked faintly uneasy. His round eyes became slitted like Tim's. He put his gun away.

"You're an alert patrolman, Riordan. In other words, a wise cop. You wouldn't be apt to mix up a shooting and a joke."

Riordan grinned, muttered something and walked away. Tracy went back up the street with Tim.

"Mind sticking on the corner with me, fella? This time I think I'm going to wait for a taxi."

"Who, me?" Tim said. "Sure thing." His voice indicated that mountains would fall and rivers dry up before Tim would desert an open-handed gentleman of the caliber of Mr. Tracy. He didn't say any more until Jerry was stepping into the cab. Then he leaned forward and his wise old eyes smiled.

"Didja get a flash of the punk's mug, Mr. Tracy?" he whispered.

"I wouldn't be a bit see-prised if it rained, Timothy."

Tim chuckled. "If it does, I bet somebody gets drowned. Me, I don't mind rain."

"That's because you don't walk around with your mouth open. So long."

THE CAB ROLLED. There was little traffic abroad on the dark windy avenue and in a few minutes' time Jerry was ascending a thousand feet per minute towards his expensive penthouse apartment.

The names of two men were congealed in his mind in letters of ice. Otto Korner was one of them. The other was little Willie Frisco.

Willie Frisco was the guy who had gunned at Tracy from the lot. Jerry had had only that one lightning glance over his shoulder to make the guess. Guess, nothing! That wrinkled and bloodless phiz behind a leveled automatic was something to remember.

Willie Frisco was a little guy with an old man's face on the body of a boy. He ran to tan shoes with perforated designs on the toes, skimpy suits with built-up shoulders, imported neckties like Turkish rugs. A handy little guy with a .38. He was on the Korner payroll.

Dutch Otto Korner—O.K. for short. That's what the underworld called Otto—O.K. A fat hammered-down Dutchman from the Bronx, with eyes like gray marbles. Otto had moved down to Manhattan and made the grade by rubbing out Manny Gross. He had a big payroll now, a swell income and as nice a murder organization as you'd want to see. The police biography of Otto would fill a newspaper column with "charge dismissed" and "sentence suspended." He had paid a ten-dollar fine once for parking near a hydrant. That was before he moved to Manhattan.

Cold rage burned in Tracy's eyes as he stepped into his suite.

He snicked on the lights in his living-room, unlocked a modernistic chest of pale silvery wood. He took out a bulky book with lined pages and a lettered index. His hand was as steady as a rock as he picked up the telephone.

He called a number and said: "Hello, yourself. Get off the wire and tell Otto Korner I want to talk to him. Tell him the name is Jerry Tracy. If you like jokes tell him T as in Tag."

He waited. Then: "That you, Korner?"

"Hello, Jerry. How's the kid?" Laughter gurgled in the receiver like greasy bubbles floating on oil. "How's my old pal, Jerry? What's new?"

"Plenty, Korner. A little rat emptied an automatic at me a short while ago. I thought I'd tell you about it."

"Yeah?"

"Yeah, I'm in a hurry, so talk fast. What the hell do you mean by handing Willie Frisco orders to bushwhack me with bullets? What's the idea of trying to rub me out, you fat Dutch louse?"

Silence. More silence. Then the laughter on the wire bubbled again. From the ugly sound of it Jerry knew he had guessed right.

"You're drunk, Jerry, old boy, old boy. It musta been two other fellas. Willie Frisco's playin' pinochle with me right now. He's been here with me all evenin'. Take an aspirin an' get back to bed. Call me up some time when you're sober."

"That's your story, eh? I'm drunk and Frisco's a pinochle player with a swell alibi."

"Go to bed, laddie." The voice hardened. "An' listen, kid: a bit of free advice. Cut out that 'Dutch louse' stuff! You newspaper guys are all alike—feed 'em a drink or two an' they turn snotty. First thing you know, you'll be gettin' me sore… So long, kid; I'll be seein' yuh."

"You're damn' right you'll be seeing me," Jerry told him curtly and hung up.

He stared at the instrument for a moment or two and then called up Harry Wilkie. Wilkie was a detective sergeant, a veteran flat foot who had climbed the rungs from patrolman to a plain-clothes tour and on to a soft daytime job at headquarters. A square dick with a straight spine. He was Tracy's link with the police department and what's more, he was Tracy's loyal and unswerving friend. Each of them was deep in the other's personal debt.

Tracy said to him: "Can you come over to my place right away, Harry?"

The columnist could hear the sound of Wilkie's slow methodical breathing. He had a chronic impediment in his nose that made him snort faintly.

"Sure, I'll come over—if it's important."

"It's important to me."

"Okey," said Wilkie. Verbosity was not one of his faults.

The *Planet's* columnist made a third and final call; this time to the garage where he kept his car—an imported thing with a bloated wheelbase, christened ruefully by himself after the first five hundred miles as *The Gashouse.*

He explained to Sam, the puzzled night man, that he didn't want *The Gashouse;* what he wanted was a small car; a roadster or a convertible coupé. Sure, he knew it was a cold winter's night and a chill gale blowing, but that's what he wanted—an open car.

It appeared that Sam had a convertible of his own with a lousy paint job and a bum fender.

"Fine," Tracy said. "Yank down the top, gas it up and get it over here right away. Park it at the curb outside and leave the key with the hallman."

"Awright, Mr. Tracy. I guess you know what you're doin'."

"I guess I do, Sam. 'Night!"

He was midway through his first cigarette when the hall-man's sleepy voice: reported a coupé for Mr. Tracy at the curb. He was crushing out his third butt when Harry Wilkie arrived.

Wilkie gave him a keen glance. "Something?" he asked lazily.

Tracy tossed him the hat with its bullet-torn brim.

"Yeah, something. Sit down, Harry."

The detective sergeant was a big man. When he grinned his mouth was pleasant, but when he stopped grinning his lips pulled tautly together as though they worked with a zipper. Plenty of meat between his breastbone and spine. It would take a strong breeze to blow Harry Wilkie over.

Tracy talked and the big man listened. At the end he nodded.

"Like that, eh? Otto Korner's little boy Frisco tries to slip you the heat. Otto laughs it off. But a guy in your business can't afford to have things like that laughed off."

"Right. The very minute I let anyone in New York—and

by ——! I mean *anyone!*—put me on the run, I'm licked—I close up shop. Korner's the first mugg to call my bluff with bullets. I'm not sure why, but I think I know… I print what I —— —— please! I'm no lousy little legman for a cheap tab. I'm Jerry Tracy, the million-dollar news buster. And I'm not taking any trains out of New York."

Wilkie's blunt forefinger made a sand-paper noise on his chin.

"So you're going right over to Korner's place and tell him no."

"Yeah." Tracy was sliding into his overcoat.

"You sound tough. Packin' a gun?"

"Nope."

"What's my angle?"

Jerry grinned. "You pack the gun, sweetheart. You're the life insurance." His grin faded. "Kidding aside, it's my party. All I want you to do is to wait outside Korner's joint in the coupé. Park under a light if there's one handy and keep your coat collar down. Let the well-known Wilkie features be prominently displayed. If I don't come out in a half hour, you go in."

"The hell with that," Wilkie muttered. "You call that a party?"

Tracy nudged him to the door. "Out," he said sweetly.

It was freezing cold on the dark street. The columnist took the wheel of the open car. Wilkie shivered as the icy wind bit his face and slashed sparks from his cigar.

"Nix on the half hour stuff," he snapped. "Fifteen minutes, brother. That's all the cold I can stand."

"Fifteen'll be plenty," the newspaperman said.

They parked the old rattletrap under a street-light. Jerry hopped out, walked briskly along the deserted sidewalk. He climbed the stoop of a squat four-story dwelling house, rang the bell and opened the glassed door of the vestibule.

The inner door was solid oak timber. A peephole opened and an eye peered. The metal eyelid closed with a click and there was a long wait. Jerry's mouth grimaced a little. The wait meant a hurried conference inside, uneasiness. Korner's bullet targets were not in the habit of calling on him to find out why. The Dutchman was probably feeling a mild species of alarmed wonder.

A moment later it was Jerry's turn to be surprised. Otto Korner opened the door himself. In person. He was smiling expansively but his eyes looked shrunken and hard. He kept his left hand in his pocket.

"Well, well! My old pal, Jerry! A pleasure, Mr. Tracy! Come on in."

He shut the door and Tracy saw the steel bar of the special Fox lock slide into place and click rigid.

Cigarette smoke drifted through the doorway of an inner room.

"Come on in and meet the boys," Korner smiled.

Tracy didn't smile back. He walked in. Stood in the middle of the room with a deadpan countenance. A tall man with light taffy-colored hair drifted behind him and closed the door. Otto Korner went over to a battered-looking desk and sat down. He waved his left hand vaguely.

"Boys, meet a dear old pal of mine. Jerry Tracy. Get him a drink, Sid."

"Never mind the drink," Jerry growled. "And forget the pal stuff. I don't pal with rats."

Silence flowed into the room. The faint ticking of a clock

became audible. Tracy glanced leisurely about him. He looked at Korner's henchmen. There were four of them. All on their feet and watching him. He knew them all. Besides Sid he saw Tubby Cohen, Al Carmody and sleek little Willie Frisco. Frisco's wrinkled face was the color of gray parchment; his eyes were dull with a sullen and vindictive hate.

"Frisk him, Willie," Korner breathed.

Willie's gat came out of his pocket. He moved forward with alacrity. "Up!" he snarled briefly. With his free hand he gave the columnist a quick overhaul. "Nope." He stepped back and Tracy lowered his arms. Tracy ignored the henchmen and walked over to the desk. He stood there, staring down at Korner.

"Okey, kid," the racketeer said softly. His voice purred. "I'm a rat and the pal stuff is out. You're here and I'm listening."

"Just why," Tracy asked him, "did you order that mummy-faced little —— Frisco to push lead at me tonight?"

"Well, well, well," Korner said smoothly. "Ain't the little Broadway garbage man tough tonight? And all by himself, too!" His voice changed suddenly. "Or is he all by himself?"

Jerry smiled mirthlessly. "Do you think I'm a sucker?" he asked flatly. "Did you think I'd come here alone? Put myself on the spot for a murdering heel like you? Be yourself, Korner!"

The Dutchman glanced towards the front room. "Take a look, Sid."

Sid's mouth was nasty when he came back.

"Yeah. Harry Wilkie's outside, Chief. The big stiff's parked across the street in a car. He's the only one I could see."

"In other words," Tracy said, "I never walk on one-way streets. I walked in here and I'm going to walk out. And if I don't walk out pretty —— damned soon, there'll be a committee of nosey cops ringing your doorbell to find out why."

Willie Frisco's lips snarled: "Let's smoke the louse and take a chance on the break."

Korner said: "Shut up, Willie. I'll do the talking."

"Willie did his talking earlier tonight," Tracy said. He leaned over the desk with his face close to the gangster. "Now it's your turn, Otto. Suppose you talk! Whatever made you think I'd take hot lead and like it? I'm still asking."

"Oh, you're askin', are yuh?"

The Dutchman's heavy fist shot out and caught Jerry flush on the jaw. The little columnist sprawled backward on the floor.

He was on his feet again in a moment, his face grim. There was a red mark on his jawbone just below the corner of his mouth.

Before he could say a word, Korner said: "How did it feel to be hit by a man—you lousy little blabber-mouth? How do yuh like it—you dirty yeller little newspaper spy!"

The words died away as he saw the look on Tracy's face. There was a long silence. Then Tracy spoke. His voice was low, hard:

"Okey, Korner... I know what's on your mind now. Well, let me tell you something... That little item you're referring to was blue-penciled, get me? It was out—in the basket—I was actually giving you a break... Well, all right! A minute ago I asked for it—and you handed it to me. Now you're asking for it; and by ——! you're gonna get it!"

He picked up the telephone from Korner's desk. He began dialing a number. Willie Frisco bounded forward. Korner growled and waved the killer back. There was a queer look on the Dutchman's fleshy face.

"Nix, Willie! Let him talk. I want hear him talk."

Tracy's nasal voice cut in with staccato speed. "City desk, child… Hello—Fielding? Tracy calling. That's right; Mrs. Tracy's headstrong little boy… Last minute change, Fred! I blue-penciled an item this morning on Otto 'O.K.' Korner. Yeah, the big Dutch professor with the A.B. degree from Oshkosh—Alcohol Baron… Right; that's the yarn, Freddie. Rip a hole for it and shove it in big. As is. Just as I wrote it. And Fred—listen to this!"

His chuckle was as mellifluous as strained honey.

"Here's a laugh for the dramatic department. I'm telling you over Korner's own phone… The hell I'm kidding! His smiling face is just about six inches away from mine and— Why, Fred, you skeptical old journalist!… Right; shove it in, commas and all. S'long."

He hung up.

"That, Otto my friend, is that."

"If that thing is printed," Korner said slowly, "you'll take six in the gut. Not from Frisco. Me. If it's the last thing on earth I do."

Tracy gave him a long level stare, turned his back on him and walked to the door. He said to Frisco: "Open up, lousy. I don't like the air in here."

"Let him out," Korner said thickly.

Frisco hesitated. His raging eyes fell before the Dutchman's. He unlocked the door. As Tracy passed into the hall Korner's husky voice drifted out after him. "Remember! If that crack gets out on the streets—it's either you or me!"

DETECTIVE WILKIE PUT his watch away as Jerry climbed into the parked automobile. The big plain-clothesman was shivering with the cold.

"Fourteen minutes!" he growled. "I might have known you'd keep me out of it!"

Jerry took the wheel and drove off in silence. Wilkie continued to stare at him belligerently.

"You're a crazy little —— to go jamming in there like that. What good did it do? Will you please tell me what in hell it got you?"

"Self-respect," said the somber voice behind the wheel.

It was less than an hour after Jerry had returned to his penthouse when the doorbell rang. He rose jerkily from the deep leather chair and picked up a gun. He stood tensely for a second; then the bell buzzed twice again. He sighed faintly, laid down the gun and walked towards the foyer.

He heard McNulty's bedroom door open and the pattering of slippered feet. The Chinese butler was in a weird-looking Oriental nightrobe; but there was no sleepiness in the almond eyes. His hands were concealed in wide flowing sleeves.

"Me go," he said quickly.

"The hell you will!" Tracy snapped. He elbowed the old fellow aside and answered the ring himself.

The night elevator man was outside with a fresh folded newspaper. Tracy took it and went back to the living-room. McNulty was there, pretending not to see the gun on the table. The newspaperman turned the pages of the smudgy *Planet*, ran his eye down the column. He read the thing with a detached professional stare. It was there, all right; Fielding hadn't muffed a comma. Mechanically, he read it a second time.

The Chinese said gravely: "Why hell you no go bed, Boss? You no tired, hey?"

"I'm not tired. I'm staying up a while. I won't need you, old boy. Scram back to bed."

McNulty shook his head. "Me stay."

"You—what!" Anger snapped into Tracy's voice. He tossed the *Planet* aside. "Listen, Bum, when I—"

The phone rang. He walked over and picked it up. He said, dryly: "Tracy. Yeah…" And in an even dryer voice: "Talk slower, Korner. I can't understand you the way you're shouting… You telling me? I just read it this minute, sweetheart."

His smile wavered but he added steadily: "You a betting man, Otto? I'll bet you an even grand that Manny Gross' brother figures it out and pots you in three days. What do *you* think?"

"I think," the voice on the wire screamed, "that you're a dirty, double-crossin' little ——!" It bubbled into a thick barrage of profanity. Korner sounded well liquored. "I'm gonna fix you for that—an' I'm tellin' you right now I don't give a damn—"

"Why should you, sweetheart? You're washed up in this town no matter what you do—and I'm the guy that did it."

Deliberately Tracy egged him on, explained in mocking detail just what the squib would do to Otto, to his leadership. Jerry smiled with a grim satisfaction. He could hear Korner bellowing with rage at the other end of the wire.

Jerry cut in. His voice was thin, steely.

"What are you going to do about it, Tough Guy?" Deliberately he parroted the scornful challenge that Korner had hurled at him earlier in the evening. *"How does it feel to take it from a man, Korner? A newspaperman! How does it feel to take it on the chin from a lousy little blabber-mouth?* Maybe you'd like to change your mind now about yeller little scandalmongers."

Korner's frenzied roar vibrated in the receiver. Again Jerry cut in icily.

"Well, what are you going to do about it? Just roar like an ape with the bellyache?"

"I'll tell yuh what I'm gonna do!" Otto howled. "I'm comin' over there an' I'm gonna spill your guts! I'm gonna tear yuh apart, yuh little rat!"

"I don't think you will," Jerry jerked. "You're not man enough to." His eyes narrowed to mere slits. He heard the receiver slam at the other end of the wire. He smiled a little breathlessly and hung up.

McNulty was watching him, his yellow face expressionless. Tracy had an idea there was probably something cold and sharp concealed somewhere in those wide flowing sleeves. He said gently: "Go to bed, Kid."

He threw an affectionate arm around the old man's shoulder and walked him to the door of his bedroom.

"In, old fella. Fireworks are over… Savvy?"

McNulty's slant eyes flickered. He touched Jerry's arm for a moment. He went into his room and shut the door after him.

Tracy poured himself a stiff drink. He took another. Two— that was enough… Running a column—a fearless column— was no fun. Put up or shut up. Knuckle down to Korner or anybody else and you stopped being Jerry Tracy. You became two other fellas—and both of 'em were yeller. A soft snicker would roll from the Battery to Bronx Park….

He lit a cigarette. His hand was a little trembly. He walked about, eyed the quiet magnificence of the big modernistic living-room; opened the French windows and stared across the stone terrace at the faint powdering of stars. Getting hazy over the East River; dawn pretty soon….

He felt pretty good about the way he had handled the

Dutchman. But there was a strong undercurrent of uneasiness to his pleasure. Korner's threats were never idle—and Korner had been ferociously specific about what he intended to do. He was going to spill Jerry's guts! No mistake about that; he meant it. Some time, some place—from that moment on it would be watch your step, Jerry! Keep alert, Jerry! The finger on you from now on! Tracy sweated and the clock ticked slow time.

Abruptly the house phone trilled. Its sound brought the columnist up tense and trembling. Cursing his jangled nerves, he answered it.

"Who? Oh, he won't give his name, eh? I see."

Damned right, he saw!

He said carefully into the instrument: "Is he a fat, hammered-down fella? Big shoulders? Little gray eyes? Uh-huh… A bit drunk, you say? Yeah, I guess I know him… Stall him for a second, Looie."

He hesitated. Korner downstairs! Liquored. A gun on him without any doubt at all. Call the police? Jerry knew instantly he couldn't do that. That was out. It was strictly up to J. Tracy, Esq. This deadly stew was a personal dish to eat all by yourself. A two-man quarrel. Either Jerry quit—or Korner did. "If I crawl," Jerry thought, "I'm through in this town forever. By ——! I *can't* crawl! I've got to see it through.…"

He eyed his shaking hand grimly. "Am I yeller or not?" he thought.

"Send him up," he said into the telephone.

He slipped his own gun into his pocket, opened the front door of his apartment and stepped outside.

His movements were quick and silent.

He shut the door and left it unlocked. There were three penthouse doors fronting on the rectangular public hall—A, B and C. Tracy's was marked "B." A few feet away was an angle in the wall leading to the head of the fire-tower and the enclosed descent of fireproof stairs required by law.

Tracy melted out of sight like a ghost.

The elevator door clanged. "Penthouse B, sir," said Looie's voice. Another clang and a faint diminishing whir like wind in a knothole as the car went down.

Otto "O.K." Korner tiptoed across the corridor. He took off his overcoat, balled it up and threw it in a corner. Then he drew a squat black automatic. For a moment he stood there, his eyes veering cautiously. They were red-rimmed eyes. Shiny. Like water.

He crouched for a moment at the door marked "B." Then he straightened up and examined the hall carefully.

Getting the lay of the place, Jerry thought to himself. He could almost see the alcohol-whipped brain working laboriously behind those little eyes. Jerry wondered how the Dutchman was going to crash the door. To his surprise, Korner turned suddenly and tiptoed towards the entrance to the fire-tower where the columnist was crouching.

The answer flashed through Tracy's mind. Korner was looking for the fire exit leading from the roof. A wise guy! He'd step out on the terrace, locate the columnist's apartment and calmly pot his victim through a window.

Jerry stiffened. As the big Dutchman turned the corner, the columnist's plunging weight pinned him off balance against the fireproof door. Jerry's gun was a grim, ramming pressure on Korner's spine. The fingers of his free hand were clamped steel hooks on the killer's extended wrist.

Korner whirled halfway round, carrying Jerry with him. The columnist's chin was sunk in the fat shoulder.

"Drop it!" he gasped. "Drop it or I'll blow you wide open!"

There was death in that clipped cry of his—the crackle of a grim hysteria. Korner sensed hair-trigger death in the voice. His body went instantly limp. He let go of his gun and it clicked on the floor.

The Dutchman cursed obscenely and kicked the fallen weapon away. Tracy prodded his spine and marched him grimly to the door marked "B." He was afraid to try to recover the kicked gun; Korner was too deadly a customer to take chances with. It was like holding a tiger by the tail. Better get him inside quickly!

"Open up," Tracy whispered. "It's unlocked. Push it wide open. Take six steps into the foyer and stop. Whoa!"

He shut his door and locked it. Every light in the penthouse was ablaze. Korner's face looked greenish, drained of all humanity. So did Tracy's.

He said: "In, Korner. Straight ahead."

They marched into the living-room and Tracy laughed a little.

"Six in the gut. That's what you said I'd get, Otto. Six in the belly for a yeller little Broadway scavenger."

Korner leaped at him like a flash of light, his fingers clutching for the gun. Tracy was barely able to wrench it free and swing it awkwardly against the Dutchman's skull. Korner stumbled backward but only for an instant. He was on Jerry like a landslide before the columnist could point the weapon.

They wrestled in a silent primeval struggle for its possession. Korner's strength was enormous. His thick fingers were twisting the muzzle—slowly, relentlessly—so that it strained inch by inch towards the columnist's arched belly.

Suddenly Jerry's face ducked desperately and he sank his teeth into the fleshy hand of his foe. Otto let go instantly with a shrill, bestial yelp. The convulsive heave of his big body threw Jerry off balance and he dropped the gun.

There was no chance to retrieve it—Korner's fingers were already diving greedily towards the floor. Tracy took the one slim recourse left to him and he kicked at the weapon with all his strength. It flew through the open doorway of the living-room and skidded out of sight down the polished wood floor of the long foyer.

The racketeer cursed and swung a terrific blow at the columnist. Tracy bobbed swiftly away and drove his own fist into Korner's mouth. The gun was utterly forgotten now—it had never existed—they were ape-men, snarling breast to breast in an ancient jungle. They swayed toe to toe, grunting and smashing at each other's bodies. Tracy laughed pantingly, tauntingly. He was a smaller man, infinitely more agile.

No one on Broadway would have recognized Tracy's taut, dead-white face. He was a sneering madman. And as he fought—he taunted.

"Who's the yeller belly, Otto? I'm a little Broadway heel— half your size... My wind is rotten with cigarettes—I'm soft with liquor... But I'm gonna beat hell outta you—and put *that* in the paper, too!"

They fought up and down the room. Jerry was a circling gadfly—his jabs carried a sting like fire. He kept weaving in and out, dodging the smashing attack of the heavier man. Korner fought to get at close quarters. Once he almost had him, but Jerry's desperate straight-arm blow snapped Korner's head back with blood bubbling from his nose.

They stumbled against a floor-lamp and it went over with a crash and the sharp pop of an exploded bulb.

The columnist danced swiftly in at his foe. A left—dodge and duck—another left! He was cutting Korner to ribbons but he couldn't hold him off. The ponderous rushes were driving the smaller man up and down the room. Tracy's mouth was wide open; he breathed with quick, noisy gasps. Once upon a time he had been a fair lightweight boxer on a college squad, but that was a long time ago. And still Korner came at him, bloody, ponderous—and clutching, always clutching for the tight hold, the wrestler's embrace.

They reeled into a table and Tracy grabbed for a bronze statuette—and missed it—as table and contents went flying. His heels caught in the wreck and he went over backwards. He managed to roll away from Korner's kick; but before he could get to his knees Korner was on him with a thump.

The big man's very eagerness made him clumsy. Jerry squirmed away like an eel. He shut his eyes to the blows hammering at him and his threshing fingers closed on the coldness of the fallen statuette.

He swung it like a bronze club at the face above him. Swung it relentlessly till the face screamed and pulled away.

He was on his feet again somehow, but the club was gone. He had lost it as he dodged past an upturned table leg that bruised him like a sharpened stake.

In a daze he saw Korner close to him with an upswung chair in his hands. The light glinted on the modernistic metal as the chair came at him. Jerry felt the wind of it pass his ear as he leaped aside. The movement cleared his head somewhat. The Dutchman was thrown off balance by the weight of the metal chair and Jerry's fists lashed out at him viciously. Both men were panting heavily.

They backed up against the French window and Korner caught Tracy with a dazed rush. The window-catch was open; Jerry had forgotten to close it when he had gazed out at the pale stars.

The frame swung wide and spilled them out on the smooth cement of the roof.

They rolled over and over through the broad splash of light into shadow. Cold wind blew into the room and whipped the drapes horizontal. The pages of an open book on the rug ruffled in the strong draft. There was no other sound in the vacant room—except for the faint murmur of grunts and labored breathing from the darkness of the terrace.

Suddenly Tracy's voice cried out sharply in mortal fear.

Silence. The sound of men stumbling and panting.

And then—shrill and knifelike, like the wail of a child—Korner screamed. His cry lifted horribly towards the stars. And dwindled....

A SLOW SHUFFLE of steps began. Jerry Tracy came stumbling blindly through the flat splash of light. Under the mask of blood his face was purplish. He reached up mechanically and loosened the ragged necktie that had been pulled tautly into his throat. His eyes were bulging; there was a small scratch on his left cheekbone under the eye, where Korner's murderous thumb had tried to gouge him.

He didn't close the window. Instead, he turned and stumbled towards McNulty's bedroom. Before he could turn the knob the door opened and the Chinaman stood gazing at him impassively.

"What you want me do?" he asked calmly.

"Get that living-room cleaned up before the cops get here. Leave the window alone. Leave it open."

The Chinaman's breath hissed faintly. "Can do."

Tracy peeled off the ruined tie and collar, the blood-smeared shirt. He ran to the bathroom and washed his face and hands, tousled his hair.

As he rubbed the scratch under his left eye with a styptic pencil he became aware, suddenly, that his front doorbell was ringing furiously. He climbed into pajamas, pulled on a dressing-gown. At his elbow McNulty was whispering: "Eve'ting okey."

Tracy opened the front door. The elevator man was standing there, pale as a ghost. "The man!" Looie gasped. "The man who called on you, sir—he—"

"What about him?"

"He's—he's in the back court, sir. ——! he looks awful... He—he musta fell...."

"What! That's impossible! I left him only—"

"That's what I try tell you, Boss," the Chinaman cut in swiftly. "He no in room. Me hear noise and run see."

He added insistently: "Me hear. Him drunk man make one big squeal like dog. Then I run and call you."

Jerry's addled brain steadied.

"Shall I phone for the police?" the houseman quavered.

"I'll take care of it, Looie. Come in a minute."

The living-room was somberly quiet. Not a thing out of

place. Nothing unusual except the cold air that blew in through the opened window. Tracy went to the telephone and lifted the receiver. As he waited for his number he glanced back over his shoulder at the elevator man.

"You need a drink, Looie. Over there on the sideboard."

Wilkie's voice growled suddenly in the receiver. Tracy spoke quickly to his friend.

"There's been a little accident, Harry," he said. "A friend of mine, Otto Korner—*let me talk, please!* He came here to spend the night. He was drunk. I left him in the living-room. He—he seems to have fallen off the terrace… Yeah, he's dead… Do me a favor, Harry; get around here quick and take charge of things."

He hung up. "That's all, Looie," he told the shivering house-man. "Go downstairs and wait for the police. And Looie—not a word to anyone but the cops."

Looie nodded and scuttled away.

"There's a shirt and collar and stuff in the bathroom," Tracy told the Chinaman crisply. "Shove 'em down the incinerator right away. Wait a minute—Mr. Korner's overcoat is lying in a corner somewhere in the hall outside. Bring it in and put it on a hanger. Pick up his gun and get rid of it somewhere."

He dropped on the couch and relaxed. He felt all gone, weak as water. McNulty came through the room with the over-coat—all clear, Jerry thought with relief. He got up and poured himself a drink. His mind tightened and his brain began to click. He turned again to the telephone and called a familiar number.

"City desk. Fielding? Tracy again… Got a story for you, Fred; not for the column. A headline—hot news! Ready? Take it.

Otto 'O.K.' Korner, famous promoter and man-about-town, was accidentally killed early this morning by a fall from the penthouse terrace of Jerry Tracy, well-known columnist and Broadway commentator on the staff of the *Planet... Shut up and take this, you damn' fool! It's straight!*"

His voice resumed steadily: "Korner was drunk when he arrived at the penthouse and Tracy put him up for the night on the living-room couch. A short time after they had retired, Mei-No-Lee, the columnist's Chinese butler, was roused by a cry and discovered the living-room window wide open and the guest gone. The body was found by Louis Winniger, night doorman of the apartment house. It was lying in a concrete area in the rear of the building. Apparently the fuddled Korner wandered alone out on the terrace, lost his balance and fell sixteen stories to the rear court. He was killed instantly... That's all, Fred; more later."

He slammed down the instrument. He saw McNulty's round face surveying him.

"You sit down, Boss. Me fix you damn' nice drink."

"Not now." He smiled wanly. "I'm busy."

He picked up a sheet of paper and began to scribble. At last he turned around. His eyes gleamed. Even his voice was different.

"How's this sound, McNulty? 'What notorious smoke and muscle king tried to take a fall out of the well-known Fourth Estate—and wound up by finding himself just another fall guy?'"

There was a silence. The Oriental looked at him.

"No dam' good. You clazy fool."

Jerry sighed. He was like a swimmer coming up from a deep

dive. "You're dead right," he agreed. "It's automatic with me, kid. I had to get it out of my system."

He laughed queerly.

"That's one item that'll never go into the column. It won't have to. The guys it's meant for are not dumb at all, kid. Let 'em figure it out for themselves. They'll know pretty well *he asked for it.*"

He crumpled the sheet and threw it into the waste-basket. With a slow, fatherly smile the Chinaman reached down and picked out the ball of paper.

"You clazy fool," the old man repeated tonelessly.

He smoothed out the wrinkled sheet and solemnly scratched a match.

Both men were silent as they watched the flame die away and the gray ash curl.

Somebody Stole My Pal

Jerry Tracy, wisecracking columnist, finds that his wide acquaintance can be a liability—a liability to catch lead, for example

THE TALL, BONY-LOOKING MAN in the faded gray topcoat came out of the drug-store, bumped into a fat woman and without looking at her said in a mechanical murmur: "'Scuse me, Madam!"

He lit a cigarette, cupping the flame of the match against the warm gusty breeze. At the corner he hesitated; then he turned east and walked through the side street towards Sixth.

A moment or two later a dark blue sedan curved out of the avenue traffic. As it rolled eastward its speed slackened. It drew closer to the curb and continued moving slowly as though seeking a convenient place to park. Suddenly its door opened and two men sprang out.

On the sidewalk the gaunt man's head turned swiftly. Without a second's hesitation he began to run. Before he could take a half dozen steps he was clutched and halted. Not a word was spoken. He struggled silently with his captors. One of them jerked something from a coat-pocket and the tall man instantly ceased fighting. He was yanked over to the curb and shoved into the slowly moving car. The door slammed. The sedan accelerated at once and sped away with a shrill whine of its rubber treads.

Across the street a blonde stenographer in a cheap leopard coat stared open-mouthed at the vanishing automobile. She kept quiet. In a small town she'd have shrieked, pointed a dramatic finger, drawn a crowd; on West Fifty-Odd she did nothing of the sort. She gulped and remembered Manhattan's Golden Rule: *"Who, me? I didn't see nothin'."*

A young man up near the corner smiled faintly as the girl high-heeled rapidly past him. He wasn't so young when you got close to him. His name was Phil Duffy. He was a legman for the *Star*.

He said in a cynical tone: "Didn't happen to notice the number on that car, did you, sister?"

She gave him a frosty dead-pan glance and kept right on going. He shrugged his shoulders. What was the use? If he hadn't been able to tab the car's license it was a cinch that the doll hadn't, either.

The *Star* man had a speakeasy acquaintanceship with Earle, the man who had been helped into the sedan. He had spied Earle from the corner and had just decided to mooch up and make a touch when the quick snatch left him gaping. Phil Duffy rubbed his chin and considered. Was it a snatch? No sense calling his paper on a wild surmise. Besides, he was about washed up with the *Star;* he was due for the economy axe and he knew it. On the other hand, if he could do the *Planet* a favor, he might grab himself a new job and quit his own rag with profane dignity—before Wilson's patent-leather toe kicked him out.

He decided to invest a nickel in the *Planet.*

"Hello, ladybird. City editor, please… This is Duffy talking. Phil Duffy of the *Star…* Now, is that a nice thing to say? Listen, you might learn something—even from a *Star* man… Somebody just put the finger on that big raw-boned feature bum of yours. Jimmy Earle—right! Couple of fast workers shoved him into a closed job and took him bye-bye. Sure I saw him. It happened right now… How the hell do I know?"

The voice at the other end crackled briefly.

"Forget that *Star* stuff," Duffy rejoined. "I'm through with the rag. They got the skids greased for me and I'm looking out for myself. I don't know a thing about Earle's assignment and I don't care. Maybe we can do each other a favor. Wanta see me?"

Duffy grinned. "Fine. Send a boy downstairs with a buck to meet the cab. Better make it two bucks. I'm away uptown."

He hung up, stuck a hopeful finger into the return-coin cup, scowled in disappointment and strolled outside.

JERRY TRACY, THE *Planet's* wisecracker, the most famous and the highest paid kingpin of all the Broadway gossip guys, parked himself on the managing editor's desk and plucked a bit of fluff from his English topcoat.

"You don't think," he said nasally, "this guy Duffy is trying to rib us for the *Star?*"

"No, I don't," the managing editor answered bluntly. "I think we're plain lucky. I happen to know that Duffy's in bad with the *Star.* I bulled him along and promised him a job later on."

"Where is he now? Why didn't you hold him till I got over here?"

"Because I was afraid if you breezed in and cross-examined this mugg, Duffy, he'd smell a big rat. Might snoop around for the *Star.* So I gave him five bucks, thanked him for his good-will and sent him on his chiseling way. He'll be cockeyed in twenty minutes."

The managing editor rubbed moist uneasy palms together. He was a bald-headed, lean-shanked man with preternaturally bright eyes and a long sniffy nose. He looked like a worried stork dressed up in a brown bag of a suit.

"When did this alleged snatch occur?" Jerry asked him.

"About a half hour ago."

"Swell," said the famous little columnist in nasal irony. "All we have then is two fact nuggets. First, your own contribution: Jimmy Earle calls you this morning and tells you in a sober voice to forget about the 'Crimes of Manhattan' series; tells you to dig a hole in the makeup for a hot frontpage scream—and when Jimmy says hot he means volcano...."

"Listen, Jerry—"

"You listen. Next, we have Duffy of the *Star.* He sees Earle scooped up by a couple of gorillas. And it wouldn't take much imagination to hook those two facts together... Say, why pick on me? Why don't you try some of your city desk Hawkshaws?"

"You're the only man I can trust with the job, Jerry. You know everybody, where to look; whom to ask. I tell you right now that Jimmy Earle is—"

"I know what he is," Jerry said. "But I'll hand him this: he's a newspaperman! When he says front page he doesn't mean real estate notes or shipboard arrivals."

Tracy's mockery vanished. "Earle has been running that 'Crimes of Manhattan' stuff. My guess is that the lucky bum has stumbled on something hot. He never gets excited without proof. He's got his hammer all ready to nail Somebody with Something. In fact, he calls up and boasts about it. And old boy Somebody gets suddenly wise and sweeps up Earle in a hurry... At this particular moment I'm glad I'm not the well known special features man, James K. Earle."

He hopped off the desk, buttoned his topcoat. He grinned airily.

"Stay sober and keep a re-write handy. I'm going out for a walk."

HE DIDN'T WALK far; as a matter of fact his pedestrian ambition died at the curb downstairs. He hailed a cruising cab, climbed in and grunted an address. He'd try Shaney's speako first; after that Marco's joint; after that—plenty others. Mentally he tabbed all the likely spots where a boozy prima donna like Earle might leave a loose thread behind. It wasn't going to be easy to follow the footprints of the vanished feature man! And Jerry himself would have to be careful not to leave a foam of shrewd whispers in his own wake.

Lying back at ease in the speeding taxi, with one creased leg folded comfortably over the other, Tracy figured with cold-blooded glee a fantastic formula. A formula for the emotional speakeasy trade. He tried it out on Pete Shaney.

Shaney was a gimlet-eyed Irishman with hairy hands and a bald head. He said: "Haven't seen Jimmy Earle for a week or so. Why the funny look?"

"I've got to find him in a hurry. It's a damn' dirty shame!" Tracy lowered his voice decorously. "This is confidential; strictly on the q.t. His wife's having a kid over at the Polyclinic Hospital and—"

"His wife?" The gimlet eyes widened. "Are ye kiddin'? I didn't know that tramp was married!"

"He never advertised it. You know Earle, I guess… Cute little wife, too; bums like that always get the sweet ones… Something went wrong—the hospital telephoned the *Planet* office to rush Earle over there quick—she's delirious and calling for her husband—and the bum's off on a stew somewhere—"

"The dirrrty scut!" Shaney said softly. "Him married—can ye beat it! A decent kid married to a mugg like that!"

"And Earle hasn't been around today?"

"Nope… Wouldn't ye think a guy like that would lay off havin' a family."

"Well…" Jerry sighed mournfully. "I gotta beat it. Oh, Pete— keep this under the hat like a good fella. She's a proud little kid; she wouldn't want to be talked about by a lot of Broadway heels. You know how it is."

"Sure. I know. Okey, Jerry. Good luck to ye."

In the open air Jerry erased his grief wrinkles, chuckled and hopped into his waiting taxi. Inside the cab he burst into laughter. He couldn't help it—the look on the Mick's face! What an act—he'd have every hardboiled barkeep in town crying in the aisles!

He drove north and west to Marco's joint. Nothing doing.

The *Planet's* missing feature man hadn't been in there all day. Jerry spun the old hearts-and-flowers record and rushed away, with Marco's sympathetic promise to call up Tracy's man Butch if he heard anything, echoing from the basement entrance.

By the time Tracy covered a few more spots he found his voice choking realistically; he was beginning to believe in the maternity yarn himself. But he wasn't an inch closer to Jimmy Earle. Earle, apparently, hadn't been in any of his chosen booze haunts lately.

It was quite dark now; and Tracy was getting hungrier by the minute. He called up the managing editor of the *Planet,* lied reassuringly and downed a Three Decker Special in a sandwich shoppe off lower Madison Avenue.

Doggedly he picked up another taxi and continued the hunt. On the fringe of Greenwich Village, in the shadow of the swanky new Women's Detention Prison, he got his first hunch from Nino—Nino of the dark liquid eyes and the soft Italian smile.

"He was here last night," Nino said. "A little dancin' doll was with him—he told me her name—wait a minute; it's on the tip of my tongue—Dot West, that's it! Earle was feelin' high; he kept pattin' her arm and did she like it! He kept tellin' her what a swell little kicker she was, how she oughtta be spot-tin' a bill at the Apex Theatre if the managers weren't all crooked. You know, feeding her the regular line. He takes me aside and boasts how he's pulled her away from a tough mugg named Griffin—"

"Benny Griffin?" the columnist cut in swiftly.

Nino nodded. "That's just what I asked him right away. The doll shoves me off and tells Earle to close his dumb trap. They have a brandy and soda apiece and breeze." Nino grinned. "Does it do you any good, Mr. Tracy?"

"Okey, Nino. You're a pal. I'm gonna give this hive of yours a sweet puff in the column next Monday. Buy a few more tables. You'll need 'em. Good-night!"

On the swift ride uptown the case-hardened brain of Broadway's favorite snoop artist ticked faster than the meter. He'd never heard of Dot West; that meant that she was a little two-cent hoofer trying to make the grade in the cheap mucilage spots. He'd get a line on her from Moe Edelman as soon as he got to Times Square. Moe knew all the hopefuls, the hungrys and the hams.

But Griffin—Benny Griffin! Benny was a horse of another color. Where did a gunsmith like Griffin fit into the jigsaw? The columnist's heart beat faster. He began to sweat pleasantly with excitement. His mouth got cottony. He felt—never mind how he felt....

He marshaled his theory in parade formation as the taxi jounced uptown. Jimmy Earle of the *Planet* working on his Famous Unsolved Crimes of Manhattan rehash; digging into odd corners, nosing around old smells. Then Jimmy Earle meets a little dancing baloney named Dot West and gets chummy. The West woman knows—or knew—Benny Griffin; in fact, Earle boasts to Nino that he yanked her away from him. Griffin is a smoothly vicious gunman with a swell political pull and a record of plenty arrests and no convictions. Griffin is also head man and bodyguard for Jackie Herzog, the biggest card-and-dice czar in Manhattan since the unfortunate death of Solly Arnstein.

Tracy smiled like a wolf. Three years ago—come next July—

the unfortunate Arnstein had staggered stoically out of the *Rex Hotel* and died silently on the sidewalk with bullets in his entrails. His death had ripped open one of the city's biggest scandals in years; had revealed a stew of corrupt politics, crooked bets, sordid vice graft. But Arnstein's murderer was never found. The case passed into the cynical folk-lore of a cynical town. "Famous Unsolved Mysteries of Manhattan," by James K. Earle....

And the man who had wept the loudest and offered the biggest cash reward was Jackie Herzog... The fat little gambling kingpin, whose henchman was tough Benny Griffin, who knew Dot West, who knew Jimmy Earle, who discovered a front-page sensation, who got himself snatched—by a couple of rats—"

"—that lived in the house that Jack built!" Tracy growled softly. He leaned forward in the cab. "Okey, Bud! Stop at the next corner."

He walked over to Seventh Avenue, entered a crumbling red-brick dump and interviewed Moe, the greasy little dime-down agent who knew all the N.T.G. rejects, the Loew tryouts, the audition hopefuls.

TWENTY MINUTES LATER and a half mile south of 41st, Tracy rapped on a six-dollar-a-week door and pushed in when it opened.

Dot West was smaller than he expected; dark hair, grayish eyes, a bit plump for a dancer. Her voice was tough but that didn't fool him; her eyes were scared. She looked like a trapped pigeon watching a tomcat.

"Outside!" she snapped.

"No. Inside."

"What's the idea pushing in like that? Who do you think you are?"

"The idea was to say hello. And I think I'm Jerry Tracy. I run a newspaper column and I'm as famous as hell... *Uh-huh!* She's heard of me! That's fame!" His cocky smile made her taut lips relax momentarily. "I'm the man who knows all. F'rinstance: you're Dot West and I hear you're a swell little dancer."

She stared at him suspiciously. She smiled faintly.

"Somebody's been kidding you, Mr. Tracy."

"I don't think so, babe. Jimmy's not the guy that kids when he praises people."

"Jimmy?" Her eyes blinked. Panic spilled back into them.

"Sure. Jimmy Earle. Pal of mine. He works on the *Planet*."

"Never heard of him," she quavered.

"That's too bad. I was looking for him. He dropped out of sight today for some reason or other. Did I tell you—I'm a damned good friend of Jimmy's."

"Why tell me?" she said faintly. The color drained slowly from her face. She reached for the back of a chair and sat down heavily.

Tracy studied her for a moment with a shrewd eye. This kid was decent; she was on the up-and-up! She must be actually in love with the Earle tramp! Imagine that! Abruptly he changed his plan of attack. He'd shoot her the brutal truth! He did.

"Listen, Dot. A big sedan slowed up alongside of Jimmy Earle on 52nd Street this afternoon. A couple of gorillas hopped out and put the snatch on him. Kidnaped him, get me? Earle's due to be bumped because he's got the goods on a lousy murderer and he's too good a reporter to be bought off...

Got that? All right; now take this! I was lying when I told you he was a good friend of mine. Let's be sensible. Neither of us two gives a damn whether they bump Jimmy Earle or not. I don't know what you want. *All I want is to find him and get his exclusive story before they slice into his heart.* Know where he is?"

"No," she whispered. She was waxen with a stiff horror.

"What about Benny Griffin? Don't lie. Where's Griffin's hideout?"

"I don't—know—any Griffin."

"Oh, yeah?"

Craftily Tracy went off on another tack. The kid was scared stiff; afraid to talk. All right; he'd get her sore! He dangled the bait with a smile that was deliberately nasty.

"Listen, Dot. Let's be business men. How would you like to break into big-time dancing? How would you like to see 'DOT WEST' up in the lights? You know my rep, kid; slip me the dope and I can do it. To hell with Earle. Gimme Benny Griffin's number and I'll put you over with a bang. I'll ease you into a top-spot in the Apex Theatre. Why, I can—"

"You dirty, lousy heel!"

Her words flew at him in an incoherent torrent. He grabbed both her shoulders and shook the hysteria out of her.

"When did you see Jimmy Earle last? Come on! Hurry up!"

"This morning," she moaned. "We had a date for this afternoon but he never showed up. I thought he was giving me the gate. I never dreamed for a minute— Oh—I love him, I—"

"Sure you do," Tracy said. "Did you think I was blind?"

"Don't let them kill him! It's my fault. I got him into it. Benny Griffin used to take me out a lot—I played him for meals and drinks like a lot of other hungry dames without a dime. I didn't know who he was, then. And he got drunk one night and boasted about the Arnstein killing—honest to gawd, I was afraid to listen to him—and I told Jimmy Earle—"

The *Planet* columnist's laugh was short and harsh, like the bark of a dog.

"Jimmy dragged it outta you, huh? Then he went snooping. He's busted the Arnstein murder wide open or I'm a liar! Who did Griffin say was the killer? Don't lie to me; if you don't know, say so. Was it Jack Herzog himself?"

"I—I think so. Yes."

"Hot ziggedy!" His notebook flew out and his fountain pen point poised over the paper. "Gimme the address!"

"You mean Herzog?" She looked stupidly at him.

"Herzog, hell! I want the hired man—the body snatcher—Griffin! Where's his hangout?"

He jotted it down and started for the door. With one hand on the knob he turned. The girl was swaying in the middle of the room, staring at him. She had a twisted old-woman look on her face. Tracy had seen that same funny look once before: a nineteen-year-old wife with a face wrinkled like a senile old lady, sitting in the warden's office at Sing Sing and watching the clock, while out in the death house they were burning a twenty-year-old kid who happened to be her husband.

"Don't let them kill Jimmy!" the dancer was croaking.

Tracy shrugged and opened the door of the room.

"Sit tight and keep your mouth shut, I'll see what I can do about the boy friend."

ONE OF THE weather-beaten planks in the back fence was split jaggedly along the grain and the spry little columnist applied an eye to the opening.

He studied the shadowy yard and the rear of the building. The place was an old-fashioned relic of the brownstone Nineties. Basement and three stories, with a one-story outhouse leading to the yard. Up on the second floor there was a flicker of yellow light under the bottom of a drawn shade—looked like the Kicker from a gas-jet. The rest of the house was black and formless.

Tracy swung himself over the fence and dropped carefully into the yard. He wished to hell Butch was with him, but there was no sense in wishing. This job called for speed, stealth and silencer—mostly speed. Two men would double the risk; they'd only get under each other's feet.

Tracy glanced guardedly at the illuminated dial of his watch. Pretty late already. The managing editor of the *Planet* was probably still in the shop, biting his nails and watching the clock himself. Jerry shoved both hands in his pockets and felt better. There was a short-barreled .38 detective special in one pocket; a slim fountain-pen flashlight in the other.

He stared at the dark house and a ridiculous tune stirred under his scalp, Made him grin. *"Somebody stole my pal!"*

He tiptoed along the yard.

The outhouse door was locked. Tracy got to the top of the side fence; and from the fence to the shed roof. He stepped carefully, feeling for beams with his feet—damned roof was like paper!

He tried the window carefully. Locked. Jerry detached a gold pen-knife from the chain that swung across his vest. The sash was badly warped and he had no difficulty forcing back the old-fashioned catch. He replaced the knife methodically and braced his feet solidly over two adjacent beams. He lifted the window with agonized care for an inch or two.

He slid his arm through the opening and let the shade up as high as he could reach. The thin pencil gleam of his torch showed him an old-fashioned back parlor, closed double sliding-doors dividing off a front room and a smaller sliding-door that should lead to a hall.

Squatting outside on the shed roof like a shadowy gnome, he forced the window slowly up, pushing with a stiff, even pressure of his whole body. He was grinning with satisfaction when the squeak came. *E-eeeeee!* The shrill sound galvanized him into action. He jammed the window recklessly up and jumped into the room.

He could hear feet pounding on stairs. Like a ghost he flitted across the inky parlor and squatted behind an armchair near the closed double-doors.

The hall door opened. Two figures sprang in. A voice hissed: "The damn' window's open! Some mugg's been tryin' to git in from the shed!"

The window framed his bent back. "There's the ——! Down in the yard—by the back corner there!"

"Whereabouts?" The second voice was throaty. "You're nuts, Izzy. That's shadow."

Tracy's muscles cringed but he made himself rise. With his heart in his throat the *Planet's* dapper columnist slid from his cramped covert and tiptoed through the darkness towards the hall door. Six slow steps of icy fear.

The shrill voice at the window said: "Shadow, hell! There's somethin' movin' down there. I'll smoke it a couple an' see."

"I'll smoke you!" the throaty voice snarled. "Yuh wanna blow up the whole neighborhood, you dumb cluck?"

Jerry Tracy melted down the black hallway, feeling out with his left hand for the banisters. He hoped there'd be a carpet-runner on the staircase leading aloft. There wasn't—his fingertips felt bare wood.

He climbed warily in the darkness, trying to hold most of his weight on the rear foot. And on the sixth step—he lifted desperately at the last second—*eeeeeeeeek!*

He heard a yelp from the back parlor. He sped helter-skelter to the top of the flight and threw himself flat on the landing. The stairs curved inward at the top. Lying flat on his side with his legs stiffly extended, he could peer down through the banisters. The darkness had expanded his pupils; he could see better.

Two cursing figures came racing up the stairs. Tracy saw the ghostly gleam of a gun barrel. He squeezed carefully—twice— and the double roar of his .38 made his ears sing. The banister below him seemed to swell outward for an instant. A falling body crashed into the lower hall.

The second thug was invisible. Jerry could hear a faint moaning in the darkness; no other sound.

Behind the columnist's prone body a door banged open. A yellow band of light from the doorway fell across Tracy's extended feet; the rest of his body was in darkness.

A man with a gun twitching in his clenched grip came forward a step or two along the hall. He cried out harshly: "What the hell's wrong?" Then he saw Jerry's feet. "——! That you, Izzy?"

The peering eyes widened suddenly and the muzzle of the gun swung. A bullet thwacked into the floor beside the columnist's knee.

Tracy jerked at the trigger of his .38. He fired again. Limp flesh tumbled on top of him. He rolled the body off and leaped, catlike, to his trembling feet.

Jerry sprang into the lighted room. A long jagged flame burned from an open gas-jet on a wall bracket. The room was empty; his glaring eyes saw no sign of the missing Jimmy Earle. There was a cupboard-lined passage leading to a front room and he raced through, gun in hand.

The gas was turned low in the front room. A cot with a stained mattress was alongside one wall. A fully dressed man lay face downward on the cot, with one hand trailing on the floor.

Jerry rolled him over. It was Earle.

The feature man was bloody and battered and unconscious. He had been systematically and horribly beaten. His face was swollen and oozy. His breathing sounded queer; like the sharp catch of whooping-cough.

Jerry Tracy whirled grimly away from him and sped upstairs to the top floor, satisfied himself that there was no one aloft. He listened again in the hall. The moaning below had ceased; the ancient dwelling was like a tomb. It ought to be, Tracy thought harshly, as the reek of powder fumes stung his nostrils; he'd used up four well-aimed slugs!

There was no drinking glass in the tiny washroom. Jerry let the dirty brown water spurt from the faucet into the crown of his hat. He sloshed it over Earle's head.

Earle's eyes stayed shut. Jerry got an arm braced and lifted him partly. The battered reporter fell off the bed. Jerry let go of him with an oath. The guy was out cold.

Tracy began to swear shrilly—then he checked himself,

choked off the wave of hysteria. A phone! There must be a phone in the old dump somewhere—maybe downstairs!

He clicked a beam out of his toy flashlight and ran back along the hall. He stepped over the body at the head of the stairs, another one at the foot. It didn't faze him; he was beyond horror. He grinned mechanically as his torch swept across a dusty hatrack and showed him a coin-box phone on the grimy wallpaper. Must have been a furnished-room house not so long ago!

Swiftly he fished for change and found—a half dollar and three pennies... The old Tracy would never have done it but this Tracy did: he rolled the corpse swiftly and fished through the pockets. No luck. He tried the guy that had gone over the banisters. Two nickels and a dime.

Tracy leaped to the phone and called Butch.

"You know the voice? Shut up! Listen! Grab a cab—some hacker you can trust—see if Shultz is on the corner—take this address—park at the curb and ring the front doorbell—tell Shultz to wait—I'll be here...."

Bang! He hung up and called Information.

"I want the phone number of Marvin's Turkish Baths. Oh, for—M-A-R-V-I-N! West 4th and Dyker... I know perfectly well that it's in the book, sister, but I haven't got one here... Thanks. Gimme the operator! Hello? Paddy Marvin? Tracy—*Tracy!*"

He peered sidewise at his watch.

"I got a guy with me that's out cold, Paddy. Can you slap him awake and make him talk sense—I mean in a hurry?"

The old retired wrestler sounded insulted. "Jerry, they ain't no souse on earth that I couldn't—"

"Shut up, Paddy, and listen! This guy's been beaten up. Gone over pretty thoroughly by yeggs that know how. He's got a few busted ribs, I think. Can you do it?"

"Bring him down. Walk him in the side door on Dyker Street."

TRACY HUNG UP with a trembling hand. He let the torch go out and wiped sweat from his hot forehead. His knees felt like cooked spaghetti.

Abruptly they steadied. He backed against the wallpaper in the darkness.

There was someone outside in the vestibule; a shadow on the pale blur of frosted glass. Couldn't be Butch—Jerry had only just called him up! He snaked his gun out. Waited quietly in the velvet darkness.

A key grated in the lock. The street door opened and closed. A voice mumbled unintelligibly, grumbling fretfully at the absence of gas-light. Jerry heard the footfalls approach, pass him—stumble suddenly at the foot of the stairs where one of the bodies lay.

"——!" said a clipped whisper.

Silence again. Slow, endless, stark. Then a match spurted light. The man's back was towards Tracy. He stared down at the thing he had fallen over. He squealed—like a terrified pig—and the flame of the match twitched.

"Hold it!" Tracy growled. "Don't let that match go out or I'll blow your spine apart! Light the gas-jet and keep your hands up."

Fweeeeep! went the gas. It burned wanly, like a crooked yellow fang, with dust flicks dancing at its tip. There was no gun on the pudgy intruder. Tracy turned him around. It was Jack Herzog, the shrewd, paunchy gambler—Arnstein's foxy murderer—meat for the unconscious claws of poor battered Jimmy Earle upstairs....

The columnist had to grit his teeth to stop a silly cackle of laughter. It was so damn' funny... He kept his gun steady. Herzog didn't say a single word; just stood there.

They both jumped when the doorbell rang. Tracy said harshly: "I'd just as soon kill four as three, fella. Don't move."

He admitted Butch with a turn of his left wrist. Butch took one incredulous look at the place and said: "Jeeze!" His eyes swung from Tracy's .38 to the body in the entry, to the dead man under the banisters, to the dangling feet at the top of the stair curve.

Butch's voice got dry: "Yuh'll hafta cut that stuff out, Boss. First thing yuh know yuh'll be gettin' a tough rep aroun' town." He stared at Herzog without any interest whatever. "What do I do?"

"Upstairs!" the *Planet's* columnist told Herzog. "Got something up there I want to show you."

Herzog cleared his throat. "You got me wrong," he said, thickly. "I never been here before." He looked green, cheese-like.

"Where'd you get the key?" Jerry grated. "I s'pose a little bird flew over and dropped it in your hand."

"Don't be that way. A—a dame gave it to me. Told me to meet her here. You—you know how it is. I—I—"

"Upstairs!" Tracy said evenly.

Jimmy Earle was still unconscious on the floor. He looked pretty bad. Tracy grabbed him by the hair and jerked his face up.

"Know this guy, Herzog?"

"Why, sure. Sure I know him." Herzog was getting his nerve back. "One of your bum reporter friends, ain't it? What's he gotta do with me?"

"He's gonna sit you in a hot squat up the river for the murder of Solly Arnstein," Tracy said. "You know that without me telling you—or you wouldn't have had Griffin and Izzy and the other gorilla hand Jimmy Earle a deal like this."

He grinned faintly at the gambler.

"You fell over Benny Griffin downstairs—remember? Izzy's kinda dead, too. So is the other monkey. And you're next in line Herzog. In the first place, because you're a lousy murderer and justice is justice. In the second place—and I wouldn't kid you for the world—the *Planet's* in business to sell papers."

His gun lifted as the gambler sprang. Butch's ponderous fist knocked Herzog sprawling and dazed.

"Stick him in that closet over there and turn the key," Jerry said curtly. "Hurry it up, Butch; we're late... All right; now gimme a hand with Earle."

"Let go of him a minute, Boss," Butch said mildly. "Lemme show yuh how it's done."

He heaved the unconscious reporter over his shoulder in a fireman carry and tramped heavily downstairs. At the front door Butch lowered Earle's heels to the ground; and they got on either side of him and took him by the armpits. His feet bumped down the steps to the sidewalk like a trailed broom.

There was nothing in sight along the murky street except the cab at the curb. The driver hopped out and helped stow Earle inside. He said: "Hi-yuh, Mr. Tracy?" with elaborate unconcern and slid swiftly back again to his wheel.

Tracy shoved a palm at Butch as the big fellow started to get into the cab.

"Wait a minute, Bum." The columnist's eyes were a dead, even lustre; like wet, gray beach pebbles. "You know what cops do when they catch a cop killer, don't you?"

"Huh?" Butch's jaw got lumpy. He looked interested.

"Personally I don't like Earle," Tracy said. "I don't like the guy as a pal; but he's a newspaper man, Butch—a hell of a good one—and so are we. And he took a pretty tough goin' over… We newspaper guys don't stand for stuff like that, do we?"

"Damn' right we don't!" said Butch, who could barely write his own name.

He hesitated. Tracy was silent. "Maybe I better stroll back again, huh?"

"Maybe you better. Hop upstairs. Yank Herzog out of his closet and put him back again when you're done. If you get careless and bust a rib or two, I won't cry. And if you think he might walk away on us when you're through, you better leave him tied."

Butch stepped away with a pleasant sound in his throat. As he lumbered up the front stoop Tracy called softly:

"Don't forget to lock the closet. Then go straight back to my place and read the funnies. I'll phone the cops when the edition is on the street."

He slammed the taxi door and the cab shot away. At the corner Shultz slowed up.

"Where do we go, Mr. Tracy?"

"Marvin's Baths. Know where it is?"

"Paddy Marvin's? Sure thing."

"Stop at the side door on Dyker Street."

JERRY TRACY LIT another cigarette from the stub of the last. He kept on walking up and down. Marvin's office was bare except for a couple of white chairs and a desk in the corner with a phone on it. Tracy's eyes kept jerking irritably from his watch to the phone and back again.

A swinging door opened and a tow-headed Swede emerged. He had on white pants and sneakers and a soiled singlet with a torn armhole. He carried a pail of discolored water in one hand and a sponge and a couple of bloody towels in the other. He went down the hall and came back, whistling pleasantly, with a long brown bottle and a glass. He butted the swinging door open with his hip.

"Tell Paddy to hurry it up," Tracy snapped.

Paddy's voice roared from within: "Keep your shoit on! We're all set right now."

"Can he talk yet?"

"Jist about."

"Drag him out here. We've got to get him on the phone."

"Okey. Hold that door open. Grab an end, Svenska!"

Jimmy Earle came out feet first on a narrow rubbing table; Paddy and the Swede set him down with an air of conscious pride. Tracy bent over him.

"Hello, Wealthy," the feature man said wearily.

His eyes were clear but he looked bloodless and shrunken. His naked body was spotted generously with iodine stains and lumps of gauze. His whole right flank was corsetted with broad strips of adhesive tape wrapped in overlapping layers. He still breathed with that curious whooping-cough catch.

"Where's your damned phone?" he whispered to Tracy.

"Take it easy, Bum. Got your facts straight and your story clear?"

Earle's jeering laugh made him cough and wince. "You and your cheap, lousy dirt column! What do you know about a front-page story, you—you *plumber!* Gimme the phone!"

"Attaboy!" Tracy crowed with delight. He jumped swiftly for the phone and dialed the *Planet's* number. His left thumb jerked. "Move that conceited ape over here, Paddy… Hello? Gimme the desk… Tracy. Yes, yes, yes! He's right here—I got him—and he's leaking story from every orifice. Shove a good man on the wire and don't drop a comma… Right. Take it!"

He laid the telephone on the cot next to Earle's pale lips and the Swede held the receiver against the feature man's ear.

"Who's taking it? Okey, Brady. If you bungle it I'll cut your heart out. And don't forget the most important thing in this yarn… Correct. The James K. Earle by-line."

He grinned insultingly at the *Planet's* columnist.

His voice was low, fragile; but the words flowed clearly, without emphasis—like a child's thin voice reciting a familiar memory-gem.

Tracy thought: no wonder we hate each other; we're the only prima donnas in the shop! He listened with grim awe to the man's easy competence. The first wallop sentence, with its damning smash. The easy paragraph of transition; the marshaling of names and facts; back to the steady smash of proof.…

"—— But Jack Herzog didn't leave New York on the 5:27 from Pennsylvania Station on that afternoon of July 14th, the day on which Arnstein was shot to death. Instead, Herzog sent a craftily worded message to his intended victim that lulled Arnstein's growing suspicion of his partner. It was this message that led to the subsequent farce of Smoky Dolan's trial and acquittal. Smoky Dolan was privy to the scheme; he was well paid for his trouble. It will be remembered that late in the afternoon on the 14th of July it began to rain. Herzog telephoned to his garage...."

Jerry Tracy could hardly tear himself away; but he stepped noiselessly aside and plucked at Paddy Marvin's sleeve. The ex-wrestler listened and nodded.

"When Earle gets through," Jerry whispered, "give him another drink and slip him a dream-powder till I can arrange to transfer him to a safe spot where he won't be apt to get a bad relapse from bullets. Don't let anyone see him unless I call up first and say okey."

"Bad as that, eh?" Paddy muttered.

"You've got ears. What do you think he's throwing at Herzog and his clique—roses? Make sure that Swede of yours locks the side door."

He squeezed Paddy's arm briefly and slipped away. There was a drug-store a little ways down Fourth and he popped in and called the *Planet*. The managing editor was still in the shop. Good sign. He said to Tracy: "Go to hell. Don't bother me. I'm busy," and banged the receiver down.

That was all Tracy wanted to know. He grinned happily. The old wheels were turning, throwing off sparks!

He grabbed a taxi at the corner and gave the driver the *Planet* address. He rode four blocks or so, grinning like a monkey; then he stiffened suddenly. The grin wiped off his face.

He told the driver: "Never mind that first address. I forgot something. Go on straight up Seventh Avenue. I'll tell you where to turn."

Ten minutes later he climbed rickety stairs and barged down a dusty hallway.

Dot West was lying fully dressed on the bed when Tracy rapped at her door and shoved buoyantly in. At sight of him the dancer sprang up without a sound. Her eyes were red-rimmed. Her mouth flew open but her haggard eyes did all the talking.

"He's safe and okey, baby," said the columnist gently. "You can take my honest word for—Whoa! If you faint, I'll sock you!"

"Where is he? Where? Where?"

"Marvin's Baths. West Fourth and Dyker. Slam a little powder on and go down, dope! Tell Paddy I said it's okey. I'll phone him you're coming. Hell—I'll go down with you!"

He smiled oddly as he watched her jumping crazily about the room, spilling powder, fighting with the loose sleeve of a coat, plucking on a hat over one ear. Crazy in love, he thought moodily. With a tramp like Jimmy Earle, out of all the people in the world! No sense to it.

He forgot her as he stared at a frayed spot in the carpet.

The frayed spot danced and became a newsprint headline:

ARNSTEIN SLAYER SEIZED!
POLICE NAB HERZOG!

Tracy leered at the carpet.

"And do we sell papers tomorrow!" he said aloud. *"Do we sell papers!"*

An elbow dug into him. He turned like a sleep-walker and nodded at the impatient girl. Women got all worked up over nothing, he thought moodily. One idea was all their skulls could hold. He was impatient to get back to the *Planet* and dive headlong into the roar. The kid made him sick with her one-track mind. How did people get that way?

Smoke

*Where fires burn, smoke rises and gets
sometimes even into a killer's eyes*

JERRY TRACY SIPPED DELICATELY at the alleged *cointreau,* wrinkled his thin nose at Clarkson like a rabbit and said with utter disgust: "Exquisite."

Clarkson nodded glumly. He was a fleshy young man with a premature bald head, sad eyes and a pouting lip. Broadway's busiest theatrical ghost writer and perennially broke. A sucker for the wheel. If you showed Clarkson a wired roulette layout he'd promptly borrow a hundred from you and lay it on the line. He always looked puzzled when he lost.

He set down his *cointreau* untasted and his eyes swept listlessly across the noisy restaurant. Suddenly he turned on his sad, fleeting grin and turned it off again.

"Reminds me. I've got a brand-new; red-hot for your column, Jerry."

"Swell." The columnist's voice sounded utterly dreary.

"Sam Volga is carrying the torch."

Instantly Tracy's well-tailored shoulders stiffened. He moved in his chain but he didn't turn around. He stared at Clarkson with a quick and alert incredulity. "Stop horsing."

"Okey. I'm a horse. Have it your way."

"Your red-hot doesn't make sense, sweetheart."

"Does it have to?"

Tracy thought that one over for a second. He said meditatively: "Sam here by any chance?"

"Yeah. I thought you saw him come in. Corner alcove. With the number. I think she's scared about it in a quiet way."

"Big time?"

"Nope. Pork and bean—and pretty as hell. Shut up a sec and I'll place her." He closed his eyes and blew out his cheeks slightly. "Oh, yeah. I remember now. Maxie Bloom's tinsel spot on 51st. Sings one lousy number and makes it sound even lousier. Does a tap like a blind man on a strange street. She's got something, though—don't ask me what; I'm tired of geography. Try tipping your hat to her and calling her Flip Kern."

Jerry Tracy laid ten manicured fingertips on the table edge and drummed delicately for ten seconds.

"Yes, yes; go on—you interest me strangely." He stopped kidding. "Are you absolutely sure the smoke is rising from Sam and not the kid? You couldn't be wrong, by any chance?"

"I said it was one for the column, didn't I? There always has to be a first time for everything. Sam Volga, the big icicle and bullet man, has been burning quietly for a week or so. Maxie Bloom giggled it to me on the q.t. yesterday, but I thought it was a gag."

Tracy touched his lips fleetingly with his napkin. There was a faint frosty spark in the eyes of the *Daily Planet's* dapper little columnist. He shoved back his chair.

He said softly: "Be a good fella, Harry, and don't spread this thing around. I don't want to spill it in the column just yet. There's a couple of angles I want to play with—see what I mean?"

Clarkson said, "Sure," but he looked puzzled. Tracy snapped flame at a fresh cigarette, said carelessly, "I'll be seein' you, sweetheart," and moved unostentatiously away among the noisy tables.

Volga was parked pleasantly in the corner alcove. His eyes

were glued on the girl opposite him. He was leaning forward, toying with a wine-glass, and there was no tension in his body. Light glinted lazily from the square-cut emerald in his ring. He didn't see Tracy until the columnist spoke.

" 'Lo, Sam."

The big head turned. A quick, stabbing scrutiny. Then the eyes went expressionless; veiled and pitiless.

"Hi-yuh, Jerry."

Tension flowed back into the big shot's shoulders. He grinned with a faint ripple of his lips and said, "How's tricks?" His icy eyes didn't join in the grin. They said, unmistakably, "Scram, pest; you're bothering me."

Sam Volga didn't offer to introduce the dark-eyed number. The kid was a little beauty. Cute figure, skin like cream, no jewelry. V-e-r-y nice and very young. And scared about something—if you'd been tipped off in advance and were looking for the small repressed signs. Her chin, for instance. Her hands.

She sat smiling uncertainly while both men looked at her.

Volga said dryly: "You're an expert, Jerry. Like her?"

"I'd have to hear her talk, Sam." He sounded casual, bored.

"Talk, baby," Volga said with a cool contempt. His tone matched Tracy's; but there was a flame in his somber eyes. The skin of his heavy forehead looked moist. There was a subtle uneasiness inside the man's hard shell.

"Say something, baby," Volga sneered.

The girl's laughter made brittle sound. "Well, of all the nerve! I never heard of such a thing. What's the point to all this kiddin'?"

Her voice was flat, metallic, unbeautiful. She said "noive," "pernt" and "hoid."

"Like it?" Volga said.

"I love it, Samuel."

"You wouldn't lie to me, pal?" A sudden thought seemed to strike him. He looked at Jerry curiously from under heavy lids. "Fifty to one you can't name it."

"Who, Flip?" Tracy laughed indulgently. "Don't be that way. Flip is the flashiest bit of tinsel in Bloom's spot on 51st."

Volga passed over a neatly creased fifty. He became at once two shades more jovial. Tracy was struck by the resemblance of the big shot to Clarkson, the bald-headed and impecunious ghost writer. Except that Volga had a mop of thick curly hair, jet-black, and his flesh was solid and hard-packed on his body.

"Sit down, Jerry," he urged. "How 'bout a li'l drink?"

"Sorry. I'm on the way out."

"Okey. Bloom say anything else?"

"What else is there?" Jerry grinned impudently. He jerked out a small notebook and clowned a bit with poised pencil. "Do you think beer will come back, Senator?"

Volga waved his cigarette impatiently and made a crooked tangle of blue smoke-threads above his cuff.

"Don't," he said distinctly.

"Don't what?"

"Put her in the column. Or me, either."

"I was thinking I'd save it, Sam."

"I would."

Flip laughed thinly. "I'll take horseradish. What is this—a cross-word puzzle?"

"This lad Tracy has a long nose, kid," Volga said. "I'm helping him to keep it clean. Stick to me, Babe, and you'll wear diamonds."

His eyes were on the girl but the words were for Tracy. Barbed words of challenge from a man that Tracy hated and despised. Something in their purring nastiness overbore Tracy's caution. He thought of dead men—and a dead woman. He looked straight at the big shot.

He said: "Stick to him, Babe, and you'll land smack in a side-walk ashcan."

He laughed as he said it. An exultant feeling as though he tasted blood. His words carried meaning under the commonplace jest, and Volga took the meaning. He blinked and his florid face went muddy with fury. A spasm of movement jerked his right hand out of sight. His forearm was a steel bar against his coat. He was like a granite carving of death. He didn't say anything, just sat there.

Music from the hi-de-ho orchestra battered at the silence in the little sheltered alcove.

"I ought to hand it to you right here and now," Volga breathed softly.

Slowly the steel forearm relaxed and the hand came back from invisibility. The *Planet* man sighed and didn't know it. His cramped lungs started in to breathe again.

"Look me up some time," Tracy said to no one in particular. His smile was glassy and idiotic.

He turned on his heel and walked away, with his back crawling. People at tables looked at him curiously as he passed.

HE BOUGHT BACK his hat and coat from a blond smoothie in black satin and pushed out into the biting cold air of the sidewalk. The dim street glittered with ice. The wind strummed like a harp.

"Twelve below zero," the doorman mumbled. He spoke proudly, as though he had something to do with it. His face was purple.

Tracy breathed deep of the icy air and shook off the moldy smell of death. Assurance came back to him.

"How about a cab, Cap?"

"Dunno, Mr. Tracy. Ain't many rollin'. They're still kinda scared account of the strike… Uh-huh—you're lucky. There's an independent!"

His whistle bubbled shrilly and Tracy climbed into the rickety taxi that slid alongside the curb with brakes set.

There was a torn square of cardboard pasted against the side window, crudely lettered in crayon: *Owner-Driver.*

Tracy leaned forward and gave the address. The driver

hunched around and gave his fare a swift, piercing scrutiny.

"Like me?" Tracy said.

"Jist a habit, Mister." He should have laughed apologetically but he didn't.

Tracy felt a mild curiosity about the guy. He made talk.

"Strike still on?"

"S'posed to be over. Some o' the Bolshies are still out making plenty trouble. They toined over a cab on Eighth and 54th a little while ago. You scared about it?"

"Nope."

"Me neither... Wanna hear the radio?"

"Nope. The hell with it."

"Most people like to listen. It ain't a bad set."

The cab whirled round a corner, pelting the frozen sidewalk with a spray of snow from the slap-slap of its chains.

"Not worrying about strikers, eh?" Tracy said.

"I ain't thinkin' about 'em at all."

A red light bloomed down the avenue and the driver braked. Suddenly Tracy heard him swear softly.

Two shadowy figures were racing out of the shelter of a dark doorway. They ran pell-mell into the street towards the motionless cab. The foremost man carried a short length of pipe. The second was palming a knife; he moved warily towards the right front tire. The hi-jacker with the pipe jumped to the running-board of the taxi. His teeth were chattering with the cold. His breath made quick little puffs of vapor.

"Git rid o' yer fare, you chisellin'—— and go hunt yourself a garage!"

"Okey," said the hackman. His hand appeared swiftly and the startled gorilla gasped and jumped backward. The fellow at the front tire saw the stubby automatic swing towards him and he swerved away so hastily that he slipped on the packed snow and went awkwardly to one knee.

"I gotta mind to hand it to you both in the belly," said the hackman bitterly.

"Scram! I got no time for ——s like you!"

The traffic light had clicked green. The cab rolled. Profanity dwindled in the icy air. The dim avenue rushed backward past the speeding taxi with a sighing, tinkling sound.

Tracy found himself more and more interested in this driver who gunned strikers away so casually.

"Nice work," he suggested.

"Yeah."

"Kinda cold tonight."

"Yeah."

"Run into much of that strong-arm stuff?"

"Nope. Yeah. I ain't thinkin' about it."

"What does a guy like you think about?" Tracy persisted.

"You wouldn't know."

"Would five bucks help me to know?"

The muffled face of the driver swung abruptly sidewise. A gloved hand touched the edge of the glass panel. "Save your five bucks, pal, and buy a racehorse." The frosted panel slammed shut with a bang.

The ace columnist of the *Daily Planet* sat back with an amused grunt. He glanced at the illuminated hack license. Joseph Antonelli. The usual taxi face. Sullen eyes. Wooden expression.

Jerry Tracy shrugged, shut his eyes and dismissed taxis and wop chauffeurs from his mind. He began to think about Clarkson, the bald-headed ghost writer, and his screwy tip about Sam Volga. Screwy tip, hell! Volga was blazing under the floorboards; no doubt about it. Jerry's sensitive nose had detected the thin, acrid stink of love smoke. And it wasn't whiffing from the gal, either. There was no fire there. She was scared about something.

Yow-suh! The fire bells were ringing for Sam Volga at last! Maybe that was why Flip was so scared. She oughtn't to be, by all the rules. In a four-alarm fire a wise gal could do herself plenty good. But Flip wouldn't angle the business that way. Flip was umday. Tracy thought of that frying-pan voice coming out of her soft white throat and grinned crookedly. If Volga could stand that, the ice-cold big shot was sure softening up. Maybe soft enough to pluck. Inspector Burch would be interested in that angle.

Tracy's mind switched automatically to the inspector. Volga's political pull had shoved Danny Burch into Staten Island in the stock market days when a square cop had no friends. Now there was a new guy in the seat with funny ideas about decency—and Burch of the grizzled gray skull and alert blue eyes wasn't riding ferry-boats to work any more. He was a deputy inspector with a grand old record and a new broom in his honest old paws. And on more than one occasion the dapper little columnist of the *Daily Planet* had helped Danny to sweep up dirt.

But that was off the record....

WHEN THE TAXICAB STOPPED before the huge stone hive that housed Tracy's expensive roof castle, the columnist added a crisp five-spot to the taxi fare showing on the meter.

"I won't need it. I got a racehorse," he told the hacker.

"Okey by me, Bud." The eyes were still sullen, unsmiling.

"Do you always carry a gat, friend?"

"Yeah."

"Why?"

"I might need it."

"I getcha."

"The hell yuh do," the hacker clicked out grimly, with a harsh venom in his voice.

He meshed gears and rolled, his exhaust spurting like a pale gush of steam in the freezing air. Tracy stared after the ruddy tail-light for a second or two. Then his teeth began to click together and he shrugged and hurried into the warm lobby.

"Gone down two more, Mr. Tracy," said the elevator man cheerfully. "Fourteen below zero. A record, what I mean. I looked at the thermometer a minute ago."

"Why?"

"Beg pardon, sir?"

"Nerts," the columnist snapped.

In the penthouse foyer McNulty, China's greatest gift to man, took Tracy's hat and coat with deft speed and a complete lack of interest. His Chinese face was plump and serenely yellow like a harvest moon.

"Got any idea what the exact temperature is outside?" Tracy growled.

The almond eyes blinked. "Me no give dam'," said McNulty with grave courtesy.

"You and me both. I knew I could trust you... Got anything good?"

"Mebbe so. You want um?"

"Me want um dam' quick like hell. Me belly freeze. Me cold."

"Can do," McNulty said.

He brought a dressing-gown and a tall glass of pale amber refreshment that steamed pleasantly and was hot to hold. Tracy yanked a chair over to the crackling sizzle of the fireplace and sat down with a pile of the late news-papers. He sipped lovingly at the drink and looked through the papers, tearing out items here and there, throwing each newspaper carelessly aside as he finished with it.

Over his shoulder he called: "Fix me up a hot bath, keed."

He was in the tub, pink and parboiled and drowsy, when McNulty walked in.

"Lady come. Want see you."

"Goody, goody. I was afraid of that. Does the husband look sore?"

"She come alone."

"That's a point in her favor."

Broadway's favorite columnist lifted his right foot above the water and watched the steam rising comfortably from his naked wet toes.

"The hell with her, aged servitor. Tell her to come back in July. What's her name?"

"No tell um. She velly excite. Make funny noise. She cly a little, I t'ink."

"That's a point against her. Tell her I've got soap all over my character. Tell her to scram."

McNulty padded away.

Tracy sat scowling in his bath for possibly ten seconds. He said "Hell!" in a petulant voice and swished suddenly out of the tub. He toweled his lean body with three quick lunges and pulled on his robe.

McNulty was talking into the apartment telephone with perfect courtesy:

"You go way, plizz. You come back next July. He sleepy."

"Hey, wait a minute, dope!" Tracy called. "Tell her okey. Tell her I'll see her."

"You come up, plizz. He no sleepy now. He see you."

The girl came in hesitantly. Tracy grinned with interest as he recognized her. He drawled lazily from his armchair: "Well, well! Pretty showgirl makes early morning call on noted Broadway maestro... Hello, Flip!"

He saw instantly that something was wrong. The girl was overwrought, trembling jerkily. Her eyes were wide with fear. She was crawling with it. Her voice was a croak. She couldn't talk intelligible words.

Tracy said, "Whoa, mama!" in a crisp murmur, and came alertly out of his chair. He put a hand lightly on her shoulder and steadied her with an insistent pressure of his muscular left arm. "Easy, Babe! Slow down for crossings. What seems to be the diffugilty?"

"I—I hadda come. You said to look you up. You're an important guy. I—"

"Sure, sure. Take it easy. Plenty of time."

She twisted to face him and talk came from her in panicky spurts.

"It happened tonight. On the way home. After you left. He'll *kill* Fred! I know he will. Fred hit him in the face. He hit him awful hard. His face bounced. Oh, Gawd A'mighty, Mr. Tracy, don't let him hoit Fred! Don't let him kill him. I couldn't bear to live if he—"

An Oriental voice said imperturbably: "You want um drink, mebbe?"

Jerry craned his neck. "Yeah. That's fine. Put 'em on the small table and take a boat-trip somewhere... Wait a minute—grab these things first."

He relieved Flip of hat, coat and gloves with a suave persuasion. McNulty vanished.

"Sit down, keed. Over here by the fire. Your fingers are, freezing." He handed her a tall glass, brimming with McNulty's pale amber masterpiece that steamed faintly. " *'Drink, pretty creature, drink.'* A guy named Wordsworth said that once. A poet, sez me. Who cares, sez you."

Her hand twitched. Some of the liquor slopped into her lap. She struggled to speak.

"Shud-dup! Sip it, Babe. It's hot."

Twice she began to talk and twice he shut her off with brusque wise-crack comedy that was as insistent as a steel padlock. He made her drain the glass. He took back the empty. Sweat showed under the tendrils of hair at her temples.

"Gawd, that was good," she whispered.

"You telling me, sweet? Now let's hear about things—and if you gallop words at me again, I'll slap you down, Big Eyes... Whose face bounced? Volga's?"

She nodded faintly.

"By a guy named Fred, you said. I think I like Fred. Who is he? Boy friend?"

"Yeah. Him an' me—we both—" Her voice broke fiercely. "I'd go to hell for him in a bucket, Mister!"

"Okey, okey... Say, you *have* got big eyes, sister. Stop winking water and let's hear the dime novel."

It came out bit by bit under his shrewd questioning. Fred was Fred Bundermann. The swellest looking young master plumber up on Tremont Avenue in the Bronx. Fred nuts about Flip and vice versa. Both of 'em working like mad to save dough because Fred was an old-fashioned guy who wanted a wife, not a toe-dancer in a hot spot on West 51st. Fred had his eye on a two-story frame with a backyard and an honest job of solid brass plumbing. And Flip kinda liked the idea of having kids with Fred's eyes and Fred's sandy hair. So....

VOLGA HAD CRASHED into the picture three weeks ago. He heated up the first time he saw Flip. Made a play and was thrown for a loss. After that he was hotter but he changed his tactics. Respectful, no hands under the table, the real thing. That made it tough for Flip because she could have handled a wise guy on the make. This guy wasn't on the make. He began to talk marriage—fierce, crazy talk that scared her sick. She knew all about Volga's ice-cold rep and his unproved murder record; and what she didn't know the other gals in the floor show whispered to her. She was in a tough spot. Straddled on a razor blade.

She tried to stall Volga but he couldn't be stalled. He was like velvet. Suave, insistent, low voiced; but the voice was a hot, whispering flame and the eyes were adamant and eager. She lied to him about Fred, said there was no one else. Volga took her out places and was icy and careful with her in public, except for the hot coals in his veiled eyes. And she made excuses to Fred and stalled him on dates because Fred was a big guy with hard fists and he wouldn't understand if he saw her with Sam Volga. On the other hand, if Volga ever heard about Fred and the two-story frame and the four kids Flip figured on—two boys and two girls—and a dog, maybe a Scottie, they weren't sure....

In three agonized weeks Flip had reached the hysterical pitch where she'd lie in bed nights with her hands clenched in the darkness and think fiercely of different ways she might kill Volga; kill him dead, quiet and harmless; kill him craftily and safely and get away from the rustle of the big shot's whispering desire... Get back, somehow, to Fred.

"I gather that Fred got wise to the competition tonight," Tracy said grimly.

"Yeah. It was my night off and Fred wanted a date, but Volga pinned me down this aft'noon an' I phoned Fred and told him I hadda work. He mustta come downtown anyways; because he steps outta the late Newsreel show just as our cab stops alongside the curb on a red light. I was lookin' out an' he seen me. He got awful white but he didn't say nothin'. He quick yanked open the door, reached over me an' hit Volga in the face with all his might. Volga fell over sideways, kinda stunned. Fred called me a—a doity rotten name an' slammed the door. An' the light changed then an' the chauffeur looked kinda scared an' funny an' we rolled an' left Fred standin' there."

Flip gulped miserably and began to cry.

"Quit that stuff. Bawling gets you nowhere. What happened then?"

"I—he—Volga come out of his daze a block or two away. He wiped the blood off his lip an' he started cursin' to himself low an' terrible, like he was tearin' the oaths outta his stummick. He made the driver toin around an' go back; an' we cruised along lookin' for Fred. Volga had a gun out, down between us, on the seat. But, thank Gawd, Fred was gone. Volga asked me who the guy was. He only asked me once. I was cryin'. I didn't say anything. An' Volga says low, like he was embarrassed: 'Okey, sweet. Forget it. Cut out the weeps, Babe. I'll find out about the mugg myself.' An' then he dropped me off home— an' I come over here soon as I got noive up. Gawd, Mr. Tracy, I dunno where to toin or what to do. An' I'm licked with Fred. I—I just *know* it! His face was like marble an' he called me a doity little ——!"

It was a curt, nasty word. Her mouth whispered the ugly epithet with a sick, unbelieving horror. Tracy's metallic voice cut into her hysteria and steadied her.

"All right, big eyes. Let's talk sense. First, let's get Sam Volga straight. Remember what I told you at the table tonight: *Stick to Volga and you'd land slap in an ashcan.* That's literally true. Devore was one of his gals. Dot Devore dropped eight long stories and broke her back on a sidewalk ashcan. Volga did that for her—even though she took the jump of her own free will. She was a sweet little fluff but you couldn't tell her a thing. She had to find out for herself. I could tell you others. Sam Volga is poisoned ice-water for dames, keed. And I won't tell you how many murder raps he's beaten because that's neither here nor there. Tell me one thing: is he really dead nuts about you? I mean the real thing. Don't try to kid yourself. You know what I mean, Flip."

She said in a low voice: "You mean does he just wanta be my sugar? It's more than that with Volga. I'm sure of it. I— No—*I'm not sure. I'm afraid....*"

"Thanks, Flip. You're a sweet little number... Plenty gals have gone soft on Volga, but Volga never melted before in his whole icicle career. If he's melting now he's easier to handle. He's gonna do something stupid and silly—or I never wrote a hotcha column… Cigarette, keed?"

She said no and he lit one for himself.

"Can you warn Fred?" she asked him shakily. "Protect him, somehow?"

"Forget Fred. Lemme try and dope this thing out… We don't want Fred to gum up the works. Don't go near him; don't call him up. Take my word for it, Fred won't be apt to run into Volga again if you let him alone. He'll go through hell for two or three days. He'll think of a million logical reasons how you could be in that taxi-cab with Volga and still be perfectly innocent. And he'll remember the name he called you. He'll pick up the phone a hundred times and lay it down again and he'll sweat blood. He'll wait for you to call. Give him three days or so for his pride to crack. In three days, maybe, I can slant Volga properly."

He mashed his cigarette butt and stood up, looking curiously small and wizened in the voluminous and gaily colored robe. He grinned at her and made a wry grimace.

"Scram, keed. G'wan home and hit the hay or I might make a pass at you myself. There's enough of the heel in me not to make that crack funny… Hey, McNulty! Cloak and suit for the lady!"

In the foyer he thought of something. He laughed suddenly.

"I always like to guess right, Flip. That Flip stuff is profesh, isn't it? What's the real monicker?"

"Matilda Gunsdorf."

"Wow! Did you pick the Flip stuff yourself?"

She giggled faintly.

"No. That was Katzman, the dance director. I had a swell name—Gloria La Fontaine. Katzman said nuts to that, it was too long. I ask him how about Vera Van Teasdale but he kinda choked an' cursed; so I says go ahead and flip a kern, big boy, I'll leave it to you. An' then Katzman roars out laffin' and slaps me on the—on the back. He says oke—Flip Kern is oke."

Her dark eyes looked puzzled.

"What's so funny about flipping a kern?"

"I'll never be the one to tell you, dumb cluck. Beat it. Tell the guy downstairs to hunt a cab for you till he finds one. And listen. Remember this. If Sam Volga gets in touch with you, play along with him for the next coupla days. I don't think he'll ask you any more about Fred. If he does, clamp the lips. Wait— gimme your address and phone number... Okey. S'long."

"I'll never forget what you're doing for me."

"You?" His voice hardened. "My angle is Sam Volga, baby."

He went back to his big armchair and watched the dying embers in the fireplace for a long time. The gray smoke tendrils seemed to fascinate him. He watched the ascending smoke, found hidden amusement in it. Smoke! He chuckled briefly. There was no amusement in the sound he made.

DEPUTY INSPECTOR DANNY BURCH had a small and secluded office where he transacted private and confidential business. It was to this small cubby, bare of blue-coated secretaries and file clerks, that Tracy went privately to talk with the big fella. Tracy's visits to Danny were not frequent but they were always confidential. The two men understood, trusted and respected each other.

Physically they were a queerly assorted pair for teamwork. Tracy was barely over average height, quick, nervous, alert, dynamic; Broadway was stamped on his sleekly groomed person, in his wise, nasal speech. Burch was utterly different. Six foot two, with big bones and solid, wind-tanned beef. Slow of words; a deep voice with no nasal twang in it; a fist like a dark red uncooked ham. Six years' exile in Staten Island hadn't soured him; the twinkle still lingered in his deep-socketed blue eyes. His curly tangle of gray thatch made a comb and brush seem like a silly idea. He looked incorruptibly, belligerently honest—and he was. There was more chance of Diogenes turning pickpocket than there was of Danny Burch reaching out to snare a dirty dime.

He puffed vigorously on an imitation briar pipe and said: "All right, son. Sam Volga, for instance. What about him? You brought the subject up. You've got something?"

Tracy shook his head. He was smiling.

"Just curious. I like to freshen up on him every once in a while. Run over the record, Danny. I mean just the personal jobs—his own stuff. The stuff you can't prove."

"Well, there's about seven sure ones. You know 'em. Everybody does. Swinky Schwartz was one. Art Epstein. Dope Rogers. The chicken merchant—what's his name?—Isaac Pintzer. The guy from Buffalo that was gunned on the tennis court last winter—you know, opposite Grant's Tomb—or anyhow, his body was picked up there... Hell, you know the list better than I do, Jerry."

"What about dames?"

"Dames?" The inspector looked puzzled. "You mean killings? I don't getcha."

"A few fluffs got burned, I understand, playing with Volga's matches."

Danny Burch's eyes became attentive.

"You've got an angle, Jerry. Don't try to kid the old man. What's bothering you?"

"It'll keep. Go ahead and recite your lesson."

Burch sucked at his pipe. The stem bubbled and he made a wry mouth and spat. He scratched noisily at the roots of his tangled gray hair and his eyes probed Tracy.

"I don't see," he said slowly, "how the dame angle gets us anything. What's your idea?"

"A hunch. A presentiment. A funny feeling." He grinned. "You know—'*by the pricking of my thumbs, something evil this way comes.*'"

"What the hell's that? Mother Goose?"

"A mugg named Shakespeare."

Danny said, "Oh," without much interest. He frowned at the bowl of his pipe. "Let's see, now. The Devore gal went out an eighth floor winder and busted an ashcan with her back. Then there was the Mallory woman—how do you pronounce that first name of hers again?—Yoo-neece, eh? She went snow, got picked up pretty reg'lar for solicitin'; I think she finally croaked on Welfare Island, but I'm not sure. I could look it up. Want any more?"

"Never mind. Listen, Danny. Here's the news. Sam Volga's on fire. The smoke is rising from him. Not the dame this time. Sam Volga, the big icicle, the hard guy! He's still hard, but this time he's hot. Do I sound interesting?"

"You sound kinda stupid."

"Maybe. But I saw Volga off guard last night and his mind's not on business. He's thinking about words like *soft, white, warm.* I walked up to his table last night *and he didn't see me till I spoke.*"

"Who is the dame?"

"Just an umpchay. Like all the others. Straight as a string. Pretty little devil with the biggest dam' dark eyes you ever drowned in."

"He must like 'em that way. Mallory had eyes like that. So did Devore. They usually do—Eyetalians, I mean."

"Go 'way. You're wet. The kid's a Heinie from way back."

"I'm talking about Devore."

"No kiddin'. I didn't know that. A wop?"

"Sure. Her real name didn't come out; we gave the family a break. Her real name was—lemme see—pshaw, I hate to have a name like that slip when I almost—Wait a second... Antonelli! That's it. Came from Bridgeport. Funny how they all come from outside, Jerry. Don't kids born in Manhattan ever hit trouble? Seems to me—"

His voice rumbled on reflectively. Jerry wasn't listening. His eyes were shut as he groped fiercely for an elusive; mental wraith. A forgotten sound that made his mind twang feebly like a ghostly tuning-fork. Was it a word spoken, a word seen? Instantly, he saw it. Printed words—two of them. Joseph Antonelli. A taxicab with a cardboard *Owner-Driver* stuck in the window to placate strikers. A guy that carried a gat. Jerry had said to him: "I getcha," and the guy had snarled: "The hell yuh do!"

Jerry Tracy opened his eyes.

Burch said: "What's bitin' you, son?"

"Not a thing, Danny. I had a little time to waste and I thought I'd blow in and wise you on the woman thing. When Volga smokes up he's sure to get careless. There might be an in for a square cop to do the city a favor."

"What's your in, Jerry? A grudge?"

Tracy shook his head.

"I just want to play cards, Danny. Nothing personal in it at all. You want Volga out of circulation, Danny? Well, so do I."

"You sound like a cop."

That made the *Daily Planet's* famous columnist grin ruefully for an instant.

"A hell of a fine pinched-back cop I'd make!"

"Okey. Then what's your in?" the inspector persisted.

"You really want to know?"

"I asked you twice already."

"Broadway," Jerry said curtly. He sounded husky, oddly defiant. "Can I slop for a minute and give you a laugh?"

"Go ahead. I never heard you slop before."

"Broadway," the columnist repeated in a low voice. "Not the street, Danny. Not the car-tracks, nor the million lights. Not the cop whistles and taxi horns and the big shoes and little shoes going in droves north and south past the Astor flower shop—a million of 'em shuffling in short-step formation every night… The greatest street in the universe, Danny—but not the car-tracks or the chewing-gum ads."

He took a deep breath. Talk raced viciously out of him.

"Laugh, old-timer, and go to hell! Do you know what I'm thinking about, Danny? Old Pete Dailey and Lillian Russell and Georgie Cohan. Rector's and Shanley's and Murray's. Top hats and opera capes and twenty-course dinners. Guys that could spend intelligently and women that were worth it. Real theatres along the Stem, not gold-plated movie coops for sixty-cent sports. Broadway! That's what it was. That's what it should be.

"Now it's a hive. A smelly, fly-specked circus alley full of orange drinks, cashew nuts, press a button and take yourself ten lousy tin-types for a dime, gyp haberdashers, henna-topped hustlers from Second Avenue—fat-legged little bims, the kind that Denys Wortman draws every day in the *World-Telly*... Pimpled soda jerkers... Flashy as hell and cheaper than a bag of peanuts. Larceny Lane, they call it. Want to know why?"

The police inspector said very, very softly: "Why?"

"Because the lugs made it that way. The wise yids, the con men, the dips and the shills and the punks. The hired guns. The muggs that know in advance who'll cop in the third at Pimlico—and never saw a horse. Cheap guys with their cheap dames festering up Broadway, because only honky-tonks and clutch parlors can make the grade with the whole town on the make... The crooks think Sam Volga is a hot shot—and he is—he runs the works. Him and a few kingpins like him, with blue jowls and blue guns. Behind them a whole cadging army of yes-men and pimps and parasites... That's my in on Volga! I'd like to see Volga bumped, shoved down a corner sewer and shot out to sea with the rest of the garbage."

"Why?" persisted the police inspector, his voice softer than silk.

"Because—" Tracy got it out with difficulty and his face was red. "Because Broadway happens to be my home town, Danny, and I love the —— damned place."

"You and me both, sonny," said the gray-haired cop who was cradled in Harlem when Harlem was white.

Neither of them said anything more for a minute. Finally, Tracy lit a cigarette and picked up his slate-colored; snap-brim. His lips crinkled with the I old rakish grin. He was Tracy the hard-boiled, the money player, the cynical peep-hole specialist.

"Ay tank ay go home."

"What do you want me to do about Volga?"

"Hands off, Danny, if you don't mind."

"Feel hopeful about that down-the-sewer stuff?"

"Very."

"Got something special under the hat?"

"Yeah."

"Give me a buzz if anything breaks. Day or night, boy. You know how to reach me—if and when."

"Check," Tracy said.

The hairy uncooked ham reached out; and crushed the slim manicured fingers with friendly pressure.

"I liked your speech, Jerry," the old man said gruffly. "Come in again some time."

"Horse," said Tracy.

A STIFF GALE WITH A nip in it like an icy buzz-saw was boring southward down Lafayette Street, kicking stray newspapers aloft in crazy spirals and rattling at window-panes that were frosted with a thick coating of white. This was Manhattan's second unpleasant day of Alaskan weather. The mercury still hovered at zero. Pedestrians slanted doggedly along in the pale, sickly sunlight. On the corner, the face of the unfortunate traffic officer was as purple as an eggplant.

Jerry Tracy thumbed a cab without much trouble. The taxi strike was officially over. Violence was waning. There were a lot more cabs rolling.

Tracy rode three or four blocks, immersed in thought; then he tapped on the glass.

"First drug-store you see, Bud. I wanna phone."

He got out, folded himself into a coin booth and dialed a number.

"Hello? Tracy talking. How you like de culd wedder, hah? Ice wit' friz-zink wit' snow... Paul there? What?... Okey. No, never mind. I'll try it myself. Thanks."

He swore, dropped in another nickel and clicked more holes around.

" 'Lo? Yeah, in the flesh... Say, is Paul there? Uh-huh, put him on... Hi-yuh, keed? Slam on your hat and hop uptown. The Times Square coop. Right... Nope, nothing much... Yow-suh."

He banged the receiver and continued uptown to his private kennel where he transacted most of his Rialto business. It was a faded office in a faded building. The chief adornments were a subway entrance and a theatre with a grand old name. The theatre had slipped to talkie movies for people with an hour to kill. Play brokers and agents infested the halls of the office building. Except for the wise buzz of their nervous and hopeful chatter about Paramount and other holy symbols, you might just as well have been in Massillon, Ohio. But you could stand at Tracy's dusty window and hit Times Square with an easy toss.

The columnist of the *Daily Planet* glanced at his watch. Ten-thirty. He fished a folded slip of paper out of his pocket, reached for the phone and gave Flip Kern a buzz.

"Morning, keed. You sound sleepy... I should say not! You needed some shut-eye, babe. Sure; do you good... No, not a thing... He didn't, eh? He won't for a coupla days. 'Member what I told you? Yeah... If Volga phones, be nice. Sure, go out with him. Why not?... Uh-huh. Sure, I will. Yes, yes, yes, Dope!... Okey; g'wan back to bed. S'long."

Whistling cheerfully, Tracy sat down at his dictaphone machine and listened, frowning a bit, to the playback of his canned wise-cracks and embalmed dirt-nuggets.

The office door opened and a man came in. Tracy quit listening to his reproduced voice. He scraped his chair around.

"Hello, Paul."

"Hi-yuh, Jerry."

The man was smallish like Tracy. Sandy-brown hair, thin nose and jaw, thin lips. Sandy-brown mustache. He snuffled and blew his nose vigorously.

"'Smarter, Paul? Got a cold?"

"Yob. Dab stiggid wedder if yuh ask be." He studied Tracy shrewdly. "Subthig?"

"Yeah. Sit down. Nothing important. Routine job. Know anybody in the hack license bureau?"

"Yob. I doe Perry."

"Wake up, me lad. They broomed Perry out last week. This is a new administration, sweetheart."

"You tellid be! It's tough, tryig to keep trag of thigs." He sneezed.

"Listen. Go down to the bureau, Paul. Look up a mugg with a fat face and rimless eyeglasses. He's a regular old woman and his name is Dave Wein-coop. Tell him the favor's for me. The subject is a wop hack driver named Joseph Antonelli."

Tracy wrote the name on a scrap of paper and slid it across the desk.

"I want to find out if I'm playing with a coincidence. I'd like it if this particular wop is *not* a coincidence. In that case he'll come from Bridgeport. Owner-driver. Get all the dope on him you can. Find out where his stand is and ask questions

246 / Theodore A. Tinsley

without starting too much. You'll know how to do that. Get me a picture. And anything else you can pick up... Want any dough?"

"No. Puddid od the reg'lar bill."

He brandished his handkerchief and made soupy noises with his inflamed beak.

"So lug."

" 'By, Paul."

The columnist sat back, cupped the rear of his skull with locked palms and thought about Joe Antonelli. He tried to recall details. A wop that peered shrewdly at male passengers and said, "Jist a habit, Mister," if, like Tracy, you asked him how come. A wop that carried a gat and was quick on the draw. A wop that gunned strikers away as minor pests and growled fiercely, "I ain't thinkin' about 'em, atall." What was he thinking about? It didn't make sense unless Joe Antonelli was thinking about a pretty little kid named Dot Devore who had dropped eight stories out of a Sam Volga love-nest and jellied her bones on a hard sidewalk. Even that didn't make sense— until a square cop in Centre Street translated Dot Devore into Josephine Antonelli. Check!

Tracy wrinkled his wise little forehead and followed the line of logic.

Volga was an armor-plated big shot; he wouldn't be easy of access. But if you drove a cab and were patient, if you were willing to wait relentlessly for that one perfect interview—check again! You always had your eyes and ears open for stray crumbs of gossip about Volga. You learned in a general way the night spots he frequented. You cruised and earned a lousy nighthawk living, but you didn't care about that. Your big job was just to wait. You never heard of mathematical averages but that's the game you were playing—the law of averages. He'd be along! Some night you'd look back and you'd have a fare. Your heart would stop for a swift instant; then it would beat again, strong, happy, resolute. You'd hear blood hammering at your ear-drums with a sweet and secret rhythm that your fare couldn't hear. You'd relax slowly. You'd take things easy. *You'd have your fare!*

Jerry Tracy shivered a little. His eyes opened.

After a while he got up and put on his hat and coat. His hand was on the inside knob of the door when it turned under his fingers and the door opened.

The man in the corridor lounged and filled the opening. He was heavy and fat. His head was a size too small for his shoulders. He breathed through his mouth; someone had broken his nose along time ago. He lounged there, making audible adenoid sounds. He grinned at Tracy like a bashful St. Bernard dog. Tracy half expected to see a pink tongue loll out on his chin with a drop of saliva at the tip.

"Hi-yuh, pally? How's the colyum racket?" said the visitor.

"Pretty good, Eddie."

"Goin' out, was yuh?"

"I had thought of it."

"Ain't I the lucky stiff, Jerry? I'd o' missed yuh sure as hell in another minute, hey? Stick around. I brung yuh a message from Sam."

"No kidding."

"Yeah."

"I'm honored, Eddie. Visited in my humble abode by the king's henchman. What does Volga want? A good tip on the seventh race?"

"Naw." Eddie Ahearn laughed hoarsely and winked like a mastiff to show he understood good kidding when he heard it. "Sam wants yuh to come over an' say hello."

"Right away?"

"Yeah. I gotta car waitin' downstairs. Soivice, huh?"

"Be right with you, sweetheart. Jus a sec."

He picked up his phone and called the *Planet* number. He asked for a man named McCurdy. Eddie watched uneasily. He didn't interfere. His instructions didn't cover telephone calls.

"Mac? Say, Mac, I'm dropping over right away to see Volga. Eddie is here with the invitation... No, he didn't take it out, but I can see it bulge..." He laughed. "Of course not. Volga is a pal of mine. I'll call you back later. If I don't, please do something about it like a good boy. 'By."

He locked the office door and went downstairs with the king's courier.

On the way down Eddie turned off his vacant grin momentarily and wrinkled his low forehead in thought. He peeped sidewise at the columnist. His voice sounded pleading.

"Hey, Jerry. You wouldn't finaygle a pal, would yuh? Honest to gawd, I never know when you're kiddin'. Have yuh reely got a hot tip on the seventh race, pally?"

SAM VOLGA SAID, "OUTSIDE for a while, Eddie," and Eddie Ahearn went away.

The room was modernistic and expensive looking. The rug cost more than a dime; somebody must have wept a little and patted that rug lovingly when it left Asia. There were etchings on the walls, nice ones that Sam Volga had never picked out. There wasn't too much of anything and the color scheme showed brains.

"Nice doghouse, Sam," Tracy admitted.

"I sorta like it. Cigar?"

"Nope. If you don't mind I'll suck on a nail."

"Plenty of cigs in that dingus over there."

"Thanks." Tracy took out one of his own and lit up. "Well?"

"You had a caller last night, Jerry. Am I wrong?"

Tracy thought swiftly and decided to play through.

"Wrong? Hell, no. You're right."

"Sorta cryin', the Babe was. All worked up."

"You're still right… Looks like I'll have to get me a new doorman hired, Sam."

"It wasn't the doorman. And even if it was, that wouldn't get you anywhere… What's worrying Flip?"

His tongue boggled ever so slightly on the last word. Couldn't make it sound entirely casual. He sensed Jerry's awareness, guessed at the columnist's inner smile. It didn't make him happy. He fiddled with an ashtray and set it in a better spot.

Jerry said: "Why, Flip was scared, Sam. An argument, wasn't it? Something scared her."

"Yeah. Little argument. That was all."

"So I gathered. I see you cut yourself shaving this morning."

"Yeah… Flip say who the guy was?"

"What guy?"

"Oh, it's gonna be like that!"

"More or less, Sam."

"Flip didn't tell you the mugg's name that—er—had the argument with me?"

"Nope."

"You lie like hell!" Volga whispered tonelessly. His eyes held flickering hatred.

Tracy didn't say anything. He wasn't in love with anybody and his hand was steadier than Volga's. Smoke rose from his cigarette-tip like a long and solid blue icepick.

"I'm supposed to be here," Jerry said, as though explaining something he had forgotten. "I mean, people know about it. I'm not supposed to stay here long."

"Sure. That's all right. I just wanted to ask you something."

"Go right ahead."

"Something like this," Volga said slowly. "Guys that nose in on me are either too dumb or too wise to know any better. You ain't neither one. I been thinkin' a lot about you, Tracy."

"Thanks," Jerry said dryly.

"I can't figure your play, see? You earn a wad of good dough and you'd like to go on livin', I guess... How come? That's what I wanna know. What's your in on the whole business?"

Tracy's jaws clamped. He thought hard. Volga would have to be prodded, worried some more. It was dangerous but necessary if the big shot was to be softened up for snow removal. The question Volga asked was an exact echo of the one asked by Inspector Danny Burch. Tracy had answered Burch, but to Volga he merely said: "Will this help? I never did quite like you, Sam, or approve of you."

"So what?"

"So anything you like. You wanted to know my in? That's it. Our fair city is turning virtuous. Somebody is going to the cleaners some day. And I'm betting on you, Samuel."

His voice was playful but his knees shook.

"Do I die now?"

"Not now," Volga said huskily. The words were barely audible. The hatred in Volga's eyes flickered up like bright flame and again smoldered. Tracy thought to himself: Smoke!

"Maybe you won't die at that," the big shot muttered, as though musing to himself. "There must be lots of real comical things I could do... By God, I can think of a stunt right now!"

"Including the personal alibi, as usual?" Tracy asked pleasantly.

"Alibi? Why, sure. As per usual."

Without warning the killer's face purpled. He came leaping awkwardly to his feet and his roar of rage filled the apartment with sound. "What are yuh grinnin' about, yuh little ——!"

A flat automatic bulged in his clenched fist. Its snout bored at Tracy's belly. Volga lunged forward with the weapon, his finger on the trigger. For a deadly split second he hesitated, trumpeting with rage.

Tracy backed up slowly, trying not to make too much motion. He dropped his hand towards a chair. His face was very pale. The door of the room opened and Eddie Ahearn came in. Eddie looked at Volga and didn't say anything.

"Get out!" Volga said to Tracy in a crawling whisper. "Get out, before I blast the livin' dirt outta yuh!"

The columnist slid quickly into his overcoat, buttoned it with fumbling fingers, picked up his hat. He walked towards the bulky figure that blocked the doorway, his heart thumping against his ribs.

Volga said thickly: "Okey. Let the —— out!" and Ahearn moved aside, frowning.

Ahearn told the columnist with dignity: "Yeah. Scram, you —— ——!"

The cold air outside turned Tracy's sweat-bath into twitching icicles. He got uptown somehow, went to his Times Square kennel. He knocked off a couple of gigantic shots of bonded rye and went through the shakes all over again.

He tried resolutely to put his mind on newspaper work. He tried to drive himself along the familiar grooves. No use. He couldn't concentrate. The gags were lifeless, the pert paragraphs stunk. After a while he abandoned all pretense of industry. He slumped and allowed his thoughts to scamper. They were scary thoughts. They squeaked and rustled like mice. A foreboding sense of impending disaster made his heart bump unpleasantly. He was in the mess now, right up to his neck, whether he liked it or not. How the thing had widened! Flip the dumb-bell and Fred the plumber; Volga the big shot and Antonelli the wop—and now Jerry Tracy. Jerry Tracy, the snooper, the wise guy, the buttinski….

A sandy-haired man came in presently and the columnist's eyes lit up. He was glad of the interruption. Activity always keyed up the *Daily Planet's* expensive ace.

He said, cheerfully: "Hey, hey, Paul. Business improving?"

"Allatime. How's my cold sound?"

"It doesn't. What did you do for it?"

"The guy in Liggett's gave me something that you sniff. Boy, am I improved! Coax me and I'll sing soprano."

He moved a desk calendar aside and sat on part of his thigh, his foot swinging idly.

"Two Antonellis, chief. Believe it or not, yow-suh. One of 'em born in Palermo, naturalized citizen, works for the Apex fleet out of a garage on Christopher Street. An old geezer. No relation to the other guy… The other guy comes from Bridgeport, so you pay off on the guess. I brought a pic along. Look him over."

Tracy studied the photo carefully. "This is the bird, all right."

"Owner-driver. Buick 1931. Socked once on a minor traffic violation, otherwise clean as a whistle, clean as this lovely brand-new schnozzle of mine. Antonelli's stand is on West End Avenue and 97th. He nighthawks. Practically doesn't use the stand at all. Does a lot of cruising south of 59th. Not liked particularly by the two other muggs on the 97th Street stand. Kinda surly and standoffish. Smokes Camels and has one lovely little hobby."

"Cut the clowning, Paul. I'm not in the mood. You mean he carries a rod?"

"A rod? Hell, no. I didn't tab that… No, I'm talking about hobbies. He's a collector."

"Collector?"

"Yeah. And it ain't stamps. The mugg is a hero worshiper. He's got a crush on one of our celebrated citizens. Thinks his hero is quite a guy. Reads up on him in all the tabs. Tears out pictures and saves 'em. And who do you think his hero is?"

Paul chuckled. "I'll help you. It's not Al Smith."

"It couldn't possibly be Sam Volga?"

"Check," said Paul in a surprised voice. "I'll be damned!" He hesitated. "Playing some marbles with Volga, Jerry? Of course, it's none of my business, but—"

"You're damned right. It isn't. That'll be all for today, Paul. Thanks a lot."

"Don't mention it." The leg swung off the desk. "Well—I guess you're over twenty-one. Be seein' you."

" 'By, Paul."

TRACY SAT BACK again. A half hour crawled. The telephone rang. It was Flip Kern calling.

"He dated me up, Mr. Tracy. I feel awful scared and funny about it—but you said to play along with him. You think it'll be all right?"

"Sure it's all right. When is the date? Tonight?"

"Tomorrer night. Thoisday."

"How come? I thought you had to dance nights in Max Bloom's liquor spot."

"He—he told me he'd talk to Maxie and fix things."

"I just bet he will." Tracy grinned mirthlessly. "Sweet, this is important. Where is the date gonna be? Did you talk it over at all? Did he say?"

"Yeah. *The Silver Trumpet.*"

"That's fine... Heard anything from the boy friend—you know who."

"No, and I'm worried terrible. Don't-cha think I oughta—"

"NO! For gawd's sake let him alone! No, Flip! Do you want him to run into So-and-so and get killed?"

She sniffled at that and said no, she didn't.

"Okey, then. Leave it to me, be nice to So-and-so—and for crimp's sake don't worry."

He hung up and went over to his typewriter—an electric typewriter with a hair-trigger touch. He had taken the tip on it from a fiction-writer friend of his who turned out high-pressure stuff at top speed. The columnist shoved in a sheet of paper, watched the blank sheet a while. Finally he typed swiftly without a stop:

Sam Volga, the big merchant prince with the heart of gold, is being seen these cold winter nights at the *Silver Trumpet*... Which adds one more note of distinction to this smart and popular glitter puddle on old Bee-way....

He rang up the *Daily Planet*, read the squib to McCurdy and instructed him to make a place for it in the Thursday column. McCurdy beefed as usual but Tracy made it stick. He grinned thinly into the transmitter and explained this was a werry, werry special item. What you might call a collector's item....

It was still early afternoon but Tracy felt tired and spent. His head ached with a dull throb. He decided to call it a day. He squirmed into his beautifully tailored overcoat and stood a moment, eying with listless hate the untidy frowsiness of the office.

Under his breath he muttered: "Jeeze, what a rat's nest!"

He got rid of it with a vicious bang of the door and went down to the street.

Still icy cold outside. The wind bit at his tired face and woke him up. The snow remnant in the street had hardened into a dirty coating of lead-colored ice as solid as concrete. Down by the corner an unkempt little gang of unemployed were chipping with picks at the flinty ice, shoving the stuff down a sewer-opening. They worked like languid sleepwalkers.

Tracy turned up his coat collar, walked past a parked sedan and stood at the curb, waiting for a cab. He didn't see the woman get out of the sedan but he did hear the quick *clack-clack* of her heels on the pavement.

As he turned she screamed suddenly—a piercing, horrible shriek of rage. She was screaming at Tracy, mouthing shrill obscenity. She was blonde, pouchy, middle-aged. Pedestrians were stopping, staring warily.

Tracy stuttered in astonishment: "For gawd's sake, what's the matter with *you?*"

"Tracy the rat! Tracy the woman chaser! Tracy the ——

——! You'll ruin no more decent daughters, you two-timing little gigolo!"

Her hand whipped out of her muff and darted at him like a snake.

Tracy threw up a defensive arm and staggered backward. It was involuntary and awkward but his very awkwardness whirled him clear of the woman's hasty arm. He heard glass smash with a brittle tinkle on the sidewalk. All along his sleeve tiny brownish spatterings appeared like pin-point moth-holes. They were on the front of his overcoat, too. The tip of one of his shoes was wet. On the pavement fragments of glass lay scattered in a wet splash. The splash seemed to smoke faintly with a queerish gray haze.

Men began to yell and point excitedly behind the columnist. A door slammed with a bang and the parked sedan slid away from the curb. It roared round the corner, scattering the pick-and-shovel men like quail. Somebody blew a police whistle. People came crowding around Tracy. A cop shoved through the excitement after a while, began asking stupid questions.

Tracy had to go through a rigmarole. Mistaken identity. Never saw her before in his life. Blah, blah, blah. No, yes, no....

The sickening part of it was the mumblings from the crowd. He could hear it like words from a jumbled dream: "No kiddin'... Sure it's Tracy; I seen him once at an actors' benefit show... They say the little rat is absolutely girl struck... Jist before she threw it she yelled somepin' about her daughter. The dames are beginnin' to catch up with Tracy, I guess. I bet if yuh was to count all the... Jeeze, lookit his shoes. Look what it done to the leather...."

The cop said: "What is it? Carbolic?"

A voice tinged with authority interrupted: "Looks more like muriatic, Officer. Rather nasty stuff. If I were you, young man, I'd get home quickly and get out of those clothes."

Tracy looked gratefully at the precise man with the Van Dyke. "Thanks, Doc."

The cop said: "Okey, Mr. Tracy. I guess I got everything."

He waved his stick towards the gutter side of the crowd. A horn honked and a taxi butted slowly through a moving surf of arms and elbows and heads.

Tracy got into the hack. Faces peered, kids jumped up and down to get a look, fingers pointed from the sidewalk; then the gears clashed and the jumble of noise sucked backward and grew dim.

The columnist gave the address weakly. The walls of his stomach were rubbing together. It hurt.

He thought: "The wise son of a gun! I didn't think he had sense enough to pull a wise stunt like that. Volga! I got luck—but he used brains. No tie-up for him on this job... And what a jobbing he's handed me. Gawd, has he put *me* in a spot!"

Tracy shuddered. He knew to the last semi-colon and comma what he was up against now. He braced himself for a locust horde of reporters. A taste of his own medicine! Headlines in all the tabs, with the *Daily Planet* doing friendly missionary stuff to hush-hush the dirtiest of the noise. Couldn't do much, at that. The circulation would drop and the *Daily Planet* lived on circulation. All the rest of the competish would be yelping gleefully like dogs on a scent. The dames catching up at last with wise guy Tracy! He could hear the guffaws, the spiteful cracks, the crop of brand-new dirty jokes about him and his love-life. The careful, non-libelous digs by the radio comics and the daily feature boys. A stag down and the dogs tearing with bloody jaws at his flesh!

Sweat dappled his pale forehead. Not bad finaygling on Volga's part, he thought grimly.

He smiled, a thin bloodless gash without merriment.

"Okey, Mr. Volga. I still can take it. How about *you?* Do you think *you* can take it, Mr. Volga?"

THE HOUR WAS BEGINNING to get late—even for the *Silver Trumpet*. Music from the ballroom filtered dimly into the bar. The rhythm sounded thin and tired and brassy; mostly trumpet and cornet; the rest was a murmuring haze that flowed or ebbed when someone opened or closed a door. The air was bluish tinted and much too hot.

Tracy was at the bar. He sipped Scotch and soda. He had already sipped a lot of them but they weren't doing anything to him. People said hello to him and he was politely and briefly affable. He kept on sipping. A man came in with a tabloid sheet and the barkeep coughed. Jerry saw the black headlines before the tab discreetly vanished. That was the *Sphere*. An eight-word head, featuring *"hurls acid"* and *"columnist playboy."* Not a bad job, although Tracy thought personally that the *Record's* headline had copped first honors.

A pudgy man with a soft gelatine stomach, pink scrubbed hands and faultless starched bosom, came in. He carried a folded menu card in his left hand. Except for his deferentially drooped shoulders he might have been a bishop.

He went across to the bar; the bar-keep moved away, picked up a glass and began polishing.

The pudgy man said in a low, smiling whisper: "He just called for the check, Jerry."

"Thanks, Julius. I'm learning who my friends are. Nice crowd tonight."

He finished his Scotch, set down the empty glass, said, "Night, Otto," to the barkeep and walked out by the corridor door. Somebody said, "Night, Jerry," as he passed but there was mostly silence in the bar. He knew, wryly, that the moment he vanished the *Sphere* would come out again and there would be smirks, whisperings, wise surmises about Tracy and his love-life. Jerry knew this with a feeling of no emotion whatever. He knew now that he didn't give a damn.

He got his hat and coat, patted the hat-check girl's face softly. Her eyes gave him the sympathy she dared not put into words.

He said: "You look sweet tonight, Anita. Go easy on the eyebrow-pencil, keed; you can't stand too much of it."

A uniformed attendant placed a gloved hand on the revolving-door and stood there, respectfully alert, waiting to twirl. Jerry lingered, drew on his gloves slowly. Then he turned and said: "Well, well. Fancy meeting you here."

Sam Volga guffawed openly. "How's everything, pal?"

"Smooth as silk, Sam."

"Oh, yeah? Where do you buy *your* silk? Woolworth's?"

He guffawed again and turned away to help Flip with her wraps.

"Hello, Jerry," Flip said. Her eyes were scared, interrogative.

"Sort of celebration night, isn't it?" Tracy said. "I suppose you two chillun will be tap-dancing for hours yet."

Flip said quickly, "No—I—" She finished, lamely, "No."

"The kid's tired," Volga said. He looked at her with hot, smoldering eyes. "Pretty tired, baby?"

"Awful tired, S-Sam."

Tracy said in Volga's ear: "Nice job yesterday, but your boys bungled it."

"Give the boys time," Volga purred. He was in high good humor.

The revolving door clacked round and round and pushed them to the sidewalk.

There were four taxis waiting in line along the curb. Tracy glanced across and looked away again. He kept up a brisk friendly chatter. He seemed in no hurry to break away from Volga and the girl. Flip helped along with inconsequential small talk. She was afraid of her bulky escort, afraid to lose Tracy's protective presence.

Finally, Volga nudged her. "You're shivering, kid," and all three of them moved towards the curb.

Flip said: "I'm not cold, really. I think the air's grand."

Tracy stood closest to the open cab door. He looked down the line, saw the driver of the second taxi. The driver was hunched slightly forward, staring at the three on the sidewalk. He seemed asleep. He was carved in quietness. Like a stone.

It was Joe Antonelli.

Volga didn't see him. What matter if he had? He'd have noted no resemblance. Dot Devore's broken body had moldered in the earth far less swiftly than the memory of her face in Volga's mind. Volga was laughing softly. He was saying something confidential to Flip in a soft, furry voice.

Tracy said, suddenly: "Well... I'll be seeing you," scrambled headlong into the first cab and slammed the door.

He heard Volga say with a slow, angry distinctness, "Well, of all the —— damned gall," then the cab rolled—and Tracy's eyes were on the rear window.

Over his shoulder he grunted: "Straight over west. Ninth Avenue."

He saw the second cab moving up, sliding to where he had stood a moment before. Flip was getting in. Volga bent his sleek head. Volga was getting in… The quick corner-turn swirled the rest out of sight.

Tracy swallowed hard and gave his hacker the exact address. The cab rolled west to Ninth Avenue, swung north and followed Ninth till it became Columbus. Kept going north. Tracy thought about Flip and gritted his teeth. He was gambling desperately on the depth of Volga's passion for Flip. The suave Volga would be afraid to press her too hard. He'd go easy, make the kid think—as Dot Devore had thought—that Sara was really a nice boy; just a little tough, but nice. Sure, he'd go easy. Sure he would! He'd have to, wouldn't he? He'd play safe for later on; he'd tip his hat to Flip; and Antonelli would be waiting at the curb. Antonelli had waited a long time already. Flip was safe enough. Don't worry, keed!

But Tracy's armpits were wet and his knees trembled.

In the Seventies the taxicab made a left turn and sped along a dark side street.

Tracy said, "Whoa! Far enough!" and they stopped. "Park here a while, Bud. This is your lucky night. You're gonna make some money."

He passed over a creased ten-dollar bill and the driver took it; yet he held it doubtfully and looked troubled.

"Listen, fella. Your dough's nice and I like it, but I'm married and I gotta coupla kids. You on the make? You figgerin' on a blast?"

Tracy shook his head impatiently. "It's okey. Newspaper stuff.

Give a look, sweetheart."

He passed over the *Daily Planet* identity card. The driver looked at it, passed it back.

"I guess it's oke. What's the lay? You're plenty excited, brother. You're tremblin' like a leaf."

"Listen and shut up. I expect a cab along in a few seconds. A guy and a doll will get out. The guy'll get back again—I hope so. When he does, follow him and don't ever lose him. Hang back a block or two. I'd rather lose him than have the hacker that's driving him get wise we're tailing… And don't forget something else. That ten-spot of mine has lotsa brothers and sisters for the right party."

"Sounds oke by me." He pondered. "Lemme get it straight, chief. S'pose the guy don't git back in the cab again? Yuh said you *hope* he does."

"He will! If he doesn't—I'll have to think up something to do about it. You be ready to roll!"

Tracy was staring backward towards the dark straddle of the "L" structure on Columbus Avenue. Suddenly headlights bounced into view and came west. Tracy went instantly down on the floor of his own cab.

Volga's taxi sped noisily past, went almost to the end of the block and stopped.

Tracy growled: "Tell me about it."

"Both of 'em gittin' out. Goin' up the stoop… I think he's tryin' to make a little play for the dame. They're chewin' together on the top step. He's got his hat off… The goil's goin' in—*oops!*— so is the guy—"

Tracy said, "Damnation!" in a harsh whisper and felt swiftly at the lump under his coat that was a gun. "Are you sure?"

"Wait a second—nope, that was just a playful gag he was pullin'. She pushed him back… Here he comes down the stoop."

Tracy said: "You've earned ten bucks more already. Take it easy when you roll, sweetheart—and don't lose him!"

SAM VOLGA CAME DOWN the stone stoop with a springy lift to his feet and a joyous feeling that he was eight feet high and four feet wide. He felt that he filled the whole street.

He leaned his big hand on the taxi door. "If I shoved just once," he thought, "I could turn this —— damned can over!"

He got inside and sat back. Antonelli's radio tinkled pleasantly with a suave dance rhythm. Volga liked it; it flowed evenly along with the rhythm in his own blood.

The driver didn't turn. He said, huskily: "Where to, sir?"

"Wait a minute, mugg. Don't bother me a minute. I gotta think… What are yuh shiverin' about? Cold?"

"Ugh… Y-yeah."

"Boy, am I hot!" Volga laughed with rumbling amusement.

A tinny voice from the radio identified the station and the orchestra. "—in N'Yawk Ciddy." A soft soprano began to croon:

Jevver see a dream walking? Well, ah deed!
Jevver hear a dream talking? Well, ah deed!

"That's me, a dream walking," Volga thought. An idea touched him and his blood buzzed.

He said, suddenly: "Down to the Village, mugg. I'll give you the address when we get there."

He jounced with the cab's sudden motion. He cursed Flip softly. She could wait; he'd save her for dessert later on. Gwen was the baby for a big shot. His smile became warm, eager. He hadn't seen Gwen for two weeks or so. Gwen's clothes and Gwen's nutty idea of furniture was costing him plenty dough, anyhow. The thing sure ran into money! He whispered: "Gwen, yuh little hellcat!" and swore thickly. Gwen fitted his mood tonight....

The cab turned through 57th, went south again on Sixth. At 53rd Street the frowning Elevated structure swallowed the taxi like a long, deserted tunnel. The avenue was icy and bare. It was very late. A trolley car clattered past, its ugly yellow-cane seats all empty. Overhead, a three-car train slammed northward and tiny particles of frozen snow sifted down from the steel crossbeams.

A red light bloomed on a distant "L" pillar and the taxi slowed. It swerved out from under the structure, idled onward to the corner and stopped. It stopped close to the curb.

The driver glanced swiftly left and right, up and down the side-street. He turned and shoved back the glass panel behind his own seat.

He said, in an uneven voice: "Little trouble wit' the motor—distributor-points ain't—"

His gun rested suddenly on the sill, steady, rocklike.

"Keep quiet and don't move them hands!"

"Why, you—" Volga's anger changed to amused impatience. This amateur stickup was delaying his head-on collision with Gwen. He didn't move his hands but he laughed throatily. "Stick-up, eh? You gotta live, I s'pose. Put the rod away and I'll forget about it. I'm Sam Volga, you mugg! People don't rattle the tin box at me. You picked out the wrong guy."

"The right guy, mister."

The radio music persisted dimly. Neither of the two men heard it. The wind sighed along the barren avenue. The "L" structure sprawled overhead in the darkness like a long rickety ghost.

The traffic light winked green but the cab didn't stir an inch.

"My name is Joe Antonelli, mister. You killed a sister of mine once. The kid's name was Josephine. You killed her, mister… Keep them hands quiet or you'll get it right away! Her name was Josephine, mister. You killed her."

Volga said unsteadily: "I never heard of her, pal, and that's the God's truth."

"She called herself Dot Devore."

Volga said, "Ah." A tiny exhalation of sound. He looked at the eyes over the gun and the warmth began fading out of his body. The gun didn't move. He watched the eyes; they were graveyard eyes.

Words came out of the mouth; flat, lifeless words:

"I seen you once before, mister. You rode in my cab. You were lucky that time. I didn't get a chance. I let yuh git out. I didn't mind waitin'… Did yuh think I only just started lookin' for yuh tonight?"

A dry sob rattled in Volga's throat.

"Listen. You're sore. You're excited. I didn't know she was your sister. She got a tough break. I wanna be fair. I wanna make things right. I didn't kill her. She killed herself. Gimme a chance. I got plenty dough. I swear I'll—"

"Dough!" He laughed. *"Dough!"*

"You can't get away with it," Volga whispered wildly.

"No? I'll take a chance. I'm talkin' now because I want yuh

to know what hit yuh—*before* it hits yuh... I'm gonna plug yuh, mister. Right between your —— damned eyes. Then I'm gonna run yuh right smack into that next electric-light pole. Somebody hijacked us. We was sideswiped by a car, see? They were after you and they let yuh have it. A gray moider car."

His bitter laughter rattled like rain.

"You can't get away with it, pal," Volga pleaded. "Don'tcha see how yuh can't? You can't ditch the gun. You can't fake it, I tell yuh." His teeth chattered. The muzzle of Antonelli's gun seemed frozen on the sill. "For God's sake lemme square things. You can't beat the rap. You'll burn. I tell yuh, you'll burn!"

Volga's cunning hand moved a full inch under his coat. His trembling body masked the movement.

"I'll count three," he thought harshly. His hand crawled further. He could feel the butt.

"We've got him, Josie," said the icy voice. Joy lingered and crawled under the ice. "Are yuh waitin', Josie? Are yuh watchin'?"

Volga's terrified brain began to count.

One... Two....

TRACY HEARD THE SMASHING echo of the shots. Three of them that blended almost into one.

He saw Antonelli's cab leap forward heard it clash into second, into high. It roared headlong down the avenue, then suddenly swerved sidewise, straight for an electric-light pole.

The wheels jounced over the curb. They skidded on the icy sidewalk, skewing the cab broadside. It struck the metal pole with a glancing impact and bounced forward like a projectile at a dimly lit plate-glass window. The loud jangling of glass was swallowed instantly by the louder concussion. *Brrrooooooomp!* Then there was no sound at all. Just silence.

Jerry Tracy stood for ten paralyzed seconds poised stiffly on his toes, with his mouth agape. He whirled, then, and ran swiftly back along the side-street where his own taxicab was parked. He dived inside and slammed the door.

"There's been an accident," he croaked. "Keep your mouth shut. I'll do all the talking necessary. We heard the noise, see? Come on; get going."

"Oke. You're the paymaster."

Heads were beginning to poke out of the dingy windows that fronted the Elevated structure. Jerry's chauffeur braked hard. He took one good look at the mess in the shop window and said, "Jeeze!" in a small voice. He didn't get out. Tracy did.

Antonelli's car had gone smack into the dimly lit show-window of a neighborhood butcher shop. It had nosed diagonally into the wall but it hadn't crumpled badly; hadn't been able to get up much speed.

From the sidewalk Tracy could see neither the chauffeur nor the passenger. He noted mechanically that a leg of lamb had been tossed on the cab's rear fender and there were curved links of pork sausage on the sidewalk.

He turned towards the gutter and his shoes crunched on shattered glass.

"Hold your hand on the horn button," he ordered grimly.

As he spoke he heard the slap-slap of racing feet and saw the panting blue-coat.

"Accident, Officer. Heard it three blocks away. Just got here. I'm a reporter. *Daily Planet*." He flashed the card and the cop looked at it and nodded.

"Okey, brother. You guys are like lice. How do yuh do it?"

There were long jagged sheets of glass sticking up from the lower sill of the butcher-shop window. The cop batted them out with his nightstick. He climbed inside and Jerry followed him.

"Look out for your shoes, *Planet!* You can get a hell of a cut that way. I loined that at a fire once."

His voice changed.

"Cripes, *that's* nice. One look at that guy is plenty."

Antonelli's arms were wrapped around his forehead and the top of his head. The steering-wheel held him upright. Under the wrapped arms the eyes were wide with a kind of amazed, sleepy wonderment. He hadn't expected that skid into plate glass. His head was nearly severed from his body. It wasn't nice.

"You took it sweet and sudden," Tracy thought, with a clutch of helpless pity at his heart. "I kidded myself you could have squared it; but you really couldn't. You had good reasons, Joe—but it was still murder. You're safe now... I hope to God mine comes sweet and sudden like that!"

The cop was peering through the cab's rear window.

"Hey! This guy is *shot!*"

"*Yeah?*" Tracy came out of his trance. "There's a phone in here. On the counter, under the droplight. Just a second."

He grabbed the instrument himself and eagerly called a number. There was a swift crunching of police brogans.

"What's the idea?" growled the cop. "Let the paper wait."

"This isn't the paper... Inspector Burch? *Danny!* This is Tracy. Murder. Take the address... What?... Come in your drawers—stark naked if you like. It's *Sam Volga!*"

He pronged the receiver with a bang.

The cop said slowly with a queer, attentive note in his voice: "You a personal friend of the Inspector's?"

"Yeah. Don't bother with the homicide boys. Danny'll flash 'em." His ears cocked. "What the hell's that noise?"

"Radio. In the cab. The damn' thing is still running. Can you beat that? I left it alone. Say, you sure that guy in the back is Volga?" He whistled softly. "I'm glad I didn't touch nothing."

He clumped suddenly out to the front.

"Git back, you people! Wanna cut yourself to pieces? G'wan back to bed. Whaddye think this is—a show?"

His club prodded.

"G'wan! Git back!"

Jerry Tracy was on the telephone again. He got the *Planet,* stunned the City Desk with a brief sentence, woke up the whole lobster trick and set 'em scuttling like roaches. He kept his wire open and fed 'em details. A running account. Short flashes they could fill.

Two police cars arrived almost simultaneously. Inspector Burch whizzed into view in still another—a commandeered sedan.

Tracy was beside Danny Burch when he opened the taxicab's door. The big gray-thatched Irishman took one keen look at the dead passenger and sighed softly.

"Nice. Very nice. I was afraid it wasn't true. Looks like the City is getting a break at last."

There were three holes in Sam Volga. One in his forehead, right between the eyes. One under his left cheekbone. A third had torn his upper lip and taken out two teeth. His eyes were perfectly: wide open. The whites were speckled with tiny powder marks.

Inspector Burch looked at Tracy. Tracy pointed. The inspector glanced obediently at the hack license and his big shoulders stiffened.

"Antonelli, eh?"

"Dot Devore's brother," Tracy said.

"Mmmmmm… Like that… The poor devil! I wish I could have shaken hands with him before he died. He done a good job—and he went out clean."

"Listen," Tracy said suddenly. Sharply.

His face was staring, incredulous.

"What's that? Wait a minute!"

He pointed to the cab's radio. The all listened. A voice was singing. Drowsy, soft. The orchestra beat was blurred in the background but the word of the song came clearly, hauntingly:

… when your heart's on fiiiire,

You must reeealize,

Smoke gets in your eyes.…

Tracy looked at Sam Volga, at the sleek, well-fed jaws, at the faint smudges of black on the whites of the wide eyeballs.

He said, "Yeah," in a flat, empty voice.

He turned off the music.

Keep On Asking

*Jerry Tracy plays big tough
brother for a little lost gal*

AS THE DOOR OF the inner office opened Jerry Tracy jerked a lean worried face across his left shoulder. "'Smatter, Butch? What do you want?"

Butch ducked his big shoulders defensively.

"Listen, Boss. There's a kind of a screwy dame—"

"Chase her! Haven't you been hanging around me long enough to know that all dames are screwy?"

The cloudy, preoccupied look vanished from the columnist's eyes, leaving them bright with mockery. With Tracy mockery was merely a veil to cloak his affectionate regard for this large-fisted simple-minded ex-pug who had annexed himself to Tracy's life by the simple expedient of falling into step with the famous little columnist and refusing to be shaken off.

The columnist grinned briefly and gestured.

"Beat it, sweetheart. I'm busy."

"Like I just told you, Boss," Butch; said calmly. "There's a kind of a screwy dame outside and—"

"And she wants to see me without undue delay on a matter of considerable import?"

Butch's thick lips grinned admiringly. "Jeeze, you took the woids right outa me mouth!"

"I'll bet I did. Mmmmm... What's the dame look like?"

"Well, she's got sorta—orange hair."

"Orange?"

"Yeah."

"Young and shapely?"

"Nope. Looks more like an old bum to me."

"Why do you think I ought to see her?"

"I—I was gonna give her the bum's rush," Butch muttered. "But there was something about her… Jerry, she means business! She's gonna *see* you, what I mean."

"Did she say what she wanted?"

"Yeah. That's the dopey part of it. She says she wants an audition."

"Audition!" Tracy looked incredulously at his faithful bodyguard. "You mean she wants to go on the radio!"

"You got it. She says she wants to go on the Krumby Krackers amateur program tonight. Says you gotta give her an audition right away and fix things so she can go on tonight."

"Isn't that swell! But why does she come to me?"

"That's just what I ask her right off the bat."

"And?"

"She says it's a matter of life and death. No kiddin', Boss, that's just what she said. She says she's gotta go on the air— that you're a good, kind guy—and please God, will yuh help her? And all the time she's got them gummy eyes of hers glued tight on my pan—and she talks low and funny—it's almost like she's praying… That's her story, What'll I do? Brush her off?"

Tracy's contemplative smile deepened. "Cease kidding, Butch, my lad. Show her in."

A moment later Butch said in a solemn tone: "This here is him, lady."

Jerry Tracy's eyes widened incredulously. The door closed.

"How do you do, madam. Sit down, won't you?"

Her hair was orange, all right; and badly in need of a comb. She didn't appear to hear Tracy's polite invitation. She came

towards him with a tremulous little rush and stood stock-still in front of his desk, pouring out words at him in a barely audible whisper.

"For Gawd's sake, Mister Tracy, don't gimme no runaround, will you? You're the only man in the world that can help me. You're a good guy—everybody knows that. You wouldn't toin down a person who was on the level, would yuh? An' I gotta go on the air tonight! I just gotta! You can do it if yuh wanta. You know all the big shots and the right parties. Please, Mister Tracy—please, please...."

She's wringing her hands, Tracy thought dazedly. I've always wondered just what the devil that meant. And she's doing it right here in front of my desk!

Watching her, he felt a queer chill of helpless compassion. Her dyed hair was streaky and stringy. Intuitively he guessed that she was nearer forty-five than sixty; but it was intuition, not observation, that told him. A bum, washed into his office from some doorway on the Bowery. In ashbarrel finery and dyed hair. Fantastically beseeching him—not for a dime, but for an audition!

HE SAID, GENTLY: "I'm not sure that I quite understand you, madam. You mean you want to go on the air? You want to broadcast?"

"Yessir. I—I—Yes!"

"Er—anything special you had in mind?"

"The amateur hour, Mister Tracy. You know the one—with the funny master of ceremonies and the Wise Cracker Band—and the Cracker Barrel Philo-philo-soffer at the end."

"Of course." Tracy nodded politely. "You mean the Krumby Kracker Amateur Hour."

"That's the one. Yessir."

A gag, of course. A buildup. A comedy blackout. In a moment, if he played straight man and kept his pan wooden, she'd yank off that orange floor-mop and the door would open and spill in a bunch of hysterical wise guys with horns and rattlers—and the party would be on till 4 a.m. with the drinks on Tracy!

He said, in a thickish growl: "Nerts to you, baby. It's a good act but I'm tired. Call in the gang."

She leaned over the desk and her fingers hurt like hell. They bit into his forearm. He had to pry them loose.

"Can't yuh write me a note—a little hunk of paper, or some-thin'. So's I can get in? It's gotta be tonight—'cause I'm afraid

I'll die. Gawd wouldn't let me die, would He, Mister Tracy?"

He walked deliberately around his desk, applied downward pressure until her knees bent and she sunk with docile obedience into a chair.

"What are you after sister? The ten buck prize?"

"Ten bucks. Yessir." She didn't look at him.

"What do you do?"

"Huh?"

"I mean, what's your act? Do you imitate guinea pigs or play a xylophone—or what?"

"Well, I—I sing."

"What do you sing?"

"Anything. Just songs."

"What's your name?"

Her eyes swung upward to meet his. By some miracle of nature color flooded faintly into her grimy old face.

"Angel La Farge," she said, and outfaced him and made him look away.

"Ever been on the stage?"

"No, sir."

"Mmmmm… What's your real name? I got no time to fool."

"Will you help me?" she whispered, "if I tell you?"

"How do I know? Come on—what's your name?"

"Annie Brenner."

The name meant nothing whatever to Tracy. His smile hardened into Broadway gutta-percha.

"Okey, Annie. You want to go on the air. So why?"

"I—I wanta sing songs on the amateur hour."

Tracy raised his voice. "Hey, Butch! Oh—Butch!"

Instantly Annie Brenner came springing out of her chair like a tigress. She clawed at his sleeve, clutched beseechingly at him so that he staggered and almost fell. He recoiled, his left arm shielding his face from her curved fingers.

"Something, Jerry?" Butch asked from the doorway.

Tracy stepped clear of the woman. Drew a deep breath. Straightened his tie, dusted a bit of imaginary fluff from the knife-edge of his trousers.

"False alarm," he told Butch calmly." No dice. Out!"

Butch stared, said "okey" in a puzzled voice and shut himself out.

Annie Brenner was weeping soundlessly—a pantomime of noiseless grief that was horrible to watch. The *Planet's* dapper columnist leaned above the bedraggled forlorn woman.

"Annie," he said slowly, "I've got a hunch or an idea—or something I thought for a minute you might be a Canadian dime, but I was wrong. The chances are I'm gonna help you. Maybe. If I do, you've got to play ball. Just what is this radio stuff? What's your real angle?"

"I hafta see somebody," she whispered. "Somebody I gotta see real bad. He makes lotsa money. He has bodyguards—men that push you away, knock you into the gutter if you try to get near him. But if I could get into the radio place, I—I could see him."

"And it's got to be the amateur show and none other?"

"Yessir."

"Guy makes lots of dough, eh? Krumby Kracker show. Mmmmm... Would it by any chance be the master of ceremonies, Annie?"

She nodded haggardly. "That's him. The comedian. Willie Zigger. The man that makes all the jokes."

"Zigger, eh?" Tracy's gnomelike forehead wrinkled. "The

little gag and patter man. Do you know him?"

"I usta know him. He wasn't so—so famous then."

"Correct. We'll skip the part about low he got his break on radio. I know all about that—all the smelly details." Tracy studied her with cloudy eyes. "Suppose I fixed it so you could get n the studio tonight. Would you say hello to him, shake hands, chew the at about old times?"

"I want to kill him," she breathed.

"That's what I thought. So why, Annie? Has he—hurt you?"

"Not me, Mister Tracy."

"Whom?"

"Ruthie."

"And Ruthie, of course, is?"

"My little girl."

"Mmmmm… How about a quick synopsis, Annie? I mean can you give me a rough outline?" He checked her suddenly with upraised palm. "Wait. I… Knowing Zigger, I think I'd like to make a guess. Ruthie is about—ummmmm—seventeen. Right?"

"She was not quite sixteen, Mister Tracy, when—"

"Yeah. Sounds like Willie Zigger. Where's the girl now? Dead?"

"I don't know. I think he may have her in his penthouse but I'm not sure. I tried to get in but his—his lawyer did something and they sent me to the Island. I couldn't talk to anyone. No one would listen. I—I thought if I came to you—"

"You came to the right shop," Tracy said curtly. "I never liked Zigger and his bum jokes. And I know what he did to get into radio. And about how long he's going to last… Tell me about Ruthie."

GUIDED BY THE columnist's gentle questioning, Annie Brenner's husky voice supplied the familiar facts. Always so prosaic, Jerry thought, always the same! A year or so ago—on the Greer Turnpike. The Greer Turnpike was a state highway not too far from Philly. Mrs. Brenner ran a tourist camp; and sometimes Ruthie and her mother ate regularly and sometimes they didn't. It was that kind of setup.

Willie Zigger arrived one warm, rainy day with a what ho! and a merry ha! ha! A great guy, Willie, in spite of his ups and downs. He blew into the tourist camp with a rented car and a pasteboard suitcase. He was stony broke and looking for a comfortable cyclone cellar. Radio was just around the corner for him—but Willie didn't know it yet! His vaudeville act was stale and sour; and besides, the big movie houses had skimmed the cream off vaudeville and had thrown the rest down the sink. That's where Willie and his pasteboard suitcase were—down the sink—playing quick tank hops for crullers and coffee. A threadbare personality boy looking for ease and entertainment. His canny eye told him instantly that in Mrs. Brenner and Ruthie there might be possibilities for both.

Ruthie had never met a free and easy little zany like Zigger. His worn-out comedy routine went over big. Ruthie gurgled at his gags, got to squeezing his hand timidly whenever Ma wasn't looking, asked wistful questions about the Big Town and the Big Time. Zigger dramatized both. He eyed the taut outline of Ruthie's figure as she stretched tiptoe, hair flying in the wind, to hang the family wash. The kid was sure a nice bet. And instantly, Zigger's cheap and tawdry little mind whispered gloatingly: "Why not?"

When he breezed one night, he sneaked away with Mrs.

Brenner's pocketbook. And Ruthie.

Listening to Annie Brenner's dreary narrative, Jerry Tracy frowned. He couldn't place Ruthie in his gossip memory. He had never heard of her. Zigger must be a very, very wise gent. Radio success had lifted him to a spotlighted national pinnacle—but with no hint of a captive or—dead—Ruthie. Plenty of tales were current about the comedian; a few funny, most of 'em dirty. But Ruthie? Not the least hint. Nothing!

"Ever had a letter from the kid?" Tracy asked. "Not even a postcard?"

"Nothing, Mister Tracy. She—she just—disappeared."

The columnist lit a cigarette and pondered.

"And you only got to Zigger once, eh? And that did no good because his hired gun gave you the old brush-off, had you vagged at the Island for a ninety-day stretch... And then— times get tougher for you, eh? And you can't do much about Ruthie, because your big job is just to keep alive. Long enough to get Zigger in a corner somewhere and *make* him talk! And that's not so easy now, because Willie Zigger is on a solid-gold bandwagon, while you are just—"

"Just a bum," she whispered drearily. "A frowsy old bum— that's me."

Tracy's throat made a brief, growling sound. "Cut that out, Annie. I don't like it and besides—it's not true. Let's see... First of all, you've gotta have some dough. Just a small loan, eh?"

She pushed the roll of bills aside.

"Don't want money," she muttered. "Don't need money."

"Where have you been sleeping lately?"

"Municipal lodging house. Salvation Army. Last night I flopped in a doorway." Her laughter made a brittle cackle in the room. "Somehow, it's easier to remember things when you sleep in a freezing cold doorway."

"Excuse me," Jerry murmured suddenly.

He went into the outer office and dug a vicious thumb into Butch's ribs. There was a brief whispered conversation between the columnist and his beefy shadow. The roll of bills that Mrs. Brenner had spurned went into Butch's pocket. The ex-pug came into the inner office presently, hooked the old derelict's arm under his, nudged her gently towards the door.

"You go right along with Butch," Tracy reassured her. "Do whatever he says. Butch is a good guy."

She nodded dazedly. "I'll do anything you say, Mister Tracy, only— Do you think that, maybe, you can—"

"You leave it all to me, Mrs. Brenner... Maybe I'll have some news for you by tomorrow." He jerked his head towards Butch. "Remember what I told you. Some food first of all. Then the rest of it. And hurry it up back. We're going places, sweetheart!"

DUSK WAS DEEPENING into early evening when Butch returned. The *Daily Planet's* dapper little columnist shot a piercing glance at him.

"Oke, little man?"

"Oke."

"That's very swell. Keep your hat on. I feel in the mood for a social call."

"Hey! Don't we eat first?"

Jerry grinned at him. "You can buy a chocolate bar from that curved blond menace in the lobby downstairs. The one that's been giving you goose-pimples lately. Come on. Let's amscray."

In the taxi Butch studied his employer covertly. He bit off

half of his chocolate bar and made swampy noises with his lips. "Where we going, mongsoor?"

"We're calling on a bigshot, my lad. A heavyweight customer. An important figure in the amusement world."

Butch's throat went *zzzung!* and the chocolate disappeared.

"Not Maxie Baer!" he gasped.

"I said amusement, dope… Can't you ever get fight out of your mind?"

"He socked me once," Butch said dreamily. "I mean Maxie. Over at Stillman's gym. Just in fun, y'unnerstan'. A little playful shove in the belly. Jeeze, I went cold all over." Butch finished the rest of his chocolate and sighed. "What a man!"

"Ever listen much to radio, Butch?"

"Oh, sure."

"Ever hear of a redhot named Willie Zigger?"

"Did I ever hear of him! You mean the Krumby Kracker program? Say, that guy is tops! I tune in for him every Thoisday night. I mean, the guy's good. I wish I had the apples he shakes down once a week. He's worth it, what I mean."

Butch grinned sheepishly.

"I was in a delicatessen one night and I seen them Krumby Krackers on the counter—and darned if I didn't buy a box. Can yuh beat that?"

"How were the crackers?"

"Lousy."

Tracy shot a pinched smile at his companion. "By the way, Zigger is the lad I'm calling on."

"No kiddin'… Willie Zigger? Say!"

"What's the matter?"

"Well—jeese… Ain't I been tellin' yuh? Zigger is the nuts!

The guy is reely funny. Did you hear the gag he pulled last Thoisday night? The one about the ———"

"If you don't shut that trap of yours," Tracy said with cold fury, "I'll poke you right in the lip. Willie Zigger is a cheap little rat and his gags smell. And he won't be so damn' funny when I finish talking to him tonight."

"Maybe I'm wrong," Butch muttered.

"I'm damn' well telling you that you're wrong. We're going over to his penthouse right now—nail him before he leaves for the broadcast tonight. I'm going to lay a finger on wise little Willie—and hold it there till it hurts."

Butch nodded at Tracy, chuckled briefly to show his intelligent comprehension of the situation.

"Right with yuh, Boss. Only lemme get it straight. You want me to ice up Zigger wid a quick left an' right?"

"No, dope. You stay downstairs. I go up… Got the proper slant on things now, sweetheart?"

"Oh, sure. It's like them crackers I bought, huh? Zigger's lousy, too?"

"Too—and also."

Butch studied the craggy fist in his lap. The puzzled look left his low forehead. "I'll shove Zigger's nose back in his hair any time yuh say. That little rat ain't gonna get away wid *nothin'*."

Jerry Tracy paid off the taxi driver at a certain roaring corner of the town; a section he had long since immortalized in his *Planet* column as the "Sexy Sixties." With Butch hulking along at his side he walked west along a dark, canyon-like street; a place of swanky restaurants, a few not so swanky residential hotels; a couple of intimate theaters that had long since gone dark—and still were. Here and there a loft building stretched its gaunt, ugly length against the chilly stars of Manhattan.

It was in the shadow of one of these buildings that Willie Zigger maintained his elaborate hideaway.

An expensive foreign-built sedan stood empty at the curb, its parking lamps a dim, filtered glow. Zigger's. The thing looked like a portable cathedral.

Butch glanced at it and said, "Uh-huh!" in awed admiration.

"Yeah," Tracy said dryly. "You wait down here, Butch. And try and make that big shape of yours as inconspicuous as possible."

"Kinda cold, Boss." He pulled his coat tighter around his throat and blew on his numb fingers.

Tracy pointed towards a small concreted recess beyond, and adjoining the building wall. It was closed off in the rear by a grilled iron gate that gave access to the rear of a theater in the next block.

"In there for you, sweetheart. You'll be out of the wind. Stick around. I may have to go other places. S'long!"

THE DAPPER LITTLE columnist hunched his shoulder against a shabby-looking revolving door and shoved inside. There was nothing shabby about the lobby he entered. Dim lights, a tapestry that belonged in a museum, an oil portrait of a whiskered financial gent—a very notorious old boy away back in Grant's administration; an oriental rug that you didn't walk on—you *waded*.

Tracy strolled across to a small desk under the tapestry. A stout, sleepy-looking man in a grey suit of excellent cut smothered a yawn and glanced up. He smiled instantly—deferentially—as he recognized the visitor.

"How do you do, Mr. Tracy? Haven't seen you in weeks...."

The columnist's eyelids flicked. "This is a confidential call, Anderson. Has Zigger gone out yet?"

"Not yet. He should, pretty soon. Broadcast tonight, you know. Show doesn't go on till nine-thirty—but they dress the show about eight-thirty, I believe."

"Okey. I'll shinny up the shaft and say hello to the bum. Don't forget what I said about confidential."

He swiveled on his heel, stepped into a tiny elevator, said languidly, "P.H., my lad," to a pimpled youth in a tight plum colored uniform. The elevator whisked swiftly upward to the penthouse level. The operator lingered with his door open, staring at the most famous little personage on Broadway, until Tracy's lips creased satirically and he murmured: "May I offer you a cigarette and a deck of cards, Egbert? Or are you just in the mood for a simple chat?"

The operator said, "Uhp... Excuse me, sir." The car departed. Tracy walked towards the ornate portal of the very funny, the very, very laughable Mr. Zigger.

Zigger's door seemed to be one of those mysterious and little understood masterpieces of art and industry. To Tracy it looked exactly like a Welsh rarebit of chromium and glass. In the lower left-hand corner was a something or other in faded brown and sepia that might be an Italian primitive—or maybe the Zigger coat of arms. The bell was a chromium chain attached to a long metal gadget that looked like a polished walking-beam.

Tracy eyed it with a mild amazement. He reached out his a hand to yank the contraption. Before he could yank he heard a fumbling sound on the inside of the door and he stepped back and waited.

The door opened. A dry little voice like a petulant cricket said peevishly: "Come on, Phil... Jeese, do I feel *nnyyyyyyah!*"

Willie Zigger appeared suddenly. Spick-and-span except for his eyes. His beady little eyes looked pale and rumpled. He saw Tracy standing there looking at him and his jaw dropped.

"Oh—hello."

"Hello, Willie—you big old famous comedian."

They eyed each other warily. No love lost between these two. Both about the same height, same build; except that Jerry Tracy was too busy at his *Planet* office to have the time to build up those mousy looking things under the eyes. Also, his jaw was less fleshy, his hands noticeably steadier.

A distant voice growled indistinctly: "Right with you, Willie."

"Hurry it up, Phil." Zigger sneered pleasantly at the newspaper columnist "Nice of you to call, Tracy. My old pal and well-wisher. Tracy the great! Helper of the afflicted; scourge of all rascals... You weesh something, my firaaaand?"

"Yeah. Let's all turn around again, Willie. And go back inside. I want to talk to you."

"Can't."

"Why not?"

"Because I can't be bothered. I'm busy. Got a show on at nine-thirty."

"I heard it last week. It was lousy."

"Glad to hear it. Give it a nice roast in your column, will you, pal?" Zigger's pale eyes were blazing but he laughed pleasantly. "A roast I could use, my fraaaand. Maybe bear down on Moe with it. Moe's got a funny idea that his scripts are good. Maybe I could chisel him a little on that guaranteed cut of his."

The glass door behind him clicked shut. Zigger grinned at the sound. The strained look left his eyes.

"All set, Phil?"

"Yeah." Phil glanced at Tracy without much expression. A sandy-haired mastiff of a man in oversize Chesterfield, dark derby, grey mocha gloves.

Zigger stepped forward past Tracy. Tracy shoved him backward on his heels.

"I said in," he growled. "Not out, Willie."

"Who's this nosey monkey?" Phil queried mildly.

He inserted four fingers without any violence inside Tracy's coat collar. He tightened the fingers and anchored Tracy rigidly on tiptoe.

"Shall I slough him right here or downstairs?"

The radio comic licked his lips. "Downstairs, Phil. We'll take him down in the elevator. When you get lout on the sidewalk, kick this nosey little —— about eight blocks!"

"Only eight?" Phil grumbled. He grinned a little. It was the first time an expression of any kind had appeared on his oatmeal countenance.

"Wait," Tracy said. He twisted his head painfully so he could look sidewise at Zigger. "Hadn't you better listen to my news flash before you do something foolish?"

"Can you gimme your news in about two words?" Zigger smirked.

"Sure I can. Capital R for Ruthie. Capital B for Brenner."

He watched the radio comic wilt. The smirk lingered stiffly on Willie's mouth but the face changed like putty. Seemed to slip a little. For a second his face drained absolutely white, then the blood came back and made it muddy and patchy looking.

The pale eyes bulged with panic—and a crawling hate.

"Let him alone, Phil," Zigger whispered. "Let go of him."

Phil let go reluctantly. The columnist stood there, rubbing his neck to take away the paralyzing stiffness.

"Unlock the door, Phil," Zigger said. "We're going back inside."

"But—hey! The broadcast! What about that dress rehearsal?"

"It'll have to wait," He glared stonily at Tracy. "Inside, pal."

HIS GLOSSILY SHOD feet led the way to an ornate, high-ceilinged living-room. The massive Phil brought up the rear with a *plunk-plunk* of his oversize shoes that made glasses rattle.

"I got a hunch," Zigger told Tracy slowly, "that you've shot your mouth off once too often. I think I'm gonna let Phil do something to you right here. Something permanent!"

"You always were a dope," Tracy jeered. "I knew all about your layout here—all about that nasty plug-ugly in the derby—before I walked in here. Do you think I'm the kind of sap who looks for a gas-leak with a lighted match? Grow up, Stupid!"

"You're not kidding me, Tracy. You thought you'd catch me here alone."

"You think that's the way I work?" Jerry chuckled. "I can see that you don't."

"He's bluffing," Phil snorted. "The little mugg is handing you a line."

Zigger glared uncertainly at Tracy. "Okey. What's your out?"

"A big guy named Fitz—Inspector Fitzgerald to you. Fitz knows I came over here to get a couple of answers. Fitz has a date with me in about an hour. He'll get very curious if I fail to show up after seeing you."

Phil kept watching the *Daily Planet* columnist with an eye like a hawk. "The guy is bluffing," he said again. "He's trying to talk himself out of a spot."

"Keep on thinking so," Jerry murmured.

Zigger hesitated, licked his dry lips.

"All right, wise guy. What do you know about Ruthie Brenner?"

"Plenty. Where is she now?"

"Why ask me?"

"Because you're the guy that knows."

"Who says so?"

"The kid's mother, Willie. Annie Brenner."

Zigger's laughter was raucous, jeering.

"That old harridan? Is she out of the can again? Next time she bothers me, I'll have her shoved in the booby-hatch where she belongs. Her and that dippy yarn she's trying to peddle! I tell you, the old tramp is a nut, Jerry."

"Forget that Jerry stuff," the columnist said evenly. "Or I'll hang one right on your lip—Phil or no Phil." He lit a cigarette very deliberately and sat down. "If you think for one minute that I'm moving out of this phoney-looking dump of yours before you tell me where Ruthie Brenner is—you're crazy in the head."

"I don't know a thing about her. Never heard of the kid."

Tracy smiled at him. Grimly. "Kid is correct, Willie. She wasn't quite sixteen the night you sneaked her away—along with Mrs. Brenner's savings. That was about a year and a half ago—before a lucky radio break put those weasel hips of yours in the butter-tub... I've panned you plenty in my column because I know exactly what you are. But, by the Lord, what

I've done before won't be a nickel's worth to what I'll do to you now—if you don't tell me damned quickly where Ruthie Brenner is. Is she here?"

The radio comic smoothed his patent-leather hair with a trembling palm.

"Okey," he said softly. "You're a smart guy. I won't try to kid you, see? I'll tell you what I know about Ruthie; and it ain't a hell of a lot. But, pal—brother—sweetheart—" His eyes flamed briefly and then got cold with hate, "—if I were you, I'd forget right away about bothering me or my sponsor. I'm in the jack, palsie walsie—got plenty of friends. A few grand peeled off my bankroll could start the worms chewing on you *tonight*. So don't get me sore or somebody is apt to find you in a vacant lot—without a face."

"I'm still asking for it, Willie. Where's the girl?"

Zigger didn't reply for a moment.

"I did know her," he admitted finally. "That part's okey enough. But the stuff about me running off with Ruthie is the bunk. Matter of fact, the kid was a pretty hot little *tamale*. She followed me the next day, see? Blew into Philly with that pocketbook you've been squawking about—"

"How did you know about the pocketbook?" Tracy asked him gently. "I didn't squawk about a pocketbook. I didn't even mention it."

"—so the kid blew into Philly like I said and hunted me up at my hotel. Plopped herself into my lap and said: 'Let's go places together, honey. You and me both.' Honest to Gawd, I was so surprised you could have knocked me over with a feather."

"Yeah. So I imagine," Tracy murmured. "Where is she? Here?"

The stolid bodyguard over by the door shifted his feet uneasily. "This guy oughta be handled," he suggested harshly. "The guy knows too much."

Zigger shook a harassed finger at him.

"You keep out of this, Phil. Tracy's a regular guy. He knows Gawd's truth when he hears it."

"I know liars, too. Where's Ruthie? Do you want me to put that question on wax and play it all night long?"

"I told you once. I don't know where she is."

"When did you see her last?"

"Oh—about—say, two months or so after she breezed into Philly and told me she was—"

"Skip that, you liar. What happened then?"

"The usual thing." Zigger grinned in jaunty man-of-the-world manner. "The kid was too hot to handle. Two timed me almost from the start. I paid her off and told her to scram."

"Just a sixteen-year-old bum, eh? But you were big-hearted and paid her off."

"Yep." Zigger shook his head mournfully. "Now you can see how it gets me sore when that old hophead with the henna hair butts in on me when I'm tops in radio—and tries to finger me for some hush-hush about that tramp daughter of hers."

Tracy got up and squashed out his cigarette in an enormous lacquered tray. He stood there, a queer half smile on his lips.

"Didn't you ever worry about Ruthie? Wonder, maybe, what happened to her?"

"Why should I worry, pal? I paid for everything she offered me."

"And that, Willie, was—what?"

"Cheapest thing in the world," Zigger grinned. "All she had to offer was—"

Tracy sprang forward as Zigger's lips framed the word. His lean fist smashed the comedian squarely on the mouth, drove him backward with blood spurting from a split lip. Tracy's own face was a taut mask of fury and contempt. He heard the rumbling shout of Zigger's bodyguard and disregarded it to get in another blow. Again his skinned knuckles pumped pistonlike into Zigger's bloody mouth. As it landed, something smashed against Tracy's skull. A flame seemed to spout suddenly inside the columnist's head. Zigger's face, the room, the world itself, spun into invisibility—into nothingness....

FOR THE SPACE of sixty seconds or so the room was dead quiet. Then the body-guard grunted. The wet slobber of Zigger's breathing became audible. He pushed Phil's protecting arm away from him. He was watching the motionless body on the rug, staring at it with a terrified fascination.

"You've killed him, Phil. You've cracked his neck."

"Nope," Phil said. "Didn't sock him hard enough for that. I sorta figured you wouldn't want the guy croaked right here in your own dump."

His gruff voice was melancholy, tinged with a vague regret....

Jerry Tracy groaned faintly. He could hear the faint slur of voices; a meaningless murmur of sound that seemed to drift unintelligently into his ears from a vast distance away. He tried to open his eyes but the lids felt heavy as lead. A sudden phrase pricked through the film of his stupor and made sense in his dulled mind. He lay very still on the rug, his eyes tightly closed.

"—come to any minute," the harsh voice repeated.

Phil. The big guy. Talking to Willie Zigger. Urging something.

"—pretty lousy any way you roll the dice. The guy's got you in a tough spot, no kiddin'. He don't look to me like he scares worth a dime—and he sure hates your guts."

"How about lugging him out of here?" the cricket voice of Zigger whined tremulously. "Can't you dump him somewhere, Phil?"

"Sure I can dump him. And what good'll that do? I tell yuh, this guy is all wound up to squawk! If he ever finds out what happened to that kid, he'll squawk, you right off the airwaves— into the gutter… and you damn' well know it."

Zigger moaned softly. "What'll we do?"

"Croak him! Stiffen him somewhere and shove him face down in a hole in the ground. Then start the dirty rumors flying. The guy's got plenty of enemies. You can handle that part all right. But Tracy has to be *dead*—and no foolin'! And if we're ever gonna do the job, he'll never be wrapped up for the worms no prettier than he is right now."

Zigger groaned again.

"Whaddye say?" Phil persisted. "The car is waiting at the curb downstairs. I can coke up this gink so that he'll walk out with us like a little man."

"Anderson and the elevator operator will remember that he was here."

"So what? You got dough. Plenty of it. Who's gonna pin anything on you? We met Tracy okey—sure—but we dropped him off somewhere, see? Any old place we wanta make up. And zooie!—he musta taken it on the lam right after he left us, for any one of a million dirty reasons… Who's gonna know the truth? You ain't talking. And neither am I."

"Yeah? How do I know you ain't talking?"

"That's a chance you gotta take, pal," Phil chuckled. "I got no kick coming. You been buttering my mitt pretty swell." His voice hardened. "Nope. I don't see no sense in anything except a quick bump for this nosy little —— of a newspaper columnist."

Silence. Tracy lay rigidly on the rug, eyes closed, muscles relaxed. He thought of Butch, waiting like a dope downstairs in that cold alley. Why hadn't he warned Butch to bust in if there was any undue delay? Too late now... Butch was probably down at the corner, gulping a hot chocolate.

"What time is it?" Zigger's voice quavered.

Phil told him.

"My gawd! We've missed the dress! It must be half over."

"Yeah. And we'll miss the show if we don't get busy. Won't *that* be nice? We done that before—remember the night I couldn't sober you up—and what the sponsor said?"

"Come on!" Zigger's voice cracked with nervous apprehension. "What are we standing here for? Grab him! Stick him in a closet somewhere. I—I gotta have time to think this out He'll keep till after the show, won't he?"

"He sure will. Git outa the way a minute."

Fleshy hooks sunk into Tracy's body. He sailed lightly aloft. The *pad-pad* of Phil's feet traveled with him. He heard the creak of a door opening. Suddenly the hands left him and a hard wooden floor hit him in the face. Fiery pinwheels whirled dizzily in his brain. He smothered a groan with clenched teeth.

"Still out like a light," Phil's voice chuckled. "Just can't take it."

The closet door slammed. A key turned in the lock. Slowly Tracy's eyes opened. He was in total darkness and something soft and invisible was tickling his bruised face. He touched it and brushed it away. It felt like the hem of a silken robe. A woman's? Ruthie's? Was she in the penthouse, hidden away somewhere—a prisoner? An icy little whisper in his brain said 'no' to that. There had been something in Phil's gruff snarl, something in the abject terror of Willie Zigger that made the *Planet's* star columnist feel sick at heart. Ruthie Brenner wasn't in the picture any more; Tracy was almost sure of it. And that meant… He refused to follow the thought any further.

He got to his knees in the closet and fingered the clothing behind him. The thing that had tickled him was a silken dressing-gown; a man's. He brushed sweat from his eyes. The closet was getting beastly hot. He tried to lunge at the locked door with his shoulder, to burst it open. No use… Maybe if he knocked rhythmically, maybe if the girl was still alive, still in the apartment somewhere… *Knock, knock, knock…* He gritted his teeth and kept it up. For what seemed like an idiotic century of time.

AND THEN, SUDDENLY, he heard an echo. *Bump, bump…* An echoing answer to the sound from his own bruised knuckles. Away off somewhere. Very faint. Still he was sure of it.

Crash… A tinkling slither of sound. That was glass smashing! Who the devil was breaking glass?

"Jerry! Hey, Boss! For the luvva Mike, where are yuh? Hey— are yuh in here, Boss?"

Tracy quivered with delight as he heard the muted sound of the familiar bellow. Butch! The big fellow had more brains than Jerry himself! He had gotten worried about the delay and had come up on his own hook. Busted right in through that fantastic glass door out front!

The sweating columnist pounded fiercely with his fist on the inner panel of the closet door. He heard the click of the turning key. Butch caught his employer as Tracy fell helplessly out into the room.

"Hey! What goes on? Jeeze—take it easy! You've been gone over, what I mean. A lump on your skull like an apple!"

"Quick! We've got to get out of here... Wait! Let's take a quick look around first. See if there's a girl locked up somewhere in this penthouse. Come on!"

He skipped nimbly away like an erratic monkey. Together the two men searched every inch of the place. Women's clothes—plenty of 'em, pink, indiscreet and frothy—but no woman. Not a sign or a trace of Ruthie Brenner.

Butch grinned suddenly at his boss.

"Was you worried any about them two guys?" he asked amiably. "They're downstairs."

"Huh?"

"Two guys. A little punk in a grey fedora. A big punk in a doiby. I hit the big guy foist. He looked like he might be kinda mean—and I didn't want no long argument with him."

"The two of them, Butch? Where are they?"

"I'm just tellin' yuh," Butch growled patiently. "They're downstairs. In that funny little alley with the big iron gate in the back. Jeeze, I sure *needed* a workout; I near froze to death waitin' for yuh."

"But—"

"They come out, see? The two of 'em together. And they're standin' there on the sidewalk with their backs to the alley. They don't see me. The mugg in the derby is laffin'. He tells the little guy: 'So that's the famous Jerry Tracy, huh? He goes to sleep like anybody else when he gets clipped on the dome.' And the little guy kinda groans an' says: 'Shut up! Let's climb in the car and scram. We're late!'"

Butch chuckled.

"But they don't *get* into no car. I *lay* 'em in. I socked the big guy foist and throttled the little fella before he could squeal an' run. I dug the keys outa the little guy's pocket. Shoved 'em both inside the car on the floor, under that black bear-robe in the back. Then upstairs I come and—"

Tracy plucked fiercely at the sleeve of his garrulous helper. A grim joy danced in Tracy's eyes, made his voice crackle unevenly.

"Out!" he snarled.

The elevator operator eyed the broken glass door of the penthouse and the faces of his two customers. He didn't say anything.

Tracy did. He said: "Did you ever get killed, Sonny?"

"N-No, sir."

"Then don't get too intelligent about this. You might spoil your record... Tell Anderson downstairs that I said there's to be no publicity. Tell him I'll be back later tonight and give him a confidential earful about the broken door. Tell him I said 'confidential' in caps. He'll understand. And so will you—after Anderson talks to you."

The lobby downstairs was as softly quiet as a cathedral. Anderson smiled woodenly behind his desk as he noted Tracy's damaged face.

"Anything wrong, Mr. Tracy?"

The columnist didn't stop. No time to wait now!

"Not a thing," he tossed over his shoulder. "Everything

serene. I'll be back later tonight and tell you why. And hold on to that elevator boy!"

The wind made cold, moaning sounds along the deserted sidewalk outside. The sidewalk was dark and chilly and very windy. Tracy opened the rear door of the glossy little foreign job at the curb. Prodded tentatively at the lumpy-looking robe on the floor.

"Get in the back here, boy friend," he told Butch. "You'll have to ride with the zoo. If the animals get restive, do something about it. See if you can't find a wrench somewhere. I wouldn't want you to hurt your hands."

He slid in behind the wheel. Butch had thoughtfully shoved Zigger's ignition key into the dash and Tracy turned over the engine. The car slid westward and Tracy's voice drifted reverently backward over his shoulder.

"Just an old tomato can, Butch, my lad. It revolts me to have to drive it."

"Yeah? D'yuh know what yuh'd hafta pay for one of these here—" Butch gulped at the sound of Tracy's uneven chuckle. "Okey! I'm the come-on in this act. Where do we go now?"

"I don't know yet. We'll loaf up through the Park while I get my two brain cells working."

They turned eastward through 57th, swung unobstrusively into the Park. Tracy kept this dream of a sedan moving along at a twenty-five-mile clip, nicely synchronized with the red lights ahead that changed monotonously to green as he passed.

As the road brushed momentarily with Fifth Avenue, away up in the Nineties, Tracy said suddenly: "Uh-huh… Yeah. Of course."

"What's that mean, Boss?" Butch wondered aloud.

"It means the George Washington Bridge, little man. Over the lordly Hudson. Westward ho! To a little gray shack in the west!"

The fur robe on the floor of the car heaved a little and seemed to mumble indistinctly. Butch busied himself professionally and the robe quieted down again. The sedan swung out of the Park and hummed across 110th to Broadway.

"You thinking about Abe Kolet's shack over in Joisey?" Butch asked the back of Tracy's head.

"Yeah. Empty—but nicely furnished, my lad, or so I believe."

"No dice. Place all locked up. Abe ain't been there for months."

"That's why we're going there, dope, Know how to break windows?"

"Sure."

"Okey. Shut up."

THE HUDSON WAS a wide blot of darkness, dimly frothed with whitecaps. A strong gale from the north made the spidery electric-lit cables of the bridge sing like zithers. Something in the chilly song made Tracy's lips curve in a small brooding smile.

A mile or so beyond the bridge he cut northward and followed a poorly paved road at a speed that made the springy car dance drunkenly. He turned into a rutted lane, followed its weedcovered curve to a high board fence that boxed in the rear of a rambling two-story frame dwelling.

The *Planet's* famous little columnist drove round to the front and snapped off his bright lights. The cold air made his nostrils ache. He was wide awake now. Eager, keen. And filled with an inexorable determination.

"For gosh sakes—look at that view!" Butch muttered. "Right on the edge of the Palisades! Another six feet—an' we'd drop down about a mile and go splash!"

"Get that meat out of the car," Tracy barked.

He glanced alternately upward and down, shivering incessantly in his light topcoat. The river surface seemed as far away as the remote stars overhead. That yellow stain in the sky, away off yonder, came from the delicatessens and neighborhood movies of Upper Manhattan and the Bronx. But the sky above Tracy's head was like black velvet. And the wind that gushed over the rocky lip of the Palisades bit at his ears like a sharp tooth.

"All set?" Butch called out. "Where d'yuh want 'em?"

"Inside. Kick that front window in and unlock the door for me."

"Attababy," Butch exulted. "This is sure my night for bustin' glass. Ain't we got fun?"

His huge hoof made magnificent ruin of the window-pane. He was inside the house almost before the jangling ceased. In a moment he had the door unlocked and open; and was escorting a large and very wobbly Phil into the front room.

"Hadda work a little on the big yum," he muttered. "Can you take the other mugg? He's pretty scared but he can walk fine."

Willie Zigger couldn't get his cricket voice articulating properly till Tracy shoved him headlong into a chair in the front room. His face looked greenish in the amber light from Abe Kolet's classy wall lamps.

"You can't get away with this!" he shouted shrilly. "I'll have you in the can for the rest of your life for kidnaping."

Tracy didn't even look at him.

"Take this other lug down cellar," he rasped at Butch. "Find some rope and tie him up tight to something. Something he can't pull loose from."

"Oke."

The groggy Phil made peculiar noises on the way downstairs that indicated he might not be walking.

Jerry Tracy shoved his gaunt, implacable face close to Zigger's and the radio comedian shrank sidewise across the padded arm of the chair.

"What do you want?" he snarled. "You got me all wrong on this thing."

"I want the truth, you rat."

"I told you the truth."

Tracy's lashing palm left a crimson welt on the side of Zigger's head.

"Do you think you can kid me like you do those moron listeners of yours? Where's Ruthie Brenner?"

"I swear I don't know."

"Is she alive or dead?"

Zigger hesitated. Tracy waited. There was will in him to wait until the second coming of Christ, he thought joyously.

The comedian's ratlike eyes darted about the room as though seeking a hole or a crevice into which he might crawl to get away from the set white face that confronted him.

"I'm—I'm afraid to tell you." He licked his ashen lips nervously. "If I give you the absolute lowdown, will you promise not to get sore?"

"Talk up—or I'll tear you apart."

"The kid is—is—dead."

Tracy's eyes bored into him. Washed him. Swept him bare.

"You're a liar, Willie. You lie like hell."

"No. I'm—I'm talking truth. Honest!"

"All right: Talk, then. What happened? I know damned well you're lying; but go ahead and talk."

"I didn't kill her. She—she died."

"Died, eh? What from?"

"From—from pneumonia."

"How come?"

"Well—it was all a mistake. The kid was sorta high-strung. She got frightened, see? And—"

"Wait a minute," Tracy snapped. "Lemme get something else straight before we go any further. Did Ruthie Brenner follow you to Philly like you said? Of her own free will?"

"Well—I—I took her along with me the night I sneaked off with the old lady's jack. I—I fed Ruthie a line of booshwah and kidded her into coming with me… But I didn't kill her. Not me."

Sweat glistening on Willie Zigger's sallow forehead.

"Where did she die?" Tracy asked patiently. "In Philly?"

"No."

"Afraid I'll check up on you, eh? Go ahead with some more lies."

"She was high-strung like I said. A kind of a nervous kid. And she was kinda scared—and—and—when I came into her room, thinking I might help her, cheer her up maybe—"

Tracy's laugh grated discordantly. He stopped after a while and said: "Don't mind me. Go right ahead."

"Well, she jumps right out of bed in her nightgown the minute I come in the door. Runs right downstairs and out of the house. With me after her, worried as the devil, trying to catch her. By the time I catch her and get her back to the house and in bed, she's as cold as a corpse. I call in a doc—for God's sake, don't *grin* at me like that!—and the doc shakes his head and says pneumonia… In five days the kid is dead."

"Where's she buried?"

"In a little cemetery—can't think of the name. I'll think of it in a second. Little dump of a place. I didn't have no trouble. They thought she was my wife."

"Mmmmm… And that's all?"

"That's all. It's the truth, so help me."

"Dunno know whether it is or not. I think I can find out."

Tracy's head nodded slowly.

"Pneumonia, eh? A terrible disease, Willie. It seems to have killed a sixteen-year-old girl and made a gutter bum out of her mother… Maybe it can make a lying little radio comic talk truth."

He swung his brooding eyes towards the stolid Butch.

"Will that big guy in the cellar stay put, do you think?"

Butch grinned. "Wanna have a look at him, Boss?"

"Nope. I'll take your word for it… Come here a minute, will you? I'm tired of talking. I want a little action now. Undress Mr. Zigger, if you please."

"Huh?" Butch looked startled and mildly shocked. "Yuh mean, take the guy's clothes off?"

"You heard me. Undress him. Yank off every stitch he's got. Strip him down to his dirty little pelt."

"Okey by me, Boss."

HE ADVANCED WITH a wide grin. Zigger squealed shrilly and jumped from his chair. Butch dove after him with a bellow of infantile amusement. His big hand tore Zigger's coat off. A second tremendous clutch ripped the terrified comedian from collar to shirt-tail. In less than a minute Willie Zigger was crouching, shrill with terror, as nude as a peeled onion in a helterskelter of ragged garments.

Butch slapped him playfully and he echoed sharply like a pistol-shot.

Tracy cut short Butch's guffaw with a sharp bark of anger. There was no smile on Tracy's lips. They were taut with purpose.

"Stop that yelping, Zigger. If you don't shut up, I'll have Butch beat you unconscious. And that won't be so good, because if you're unconscious you can't save yourself by telling me the truth about Ruthie Brenner... Is her name familiar? We're still on the same old subject, you know... Only, now, we're going to talk about pneumonia."

"What do you mean?" Zigger faltered.

"Pneumonia, Willie. The scourge of the human race. Remember how cold it was when we took you out of your car outside? It'll be just as cold in the back yard—colder. With a nice high board fence for privacy. I'm going to put you out there, Willie, just the way you are now. Stark naked. Tie you up so you can't move. And *leave* you there till you're colder than a brass monkey... Unless—"

Jerry Tracy's voice dripped with a soft, honeyed hate.

"—unless you've got some accurate news for me about— let's see, what's her name again? I keep forgetting—oh, yes... A sixteen-year-old girl named Ruthie Brenner. She died of pneumonia, so they say."

"If you kill me," Zigger wailed, "I can't tell you any different."

"Take him outside, Butch!"

There was a short tussle. Butch said, plaintively: "Hey—the guy's as greasy as a pig. Hard to hold on to him… Okey! Shall I take him rout now?"

"Yeah. I'll relieve you in ten minutes. Give you a chance to come inside and get warm. No sense in you and me freezing, too."

The columnist walked over to the door and threw it open. A draft of wind whistled through door and smashed window. The cold blast rattled the pictures on the wall, whipped a cloth off a table. Zigger squirmed like a maniac in the clutch of Butch.

"Easier to hold him now," Butch panted. "He's got a million goose-pimples already."

"Take him out!"

"Wait!" Zigger screamed. His voice was as high-pitched as a woman's. "Wait, for God's sake! Lemme talk. I'll—I'll tell yuh!"

"Hold it, Butch."

Tracy walked leisurely towards the wide-open door. Smiled at Zigger.

"Ruthie Brenner isn't *really* dead, is she?"

"No… Damn you—no!"

"In other words, she's alive?"

"Yes—yes—yes!"

"And you know where she is?"

"Y-Yes. I'll t-tell you. I swear I will."

His body was squirming spasmodically. He could hardly spit the words through his chattering teeth.

Tracy slammed the door shut with a sweep of his arm.

"Chuck him in that chair," he told Butch. "And go upstairs and see if you can find a blanket."

Zigger burrowed into the big chair, shaking like a leaf. From cold. But more from fright. Every last bit of nerve had deserted him. Without his clothes he looked curiously like a chattering monkey.

"You're a devil," he whispered. "A murderous devil."

Jerry Tracy's head shook calmly.

"Not at all. Just a bit more willpower than you, my friend. You see, I know a liar when I hear one… And you wouldn't really have been murdered. You'd have just—died. Contributory negligence on your part. Or something like that. It was strictly up to you, my friend and you knew it—didn't you, Willie?"

Tracy's eyes narrowed watchfully.

"All right. We'll start all over again. Ruthie Brenner is alive. So where is she?"

"Egmont."

"Where's that?"

"Little place not far from Philly."

"Got her under guard there, eh? Locked in? Attic maybe? Dazed with dope? Hoping she'll cave in and die, perhaps?"

"No, no. I just—"

"Yeah. I can imagine. I'll tell you why she's not dead, Willie. Because your guts weren't strong enough to have her killed. Even though you knew that if she ever managed to get away and told her story in a courtroom… Mmmm… Let me have the exact address, please."

He wrote a line or two in his notebook. Very carefully. And steadily.

"Fine. I'll have a man over to Egmont tonight. With a note in your own handwriting to whoever's in cahoots with you. A private gumshoe lad who knows all the answers and charges accordingly. You're paying for that, Willie. You're also going to pay for the swellest private ambulance that ever rolled on balloon tires. And a couple of the best nutrition experts I can find."

Jerry Tracy smiled.

"So the war seems to be over, eh, Willie? All except the indemnity. No peace terms complete without indemnity. Let's see… They'll need a home, won't they? Not in the city—Ruthie and her poor devil of a mother have had plenty of the merry old city life, don't you think? A neat little house in a cute suburb. Eight thousand bucks for the house, say. Then there'll have to be chickens, telephone, a radio, decent plumbing… Fifteen grand might do it… No, better write me out a check for twenty G's."

He delved into the wreckage of Zigger's coat and found a check-book. Gravely he uncapped his own fountain pen and presented it to the radio comic.

"And—Willie, my lad—if you hope to stop payment on this thing or cause me any heartburn whatever, I'll produce Ruthie Brenner in a courtroom, much as I hate to—and make your name stink in every newspaper in the land. I'll let you figure out for yourself how many years you're likely to spend among camphor if you force me to produce the girl."

Zigger said faintly: "I dunno whether I got twenty grand."

"Then find it. Borrow it somewhere. Chisel it. That's up to you… And hurry that check along, please. I've got to go places."

He made Zigger sign four checks before the signature looked pleasing to him, free from tremor.

"You're staying here," he told Butch. "Keep your eye on this bird. And don't forget that overgrown ape in the cellar. I'll send over some canned goods and whatever else you need. I've got to wait till a check goes through and attend to a couple of other little details. Vacation for you, Zigger. Aren't you glad?"

Zigger's eyes popped suddenly with a new terror. A despairing realization of something he had forgotten.

"My broadcast!" he wailed. "I'll miss it. Lemme go. You gotta lemme go! Please—please…."

"Dry your tears. You've missed it already."

Butch had to attend to the radio comic for a moment. Not very long; he quieted easily.

"You can't get away with this!" his muffled voice snarled. "They'll pick up your trail from the penthouse. They'll be combing the city to find me. They'll—"

"They'll do nothing of the kind, Willie. I forestalled all that with a little message to Anderson, the discreet personage downstairs. Incidentally, Anderson is the first guy I'm calling on tonight. There's a quick glazing job to be done on that glass door of yours—it's probably done already. Then there'll be a little expert perjury to be arranged. You went away, I imagine, on a drunken bat with a shapely and unidentified blonde. Boy, will *that* make things plausible! By the way, did you know that Anderson is on my payroll? And werry, werry grateful for past favors?"

Jerry Tracy slipped on the snappy-looking light topcoat, adjusted the expensive grey hat with the snapbrim.

"So long! Okie doke."

Zigger dived partly out of the chair with an inarticulate cry of anguish. Butch bounced him right back again.

The door slammed. A front window-pane flared briefly in the brilliance of strong headlights. Then the light faded with the diminishing hum of a motor.

Butch said, reflectively: "Jeeze, I sure hope Jerry remembers about *liverwurst*. How about you, keed? D'yuh like *liverwurst?*" He licked his thick lips and swallowed with an anticipatory delight. "It's grand, fried. In buffer...."

His big shoulder turned and he gazed at the rows of built-in bookcases. His eyes glazed with a complete lack of interest.

"Jeeze, I sure wish tonight was Tuesday. Nothin' to read in this dump but books! I could do with a copy of *Variety*."

So could Tracy, apparently.

ON THE FOLLOWING Tuesday the *Daily Planet's* immaculately dressed little columnist tilted comfortably back in his battered old office chair. He was reading with frowning attention a brief item in Broadway's familiar Bible. An item tucked away in a mess of wordage headed "Inside Stuff."

Butch yawned and made hopeful shufflings on the floor with his thick soles.

"Nearly finished, Boss? Anything new?"

"Yeah. Death notice, Butch. Lemme read it to you."

The columnist shifted his crossed legs and rattled the paper.

"Krumby Kracker setup canceled unexpectedly Friday (12). Reason unexplained absence from ether of Willie Zigger, m.c. and gag comic. Zigger's third offense and sponsor takes advantage of trick clause inserted in contract by mutual agreement after last Zigger outbreak. New setup reported to be about same. Name band, quartette and gag comic. Randy Yosseloff and his boys seem to have inside track on band nod. Audish for new comic Wednesday (17) with odds favoring either Walter McKee or Ray Harkins. Zigger out of town and future plans indefinite. Krumby Kracker account handled by MacTavish and Fenn, Bill Bradman directing."

Butch said, irrelevantly: "How's the kid and the old lady coming along?"

"Very nicely, Butch. Dropped in on 'em yesterday and had a look. All they need is vitamins and a chance to sleep without alarm clocks for a while."

He crackled the Broadway weekly in his lean hand and smiled.

"Only one mistake in this yarn here, Butch."

"Yeah? What's that?"

"It says Zigger's future plans are indefinite. I got a hunch that they're pretty damned *definite*."

"How come, Jerry?"

"He never was a real comic," Tracy said slowly. "Just pure accident. He got a lucky break—and clicked. He'll never click again in a million years. Watch him with his next sponsor. He won't last out the first thirteen weeks… Nope. Zigger's plans are definite. He's going places, Butch."

"I'll bite. Where's he goin'?"

Tracy's face became utterly expressionless. His voice held neither satisfaction nor sorrow.

"Right where he started, Butch. Where he belongs. In the gutter."

Murderer's Guest

Jerry Tracy, Broadway wiseguy, is asked to front for a murderer

FAULTLESSLY ATTIRED IN EVENING clothes, formally correct down to the last little accessory, Jerry Tracy rang the front doorbell of John P. Barker's imposing town residence on Park Avenue.

The Little Guy's jaunty elegance masked a complete inner bewilderment. There was no sensible reason on God's green earth why the shrewd and sensational columnist of the *Daily Planet* should be invited to dinner and a formal evening at the John P. Barkers'—yet here he was! There was a catch in it somewhere, a mysterious riddle of some sort behind that engraved invitation—and Jerry Tracy had come grimly to find out the answer. Jerry was old enough in the horn to know that blue-bloods like the Barkers had no logical reason for inviting a Broadway wise-guy. Okey; so why did they want him here tonight?

The door opened suddenly and Tracy grinned cockily at a stoutish, frigid-faced butler.

"Evening, Michael, my good man."

"Hunter, sir." The butler coughed in well-bred reproof. "May I see your invitation?"

"You may."

He watched the solemn butler glance at it. Tracy himself knew the blame thing by heart. It had arrived early that afternoon and he had studied it frowningly about two dozen times since.

The austere Hunter was smiling, thawing a little.

"If you'll kindly follow me, sir? Thank you, sir."

He led the way down the dimly illuminated length of a gorgeous 1890 corridor and threw open a huge Arabian Nights door.

"Mister Tracy!"

Eight or nine people were chatting noisily in the big room. Tracy spotted the hostess instantly. She looked about the same as her rotogravure pictures in the society sheets.

"How do you do, Mister—er—Tracy?" she said.

"Good evening, Mrs. Barker."

The old guy standing next to her, with the rounded Santa Claus belly, was old J.P. Barker himself. Financier, philanthropist, noted collector of rare stamps, lineal descendant of the

John P. Barker who left England in 1620 aboard the *Mayflower.*

He was gruffly cordial with Tracy but his tufted gray eyebrows rose slightly. He flicked a brief glance at his wife and got the same puzzled glance right back again.

It was obvious that neither of the Barkers had invited Jerry to their exclusive little shindig. Then who had? A pleasant little chill tickled the back of the columnist's sensitive scalp. This cock-eyed evening, he decided, was going to be good—werry good!

TRACY LET HIMSELF be taken in tow, nodded politely to a lot of well-dressed bozos. A manservant handed him a biscuit

and a glass of magnificent sherry. He sipped and let his eyes go to work.

Nobody here that he knew except by remembered photographs. He could look at the faces and ticket them geographically. That long, rangy lad was from points West; the hawk-nosed gent and his wife were Newport; Cannes and Lido flirting snugly over in the corner; the red-nosed dowager taking another snifter of sherry was Tuxedo Park—hospital committee, or something....

Tracy's alert eyes stopped suddenly. He knew that stunning sullen-eyed girl in the gorgeous green outfit. He had never met her—but he knew her plenty! Night-clubs, midnight razzmatazz, fox hunts, tickets for speeding... The screwy Lily, the only cheeild of Mr. and Mrs. John Barker. Bored as hell. Being nice, with an effort, to a military-looking gent who was buzzing her very quietly and watching his sherry while he talked.

The *Daily Planet* columnist butted in on them. After a while the military gent shrugged and went away. Lily laughed low in her white throat; a hard, sneering little sound.

"Thank you, Mr. Tracy. Do I know you?"

"We might start now... Er—who was the gentleman with the nice clean shave? I'm afraid I annoyed him."

Lily laughed again. There was uneasiness in that laugh of hers, Tracy suddenly discovered.

"Major Robert Griscom," she murmured. "Do you like people without imagination?"

"I don't know. In my business I never meet 'em."

"Lovely! Do you need an assistant? Your business, of course, being—"

Tracy studied the reckless gray eyes. "Suppose I tell you about it—at dinner?"

"Agreed," she said promptly. Almost too promptly. "I'll get Hunter to switch the place cards—and I hope that won't make you too conceited."

"It'll make me sparkle with brilliance," Tracy chuckled.

He bowed and drifted away. The room was filling with more people. Jerry let a servant refill his sherry glass and thought a little about this hard-shelled, glamorous Lily. More than hard-shelled, if rumor was right. Downright ugly. A girl who liked to smack down things—and people—that got too annoyingly in her way. Exclusive surroundings—if she chose to stick to them—and careful training hadn't been able to do much about it. Lily Barker was emphatically Grandpa Barker's girl—that infamous old stock market devil whose piratical millions were now being spent by the pious John P. on peace foundations and pigeon fountains!

Was Lily behind this cock-eyed social invitation? She seemed ready as rain to sit next to Tracy at dinner. Was that "Do I know you?" stuff of hers a bluff? And if not Lily—then who? Somebody had invited him to this solid-plush *soirée* for some damned good reason!

His attention moved again towards Major Griscom. The major was chatting politely with two aged ladies in a discreet corner. Watching him, an idea came suddenly to Tracy, a fantastic and dopey notion. He had a queer feeling that somebody had rubbed something off the major with an eraser.

Griscom bowed finally, left his two ladies—and Tracy had the answer. Got it from something he hadn't noticed before. The major's hip! Some undefined stiffness in that left hip of

Griscom's; a something that imparted a slight side-motion to his walk. And—bango!—a gray mustache jumped into place on the major's clean-shaven lip. That's what had been rubbed off. The mustache!

About a year or so ago; Tracy remembered it grimly now. A narrow stage. Hard white lights. Tracy, sitting next to a husky old veteran of an Irishman named O'Grady—Chief Inspector O'Grady to a lot of first-class dicks with black masks over their attentive eyes. Morning lineup at Police Headquarters.

A guy up there on the stage with a suave, sneering smile and a slightly bum left hip. Major Robert Griscom, hell! His name had been Mr. Hubert Eldrick on that brightly lit morning down at P.H. No charge against the guy; just a routine pickup for the lads in the black masks to remember. Suspicion of larceny, suspicion of extortion, suspicion of polite confidence games… A brief, formal hearing and released… And now, Major Robert Griscom, if you please! At the John P. Barkers' exclusive little rootietoot. More suavely at home, damn him, than the *Daily Planet's* mystified little columnist.

Is Griscom the guy who sent me that phoney invitation, Tracy wondered. Nuts—it didn't make sense! If the fake major was here for anything at all, he was here for a finger-finger job. Maybe a wall safe somewhere with a fat string of pearls; maybe blackmail; whatever it was, something that would need careful timing, a good front, a blandly innocent getaway. In that case why should Griscom lug in a shrewd newspaper guy like Jerry Tracy? Nope to that. No dice….

Then who *did* send the invitation? The thing was beginning to get Tracy's goat. Maybe John Barker himself—or his wife?—had some important confidential reason that would come out later in the evening. Maybe Lily Barker, with her smoldering, enigmatic eyes. Maybe even Griscom—if you could figure out why!

The phoney set-up bewildered Jerry. He looked from face to face. Somebody here needed him—for what?

LILY BARKER'S HARSH little chuckle at his ear startled the columnist.

"Frowning, Mr. Tracy? Don't tell me the dull, respectable atmosphere of the ancestral mansion is getting you down, too."

Tracy smiled at her. "Did you have any luck with Hunter?"

"Excellent luck, my friend. The place cards have been changed. In a moment or two you're going to take me in to dinner." Her voice lowered suddenly. "Careful! Major Griscom is coming over now to claim me as his table partner. I'll be very gracious—but efficient."

She was. If the major felt any disappointment over his rebuff, he hid it gallantly. The enormous dining-room doors slid apart. Hunter's rolling tones announced that dinner was served.

Tracy enjoyed the meal, disregarding the puzzled glances of the other guests, concentrating on a bright line of Park Avenue gab with Lily Barker. Underneath her careless smile she was studying him intently. She reminded him of his promise to tell her all about himself. He told her in one word. With a grin.

"Typewriters?" Lily pouted and looked baffled. "You mean you sell the things?"

"I write on 'em."

"That's better. What do you write?"

"Biography," he said dryly. "I like to study people. Like you, Miss Barker. Like Major Griscom, for instance."

The girl's face flushed queerly. "What do you know about the major?"

"Will you be offended," Tracy whispered boldly, "if I speak frankly?" He watched her reaction as he handed it to her: "The major, in my professional opinion, is a lead dime, a bit of the 'queer,' a phoney, a subway slug, a greasy quarter, a rubber check... You catchee what I mean?"

There was nothing to read in her face, he discovered regretfully; just the slow beat of a tiny pulse at her temple, the relaxed curve of her fingers around the handle of her fork. He let things go at that. Plenty of time before the evening was over. He tried one last shot.

"By the way, am I indebted to you for my—invitation?"

"You mean tonight? Are you serious?"

Smiling at her, he shook his head. "Just joking," he said.

Lily Barker gave up after a while and over the salad and dessert got quietly morose. Once Tracy caught her gray eyes squarely on him and saw what he had half expected to see— anger, apprehension, hate. It was gone in an instant like a shutter banging closed on a window.

The ladies were rising now. John P. Barker beamed from the head of the table; and coffee, liqueurs and cigars appeared for the relaxed males. Barker's fingers dipped shakingly into his pocket and he dropped a tiny white pellet into his black coffee. He caught Tracy's glance, smiled apologetically, made a pathetic little gesture of self-derision.

"Saccharine tablets," Tracy thought. "The poor old guy is a diabetic."

He tried to keep Barker's attention, to give the old guy a chance to send him a private eye-signal that would mean:

"Stick around, Jerry! We'll talk later on. I sent you that under-cover invitation myself. On the quiet. Keep it under the hat for the present."

But Barker sent no such signal. Somebody else got talking to the old man and he got busy in a long wheezy conversation. Hunter came in presently and slid back the big doors. They passed through into the music room.

Tracy found a chair and sat quietly down near the Barkers. Major Griscom was diagonally across from him, talking defer-entially to the older man. Barker listened to him without much interest, eyelids drooping sleepily, hands twined together over his fat stomach. Next to him, his wife watched the prepara-tions for the concert with a tight little smile that Tracy thought looked mean. He watched her keenly. Occasionally she turned a little to listen to some whispered comment from her scowling daughter. What a family!

A patter of applause sounded. Into the tiny circle of dim light in the far corner around the harp, came the bared, sand-alled feet of a slim girl in a flowing white robe that was just translucent enough to be interesting. Señorita Lora y Gil. A pale blonde with supple wrists and softly gracious arms. She smiled, bowed, seated herself.

And then, suddenly, the gold harp strings quivered—and Tracy forgot everything but the lovely ripple of exquisite music. In spite of himself he forgot the room, forgot the almost invis-ible guests, drifted in the darkness with glorious music....

A hand nudged him. Half drowsily, he shook it off. Again the hand nudged him. Furtively. Insistently.

Tracy's head turned. In the darkness he could barely make out the butler's livery. It was Hunter, almost invisible in the darkness. The slight backward jerk of Hunter's head said unmistakably: "If you please, sir. Back this way, sir."

He melted out of the room. The folds of a velvet curtain swayed together without sound behind him.

JERRY TRACY TOOK his time getting up. Nobody noticed him as he passed quietly behind the curtain. Beyond it a door stood ajar and Hunter was there, beckoning urgently, waiting to close it. Tracy followed the butler through a dimly lit sitting-room and into another. The music of the harp was a faint, tantalizing echo.

Jerry scowled and dropped his bored manner. "Okey, Hunter! Your turn at bat. What are we playing now—cops and robbers?"

"Please!" the butler whispered. "They'll hear you, sir."

"So what?" He eyed the man's face. "Wait a second! Don't tell me that *you* sent me the invitation?"

"Invitation, sir? I don't understand."

"To this party here, dope!"

Still Hunter didn't seem to understand. His fleshy face was twitching with nervous terror.

"For God's sake, sir, you must help! You—you really must. I recognized you the instant you came in the door tonight. Aren't you Mr. Jerry Tracy, sir—the columnist and police investigator?"

"Did I say no?"

"Oh, thank God! I told Charlie I was right! It's a lucky godsend that brings you here tonight, sir."

"Yes? Who is this Charlie that you tell things to?"

"Not a man, sir. A woman."

"Huh?"

Hunter groaned suddenly and wrung his hands. "Please, Mr.

Tracy, we're wasting precious time. I'm horribly afraid. I tell you that any second there may be—"

"Yeah? Hold your horses! Let's get something else settled first. Did you send me an invitation to the party here tonight?"

"I? No, sir."

"You didn't know I was coming until I showed up here tonight?"

"No, sir. I recognized you instantly and I told Charlie that she ought to—"

"Okey... Tell me something else: who is this Charlie that turns out to be a woman?"

"Charlotte, sir. A lady's maid employed here. I sometimes call her by the shorter nickname for convenien—"

"Sure. Charlie over the water, Charlie over the sea." Tracy was watching the butler intently. The guy was scared sick; shaking with a genuine case of the jitters. More than scared—terrified! Tracy had seen too much real terror in his dealings with the police not to recognize it instantly when he saw it again.

"Exactly what is wrong here, Hunter?"

"I'm terribly frightened, sir. Mr. Barker—"

"What about him?"

Hunter's face quivered. The fool was sweating, Tracy saw, like a pig in an icebox.

"He's in danger of being murdered—tonight. Charlie begged me to tell you. Will you come with me and talk with her— and *do* something? Neither of us dares to speak to anyone else here. No one would believe us—and it would create a frightful scandal in the household. It's—it's awful—and Charlie has no proof—but maybe if you watched the master and kept an eye on him until this damnable evening is over—"

Tracy's fingers dug into Hunter's wavering arm.

"Where is this Charlie right now?"

"In the dining-room, sir."

"Can we get there by some sort of side entrance?"

"Yes, sir. That's why I—"

"Oke," Tracy snapped alertly. "Let's go!"

Hunter led the way. They crossed a narrow hall, went through a well-stocked pantry and on into the kitchen. A tremendously fat Irishwoman in a spotless white uniform was busily superintending the dishwashing activity of two younger women, up to their wet elbows in soapy water. At sight of Tracy's faultless evening attire the clatter of dishes stopped abruptly. The cook eyed Hunter with frosty hostility and curtsied briefly to the guest.

"It's all right, Ethel," Hunter said quickly.

Hunter pushed open a swinging door and Tracy followed him into the vast empty dining-room. A girl in the trim uniform of a lady's maid rose quickly from a chair and stared timidly at the two men.

"This is Mr. Tracy, Charlotte," Hunter whispered. "He was kind enough to come, thank God!"

She glided swiftly forward like a pale, haggard ghost.

"You know?" she whispered. "Has Hunter told you what I—"

She was a woman, not a girl. In the half light of the empty dining-room, the slimness of her figure had deceived Tracy. He saw now that the face of Charlotte was definitely middle-aged. Her eyes were crawling with the same swirl of nameless anxiety—terror—that he had seen in Hunter's. For a moment they stared at each other, the newspaper columnist and the lady's maid; and the air of the dining-room throbbed softly with the muted echo of harp music from the room beyond the closed sliding doors.

"You've got to help us, sir," Charlotte gasped.

Tracy said curtly. "You suspect murder? An attempt at murder—here, tonight?"

Charlotte's face was like marble. "God knows, sir, I hate to accuse anyone, but—" She drew a long, shuddering breath. "Mr. Tracy, as the Lord is my judge, I'm afraid Miss Lily is going to murder her father tonight!"

"What makes you think so?"

"She's hidden the poison, sir. Took it from the medicine chest in the bathroom. Her own medicine chest. That's where I saw it this morning. I—I thought I might have mislaid it myself, but it was gone. I was afraid and I searched her room while she was taking her bath. I found it in the second drawer of her dresser. I didn't touch it. It's—cyanide of potassium, sir."

"Well? What of it? Miss Barker might have wanted the stuff for any one of a million different reasons."

"Not Miss Lily," the maid breathed. "She's a devil. A cold, calculating devil."

"You hate her, don't you?"

"Yes, I do," Charlotte gasped. "I do! And why shouldn't I? Her father hates her. So does her mother. Grief and sorrow is all that she's brought them. I tell you, terrible things are going on in this old house. If you don't believe me, Mr. Tracy—look at this!"

SHE PULLED THE starched uniform away from her shoulder and Tracy blinked as he saw five little scabs of dried blood on Charlotte's pale skin.

"That's where she clawed me like a—a tigress this morning, sir. While I was combing her hair. You see, she got another one of them phone calls this morning—and she's always a demon after she finishes talking to that—that man."

"What man?"

"I don't know, sir. Whoever he is, he's trying to get money out of her, sir—that I'm certain of. For the last week, every single day, sir—she's been begging and storming at her father to give her fifty thousand dollars."

"Fifty grand, eh?" Tracy whistled softly. "You absolutely sure about that?"

"Ask Hunter. He heard the quarrels and the goings-on, too. They carried on terrible, sir—Miss Lily and her father. He's a grand old man, lovable and kind—if you forget his foolishness about the stamps—"

Swift interest flared into Tracy's eyes. "Stamps? You mean postage stamps?... Never mind... Tell me more about Lily."

"She raved at her father, sir, about that money she wants. Told him he was depriving her of her rightful inheritance. Said he was treating her like an infant, doling out pennies to her that should be dollars—and dollars in her own right. Said she'd have that fifty thousand dollars, if she had to take it from him as his legal heir."

"Did you actually hear Lily say that, Charlotte?"

"I did," the maid whispered. "So did Hunter."

The butler nodded slowly. There was dignity in his bearing, no evasion.

"I listened at the keyhole, sir," he said gravely. "I love the master. I'd do anything to keep him from harm."

Something in the haggard contour of Charlotte's face seemed

to interest the *Daily Planet's* columnist. A vague thought grew in his mind.

"You sure you didn't send me my invitation, Charlotte?"

"Invitation?" His ignorance made her smile wanly. "I'm only a lady's maid, sir. The social secretary attends to that. Miss Dalton."

"I see. And either Mrs. Barker or Miss Dalton should know all about it, eh?"

"Of course. The mistress always tells Miss Dalton exactly who she wants."

Tracy nodded. "Now about the poison. The missing potassium cyanide. Is it still hidden in Lily's dresser, Charlotte?"

"I don't know, sir. It was there while she was taking her bath this morning. It was there before she dressed for dinner tonight."

Tracy's voice sounded confused, nettled. "Mmmm... What do you want me to do? Blow a police whistle?"

"You're a guest, sir," Hunter said faintly. "You can—watch things, if you will. Keep at the side of the master, see that—" He shuddered slightly, "—that the master doesn't drink anything that might—"

In the tense silence Tracy could hear the faint, muted ripple of the harp beyond the closed dining-room doors. Vaguely sweet it sounded, like an endless ripple of golden rain.

He looked at the maid and the butler; and again, temporarily, he put from his mind a shrewd guess he had made.

"You said something about stamps," he suggested.

"A hobby of the master's," Hunter murmured. "I only mentioned it because of the presence here tonight of Mr. Carron, who also is a collector of rare stamps, sir."

"What's he look like?" Tracy snapped.

"He's rather a tall man, sir. You must have noticed him. Sandy hair. Light complexion."

"Walks with a slight limp?" Tracy asked suddenly. "Something wrong with his hip?"

"Oh, no, sir. That's Major Griscom. Mr. Carron is thinner, taller. Surely you must have—"

"Yeah, I remember him… What about the stamps? Carron and Barker have an argument about stamps lately?"

"Well—in a way, yes. They both wanted an extremely rare Siamese one, with a native tree of some sort that has something to do with the cure of leprosy, I believe. This particular stamp, I heard Mr. Carron say once, is so valuable that it's worth more than a hundred thousand dollars."

"And Barker grabbed it off for himself?"

"The master bid it in—played a small financial trick on Mr. Carron, I'm afraid. They had a nasty scene or two, but Mr. Carron got over it and they're still the best of friends."

Mmm, Tracy thought, I wonder could it be possible that the very forgiving Mr. Carron is the kind friend who fixed it for me to get that invitation here tonight?

Harp music beat like the rush of a distant waterfall at the closed oaken doors of the dining-room.

"By the way, Hunter," Tracy said in a quiet, conversational tone, "how long have you and Charlotte been brother and sister?"

Hunter's face drained to a chalky white. His jaw sagged. He said thickly: "Sir?"

"You heard me. Come across."

"I—I don't understand."

"Tell him the truth, Edward," the maid whispered. She untwisted her hands, squared her tired shoulders. "We have nothing to hide, nothing to be ashamed of."

Hunter's eyes glared haggardly at the *Daily Planet's* columnist.

"Is it a crime, sir, to help one's own flesh and blood? One's own sister?"

"Not in my book," Tracy said gently. "We'll just forget about this private little personal angle."

"God bless you, sir," Hunter breathed.

Charlotte didn't say anything. Her brimming eyes said unspoken things that made the columnist feel pretty good.

Tracy shrugged. "I think that I'll—"

A SCREAM, A horrible, knifelike wail, cut across Tracy's whisper and killed it. Deadened by the closed doors of the dining-room, that shrill screech sounded eerily like a woman locked in a sealed tomb.

"What—what was that?" Hunter faltered.

From the music room there echoed a confused jumble of shouting. A dull thump, like the sound of a heavy chair being overturned, made the dining-room floor vibrate.

"Lights!" a hoarse voice was shouting. "Where are the lights? For God's sake, turn 'em on!"

The stupor left Tracy's limbs. In three swift jumps he had reached the closed doors. A jerk of his muscular wrists sent the heavy sliding doors crashing apart. Hunter darted past him, rushed towards the dim, tapestried wall. There was a faint click and the lights came on.

All that Tracy's brain seemed to register at first was the overturned harp. It had fallen to the floor in a dented ruin. The blond harpist in the white robe was trying hysterically to free her imprisoned left foot. The hem of her flimsy robe had caught on one of the big gilded pedals and was ripped halfway up her thigh. Unaware of her near nudity she was struggling hysterically to get her bleeding foot free. Tracy propped up the harp for a second and got her over to a chair.

At the other end of the room, Mrs. Barker was still screaming, pushing feebly at a suave gentleman who was trying to restrain her. On the rug in front of them both, flat on his face, lay John P. Barker.

"All right!" Tracy called out suddenly in a hard, clear command. "Stop all that noise in here! Everybody!"

He advanced slowly towards the motionless figure on the rug.

Successively, like quick motion picture flashes, the columnist's eye registered the various marionette figures in the music room. Major Griscom was wrestling gently with the wife of the man on the floor, pushing her soothingly into a chair. Lily Barker kept staring at the body of her father, with a pinched, white look about her intolerant nostrils and a hysterical tremor at her lips. Hunter was still over by the wall, his fingers still resting uncertainly on the light switch. Carron, the stamp man, a bare two feet from the body, was staring down at John P. Barker with a peculiar grimace on his calm lips, that might have been the faintest of sneers. Carron seemed to have his nerves well in hand; he was noticeably steadier than Griscom.

It was Major Griscom who first dropped to one knee beside the body. Tracy promptly shoved at him, knocked him off balance.

"Get away!" the columnist ordered. "Keep your paws off him!"

"Why, you bounder—what do you mean by—"

"This might be murder," Tracy snapped. "If so, I'll take charge until the police get on the job."

An elderly, efficient-looking man rushed forward. "I'm the family physician," he told Tracy. In a soberly quiet silence, he tested swiftly John Barker's heart, pulse, respiration. He pronounced the man stone dead.

Jerry's eyes lifted slightly, measured the assembled company.

"And don't any of you people go telephoning for an ambulance," he said with a premeditated harshness. "We won't be needing any tonight, thanks."

He watched Mrs. Barker take the news. She hadn't fainted. She didn't now. Lily's eyes were still darkly enigmatic; she looked sick with horror. The major very watchful; not half so angry as he had pretended to be. Carron, the stamp collector, was definitely grinning at the columnist.

"Exactly what happened in here, Mr. Carron?" Tracy asked him.

"Hard to say," the stamp man replied calmly. "For one thing, it was infernally dark in here—just a dim circle of light around the harp, the rest of the room pretty vague." He stared coolly at Tracy. "Matter of fact, I didn't even notice when you left the room, my friend. May I ask when that occurred? And why?"

Tracy frowned. "Suppose you let me attend to the questions, Mr. Carron. Did Mr. Barker cry out at all?"

"No. I thought he was asleep. He usually dozes at—er—musical affairs like this. The first thing any of us I knew was when Barker slid quietly out of his chair and hit the floor with a thump. Then Mrs. Barker screamed and we all—"

"But you didn't see or hear anything unusual before that?"

"Nothing at all. Not a thing. Sorry."

"Thank you, Mr. Carron." The physician moved close to Tracy. "You suggested it might be murder. Had you any reason to suspect that?" he asked.

"Suppose you tell me what you think," Tracy countered.

"It is impossible to tell at once," the physician answered slowly. "There is, however, a suspicious odor that might be cyanide."

"Is there a phone handy in here?" Tracy asked Hunter.

"Not here, Mr. Tracy. I can plug in a portable directly, sir."

"All right. Go ahead."

The butler turned obediently and Lily Barker's voice hit him in the back like a hard, icy hand: "Don't!"

Tracy said, with the mildest of smiles: "Do you want to climb into a patrol wagon, Miss Barker, and ride to a cell and perhaps have to answer a whole lot of questions—or do you want to behave sensibly?... Go ahead, Hunter. Plug that telephone in."

"Do you happen to be a policeman, Mr. Tracy?" Lily sneered. "I should have guessed it earlier—when I first saw the cut of your evening clothes."

Mrs. Barker shrugged and sat up straighter in her chair. "Who is this man? I've been wondering all evening how he got in here."

"You'll find my invitation on your tray out in the hall, madam," Tracy said. "As to who invited me—I'm as interested in that angle as you are. Did you invite me?"

"Certainly not!"

"Did your husband?"

Mrs. Barker didn't answer, just glared at him. Very definitely in a shrewish mood. Not so wrought up over the unexpected death of her husband as Tracy had first surmised.

With a gently quiet mockery the *Daily Planet's* wizened little columnist scanned the rest of them.

"Did you invite me, Major Griscom? Did you, Hunter? Did you, Mrs. Bascomb? Did you, Lily? Did you, Mr. Carron?"

He repeated the silly query patiently. Nobody answered him.

Jerry Tracy grinned. "All right—I'm here. What I'd like to know is: Who asked me to come? And why?"

He took the portable telephone from Hunter. Smiled over the transmitter at the assembled company.

"And what's more, radio listeners, I'm gonna stick close to this house till I find out what goes on."

He called Police Headquarters, and asked for Inspector Fitzgerald. Fitz was not there. He waited patiently until a switchboard relay carried his voice to Fitzgerald's modest home up on Cathedral Heights, in the shadow of Columbia University.

"Hello, Fitz? This is Jerry. Jerry Tracy."

He heard a low, angry gasp from Lily Barker.

"So that's who you are!" she said harshly. "Jerry Tracy! A cheap tabloid columnist! A keyhole snooper! A—a garbage collector!"

"Right," Tracy grinned. "With a proud record of always delivering the garbage. Never muffed a bum tomato in my life... Listen, Fitz! I'm down here in the John P. Barker residence. Somebody just bumped the old man... Looks like it. Poison, says little Jerry, and I don't think I'm wrong... Huh? Sure thing. I'll be werry glad to tell 'em, all of 'em. Be seeing you, keed."

He gave the telephone instrument back to Hunter.

"That was Inspector Fitzgerald, folks, in case you tuned in late. He wants me to tell you that if anybody present tries to leave this house before he gets here, he'll pick 'em up with a warrant and heave 'em in the can—jail, to you."

He walked about the room, leisurely examining the rug. They watched him bend over suddenly, pick something up. He examined the object behind his cupped palm, then placed it carefully in his pocket.

"If necessary," he told the watchful faces, "I'll put Hunter and a few of the boys in plush on the doors. But if you'll take my advice, you'll forget all about the exits. All people will sit yourselves quietly down and start chewing your nails very thoughtfully. An alibi isn't going to hurt anybody in here."

THE POLICE WHEELS began turning presently, without much confusion. Inspector Fitzgerald took charge, with the inevitable Sergeant Killan at his elbow. The guests were assembled in the library and a uniformed patrolman went on duty at the front door.

Max Goldfarb, the chubby little medical examiner, got professionally chummy with the corpse. He took his time, examined John Pennington Barker with slow, painstaking thoroughness.

"Dead very recently," Max said. "Within an hour, maybe even sooner. Drugged first. Poisoned afterwards. The guy's a diabetic; I thought at first it might be an insulin collapse. But it's a poison job, all right. Potassium cyanide or a derivative. Administered hypodermically in the side of the neck. A needle or a long slender pin of some sort, coated with the stuff—probably made a paste of it with glycerine. Hole in the neck closed up almost instantly; but there's a tiny drop of coagulated blood to show where the jab went in."

"Jabbed while he was drugged, eh?" Fitzgerald growled. He glanced at the *Daily Planet* man. "You were on the spot, Jerry. Any slants?"

"Call Hunter in," Tracy suggested.

Sergeant Killan got the butler. Tracy smiled faintly and showed the butler the object he took from his pocket. It was a long, slender pin with a round white head. The head was soiled and indented slightly on one side, as though someone had stamped hastily on it with a hard leather heel.

"Recognize this pin, Hunter?"

"I can't say that I do, sir."

"Is Miss Barker still wearing her spray of orchids?"

The butler hesitated, looked uneasy. "I—I don't think so."

"Ever seen a pin of this type before?"

"I believe it's the sort of pin that—er—"

He stopped talking, looked white and unhappy.

Tracy nodded. "Okey, Hunter. That's all. Beat it."

"Orchids, eh?" Fitzgerald muttered. "A corsage pin. Is that what you mean?"

"Correct, me lad. Couldn't possibly be anything else. The kind of pin that you get nowhere else on earth but from a florist. I picked the thing up back of Barker's chair. It was crushed deep into the rug." He added, absently: "I noticed that Lily Barker wasn't wearing her orchid spray when the lights went on, Fitz."

"Yeah? Come on, Sarge."

"Wait a minute," Tracy said. "I'd like to make a small guess about the drug angle before you go." He smiled at little Max Goldfarb. "You were right about the guy being a diabetic. You might try analyzing a couple of the poor old fella's saccharine pills. You'll probably find 'em very sleepy-sleepy. He had one of 'em in his coffee tonight."

He glanced at the inspector.

"And Fitz, before I tackled that hard-boiled daughter of Barker's, I'd talk to the maid, Charlotte, first if I were you. Then Hunter."

"Anything else on the ball, Jerry?"

"See what you make of Carron, the stamp collector. And don't get too excited if I tell you that Major Griscom is a guy who could stand a lot of questioning. He dates back to the time before you were in favor down at Headquarters. If you can't get him to talk much—ask Inspector O'Grady."

"Hey—where are you going?"

Tracy stopped at the door. "Just looking around. Page me after you've lined up all your dope."

Fitz nodded to Killan. "We'll examine 'em all in the dining-room, Sergeant. One at a time. The maid first—get the Barker girl's maid."

"Name's Charlotte," Tracy murmured and closed the door behind him.

He wandered out to the front hall, nodded genially to the cop on duty, poked unobtrusively about. Hunter went by, looking pale and distraught, and Tracy buttonholed him. He asked the butler questions, and on the answers drew a roughly penciled floor plan on the back of an old envelope, marked the various rooms with quick, nervous scrawls.

After a while he walked leisurely upstairs to the second floor.

Lily Barker's room was about midway from the end of a long carpeted corridor. Tracy rapped briskly on the panel. No answer. He rapped again. Not a sound. He was turning the knob softly when the corridor plunged suddenly into total darkness. He heard the soft *thud-thud* of feet, tried swiftly to turn—and received a smashing impact on the back of his skull.

It was a hasty blow, poorly aimed, but it dropped him to the floor in a dazed huddle. Dimly he heard the soft patter of retreating feet. Someone was screaming faintly.

"What's the matter? Is anything wrong?"

The lights came on suddenly and flooded the corridor with brilliance.

Lily Barker was the one who had screamed so half-heartedly. Her door was wide open. She was standing there looking at the dazed columnist. Staring at him with an expression that Tracy couldn't be sure was relief—or disappointment.

HUNTER CAME RUNNING down the corridor. The blond Mr. Carron was right at his heels. Together, they helped Mr. Tracy to his feet, murmuring shocked and puzzled words. There was a ragged gash in Tracy's scalp and he dabbed at it gingerly with a handkerchief.

"What in the world has happened to you?" Carron said suavely, with the faintest tinge of mockery in his voice.

"Who just turned on those corridor lights? Did you turn 'em on again?"

"Not I, my friend."

"I did," Hunter said slowly. "I heard someone scream—sounded like a woman—"

"It was I who screamed," Lily said. "Pardon the emotional outburst." She kept staring at Tracy. It was disappointment,

Tracy decided, not relief. Behind the mask of her smooth face, Lily was grimly disappointed about something.

"—ran upstairs from the main hall," Hunter was saying. "Saw that the corridor was dark. So I threw the hall switch properly—and there you were, sir."

"Yeah. There I was… Whose room is that by the corridor switch? Barker's, isn't it? The dead man's room?"

"Yes, sir."

"Anyone in there?"

"I couldn't say, sir."

"Maybe I can. Stay here, all of you."

Tracy went down the hall, opened the door. There was nobody inside. Everything quietly normal. However, to Tracy's morose eyes, the picture on the south wall looked the least wee bit askew. He lifted it and smiled briefly as he saw the tiny wall safe behind it. The safe was closed and locked.

He went back to the group in the hall. "Battle's over, folks. Not much of a battle, at that. Too small for Fitz even to hear it downstairs. Which may, or may not, mean something."

Lily Barker started to close her door and he laid a sternly detaining hand on her arm.

"May I come in and chat a while?"

"Is that a request or a command, Mr. Tracy?"

"What do you think?"

She shrugged and turned her back. He followed her inside and closed the door.

"Why didn't you answer my knock before, Miss Barker? I knocked twice, you know, and got no answer. Were you—afraid?"

"I'm afraid of nothing," she told him gravely. A flame blazed briefly back of her coldly somber eyes. She glanced at his cut scalp. "Not even of you, Mr. Jerry Tracy. Or weren't you going to ask me about that?"

"Did you poison your father, Miss Barker?"

She laughed at him. A hard and musical little jeer. "Do you think it's the usual thing for daughters to murder their loving parents? Oh, I forgot—you're Jerry Tracy, of the dirty little *Planet*. Of course I murdered Dad! Picture on page two! Have you your camera all ready? A small one—hidden in the leg of your trousers, perhaps?"

"Leave the sarcastic cracks to me," Tracy said. "I do that stuff much better. They pay me dough for it."

Again Lily Barker laughed. She was holding herself in check with an iron will. But she was horribly nervous.

"Have the servants told you about my shrewish temper, Mister Dirt Gatherer? Have they told you how I hate this horrible old tomb of a house—and everyone in it? Have they told you that I think my sainted mother is a pious fake and my father a tyrannical old fool? If they haven't, Mister Tabloid Columnist, I'm telling you now. And you can tell your moron readers of the *Planet* that I'm bearing up bravely under the shock of my father's unfortunate demise. Tell them that, Mister Snooper."

Jerry was completely unimpressed.

"A little old-fashioned bawling act would make you feel a whole lot better," he growled. "You're on the verge of hysterics. You hardboiled dames give me a pain."

"Finish talking and get out of my room, damn you!" she shrilled at him.

"Okey. Let's both stay hard. We'll skip the murder charge for the present. I came in to see you about something else."

She got calmer all of a sudden. Watched him warily. "Hadn't you better talk about the three things you haven't said much about?"

"All right." Tracy chuckled. "Name three."

"A motive. A weapon. An opportunity."

"Make it four," Tracy said. "Add an accomplice."

"May I ask what you have in mind now?"

"You may ask, Dollink, but you won't get any answers." He pointed negligently towards her dresser. "Mind if I get nosey?"

"Not at all. Try and not leave any dirty thumb-marks on my underthings. I'd hate to have to burn them."

He went through the dresser very carefully. She watched him with a sneering, triumphant smile.

"Find what you wanted, Mr. Keyhole?"

"Nope. I was looking for a bottle of silver polish."

"I should think brass polish would suit you better. Why not look downstairs in the kitchen?"

"Or your bathroom?" Tracy suggested. He drew a blank on that. She didn't register a thing.

"By the way, what happened to your orchid corsage? Wilted?"

"Yes. I always throw flowers away when they wilt. I can't bear to wear them after that."

He bowed suddenly. "Sorry to have disturbed you. If you'll excuse me, I'll run back home to my newspaper cesspool."

Lily Barker made no comment to that. Walked to the door with her back as straight as a poker and shut him out.

The servants' stairs were at the rear of the hall. Tracy went down the flight and paused on the landing, his brow furrowed thoughtfully. Suddenly he stiffened, his ears became alert. Was that a groan he had heard or did he imagine it? It was very faint; but he was sure he had heard a groan. A man this time, too, not a woman!

His tensed fingers undamped from the stair-rail. He bounded upstairs to the second floor and stared down the long carpeted corridor. Lily Barker's door was still closed. The corridor was very quiet, bathed brightly in prosaic yellow electric light. Everything seemed exactly the same as it had been a minute or two before. Except—

The little columnist's breath sucked in sharply. A bedroom door was open! One that he had carefully closed himself. John Barker's door. The dead man's room!

Tracy sped silently down the corridor. An idea ran hand-in-hand with him; the memory of a framed etching hanging slightly askew, with a wall safe behind it. Was someone at it again? The same guy who had tried it before?

The bedroom was dark, the shades tightly drawn on the windows. The light from the hallway showed Jerry a dim figure lying face-down on the floor, beyond the bed. The *Daily Planet* columnist sprang into the room, fumbled for the light button, clicked the room into sudden brilliance.

He turned over the man on the floor and grunted disgustedly. It was Hunter, the butler. Hunter's eyes were closed and his face a pasty white. The back of his scalp was damp with blood where someone had struck him. The same sort of ragged little gash as the one that still throbbed uneasily on Tracy's own scalp.

HUNTER'S EYELIDS FLUTTERED. He groaned weakly: "I believe I've been—hit, sir."

Jerry got an arm under him and helped him up to the chair.

The butler's eyes widened with horror as he saw the framed picture lying upsidedown on the bed. He pointed weakly.

"The picture, sir. Someone—"

"So I gather," Jerry said shortly. His glance jerked across towards the tiny safe in the wall. The door of the safe was still apparently shut. He walked over, reached up and tried it. Locked, as before.

"Feel all right now, Hunter? Can you talk now?"

"I'm—I'm all right, sir."

"What happened?"

"I—I scarcely know, sir." He put a shaky hand to his scalp and winced. "I was on my guard, sir, so to speak, after what had happened to you. I loitered down below stairs, wondering whether the fellow who had attacked you might not be still hiding somewhere up here. I thought that perhaps I might watch to see whoever came down the stairs later and make a mental note of it, sir, for your information."

"And it turned out to be a bum idea? Go ahead, Hunter."

"And then, suddenly, it seemed to me that I heard a tiny noise—like someone tapping with a hammer on metal. It came from up here. There was no policeman in sight, I didn't know where you were—so I crept silently up the stairs. The master's door was closed. I opened it very cautiously, stepped inside to investigate—and someone struck me from behind and—well, knocked me silly, sir, if I may use the expression."

"Who was it? Get any kind of a look at the guy?"

"No, sir. I didn't. You see, the fellow sprang at me from the rear and—"

"Okey. Or rather—nuts!" Savage disappointment rode high in Tracy's eyes. "Tell me something, Hunter. Who else besides the dead guy—this John Barker gent—knew the combination of that wall safe?"

"No one, sir." The butler shook his bleeding head positively. "It's the master's own private safe."

"No one? Are you sure? His wife, maybe? How about his daughter? Wouldn't they know?"

"No, sir. To my own personal knowledge, no one had ever closed or opened that safe but the master."

"Any idea what's in it?"

Hunter hesitated. "I'd be only guessing, sir."

"Go ahead and guess."

"Currency, perhaps. Securities, maybe. Possibly stamps."

"Postage stamps, you mean?"

Hunter nodded. "I'm familiar with most of his collection, sir. That is, most of them are kept in large books with no attempt at concealment. But some of the more valuable ones might be in the safe."

Tracy's eyes got narrow and thoughtful. "Like that Siamese one, for instance?"

"I don't know, sir. He never showed that stamp to me."

"And he never told you—or anyone else as far as you know—the combination of the safe?"

"No, sir."

"Check." Tracy grinned ruefully. "Let's get the hell out of here and find us a place to wash. We can both stand a bit of scalp-scrubbing, I guess."

Sergeant Killan almost bumped into them as they stepped into the hall. The sergeant stopped short and his eyes bulged with blank amazement.

"Hello! What the hell have you lads been doing? A fight, or something?"

"Yeah," Jerry said dryly. "Didn't you hear it?"

"Not me. I was just coming up here to get that young Barker dame. Fitz wants to talk to her." His eyes narrowed. "What goes on, Jerry? This lad Hunter been pulling a fast one?"

"Nope. Someone has been bopping Hunter and me on the dome—one at a time."

"Yeah? Something phoney up here, eh? Stick around a second. I'll get Fitz up here right away."

Jerry shook his head to that. "Don't bother. You go ahead and get the girl down to Fitz. I want to go downstairs myself. Got an idea I'd like to look around. How about you, Hunter?"

Hunter shuddered and nodded wanly.

"Downstairs will surely seem a lot more comfortable to me, sir," he quavered.

They waited at the head of the stairs for Killan and Miss Barker. She looked at the butler's bleeding head with a small, tight smile.

"What in the world has happened to you, Hunter?"

"Someone struck me, Miss."

"What—again?" She laughed out-right, spoke jeeringly to Tracy: "You two gentlemen really ought to be in a shooting gallery. Don't you *ever* remember to duck?"

For once in his cocksure life, Jerry Tracy had no comeback. Instead, he said gruffly to Killan: "Keep all this stuff under the hat. I'll talk to Fitz about it later on."

They all went downstairs and Hunter walked unsteadily back to the kitchen. Tracy wandered soberly through the music room and the library, scowling at the scattering of men and women who stole silent, interested glances at his damaged pate.

The faint chuckle of Major Griscom infuriated him, but he

managed to keep his rising temper in leash.

"Seen Mr. Carron anywhere about, Major?"

"Why, yes. He was in the dining-room answering questions for your jolly old inspector friend a little while ago. Then he took a book, I believe, and went into the library… What happened to the head, old fellow? A lump, by Jove! You've an egg on the scalp, old fellow, like a bloody ostrich affair."

Tracy whirled irritably away from him towards Mrs. Bascomb.

"Tell me, madam, has this alleged British humorist been in here during the last five minutes or so?"

"Why, no." Mrs. Bascomb stared at him mildly. "Major Griscom came in here just before you did."

"I see. Thank you, madam… Where were you, Griscom?"

"Oh—just knocking about. Rather a bore here, don't you think?"

"Upstairs, maybe? Were you, Major?"

He chuckled musically. "Oh, dear, no. Wouldn't think of it. Slight imperfection of the jolly old hip makes stair climbing a bit of a nuisance."

He was manifestly enjoying himself. Tracy nipped his chuckle neatly in half. "Tell that gag to your friend, Mr. Hubert Eldrick."

The major's eyes glared suddenly, then went dead and fathomless. "Beg pardon, old fellow?"

"The inspector is saving it, I see," Tracy murmured. "Were you ever on the stage, Major? A narrow stage where the lights are very bright and very concentrated; where the audience is always very, very attentive? Think it over, Major, and give my regards to Mr. Hubert Eldrick."

"I—I still fail to see your point, old fellow. I assure you that I've never been on the—the theatrical stage. I don't think I'm being stupid when I say that I—I fail to see just what you're driving at."

"You've been a lot more stupid than you realize, Major," Tracy told him curtly and walked on into the library.

CARRON WAS ALONE in there, listlessly turning the pages of a popular novel.

"How long have you been in here, Carron?"

Carron laid his book aside, yawned deliberately. "I must say I don't like your tone, Mister—"

"Tracy. Jerry Tracy, of the *Daily Planet*. You damned well know who I am! How long have you been here in the library?"

"Oh… matter of ten or fifteen minutes."

"Didn't you just come in?"

"Of course not. As you can see, I've been curled up comfortably with a good book."

"You wouldn't lie to a pal, would you, Carron?"

"I might," Carron said with easy impudence, "if I thought it would relieve me of the annoying attentions of the tabloid press."

"I get it." Tracy grinned suddenly. "You'd feel better, you mean, if I were a lot of miles away. In Siam, say. Where the Chaulmoogra tree grows."

The effect on the suave Carron was astonishing. His face went as black as a thundercloud. He came leaping to his feet, the cords in his lean neck suddenly tense. He shook his fist wrathfuly in Tracy's face.

"If you try to mix me up in this—this mess," he snarled, "I'll break every bone in your cheap, gutter-newspaper body."

"Got a rotten temper, haven't you, Mr. Carron?"

Tracy didn't move back an inch from the furious stamp collector.

"Don't like to give up things, do you? Stamps, for instance. Got blackballed from a club once for beating up a rival collector in a quarrel over your damned stamps... I've got an idea, Carron, that in your own quiet little way, you're dangerously close to being a monomaniac, aren't you?"

He moved the collector's trembling fist away from in front of his nose.

"And don't try the tough stuff, sweetheart. I've mixed with tougher guys than you'll ever see in a carload of blue moons. Get that paw of yours down or I'll turn you into a pinwheel."

Carron's forehead was pale and moist. His sudden rage spilled out of him and left him a little smaller in stature, a little scared.

"You mustn't take my—my temper too seriously," he muttered with a forced smile. "I'm an excitable man. I mean you no harm, Mr. Tracy. And there's no reason in the world why I should lie to you about my recent movements. I—I really wasn't upstairs."

"No?" Tracy said, and chuckled softly. "If you'll think back, Mr. Carron, you'll realize that I didn't ask you if you were upstairs. I merely asked you how long you had been in the library here."

The *Daily Planet's* little columnist turned on his heel and left the discomfited Carron staring after him. The bump on Jerry's pate was forgotten now. He was in high good humor. He walked back through the music room and on towards the drawn curtains through which he had passed earlier in the evening, when Hunter had beckoned him.

A hand touched his arm hesitantly. It was Griscom, looking at him with a curiously haggard eye.

Tracy shook his head curtly. "Sorry, Major, I'm busy."

"Just a sec, old fellow. There's something that I—I— The truth is, I lied to you about Carron."

Jerry gestured towards the closed dining-room doors behind which Inspector Fitzgerald was interrogating the widow of the dead man.

"Go in and tell Fitz. Don't bother me."

The thought of Inspector Fitzgerald suddenly reminded Tracy, with a feeling of grim incredulity, that the inspector had hardly begun his routine questioning of the witnesses to the murder. Tracy's bizarre dashing about the house had occupied not more than—he glanced at his watch—not more than a bare twenty minutes!

Griscom tugged again at the columnist's sleeve.

"Listen," he whispered. "Carron was upstairs. I can swear to it. I saw him sneak down."

"Yeah? That's funny. You both seem to have been up there."

"It's a lie," Griscom said faintly. "If Carron said that about me, he's lying to save his own skin."

"Carron didn't tell me."

"Who did?"

"Maybe I told myself. Or maybe—" Tracy's voice got low and confidential "maybe I was told by—Lily Barker."

He looked full into the white face on the pseudo Englishman. Watched raw terror writhing there. Then he walked onward to the curtain, lifted it and went quietly along towards the pantry to find Hunter.

The butler sighed with relief at sight of Tracy.

"What's the matter, Hunter? You look a little sick. Head still bothering you?"

"No, sir. It's—it's my sister I'm thinking of. I'm afraid she's in danger. Do you think that whoever struck down you and me might try to—to silence Charlotte, sir?"

"Mmmm…" Tracy's brow furrowed. "Where is Charlotte now?"

"In her room, sir. She came to me rather unnerved after the inspector finished questioning her, and I told her to go upstairs, take an aspirin and lie down."

"Where's her room?"

"Servants' hall. Two rooms from the end. Second door on the right. Just beyond the laundry chute, sir."

"I see. By the way, there's another angle I forgot. Have you seen anything of that discarded spray of orchids? Miss Barker's corsage, I mean."

"No, sir. Shall I look for it?"

"Don't bother. I want you to do something more important. You go ahead up front where the guests are. Saunter in and make a bluff at picking things up. Or you might ask 'em if they'd like a cup of fresh, hot coffee. The trick is to keep a sharp eye on two people in there—Major Griscom and Mr. Carron. Don't let either of 'em get out of your sight. You don't have to be too obvious about it. Just be discreet and hang around. If either Carron or Griscom takes a sudden sneak, let me know about it right away."

"Where will you be, sir, in case—"

"I'm going upstairs. Got a couple of questions I'd like to ask Charlotte. And incidentally, to make sure that she's all right."

"Tell her to lock her door," Hunter paid in a worried voice. "And you, sir—better be careful."

Jerry's smile got sunny and quite cheerful.

"We're coming out of the fog, Hunter. The killer is the lad who's got to be careful now. Pretty damned careful, if you ask me. He's in what you might call a spot. As a matter of fact—" Jerry's voice purred with satisfaction—"as a result of a little heavy bean work, I've finally decided just who the party is who invited me to this murder shindig tonight."

He jerked his head towards the front of the house.

"Keep your eye on those two birds while I'm upstairs."

A voice said, suddenly: "Good evening, gentlemen. Is there any chance for a cup of hot coffee, Hunter?"

It was Major Griscom, smiling and affable, with no trace of the terror that Tracy had observed a few moments earlier in his eyes.

"Coffee will be ready in a minute, sir," Hunter murmured.

"Save a big cupful for me," Tracy smiled. "Excuse me, Major. See you later."

Griscom shrugged, matched Tracy's smile, walked back with the columnist as far as the library. Tracy finally got rid of him and slipped away. He went through to the rear of the house and out the back door. There was a little breeze stirring and the air felt sweet and cool. A low moon hung over the ornate private garage of the Barkers, like a segment of golden coin. The garage was locked and dark; no noise came from the big house. Murder seemed suddenly as remote as the pale scattering of stars overhead.

Tracy got quietly busy with the prosaic job of looking through the garbage cans. He poked thoughtfully through the trash bin, examined a multiplicity of bedraggled objects with finicky care. He looked up from his task finally, and listened. After a while he went back into the house.

Charlotte's door was not hard to find upstairs. It was closed and he knocked softly.

He got no answer and knocked again. Finally, with a frown, he turned the knob and the door opened easily. He reached inside the casing and switched on the light. The room was empty. No sign of Charlotte. Just a chair, a rumpled bed, a plain dresser and mirror, a closet.

Tracy thought of the butler's anxious forebodings of peril.

"I'd like to know where the devil Charlotte is," he muttered. "If she came up here to go to bed—and evidently she did—she must have changed her mind in a hurry. Or somebody changed it for her!"

He stepped into the maid's room and closed the door softly behind him.

TEN MINUTES LATER the *Daily Planet's* wizened little columnist reappeared in the hallway.

He walked slowly towards the stairs, concentration. An idea occurred to him and he stopped short. Turned, and came back towards the laundry chute in the wall. He unlatched the square door and swung it open. Stuck his head in and tried to peer down the dark maw of the chute.

A sudden plunging attack threw him off balance, drove the breath from his body.

Steel fingers clamped on his throat. His startled cry died unuttered. Desperately he tried to squirm about, to confront his assailant; but the grip on his throat was as tight and immovable as a vise. His lungs burned with agony. He forgot his mysterious foe, the peril of death, everything! All his fainting brain could think of was to *breathe,* to suck horribly for air....

Dimly he felt his body lifted from the floor. His convulsive fingers clawed at wood, were torn ruthlessly away, but the momentary hold had kept his body head up. He fell, feet foremost, down the chute, into space. He had barely time to think, when a jouncing, curiously soft impact laced his ribs with pain and sent him bouncing headlong against hard concrete. Instantly, all thought and feeling left him....

CONSCIOUSNESS RETURNED GRADUALLY to him. His tongue felt heavy and slimy, as though coated with cobwebs. His body ached when he tried to move. He couldn't see anything in the gloom that surrounded him, but he knew, of course, where he was. In the cellar. By some miracle of God he had plunged feet first down the laundry chute—and was still alive!

His groping fingers reached out and touched the soft mound that half buried him. Soiled linen, a huge hamperful that stood under the chute, had broken his fall and saved his neck. Mechanically, he touched his throat—and remembered the murderous fingers that had squeezed his windpipe from behind.

He fumbled weakly for a pad of matches, lit one, held the flame tremulously aloft. The cellar, all right! Tubs, a washing machine, a long, narrow table, covered with a white, shroudlike sheet... The flame burned his shaking fingers and the match dropped and went out.

He was reaching for another when the rustle of stealthy footsteps reached his ear. The sound seemed to come from below the dark underslant of the staircase. A beam of light—thin, pencil-like—snapped briefly into view. It jumped across tubs and table and stabbed vividly at Tracy's slumped body. He couldn't see the face of the intruder a the flashlight was held carefully low and carefully shielded.

A faint chuckle sounded and the beam snapped out.

Tracy tried to kneel, tried to brace himself with his left hand—and went over backwards like a ninepin as the shadowy figure dived murderously at him. Blows rained on his undefended head. He tried to squirm away, to crawl....

And, gradually by some queer magic, he was all alone again in a pain-filled darkness that seemed to throb with a peculiar hum as though in tune with the beat of his own pulse.

Concrete was still under Tracy's fingers. It felt greasy and for a moment he thought it was blood. He sucked his smeared finger—grease, a taste like oily sludge. He could hear that rhythmic throbbing in the air more clearly now. The bulky monster beside which he lay took slow form, became familiar and coherent. An automobile Beyond it were dark, heavy doors. He was in a garage, locked up alone with that shadowy car that kept purring like a fool kitten... By God—the engine! Running!

He froze suddenly with cold terror. *Carbon monoxide!* He was trapped, sealed up for death. Colorless, odorless, tasteless! Swift—sure death!

It took him years to hang to the running-board and get the car's door open. It took him centuries to grope for the ignition key and find it gone.

He was lying in a tangle on the floor of the car, his cheek pressed against the cold metal of the clutch. He got up like a floating feather, clung fuzzily to the circumference of the steering wheel. He laid a hand that felt absolutely devoid of weight or feeling on the horn button.

To his amazement the horn began to blare monotonously.

He wanted to laugh, it was so silly. How could the thing yawp like that, when his hand on the button didn't weigh a damned ounce! Funniest thing God ever heard of, Tracy said stubbornly to himself, away off in sleepy space, higher than the dimmest, drowsiest star....

THE BRUTALLY INSISTENT smack of a palm on his face roused Jerry Tracy. Cool, fresh air was in his lungs. His eyes opened. He was lying flat on his back on the gravel in front of the Barker garage. Sergeant Killan's heavy palm kept slapping him monotonously.

"Easy, Killan," he gasped. "I'm all right."

"Boy, I sure thought you were gone for good! Feel better now?"

Tracy groaned. "Where's Fitz? Where's everybody?"

"Inside the house. I heard that automobile horn of yours yelping and I tore out to the garage on the run. Just in time, too! Who put the finger on you, Jerry?" He swore viciously. "This thing is beginning to drive me nuts!"

"You came out here alone?" Jerry asked slowly. "Is everyone else in the house?"

"Sure. Fitz thought the horn gag might be a trick. He thinks he has the killer okey—but me, I'm not so sure now."

"Who is he arresting?"

"The daughter. Lily Barker."

Tracy scowled with a grim disgust. "Of all the crackpots—Fitz is the worst!" He got up on his feet and found that he was not as weak as he had thought. Fitz's dumb play in arresting Lily Barker acted on him like a shot of stimulating liquor.

"Back into the house," he snapped. "It's time we put the crab on this little show. Come on, keed."

"You got a slant? Who done it, Jerry?"

"Get a move on and you'll see."

Inspector Fitzgerald scowled as Killan and Tracy came into the music room. Most of the guests were assembled there, staring at one another with suspicion and uncertainty. The only one definitely smiling was Lily Barker. Her smile was bitter, ironic. The inspector didn't seem to like looking at it.

"What goes on?" Fitz asked Tracy harshly. "What the hell have you been doing with yourself?"

"Solving a murder—and a lot of other things," Tracy said calmly.

"Oh, yeah?" The inspector's unhappiness gave way to a puzzled hopefulness. "Mind telling me all about it?"

"Not at all. I'm going to enjoy putting an end to the hectic doings in this gilded dump." He felt his damaged scalp tenderly. "Somebody cracked me on the dome upstairs and did the same for Hunter. Twice somebody tried to murder me. In addition to that, three separate attempts have been made to rifle the safe upstairs in John Barker's bedroom—and two of the attempts *were successful*... Yeah, I sure think I'll enjoy talking, Fitz."

He glanced keenly at the inspector. "Everybody in here now?"

"You mean—"

"I mean everybody in the house. I want all of 'em here— guests, servants, guest towels and cockroaches. Let me know when they're all here, Hunter. Scram!"

Hunter looked at Fitzgerald questioningly and the inspector nodded. "You heard what he said. Go get 'em."

"Very good, sir."

Tracy said softly: "Come here, Fitz. Little Jerry wants to whisper some info to papa... Killan, you go out to the back of the house, reach under the wooden step and bring me what you find."

The face of Inspector Fitzgerald got wooden as he listened to the *Daily Planet* columnist. He glanced at the crowd but his eyes didn't seem to dwell on anyone in particular. Men and women watched him with a stark, puzzled interest.

Sergeant Killan came back and Tracy said: "Thanks. Put it on that table for a minute."

"Everyone is here now, sir," Hunter reported. "If I may say so, sir, the cook is quite angry."

"That's tough," Fitzgerald growled.

Jerry Tracy was facing his silent audience. A little spot of color came into his lean cheeks. Nice to be in the spotlight again! He had been an awful dope for the last hectic half hour; but now he was frankly enjoying himself.

"I know exactly who killed John P. Barker," he said slowly. "I know exactly who the guy is—or should I say the person?—who bopped Hunter and myself on the head. I know the two things that were stolen from Barker's safe—and why."

He paused and his eyes roved coolly about the room.

"More important than that—I know who sent me the phoney invitation to come here tonight—and the reason why it was done. It was done to facilitate a cowardly murder for profit. Somebody remembered that old Mother Goose rhyme: *'Will you walk into my parlor?' said the Spider to the Fly.* Somebody thought I'd make a swell fly. But this is one time the foxy spider made a bum guess."

He smiled at Killan.

"Gimme that orchid spray a minute, Sarge. Thanks… This is the corsage that Lily Barker wore tonight. It wilted and she threw it away. I found it hidden underneath the trash barrel in the rear of the house. If you'll notice, the white-topped corsage pin is still stuck in the spray. Lily jabbed it back again when she discarded her flowers. In other words, there were two pins used here tonight. Lily Barker's pin did not kill her father. A substitute pin was used. The murderer took advantage of the fact that Miss Barker always threw away flowers the moment they began to wilt."

Tracy's voice hardened. "Gimme those handcuffs, Sarge."

He began walking slowly forward. Killan walked along beside him. The columnist sauntered straight towards a small group of staring people. Towards Major Griscom and Mr. Carron. Carron was trembling badly but Griscom was like chilled white steel. Both of them stared at the blazing eyes of the approaching columnist and neither of them backstepped an inch.

"And now," Tracy said, "I think that this tragic little adventure in Mother Goose draws to its finish."

HE GRUNTED AS he sprang past Carron. His fingers closed grimly on the icy-cold wrist of a woman. He jerked her off balance and *click* went the steel handcuffs on her left wrist.

Charlotte uttered no cry but she fought like a maddened tigress. The sudden glitter of a knife slashed Tracy's coat-sleeve from shoulder to elbow. Sergeant Killan dived in, wrenched the knife away—and Tracy got plenty rough. In another second the dangling cuffs were locked on both wrists and the manacled lady's maid began to laugh. Stridently, horribly.

Inspector Fitzgerald had taken efficient care of Hunter. For a dazed second the handcuffed butler seemed bereft of his senses. Then he began to shout, to rave like a madman.

"Let her alone!" he screamed. "Take your dirty hands off Charlotte! She didn't do it! I did—do you hear me? I killed the old fool! I did!"

"You both did," Tracy panted. "Nice, sweet couple. Very lovable lice—the two of you." His glittering eye quelled the murmurs in the rest of the assemblage. "Shut up, everybody— and stand still. I'm not through with the rest of you, yet."

Fitz said calmly: "Go ahead, Jerry. The stage is yours."

"Thanks... The butler and the maid worked in cahoots. Charlotte did the drugging of the old man's saccharine tablets; Hunter did the actual murder with the poisoned pin. He coated it, is my guess, with a paste of glycerine and potassium cyanide. Did it as he passed by the old man in the darkness of the music room on his way to call me. The old man was dead in a second or two. Just gulped as the pin pricked his dazed neck—and died. The foxy Hunter then quietly attracts my attention, escorts me back to the dining-room; and he and his precious Charlotte spin me a well-prepared baloney yarn that I fell for at first like a ton of bricks. All about a noble brother and a poor unfortunate sister. As a matter of fact, Charlotte is the worse of the two—as I discovered when I rummaged around in her room upstairs. She's the one who first suggested the whole plot. She's the cold-blooded tigress behind this planned murder.

"She stole the engraved invitation from the social secretary and invited me here for the sole purpose of having a well-known newspaper man to copper-rivet her brother's alibi. So daring a stunt, you might almost call it genius. Charlotte and Hunter and I were talking nice and chummy in the dining-room when the old man's body finally slipped out of his chair. That's what gave me my first hunch. The alibi was why I was invited. And Hunter and Charlotte and I were the only ones so favored."

"And the motive?" Fitzgerald suggested dryly. "You said murder for profit."

"Greed was the motive. There's a package of $50,000 in nego-tiable securities hidden under a loose board in the floor of Charlotte's room. It was stolen from Mr. Barker's safe. Hunter tried for it once, and failed. The iron-willed Charlotte sneaked back afterwards and got it."

Tracy's smile hardened.

"Which brings me to an unfortunate angle—the part of this peculiar triangle that concerns Lily Barker and Major Griscom."

Griscom was very pale. He didn't say anything. There was a uniformed policeman standing stolidly at his elbow.

"Blackmail," Tracy whispered softly. "That's not a very pretty word, Major. Griscom had something on Lily and he put the bee on her for $50,000. She asked her father for the dough and he refused. Said he wouldn't give her a penny. Hunter told me about it and that part of his story was true. But Hunter didn't tell me the rest. Which was, that John Barker relented later, got the stuff, placed it in his wall safe to give to Lily tomor-row. The butler, with his expert keyhole system, was aware of this. Nobody knew the dough was in the house except old man Barker—and Hunter and Charlotte. A swell set-up to swipe it, kill the old man, toss the blame of his death on his daughter, who had, before witnesses, said she'd get that loan if she had to get it as her father's heir."

The columnist's finger pointed at the major.

"Griscom came here tonight to renew his demands for the payoff. I got a hunch he was in your room tonight, Lily, when I knocked at your closed door and you didn't answer. That's true, isn't it?"

"It's true," Lily Barker said drearily. "He came up to my room, threatened to accuse me to the police of father's death if I didn't shut his mouth with money. He skipped out of my room under cover of the assault on you. You were lying out in the hall, half unconscious—"

"I know," Tracy said shortly. "When I opened my eyes, Griscom had already stepped over my body and beat it—and you were standing there, staring at me, wondering who had slugged me and what it was all about… Which brings me to the third and final angle of this crazy puzzle."

He walked across to Carron, smiled pleasantly, held out his palm.

"Let's have it, Carron, if you please."

"I—I don't know what you mean," Carron faltered.

"Oh, yes, you do! Your share of the swag. You took it out of the safe. I want it."

"You're mistaken, Mr. Tracy. I never was near the safe."

"Are you going to hand me that Siamese Chaul-moogra?" Tracy rasped. "Or do you want me to get tough?"

Carron shrugged, removed a wallet from his inner pocket and tremulously laid a postage stamp in the palm of the *Daily Planet* man.

"I'm sorry about all this," he said in a dead whisper. "I really didn't mean anything criminal. Barker defrauded me out of that stamp. It was rightfully, morally mine. I—I knew it was here. I couldn't get the thought of it out of my head. The—the moment I realized that Barker was really dead, I determined to get it."

"Even if you had to sock two people on the skull to steal it, huh? Who told you the combination of the safe? Hunter?"

"Yes. I had bribed Hunter weeks before and I knew the combination. He copied it from the old man's private papers. I thought no one would miss the stamp in the excitement attendant on Barker's unexpected death. I sneaked upstairs the moment I thought everything was clear."

"Must have been a damned political convention going on upstairs," Inspector Fitzgerald commented bitterly.

"Pretty close to it," Tracy nodded. "Griscom and Lily, arguing stealthily in her bedroom; Carron down the hall, trying feverishly to open Barker's safe and swipe that blasted Siamese stamp. I sure picked a swell time to knock at Lily's door. She and Griscom must have been scared stiff when they heard my knock. And Carron heard it, too. He was afraid that maybe I'd suspect what he was up to; so he reached out cautiously and threw the hallway into darkness. Socked me on the skull and vanished. And then, by God—he got his nerve back and decided to have a second try. Showing," Tracy muttered, "that when a man plays too hard at a boy's hobby, he's apt to come pretty close to being a monomaniac."

"You mean that Carron was the guy who socked Hunter, too?" Sergeant Killan asked dazedly.

Tracy nodded.

"The butler, of course, lied and reversed what had really

happened. Hunter was at the safe looking for the fifty thousand bucks when Carron tiptoed in and surprised him. Carron socked him before Hunter could see who it was, stole his blasted Siamese stamp, closed the safe and beat it. That ended the evening's strong-arm stuff, except for a few minor affairs like—"

Jerry smiled ruefully.

"—like dropping me down a laundry chute, beating me up in the cellar, lugging me out to the garage in the rear and trying to murder me with *carbon monoxide* from an automobile exhaust. Good old Hunter attended to those details, because he was beginning to suspect from a couple of hints I had carelessly let drop, that I was getting wise to him and his sweet sister, Charlotte."

"Go to hell, you little punk," Charlotte said sweetly. "Do I move along to jail—or do I have to listen to this guy all night? He gives me a pain —— ——."

"Shut up," Killan growled and emphasized the remark.

"What am I going to do about Carron?" the inspector asked Jerry. "You advised me to let him go. He stole the stamp, didn't he? He admits it. And he socked you and he socked that damned butler."

Jerry smiled. "I don't think I'd call Carron a habitual criminal. Let him go, Fitz; I'll talk to him later. I shouldn't be a bit surprised if he quit collecting stamps from now on."

"I swear it!" Carron cried eagerly.

"I'll—I'll burn every stamp I own. I'll never touch another one as long as I live. I didn't really mean to—to hurt anyone."

Tracy said, dryly: "You do pretty good for an amateur, Carron. However, I don't think we'll press the assault and theft charges.

I don't think Hunter will, either… Besides, there's still something important for me to consider. Griscom is the guy that interests me."

His cold eye focused on Major Griscom and the major quailed.

"GRISCOM," JERRY SAID evenly, "is due for a large load of bricks on the skull. He's the one who started this whole filthy business brewing. He's a blackmailer, a cowardly whelp who makes his dirty living from the terror and shame of women. There's a word that describes him very accurately, Fitz, but I won't use it." He turned towards Lily Barker and his voice got very gentle, very low.

"It's in your power, Lily, to put this crawling little piece of boudoir vermin out of circulation."

The girl didn't reply. She stood there, looking at Tracy; straight-backed, erect, her face as white as paper. No tears, no wringing of foolish hands. A thoroughbred! Tracy admired her suddenly like hell.

"May I speak with you privately, Lily, for just a moment or so?"

Her face didn't alter. She merely nodded, turned and followed him into the next room.

"We've both of us done a little misjudging," Tracy said. "It may even be possible that I'm not the cheap little tabloid guttersnipe that you thought I was."

No answer.

"There's no way of telling," Tracy said meditatively, "just how much wreckage a guy like Griscom leaves in his wake. No telling how many people he's driven to suicide or worse. However,

I'd say the answer was plenty. You've got it in your power to stop him once and for all. I'm not asking you to testify against him; I'm merely asking you to think it over. I may be able to hush up some of the newspaper dirt but not all. You won't be able to escape all of the pain, all of the humiliating notoriety. If you don't do anything about it, Griscom will probably beat the rap. There's nothing to connect him definitely with the murder of your father. On the other hand, if you do testify against him, he can be nailed to the cross and his slimy career ended—but in that case, Lily, you yourself will take the rap. I'm not trying to kid you, you see."

No answer.

"I won't blame you if you say 'no' to the proposition. You have a free choice. If you do say 'no,' I'll promise to do my damnedest to keep your name out of this mess and to close Inspector Fitzgerald's trap... And—I guess that's all, Lily."

"It's unfair," she whispered. He had to bend close to hear her. "I've been foolish, headstrong, self-willed, bad-tempered—anything you like. But I—I don't see why I should have to suffer more than I have already, for the good of other—"

She broke off, her eyes tightly closed. There was a long pause. When she opened her eyes they were wet. She smiled forlornly at the columnist.

"Tell your tiresome inspector of police that I'll—I'll prosecute Major Griscom for extortion," Lily Barker said.

Tracy nodded at that. He took her slack hand, clasped it man-fashion till she winced.

"You sure don't belong in a stuffy old household like this," he whispered huskily. "I know what you've been up against, why you've been kiting around to night clubs and jazz hives, bored and disgusted and desperate for something real. Why don't you skip this whole set-up of hypocrisy and stodgy living with a bunch of near-men and women that haven't brains enough to stuff a scallion? You've got the brains, Lily! You've got guts, grit, courage! Why don't you stand on your own two feet? Get a job, work like hell, *live!*"

She cried, fiercely: "If I could do that, if I could—"

"Why not, Lily? You can. I've got a million friends on Broadway. Say the word and I'll spot you in a job tomorrow. A hard job or an easy one."

"Make it a hard one," she whispered. "A job where I'll have to use an alarm clock. Where I'll get so damned tired that Sunday will seem like heaven. Where I can do the first day's work I've ever done in my life."

"Lily," Tracy promised huskily, "I'll spot you in a job where they'll give you a straight shot at something—and handle you with crowbars! I'll make you a credit to your hardworking old grand-pop—and he earned forty millions."

To her manifest horror, Lily found herself sniffling.

"You're a grand guy, Jerry Tracy," she choked.

"Nerts," Tracy said. "That's because you've been in one spot too long. Haven't seen anything outside of it."

JERRY TOOK HIS time getting back to the outer room. To the silent people assembled there he was still the same grinning, impudent, cocksure Jerry Tracy, the pampered darling of Broadway. But wise old Inspector Fitzgerald saw that the smile was a feeble affair.

"How'd you make out, Jerry?"

"It's okey, Fitz." His voice sounded very tired. "She'll press the complaint."

"Swell… Feel all right now? Want a drink?"

"No. I'm okey, Fitz. Thanks." The Tracy grin got more natural. "Hell, I'm just beginning to realize that I've taken a couple of bouncings around tonight."

"Boy, I'll say!" boomed Sergeant Killan. "They done everything to you—except maybe bat you with Brooklyn Bridge… Hey, how you ever gonna explain that bump on the coco to the lads in Times Square?"

"I'll tell 'em," Tracy said with mock solemnity, "that I'm not used to million-dollar bonded liquor. I fell down after three tall drinks and bumped a gold-plated coal scuttle with the rear of my plebeian forehead."

Killan's gruff laughter boomed. "If I were you, Jerry, from now on I'd stick to the—"

"Save it," Tracy murmured, "I know the answer, myself."

He felt tenderly of the egg-shaped swelling on his skull.

"I'm sticking to the Broadway muggs, thank you. A little crude maybe, but give 'em credit: when they get mad they don't sock you—they *sue* you, God bless 'em… I don't expect to receive any more engraved invitations from Park Avenue, but if I do—guess whom I'm gonna turn it over to? Think hard, sweetheart!"

"Maxie Baer?" Killan chuckled.

"Right!" said Jerry Tracy.

About the Author

A NATIVE NEW Yorker, Ted Tinsley can't stay put in the old home town.

Traveled around the world, including Bali, then promptly married a Southern girl and moved to Florida.

He now works for the OWI in Washington.

www.ingramcontent.com/pod-product-compliance
Lightning Source LLC
Chambersburg PA
CBHW020257030726
47499CB00001B/226